P9-DMH-774

GONE

KIT CRAIG

GONE

A NOVEL

LITTLE, BROWN AND COMPANY
BOSTON   TORONTO   LONDON

First Edition

The characters and events in this book are fictitious.
Any similarity to real persons, living or dead,
is coincidental and not intended by the author.

Library of Congress Cataloging-in-Publication Data

Craig, Kit
    Gone / Kit Craig. — 1st ed.
        p.   cm.
    ISBN 0-316-15923-9
    PS3568.E367G66   1992
    813'.54 — dc20   91-37566

        10 9 8 7 6 5 4 3 2 1

MV NY

*Published simultaneously in Canada
by Little, Brown & Company (Canada) Limited*

Printed in the United States of America

For Joseph Reed
Still crazy after all these years

GONE

1

IF THERE IS ANYTHING UNUSUAL on Pequod Street, a disturbance in the night that suggests impending loss or change, a disruption or a dislocation, Clary Hale's fatherless children are sleeping too profoundly to hear it. These three would stand out as Clary's anywhere; they have the same black brushstrokes for eyebrows as their mother, those same thick lashes scoring translucent cheeks, the same brilliant, stubborn faces. They are not laid-back civilian kids, they are Navy juniors, but asleep like this, they could be anybody.

In her orange bedroom, gawky, glamorous, love-struck Teah dreams with her arms locked around threadbare George Teddy. Two doors down her restless brother Michael sleeps tangled in quilts on the floor where he landed in the middle of a violent, cinematic dream — titles, end credits; he even had lines. In the bedroom next to Clary's, her youngest, Tommy, sinks into sleep like a stone in deep water while the dog stirs uneasily. Forgotten, the child's plush Tasmanian devil turns blank glass eyes to the ceiling.

Outside the New England saltbox where the children sleep, the light changes. The moon is disappearing. As it loses itself in pale dawn skies the late spring air quickens; supersonic booms sound over the water — jet planes from the base soaring out and peeling off. Running underneath is a new sound, a distant clatter, or ratcheting, unidentified and therefore frightening — of something huge approaching, roaring down on the town like an engine of destruction. It's the kind of noise that shakes the unwary sleeper, terrifying until it gets close enough to signify — oh: an eighteen-wheeler, a lone driver strung out on speed and hell-bent on home at four in the morning. The giant truck comes barreling down on them from the north like a monster with steely jaws wide and headlights glaring. It rumbles into Broad Street, leaving the roused sleeper alert and shaking: *what was that?* Oh, it was only.

While on the quiet street in front of the house where Clary Hale's children are sleeping, the real terror begins.

The sound of something out of the ordinary happening —

A woman's voice. *Oh my children.*

Wait. What is it? What's happened anyway? Is there a struggle? Something. A stir. Nothing you could identify, exactly, but something is going on.

It makes the kind of subtle difference in the air that alerts the sleepless and brings them, trembling, to their windows. If someone heard and looked out, what would they see anyway? Could anyone make out what's going on in the shadow of the big maple? Would they understand or know what to do about it?

Can anybody stop what's happening?

But the only witness is anxious old Sarah Ferguson, whose bedroom overlooks the street, and she feels too fragile to get out of bed in the middle of the night like this. Failing now, uncertain of everything — her hearing, her balance, the sound of her voice — the old lady next door blinks and shudders. She won't know what she's heard because the thunder of the eighteen-wheeler rolls in, obliterating memory. Sarah weighs ninety-two pounds; if she did go to the window now, and saw, what could she do anyway?

The southbound semi clears Broad Street and plunges through the outskirts on its way to New London, a departing storm center that rattles windows as it passes. With a clank, the first weekend shift starts work at the foundry. Over at the base a training squadron takes off in a series of explosions and three blocks away the giant trash compactor at the hospital starts up with a whine and a thud. The unaccountable is obscured by the expected.

In the house next door, therefore, anxious Sarah Ferguson shifts uneasily, but does not get up. Instead she blinks at the watery light on her bedroom ceiling without knowing what's caught her attention.

It's already too late. If she goes to her window now she will see only the empty street, maples stirring in the wake of a departure, although she'll tell herself the breeze has left the branches clattering. She is too shortsighted to make out the white blur in the gutter in front of the Hales' house — a piece of paper, covered with a hasty scrawl and crumpled into nothing.

But something has left Sarah awake and jangling. *What,* she thinks. *What is it?* If she puts her feet on the cold floor now, even for a minute, she will be awake forever. Instead she lies still, courting sleep. *Nothing,* she tells herself. *It's nothing.*

It is as if nothing's happened.

By the time Clary Hale's children wake to find out otherwise, it will be late morning.

Yawning, Michael Hale blinks at a room bright with reflected sunlight, turns over and bonks his elbow, ow! He's landed on the floor again, rolled out in his sleep without even knowing it. Oh look, if I ever get a girl, how in hell am I going to explain this? Fifteen years old and still falling out of bed like his baby brother; some grownup I am. Enough of a kid to be stuck with a paper route. Grown enough to want a girl there in the blankets with him. Halfway between, Michael is neither one nor the other.

He rolls over. What time is it? Late, he thinks. If the alarm went off he never heard it. My papers! Two dozen families are out there eating their oat bran and Eggos without any morning paper. So why didn't his mother wake him?

Clary seldom lets him oversleep on Saturdays. With Dad gone they don't necessarily operate by the numbers, chop-chop, but the woman can make his life a living hell if he doesn't spring out on time. First she lets him have it with the pillow just the way a kid would, bonking him with that same kind of gutty laughter. She's a lot like another kid, quick and funny. Grinning, she threatens him with ice in the ear, water torture, tickling. "Ow, stoppit Ma, OK, OK, I'm coming."

"It's either you or me, kid, and you're the one who's saving for the camcorder."

He is. Michael has saved almost fifteen hundred dollars. All his conscious life he's wanted to make movies. He walks through hard times with an imaginary camera riding on his shoulder.

"Smile, Mom, and I'll put you in pictures." *And the pictures will make you really smile.* It is his dream. Spielberg, crawl off somewhere and shrivel. David Lynch and the next guy in line after him, move over.

"Really." Although she dimmed like a light on a rheostat after their father's sub was lost, Clary forgets sometimes and shines. Laughing, she turns Michael out with goofy tag lines. "I'm only being cruel in order to be kind," she'll say. ("Aw, Ma.") "What price glory?" "It is a far, far better thing you do." Et cetera. ("OK, OK, Mom, I'm coming.")

Beautiful, relentless, she pulls him to his feet, stabilizing him with her index fingers, "Ooop," "careful," "steady," pretending that she alone has the power to keep Michael from toppling. So there he is, waked and set moving by this laughing wild person who one day soon will see he is getting too old for this and stay out of his bedroom altogether.

If their family is an island, the inhabitants are friendly. It's what keeps him going. It's what's kept him going all his life. When your father is in a nuclear submarine, your nuclear family is all you have. You don't come from a particular state and you don't grow up watching the same boring people grow up in the same dull neighborhood in the same old town. Michael feels sorry for civilian kids; it must be boring, always knowing what it's going to be like when you go out. In his relatively short life Michael has moved eight times and started all over again in six different schools. Wherever the family moves, Clary unpacks and puts the same things in the same relationship in every room. It keeps their heads in place. The country they live in is the Navy — traditions Michael and Teah have been brought up in. The constants they have in life are the things they take with them: each other, their dog Fang, the matched rings — Dad's class ring from the Academy and the miniature their mom wears instead of an engagement ring.

When Michael goes out in a new place everything is different. One reason it's so important to keep everything the same at home.

The pattern on the ceiling tells him it's late. It's after ten. By this time customers on the route are usually like angry jays, squawking every five minutes, but today the phone is quiet. He yawns and stirs lazily, but the nest of covers is seductive. *Good old Mom,* he thinks, rolling over on guilt and smashing it flat, *probably she did the route.* And slips deeper into the tangle of quilts and blankets. He isn't awake, exactly, but he isn't asleep either; he's drowsing.

Right, he thinks, Mom did the route for me. He's glad but he isn't. The beach road is hard for her.

He knows he ought to keep his mother away from the damn ocean. Something in Clary's face: a drawn look, shimmering gray eyes veiled with memories, makes it clear how much it costs her. It's hard enough for Michael to take his papers along the beach road all the way to the last house on the Point overlooking the Atlantic, but he has to. Dad started him saving for the video camera before he went away. Now Michael has to follow through, no matter how long it takes, because his father wanted it.

Because Dad is in the Navy, they all are. The first rules, as set down by their father: if you are under orders, you honor them because you are helping me do my job. The last orders Dad gave him were, stay put. Sit tight. Michael adds: *hold the fort.*

Continuity is everything.

Even though Captain Thomas Hale, U.S.N., was ripped out of their lives three, going on four years ago, it's important to Michael to keep everything exactly the way they had it when Dad was home. Especially since they're basically alone here. For the first few weeks the other Navy wives came from Groton and New London with cookies and casseroles. The Hales froze well-wishers' cakes by the dozens and threw out gallons of other people's pasta salad. But the other wives looked into his mom's face and got scared of their own losses and backed off as if they thought, Hang out with her and you might lose your own husband. You'd think the Hales had something you could catch. Even civilian kids with live-in dads treated them like it was contagious: get away. He can see it in their faces. It's as if the Hales stand accused of carelessness: look what you did. Thing like that, it distances you.

So the family has been more or less on its own since the last flowers wilted and the casseroles stopped coming, but this is nothing new. Navy kids who go to civilian schools aren't really in the Navy but they don't belong because they aren't really civilians, either. They're just different. And Mom, Mom has already been different. Doesn't listen to anybody's music but her own. Which is why they live out here instead of close enough to go to movies on the base, or swim in the Officers' Club pool. But they are keeping it together here. They are.

They do things carefully, getting up in the mornings and smiling at each other in the kitchen and acting normal, *normal.* We're cool. Everything's OK. Michael spends his life on it. He'll keep the family in place with his bare hands if necessary. Tommy don't cry. Not so fast there Teah, Dad would *hate* Eddy Stanko. Be cool, Mom, I'll take care of it. Business as usual. Life the same. Michael tells himself the inconvenience is only temporary. *If we can just keep it together we can get him back,* he thinks. *But we have to keep it just the way he left it.* Michael is afraid to change anything — systems, routines, the way he combs his hair. The least thing might hurt his father's chances.

Chances? The thing about Missing in Action is that it in no way says anything final. If it did you wouldn't let anybody see you grieve. Officers' children don't cry.

So Captain Thomas Hale, U.S.N., skipper of the lost sub *Constellation,* isn't dead, OK? He's only missing. The *Constellation* just disappeared from the airwaves, radar, sonar: dropped out of sight. There's no record of a final transmission, no debris reported, nothing floating on the surface to mark the spot, Tom Hale's ship with all hands may be buried too deep to find, but show me. So what happened? Nobody knows, exactly, and if they do know, they aren't telling. The official bastards say it's classified because Dad was on a sensitive mission. For all Michael knows, it's all a cover story — you know the government.

— Look me in the eye and tell me you know he is dead.

— Be proud, son. The *Constellation* was on a sensitive mission. Can't tell you any more. It's a matter of national security.

Well, listen. Dad could have been taken prisoner by a foreign power ordinary civilians don't even know about, on orders they aren't allowed to guess at. For all Michael knows, he could be out there somewhere on a secret mission.

What do they know anyway? Thomas Hale loves his family but he often traveled with his briefcase shackled to his wrist, and going on sea duty he proceeded under sealed orders. No telling what he was out there doing under orders. For his country.

No one outside the service could understand the discipline.

All those farewells — big, square Dad with his big square sense of honor: — I love you, Mike, but I can't say.

— But Dad.

— Orders. Tom has said the incontrovertible. They are all under orders here. Stay put. Sit tight. Hold the fort. — When you're old enough, you'll understand.

It's this that keeps them all in place.

The trouble is, Michael can't stop looking for him. He can't stop going to the ocean. It's where they last saw him. Put your hand in the water and it's like touching him.

With his camera eye Michael sometimes sees his missing father unshelled on the sandy ocean bottom in full uniform, sleeping with his blue eyes wide and his bright hair rippling like a banner in the underwater currents. At other times the camera shows Michael his father trapped in his ship, alive against all odds and waiting to be rescued. Although his father put out in a sealed nuclear submarine, sleek and black as a barracuda, Michael sees Dad and his men through a giant porthole, skipper and crew, calling and waving, trapped under the ocean. So he drops papers on the doorsteps all along the beach road, paving the way to the Point, where he can sit on the rocks and look out over the ocean. All right, he's still looking for his father. He can't help it.

It may be just as bad for Clary. Some Saturdays she sneaks out in the gray dawn with Michael's papers and delivers them, spooking around houses with complete families with her heart full of questions; like him she finishes at the waterfront, going out on the Point to sit on the rocks, looking out over the Atlantic.

"I needed to think," she'll explain. "You know how that is."

He does. He doesn't.

Listen. If they look out over the water hard enough and for long enough, oh God, maybe they really will see it coming. Black, powerful barracuda shape running along underneath the ocean, could be anything. But, God, is that a periscope? Then in a rush it will break the surface, water crashing from the conning tower, splintering into a million glittering pieces, the whole damn submarine back safe after all, in another minute he'll see the hatch opening, somebody coming up the ladder, Dad! *I told you I would make it.* It *will* happen. It is only a matter of concentration.

Maybe she just wants to be close to him.

It's what Michael does, most days. Oh God, oh Dad, I still miss you.

The familiar little twist of pain drives him out of the nest he's made for himself. "Oh shit." He sits up abruptly.

And realizes something is missing. Usually by this time he hears Mom and Tommy in the kitchen, her crashing pots and his baby brother getting louder and louder as morning heads into noon. But he doesn't hear anything downstairs, not even Fang nudging his food dish across the tiles. Where is everybody?

He throws on a sweatshirt and jeans and pads out into the hall, thrown off balance by the silence and tilted into uneasiness. It's as if something is about to happen.

What makes this day different from all other days?

Nothing he can put his finger on. Something.

After Dad and everything, Michael counts on the ordinary. So. If anything turns out otherwise, at least he can handle it. He may not know much, but he does know he's going to be a moviemaker someday, or he'll die of it. The movies make more sense of life than any thousand stupid people trying to explain it. Which is why he looks at life through this imaginary camera he carries on his shoulder. It frames what's happening, so he can size it up and manage it. The camera may not explain, but it is an organizing factor. He uses it now. Cautiously, he begins the sequence.

INTERIOR — DAY — THE HALE HOUSE

In the kinds of movies Michael dreams of making the camera tilts around now, long tracking shot of the upstairs hall, P.O.V. Michael; Steadicam gliding down pumpkin pine stairs, picks up nothing at the bottom, nobody in the orderly living room as it tracks Michael's entrance. Pan living room: fisheye lens distorts the Chinese teakwood desk, the silver tray from the crew of Dad's last command, picks up a shadow moving, it's like a cheap shot out of one of *Freddy's Nightmares*, look out, something behind you . . .

Michael whirls. "What!"

It's nobody. Nothing. Besides, the dog would never let anybody . . . "Fang?" Where is the dog anyway?

The kitchen is so still it's as if nobody has ever used it.

"Mom?" The gleaming counters and the empty sink give back nothing. OK, where is she? Can't be the store, she went yesterday; morning walk, not like her; at a friend's, not really. Clary would rather talk to her own kids than waste time with most people, so except for big old grinning Shar Masters, who cleans for them on Fridays, she really only hangs out with this ancient Sarah, from next door. OK, maybe she got a rush call from her gallery down on Broad Street, some new patron wants to see her landscape paintings. But all the same oils still line the walls in the cluttered family room off the kitchen, waiting for her dealer to collect them.

Maybe . . . his breath catches. Get off this track, Mike, get off it. But he can't. Maybe she's gone down to the sub base in New London because they have some word about the *Con* . . . No. If word came she would have them all up and dancing in the night. If he came home, she'd take all the kids with her, they'd be lining the dock waving when the *Constellation* put in. "Fang?" God, he can't even find the Westie.

Out in the car, he tells himself. They're out riding around with Tommy. Or she and Fang have driven him over to play with somebody. Mom could be out back putting in those plants she bought yesterday, Clary with her dark hair pulled back in a ribbon, kneeling by the back steps with her trowel. Then in a house where nobody ever goes out the front door, why is the dead bolt still shot, and why has she left the chain lock on? When he lets himself out the spongy dead grass is as before and his mother's silly-looking pansy plants in their plastic flats are sitting where she left them. But what's that out by the garage? Fresh dirt turned over for a shallow grave, or torn up in some cosmic struggle? Then he sees it's only the new garden patch Clary made yesterday, with bricks piled next to it, where she's going to make a border. Somebody speaks but he's getting too weird to notice.

"I *said*, what's going on?"

"Ma'am?" At first he can't locate the speaker. When he does, he tries not to make a face. Funny old lady, he's never figured out why Mom is so fond of her. She probably hates him for being young. She's so short the top of her tangled steel-wool curls barely clears the fence. "Oh hi Mrs. Ferguson."

She's bobbing like a hand puppet. "You still haven't answered me."

"I *said* hi. I'm just out here getting the pruners for . . ." Michael starts to say, For my mother, but uneasiness makes him want to put her off. If anything's wrong here, he can't afford to let anybody know it. Pretending everything is fine, he is just about to begin to create a structure that will either conceal or confine him. "What do you mean, what's going on?"

"In the night I thought I . . ." Scowling, Sarah finishes in that weak little voice.

"Ma'am?"

"I-thought-I-heard-something."

Cleverly, he asks, "What did Mom say it was?"

"Your mother?" Surprise makes Sarah apologetic. "I haven't seen your mother this morning."

So much for next door at Mrs. Ferguson's. Then where is she?

But the old lady is on to him. "Now that I think about it, Clary *always* calls me on Saturdays, she usually comes over . . . Is something the matter?"

"No Ma'am," he says hastily, laying the first block in the tower of lies he must build to protect his family. "She's just. She's fine. She's just . . ." He lies! "Lying down right now."

"Probably a cold from running around without a sweater." Sarah pulls her tatty cardigan around her. "I shouldn't be outside in this. When she's feeling better, would you ask her to call me?"

"Yes Ma'am I sure will." In hell. So if Clary isn't next door, she's out in the car. If she isn't out in the car, where is she? Fleeing, he promises, "I'll tell her you were asking."

The car is still in the garage. Worse yet, on the driveway where the *Day* truck dumps them, he sees his undelivered Saturday papers still bundled. Why didn't Mom . . .

Then he goes back inside. Sees — thud. Her keys are still on the hook by the back door. And then sees the next thing. The wall phone in the kitchen is off the hook, receiver dangling. He picks it up and, irrationally, starts shouting into it. "Mom? Mom?"

God! The tail of the monster that's seized his belly flails around and smacks him.

2

FOR THIS DRIVEN MAN, this fierce engine speeding along the dark avenue of compulsion, everything is one — then and now, waking and nightmare, memory and obsession, self and needs, all inseparable. Outlines disappear. Everything fuses: his beauty and the power that drives him. Loss and desire. His body and the tree. It is rooted in deep childhood: *Oh Daddy, don't.* Running ahead of pain, the child turned in on himself and began the tree — so pretty at first, brilliant, so new. He could lose himself in its glossy leaves, spin new tendrils and watch them flower. He could forget it was happening. *You can't hurt this tree, Daddy. You can't hurt me;* he loved to watch it grow. Now it is huge. The tree is rage. He spends his life feeding it.

In the continuum in which he moves, distinctions blur. Everything is *now:* the acorn his mother planted in a paper cup on his windowsill: "Water it," his mother said, "watch it grow," and died before it sprouted. What his father did to him.

What he has done. Must do.

What he is already doing.

He takes what he needs.

His eyes are like headlamps flicking over other people's faces, blazing, terrible. The images that flicker behind the eyes are dark, frightening. They reinvent him. Fuel his power.

Clomp. Clomp. Clomp.

He will never shake the sound of his father's footsteps coming up the stairs to his room. How old was he? No matter. He is still that child. *Oh Daddy don't.* Always turned on the light. His father's harsh whiskey breath, the hands, *what he did to me* and all the time his lovely mother lay far away in the front bedroom with her black hair splayed on the pillow, *Mother,* so sick; close enough to hear him cry but too weak to come to him. "If you are good I'll let you see your mother now." Close his eyes and he can still see her, how beautiful. Listen hard and he can hear her calling, *Is anything wrong?* and in response his own voice, why can't he make her hear, with running along underneath, the knowledge of heavy, hairy hands, that face, "Come here son, I'm not going to hurt you." *Mother.*

"Water it," she had said before she got too sick to walk, "watch it grow," but the paper cup fell and everything spilled out on the floor. When she died they said he was too little to remember her — so pretty — but some part of him is ripped open in a perpetual groan.

They think he wasn't old enough to remember, but he does. *Oh Daddy, don't!*

— He tore a hole in me, ow! It bleeds. Like a dentist's drill in butter, like a jackhammer in baby flesh. Everything in me rushed away from the pain and left a hole so big that the air whistled right through the middle of me like a whirlwind in a void.

Made a hole in the middle of him that would yawn empty for the rest of his mortal life; *oh Daddy, don't.* It is bigger than hunger, graver than loss. The hole. That he has spent the rest of his life trying to fill so he can be whole again.

Cannot assuage it.

Or comprehend it. How it happened to him, or why.

— Is it something I did that drew you? No it is what I am. A living magnet. He turns the unholy attraction to different uses now. — I can make anybody fall in love with me.

Those footsteps.

Door to that little back room opening. Crash. *"There* you are."

Curled up against his father, centered around his pain, the hurt child discovered a kernel of hatred glowing inside. Suffering, he curled around it, nursing it until it sprouted. Fueled by pain, roots fed the double trunk. The hurt child could feel the tree spreading inside him, branching into his legs and arms, supporting him. *Oh Daddy, don't!* In time it was strong enough to support him. Bigger than he was. Pain and hatred fueled the tree and when it bloomed, it was lovely. *Such* pretty flowers.

And all the time his father. "There you are."

Boring a hole in his world. He is built around that vacancy. Negative space. Has spent all his life since then trying to fill the yawning vacancy his father tore in his soul. Beyond lies the void. Chaos whistling. The tree shifts to accommodate it; grows up around the hole like a sapling forked by lightning.

Together, they are dangerous.

Daddy, watch out.

"Shut up. Hold still and let me do this."

Accepted the pain with a fierce joy because it fed the tree. *Together, we are huge.* Because they are one now. And overshadow everything. Take what we want from the earth to make ourselves strong. And are invincible.

When we move out together, we can destroy everything.

Its branches are his arms, with the future spelled out at the fingertips: absolute power, and if there is a flaw hidden in the design, if it has grown up around a vacancy, that empty place where the trunk splits to put two feet on the ground, this will be corrected. He has the strength. Urgency gives them a long reach. Whatever gets in the way, they destroy.

I tried to warn you.

"Daddy, no more!"

The tree blossoms in fire.

Fire that changes everything. After the father finished and went to bed they climbed out of the crib, crept through the house until they found what it needed. Matches. Kerosene. Did what they wanted while upstairs he slept on and on. Sirens in the night: At the hospital, some woman hugged him. His smile was so bright she overlooked the scorched cuffs of the pajamas, the burnt-out kitchen matches in the pocket. "You poor child, now you have lost both parents. Oh, you poor baby. We'll find a lovely new home for you."

In her arms, he turned on the fatal charm as coolly as his father switched on the bedroom light. He can smile and *smile.* Felt her respond. "Oh, you sweet thing."

The tree takes what it needs.

It blossoms in fire, but it will express itself in blood.

The rest flickers in the background; like the pictures on the wall of the cave it is perceived but not present. What fell between him and his first attempts to complete himself, all the pain and blood and failure. How he will fulfill the design; this time he will not rest until it is accomplished. He has what he needs. The woman, after all these years and in spite of everything that's happened to him. The place is ready. Everything is rushing to completion.

The tree incandesces inside him like an armature of wire. They serve each other. What it needs, they take.

His head fills with the rush of his own breathing.

He has her now. The rest will follow.

3

SILENT RUNNING: submarines when they shut down all systems to evade pursuers. Michael goes through the kitchen. He's afraid to rouse Tommy or Teah until he knows something for certain. If he wakes Teah now and Mom turns out to be out on the point sketching or down the street borrowing a cup of perspective, Teah will never let him forget it. His sister is sixteen now, and so hung up on being older than Michael that she acts like a citizen of another country. These days his sister is like an unexploded firework, one spark and she'll go up like a basket of rockets. She'll fly out in eight directions and ruin everything.

There is a major problem here. He doesn't know what he means by *everything*.

When his dad got lost something weird happened to Michael. He needs to have everybody accounted for. Especially Mom. When he was little and stuck in the car while Clary went into the store Michael got strung out on waiting. You could never tell what might be happening to a person while she was in there somewhere, so deep inside that you couldn't see her. By the end he'd be holding his breath until she came out again. Somebody who knows says it's separation anxiety, natural, considering. *You poor kid your father.* Shut up, my father's fine. But the anxiety is awful.

He almost dies of looking in the cellar.

From the top of the stairs he sees it is neatly swept, the same. Going down he broaches a spiderweb stretched across the stairwell like an airtight seal on an aspirin bottle, guaranteeing no tampering.

Upstairs is worse. What if his mother is sick in bed, or hurt or something?

If you keep your weight on the ends of old stairs instead of stepping in the middle the boards won't creak and nobody will hear you coming. If you turn the door handle silently you may surprise the person inside, but if she's OK and she sees it's only you she won't cry out and the others won't have to know you were so silly. If there's nobody in the bedroom at all, you have to deal with a completely new set of problems.

It's never been emptier. The bed is made: tight hospital corners, spread so taut you could bounce a penny off it. The usual clutter is missing: daybook, makeup, sunglasses all removed in one swipe as far as he can tell, leaving a picture of his folks and one stray lipstick on the dresser. He's afraid to look in the closet.

He doesn't know whether to be glad or sorry everything looks the same, her clothes jumbled at one end, his father's dress uniforms and civvies neatly hung at the other, Dad's shoes at attention. The suitcases are still stashed; nothing's been moved and nothing's missing.

This is the song he sings to himself: so if she's gone, she's not planning to be away for long.

The bedside phone is off the hook. Maybe she called to explain and the phones were out. The minute he sets it down it starts ringing. When he picks it up, this rushes out: "Mom?"

"Michael?"

"Mom?" He can't stop; it keeps coming out of him in staccato, "Mom? Mom?" keeps coming out even though he knows it isn't. It's Mrs. Brancato, from the New London *Day:* all those undelivered newspapers. They've had somebody send out replacements . . . A part of his mind is already at work: can't afford to lose the . . . may need the . . . What? Why is he going to need the money? Mrs. B. is just giving him his first warning. As he apologizes, he hears thumping on the bedroom wall: Tommy's still in bed — at this hour — and he sounds cranky.

Going into his little brother's room, Michael tries to be cool. At four and a half, Tommy usually seems older, but right now he's regressing, blinking and rubbing his eyes like a baby. He's plunked in the middle of his rumpled bed, still in his jammies, and there's Fang, sprawled like a white dust mop in the covers next to him. His stuffed Tasmanian devil is lying on the floor, abandoned, and Tommy, hey, the kid is surrounded by . . .

What's he got there? Rocket base, new Legos, Slinky, who gave him all these . . . "Wuow Tom, not up yet?"

"Orders," Tommy says with a little salute that kills instantly. He's blinking fast and his voice is furry. The Westie, who usually mauls Michael's Nikes, yawns and rolls over like an upended doormat. "We had to."

Michael can hardly sort out his baby's brother's shape from the toys in the bed, there are so many. He picks up Tommy's stuffed devil and restores it to him, saying, "Hey, you forgot Taz here." Studies him. "Had to what, Tommy?"

"Be quiet," Tommy says over Taz's head. "Mommy came in and told me."

Slinky, Nerf basketball, gummy worms, giant Teddy, rawhide chewy for Fang. "Told you what, Tommy?"

"Sleep tight . . ." Tommy is rubbing his eyes. He's acting so stupid you'd think he'd been doped. *Doped?* Oh Michael, come on. His little-kid voice is dreamy. ". . . be quiet." He's still struggling back from wherever sleep took him. "Stay here till you came.

"Orders," he murmurs. But there are all these strange new toys. What else has he got here in the bed with him? G.I. Joes, Teenage Mutant Ninja Turtles. Clary said she'd rather die than buy him . . . Uneasy, Michael says, "Where did you get the new stuff, Toms?"

"Mommy. I have to pee." Tommy blinks comic-strip eyes, black circles with wedges for pupils. He looks like a cartoon toddler.

He's so sluggish Michael wants to shake him. "What else did Mommy tell you?"

"Tell me what?"

Short-tempered Teah probably would pick the kid up and shake it out of him, but he's waking up fast and getting upset so Michael says, carefully, "Where she was going, Thomas."

"I want Mommy."

Michael tries, "It's ten o'clock, Tommy, did Mommy put you back to bed today?"

"Not really."

Didn't get him up for breakfast, he thinks even more uneasily. What else does he see on the bed? Jelly doughnuts, half a box left. The dog regards him and goes back to sleep. "Where'd you get the doughnuts?"

"Last night. We had cocoa."

"Last night!"

"Fang too." But Tommy is beginning to crumble. "I want Mommy."

Michael sighs. "Come on, kid, let's go downstairs. Don't worry, be quiet and I'll take care of you."

"I want Mommy to take me."

"Oh shut up and come on," Michael says impatiently.

Going downstairs Tommy gets louder and louder, laying on the volume until Michael picks him up and thumps him down at the kitchen table so hard he drops Taz and starts crying as if his world has ended. "Shh shh, shh, goddammit," Michael says, dragging out soup bowls and filling them with Froot Loops that overflow and scatter.

"Nooo," his little brother says, getting redder. "I want Mommy to fix it."

"Shut up and eat."

Tommy swells like a water balloon about to pop and splatter everything. "I want Mommy!"

"Oh shh, oh shit, oh please stop," Michael begs, throwing a blob of ice cream on Tommy's cereal just to quiet him; then he slouches at the table next to his baby brother, shoveling food into his own face without knowing why it rolls around in there like plastic kibbles, growling, "just shut up and eat your damn breakfast." He hands him the pad and Craypas, just the way Clary always does, saying Clary's lines: "If you eat it all up you can draw monsters, OK?"

"Where's Mommy?"

"She's not here right now but . . ." If you leave your name and number after the beep she'll get back to you. "Ah. She'll be back soon," Michael says heavily.

There is no reason for him to notice that there's a page torn off the top of Tommy's pad. Alert and careful as Michael is, there's no way for him to find out that the missing page is crumpled now and blowing along the gutter in the beginning spring rain, collecting with other debris in front of old Mrs. Ferguson's house. Even if he knew to run outside, even if he went straight to the gutter and found it, the rain has all but destroyed any trace of the message scrawled there. In another hour the pulpy mass will be plastered across the grate of the storm drain at the corner.

What Michael Hale *will* notice as he cruises restlessly because he isn't feeling strong enough to face his baby brother are two fresh oven dishes in the refrigerator. Mom's left her noodle thing and her rice thing for them. Which means she stayed up cooking after they went to bed, what was it, a military secret? If she knew she was going away, why didn't she tell them?

Troubled, he goes back through the hall, checks the phone pad, but his mother hasn't left any note he can find. Hopelessly, he pushes the SAVE button on the answering machine and replays yesterday's messages: one from big, goofy Shar Masters, only cleans for them one day a week but acts like she owns the family. Shar sounds pissed about something, but, hey. There's another one of Sarah's long, boring messages that always begin, "Dear Clary," which he fast forwards. Then without preface or explanation a flat, neutral man's voice says: "Be ready."

It is this that sends Michael upstairs, shouting for his sister, whom he loves but does not always like, and discovers he needs right now. He hears his own voice getting thick with worry and confusion as he starts hammering on her door, calling: "Teah. Tee-yahhh. Ce-ceel-yah. *Tee*-yahh!"

Michael knows she is rubbing her eyes wondering: Phone for me, oh, is it Eddy? What does Teah care that their world is cracking? Eleven months apart, they are yang and yin, these two, divergent parts of the same psyche, Michael and Teah. They are so close that what one thinks, the other knows, and yet they fight, they fight.

He hammers, calling, "Tee-ah."

Idiot, in no way can she answer fast enough. He wrenches the door open.

"Go away." Teah hurls George Teddy at him and puts her head under her pillow.

Lunging, Michael grabs his sister by the shoulders and pulls her to a sitting position. To his astonishment, she's waked up smiling. "For God's sake, Michael, what are you doing?"

"There's trouble."

But Teah's trying to cling to something: whatever she had in sleep before he disrupted it. Surely Michael knows those dreams in which their dad is fine, and more good things are coming. They never dream about him coming back. That would be admitting he's really lost. Instead, in this continuum Dad is a given, and for the rest — well, Teah dreams of the one perfect person she will love forever. Waked like this, she can almost see his outlines shimmering: tall, gorgeous, with eyes she can't make out at this distance even though she can feel them on her. If only she can get closer . . . one of these nights she's going to get near enough to see him clearly . . . The image shimmers in the air between them. Dazzled, she blinks at her brother. "Let go, Mikey!"

"Shut up," he growls, low, so Tommy won't hear.

Naturally Teah does the opposite, segues from the dreamy whisper into angry shouting. "Trouble! What do you mean, trouble?"

Tommy, he thinks. The neighbors, he thinks, shaking her. "I don't know yet, now shut up, OK?"

Instead she tries to shake him off. "Leave me alone, Michael."

They grapple until Michael gets a grip on her upper arms in spite of the fact that they are swimming in the sleeves of Eddy Stanko's Shrunken Heads sweatshirt and he pins her. "It's about Mom," he begins, oh shit, why is he barking? With an effort he pulls it down to a taut whisper. "I don't know what's the matter and I don't know what to do, but I think something's happening."

Teah strains against his hands in the second before she snaps into the present; it's as if she already understands that whatever she had before he woke her up is lost, that there will be other losses and this is only the beginning. Tears slide down; she doesn't even know. "Oh Mikey, I was having the best dream."

4

SHAR WOULD DO ANYTHING for Clary Hale, but no way in hell is she going to go in and clean house for her today. Saturday, man, her one day to sleep late because part of her rehabilitation is getting up early on Sundays to sing in the church choir in the rinky-dink Congo, sorry, Congregational Church down on Broad Street. Sundays she has to wash her haystack hair and snare it in a barrette so she'll fit in with the women of the First Church of Christ Congregational, you'd think they were doing her a fucking favor, letting her sing, which leaves her only today to sleep in.

Shar Masters has a history. With a conviction plus a couple of priors she's already done three yards in the women's prison, all for a little bitty armed robbery, unfair since she only happened to go into the job carrying a gun because she had the supreme bad taste to fall in love with big old handsome Bo — Bobie March, with the gifted hands and honey mouth and the back tooth missing. Met him, oh shit! at the laundromat on Divorced Dads' Saturday. Hair crawling up his arms like a flock of live things pulling her eyes after them. "I love you, Sharlit, — do — love — you."

"I love you too, Bobie, honey, but it's Charlotte." "Oh Shar, Shar-*let*": those hands!

"Wuoow, Bobie . . ." No wonder she'd do anything for him.

You might think who would go for klunky Shar Masters with the great big shoulders and that face like a Polish ham, but, crazy, she comes off soft and fluffy because of something sweet that runs along just underneath the surface, the foster dads used to point it out to her when she was little, honey you're so sweet. Come on over here to me . . . And bongo, out of *that* foster home and into another, it's not her fault men like her. Her tragedy is always being attracted to the wrong ones.

Left to herself peaceful Shar would be living in some nice sunny place with frilly checkered curtains and the china with the rooster pattern. She would grow her own vegetables and never be brought up on charges. But she is romance-prone like some people are accident-prone. She can see trouble coming and walk right into it. That sweet, longing part of her runs ahead of her with its arms wide. *Maybe this one.* And once she falls in love she will do anything for him, no matter how stupid or wrong.

Then he stiffs her and she vows all over again that this mistake in love is the last. It never is.

She would give anything to be independent.

Like Clary Hale. Painter, mom, no man around. This is a woman who knows how to keep it all together. Shar would love to learn her secret.

In fact Shar has a lot to learn from this person. Where Shar is big and plain, dark-haired Clary is slight and beautiful, knows what to do no matter what happens, has style, this electricity — Shar can see the attraction — in spite of which Clary makes it clear she's not going to let anything touch her. Where Shar is mushy at heart when it comes to men, Clary is like steel. It is this toughness Shar would like to catch from her.

No more bars, she thinks, but goes anyway.

Some of it must be rubbing off though, she thinks, now that there seems to be a beautiful new guy coming into the picture — nice fellow, wears a white shirt. Keeps it on even when they make love. Shar thinks her life is borderline changing. Since the Hales, she is attracting a better class of men.

So she has Social Services to thank. They got this job for her, those dreary tools of the state in squidgy rubber-soled shoes and ugly dresses matching up unskilled people and dumb jobs. Nice Navy family called Hale needs someone to clean on Fridays. Me, clean house? No way. But she doesn't have much choice here. Now that you are released, Ms. Masters. Released. To what? Ugly room above a Korean grocery, flaking plaster, stained window shades and no-watt light bulbs, bad mattress. Lonely nights and bad TV and zits from the fast food she eats, breakfast lunch and Christmas. Compared to this, Clary Hale's house looks like Saint Theresa.

Of all the people she works for, the Hales are like family. In addition to cleaning, she takes care of Tommy if they go out nights. That Michael slaps her a high five, "Yo, Shar," and she thinks, Man, if you were only a little older. Half a yard older and this guy could give her serious heart trouble. But he's a kid too; when she tries to clean his room he fake-guards the door.

"Nobody comes in here."

"Sorry, but your mom says I have to." If he gives her any lip she goes: "Be glad you've got a damn mother, the state took mine away from me." And if that doesn't do it, she beats him down with the worst stories about her foster-home period. "This could happen to *you*," she says, "if you don't watch it. *Listen;* until I got busted I slept on other people's sofas." She says, "Kneel down and thank your stars you've got a mom that cares about these things. When you go on the state you lose your rights," she says, "so shut up and let me clean."

And Teah? When nobody's around she and this girl Teah hang out in the kitchen and Shar dusts off her love stories. "Bonnie and Clyde," Teah says when Shar talks about Billy from high school that stole the Porsche for her, and Bobie March, whom she is still a little in love with. But Billy is dead and Bobie is doing hard time and she has lost touch with the nicest guy she ever went with, homely Marlin Winslow from Wilmington, in spite of making love all one Labor Day weekend after they got back from the beach.

Shar feels bad about the loss, the waste, the sadness, and sweet Teah goes, There there. She wishes Teah was her sister, pretends Tommy's hers; she buries her chin in his soft hair thinking: he's just like me, neither one of us can remember our father, and can't say whether the tears squishing up in her eyes are for this poor little fatherless boy, or for Shar.

This Clary is not like any of the other women Shar works for. Her family are the only people in her life. She's even fixed it so she doesn't go to an office. The woman doesn't *do* like other people do, hang out with girlfriends over coffee, give parties, spin stories on the telephone. Picked this spot halfway between Newport and New London so she wouldn't have to hang with the other Navy wives. With him gone she has no desire to go to the Officers' Club, which Shar would think of as the ideal place to meet men.

But Clary doesn't want to meet men.

To love-struck Shar, it's a puzzle and a mystery. One guy, that's probably lost forever, and that's enough for her? Look at his pictures and you can see it, handsome young Navy officer, clear eyes, square jaw, who wouldn't love him, but. Oh, *lady*. Four years gone and Clary's not thinking of replacing him?

"What good is he going to do you, dead at the bottom of the sea?"

Clary answers with tears rimming her eyelashes, "It was perfect once. I don't want ever to do it wrong."

Everything she has Clary pours into those kids, and what she has left over she gives to these paintings she does. Wild. Shar can see the passion, but it's only paint on a board. Doesn't she ever get. Well. "But, don't you ever get. You know."

"Listen," Clary says with force. "Guard yourself. Take care. You can't be too careful in love."

She is driven by things Shar doesn't even know about.

It comes out in these big paintings, not the ones she does for sale, but the other ones, that stand along the wall in the room off the kitchen where she paints. They seem alive, like crouching animals. Most of the little stuff Clary Hale paints to sell looks like all the other little stuff people sell in beach towns during the summer season — gulls wheeling over sea oats, trawlers, sailboats, lobster pots bobbing up and down in the water, pretty patches of sand and water that make people think they can buy a piece of summer and take it home. This is her gallery stuff, that makes her money for extras, like paying Shar.

But then there are these — *others*. They are big, dark, glossy; they are in no way pretty-little, or nice. They look less like paintings than explosions. Anybody weird enough to paint these has got to be up the wall and halfway across the ceiling, but pretty Clary just smiles. Shar is scared to be in the same room with them.

They are all of this *place*. In spite of the differences in color and style and kinds of paint, in spite of Clary claiming they're abstractions, Shar knows otherwise. The woman is painting the same weird scene a dozen different ways. This ramshackle house in some Godforsaken spot: same slash of a roofline. Hurricane light in the sky, palms and pines slanting to horizontal in a hard wind.

Ask her what she's painting about and she won't say. She won't even tell you where. Works on them when nobody's around; maybe it's like making love. Now they are getting different, darker. Mention it and Clary just looks blank and says offhand, "Oh, those," as if nothing out of the ordinary is happening. But something is happening. Shar catches — what is it — a shift in the atmospherics. The hush before some huge electrical storm.

Lately, it's gotten worse.

Shar came in last Friday with something big on her mind. Usually Clary gives coffee and they sit down and jaw. So once they got talking, Shar could just let it out. But last week, when Shar most needed her, this *friend* of hers was off on a tear. No hello, just this death grip, Clary asking, "Was anybody here?"

"Listen, Clary, there's something I've got to tell you . . ."

She didn't hear; she only jerked Shar's arm. "Last week."

But Shar was filled to overflowing with it, happy, scared. ". . . That's happening with me."

"Was anybody *here*?" Clary was white around the mouth — all bent about something, but listen, Shar too has her problems, so if she fobbed her off, listen, she had a big load on her mind. Like, maybe it was a glitch in Shar's memory, or a funny need to pay Clary back. So all she said was, "Gee, not that I know of." And by the time Shar did remember who had come, the moment had passed.

"You're sure," she said; lord she was grim. Then Clary left her standing in the kitchen with her teeth hanging out and went back to slashing at one of those great big paintings.

Shar followed her into the painting room, trying to get Clary to look at her, but the woman was on some astral plane where the wind whistles and ordinary people don't belong. "Listen," Shar began anyway.

God it was crazy, Clary, cross-eyed with concentration and stabbing at that painting. "I can't talk now. I have to finish." She was over the edge and hanging by her fingernails, snapping, "Oh please just get out of here."

End of their conversation that day; end of the day, in fact. Clary paid her off and sent her home. No wonder Shar forgot to mention the one person that did drop by, unless she was so pissed she, like, *failed* to mention it? Shit, she thought angrily, it's my business anyway.

When Clary called Thursday night, Shar thought she was going to apologize, but no. All she wanted was for Shar to bag Friday and come in and clean on her goddam day off. "I'll think about it."

In hell. It is her pleasure to lie in on Saturdays drowsing in her shortie gown, and besides. Her new man may come. He may just walk in and find her in her flowered eyelet nightie, in which case she'll tell him what's happening with her. (Oh dearest, it's my baby too.) Listen, it could happen. What this sweet talker is not going to find on any Saturday morning, she vowed, is Shar Masters in another woman's kitchen, scrubbing on her day off.

Which is what she told Clary's machine.

Trouble is, now she feels guilty. How often has Clary Hale asked her to do anything special, or extra? Not one time, Shar thinks, getting up and sitting on the edge of the bed with her wide feet lightly resting on the tops of her fuzzy bedroom slippers. Clary's fuzzy bedroom slippers. They have white plush bunny-rabbit heads with pink ears. Oh here, generous Clary said, laughing, when Shar admired them. "It's just a gag, if you like them, enjoy, I never wear the things." Shar is wearing them. Oh thanks; this makes her feel like shit.

Shar would like to be the one who does all the giving. It is, she thinks, a mark of security. She is beginning to feel terrible.

She will not breach her principles and clean on Saturday, she thinks, no way, not ever, but tell you what. If her Lover doesn't come soon, if she doesn't hear a knock on the door of her single room and open it up to find the future waiting outside, if she doesn't open it on this *handsome guy,* Shar is going to have to get up and get dressed and go on living, same as before. After she's been to her Saturday matinee at the smelly little old Capitol on Broad Street, she'll, like, drop by? Maybe take Clary a present just to let her know that she has her principles about days off and all, but Shar doesn't hold a grudge.

5

IT'S ALMOST SUPPERTIME and their mother isn't back.

Michael is sitting on the back steps spitting grape seeds with tough old Shar, thinking, should he tell her, should he not tell her? He isn't even sure what there is to tell.

Inside, Tommy's on his face in front of the TV with his ass in the air, having his fourth nap of the day. Fang is asleep on Tommy's bed upstairs and Teah is off at Crystal Mall, going malling in their mother's diamond studs and her best silk shirt. His sister who he has always thought was a lot like him is diverging. It's not so much that she's doing something he thinks is wrong as that she's doing something he can't imagine either of them doing.

Teah is out malling with slouching, sinewy Eddy Stanko, who even stands on a slant leaning into you like a mother's nightmare, bad Eddy with the satin shirt open over the pecs and the black-rimmed eyes with blue stains running underneath, who knows what he is taking, at a hundred yards Eddy looks like bad news. If people wore road signs, his would have the red circle with the slash through it. What Michael doesn't know is whether Teah has attached herself to the worst possible person to prove that she can do fine in this world without their father or because she's so desperate to replace him that anybody looks good to her.

She says it's love but love has nothing to do with it. It's as if the part of Teah Michael likes is trying to commit suicide.

Teah doesn't see it. Stood by the phone looking like Snow White on a good day, in the slashed jeans and Eddy's lizard jacket and that look that makes Michael want to smack her:

"Well, me staying home isn't going to get her back here any sooner."

"But, *Eddy*."

"Listen, if he wants to, he can go to Juilliard."

Well he looks like just another bum guitarist to me. "What if something's happened to Mom?"

Teah blew him off: "This isn't a movie, Mikey. Now be cool."

"She could be anywhere."

Twirling her fingers, Teah just blew him off, Michael and all his worries. "Mothers do *not* disappear on you, when she gets back tonight she'll laugh at you for worrying."

"What makes you think she's coming back tonight?"

"She always does." Teah's one year older and always will be: superior Teah, who never lets him forget she hit the planet first.

It sounded OK. Maybe he just needed reassurance. OK, sometimes we believe what we want to. For a while.

But now the day is definitely getting old and the older it gets the uglier the taste in his mouth gets, like socks after gym class, or a room with a corpse in it. He's glad Shar's here to take his mind off it, he thinks, popping in a string of grapes in a series of *thops*. He pops a grape, sucking it in fast, *thop*. Shar pops a grape. Her bubble-gum-pink sneakers are almost as big as his scuzzy black hightops. One of the best things about Shar is she doesn't talk unless you want her to. He isn't waiting, exactly, but nothing has come along and let him stop waiting. No cab has pulled up bringing Clary back from wherever. Nobody has called to say their mother is on her way. No one has explained.

At least it's quit getting dark so early. At least he has company. Shar turned up at the front door around four today looking dressed up, for Shar, in this pink flowered dress with a shit-eating look and this holiday fruit basket that unaccountably makes him sad, perky grapes and bananas and fancy jelly and cellophane grass piled in under yellow cellophane with a big ribbon on top, who knows where she found it, when he opened the door she was working hard on a smile. "Here."

He's embarrassed about how glad he was to see her.

Shar simply waiting: "It's for your mom."

Oh thanks. Michael thinks his face was probably going all funny — should he lie about where she wasn't, or what? Could he make that muscle in his cheek quit twitching? "She's not here right now." His face felt naked.

Probably Shar didn't notice; her face was not exactly *all there,* like, not everything was right with her either. She hung in the doorway like Fang begging: Don't send me away, OK? "Tell her, ah, I'm, ah, sorry I couldn't clean for her?"

"Yeah, right."

"I had to. Ah. I was waiting for somebody." She was looking at him like, did he see anything wrong with her? Shar is always getting disappointed in love. Hocked: a-*hem*, shrugged, like: life goes on, and continued. "Then I thought, fuck it, so I came on over."

In the top of the basket were these chocolate bunny rabbits — left over from March, probably, distressed merchandise. It hit him that last Easter Clary took the family up to Newport for lobster, and the leftover bunnies made Michael so sad that he said, "So, do you want a bite of bunny rabbit or what?"

Her big, blunt face broke into a grin. Which is how they ended up sitting out here on the back steps eating grapes. "So your new man was supposed to come but he didn't," Michael says, priming her. Sometimes Shar forgets and tells amazing love stories.

"You know men, tell you one thing and do another, if you want to know the truth, that's the way they keep us down." Disappointment is rising from her like smoke. "I could have sworn he was in town last night, things he told me, you know? But he didn't call and he never came. Now it's practically night . . ." She brightens. "The way I figure it, he got held up on a job."

He is too polite to say the way her luck runs, the guy could be held up by almost anybody, because even Godzilla was cuter. "What kind of job?"

"He's in investigation," Shar says importantly.

The word strikes an off-chord. "What do you mean, investigation?"

"Asks a lot of questions, you know."

Michael can't stop his back hairs from standing up one by one, making a spiny ridge up his back. He asks carefully, "Like what?"

"Insurance, I think," Shar says, delicately extracting a grape stem from the pulp in her mouth. "All those questions. Maybe it's about false claims."

"Maybe." Insurance. Oh is that all.

"At least I think it's false claims. He never says exactly. I like a man in a white shirt," she says. "I waited all day," she says mournfully.

"Maybe tomorrow."

"Maybe," says Shar, who lapses, dreaming.

Meanwhile it's almost dark, no Mom, he's going to have to go in the damn house and put in one of Mom's casseroles, which is a form of giving in. The taste in his mouth is so bad that he doesn't think he could stand to eat without her back home and sitting at the table. His mouth cracks. "Ah."

"Say what?"

"Ah." He can't get it out. Instead he circles around the trouble. If he gets Shar started maybe he can spring into one of the gaps Shar leaves when she thinks it's your turn to confess something. "Tell me how you got stuck being a ward of the state."

Brooding, Shar says absently, "You don't want to hear that old story." But because it may help her *not* brood, she begins. "OK, it was a total accident, and I can tell you that is one accident you don't want to get into. It was like we got into a wreck. Patsy and me. Patsy was my mom."

"What happened to her?"

Shar's face darkens. "After a while you just lose track."

This is awful. "But she was your mom."

She looks into her hands. "So listen, one day the two of us were getting along fine, when she couldn't cook we would get take-out or I could open cans, and the next minute they yanked me out of there, put my mom in detox and I never saw her again, and bang, I'm a ward of the state."

"Just — like that?"

"Struck without warning. They didn't even have a warrant," she says. "Right when we were doing fine."

This makes Michael uneasy. "How did they get on to you?"

"Patsy used to take this stuff to keep from getting depressed because she had such a hard life. After a while she just kind of phased out. Everything in our house broke or quit working and we ran out of money. My school dress was getting kind of, crusty? If you spill enough stuff on anything it starts to smell, which was one thing. And then some kid got lice and the teacher took us all into the bathroom and checked our heads with a ruler and a flashlight. I guess my hair was kind of scuzzy because Patsy forgot to wash it." She looks up. "So I suppose you could say it was my fault, in a way, but I was only in second grade, and who knew I was supposed to wash it?"

"It wasn't your fault, Shar."

"It wasn't her fault, either. She just wasn't up to it." Her voice drops. "So we were just sitting home one day eating TV mix when this pinched-looking bitch from the state got inside our house. Patsy was too wasted to focus so this person got in, like, accidentally."

"That was it?"

"You got it. If it hadn't been for that, we would still be doing fine. Once they get inside, you've had it," Shar says. "You have to never, ever let them get inside."

Noted and filed against contingencies. If you arm yourself against the future you can keep a lot of bad things from happening. When they got the word about Dad, Michael was so astonished that he didn't know what to do. Did not — know. What to do. He'll die and go to hell before he ever lets himself get caught short that way again. Now he's the master of plans.

He thinks. What if Mom? He swallows air. "So what was the worst part about being on the state?"

"Right, that," Shar says moodily. "The worst part was the surprise. Like, the insult?

"The second-worst part was they didn't fucking know what to do with you. Like, in the old days, they had to live in the orphanage, with tin cups and bunk beds and all? Kids had each other. But some genius figured out if they could stash you with some grownup, it would save the state a pile of bucks, and if they couldn't find a grownup you were related to then the best thing to do was hire one. Foster parents. Sure. The nicest foster mom I ever had lived in the crappiest place but she got sick and they couldn't keep me any more. And the rest — I wouldn't give you two cents for the rest."

"You could have run away," he says.

"They always catch you. Besides, I was only eight, and, like, who would I run to? If I'd had anybody to run to they wouldn't of made me a ward of the state in the first place."

Michael says carefully, "You mean any living relatives."

"Oh shit, I had a living relative, but nobody knew where he was living."

Michael almost chokes on a grape. The part of him that plans goes running on ahead. If she's really gone, we have to keep things going no matter what, he thinks. If my route money doesn't cover food, we can always go into my stash. He will not admit precisely why he's stalling on the camera. Fifteen hundred dollars, and he can't stop waiting for his dad to come home and help him choose the right one. Mom can always pay me back. If it turns out she's gone for good, we can always . . . He doesn't know what they can always.

". . . I didn't even have my own damn teddy bear," Shar finishes. "But you guys are probably loaded with relatives."

Not really. Dad's folks died in a plane crash. And Mom's . . . God, he doesn't exactly *know* about Mom's. But Shar is waiting. "Oh sure," he lies because it seems important. "Gangs of them."

"Then you'll be fine."

They don't hear from their grandparents even at Christmas. "I don't know what it is with my mom's folks," he begins. Shar has her head turned like Tweety bird; what is he expecting her to say here? Does he really think Clary has told this goofy felon some truth about her mother and father, that she wouldn't tell him? Foolishly, he fishes anyway. "We. Ah. Don't hear from them?"

"Sometimes families don't get along."

"Mom doesn't want to talk about them," he blurts. It's strange, the way Clary's face closes when he broaches it. "Mom grew up in Wilmington."

"No shit!" She gives him a what-a-coincidence grin; it's as if they've discovered a friend in common. "My old boyfriend Marlin lives in Wilmington."

Information he files for possible use later. "That's great."

It is dusk now and the violet half-light makes Shar forget who Michael is. The way she talks, he could be some trusted girlfriend. Or confessor, accepting confidences in the twilight. "Sweet man, big shoulders, Marlin Winslow, the only guy I ever dated that didn't have a record. I don't know how it all slipped away but it did, but I always liked him. Sometimes I think if my old man had stayed around I'd be a better judge of who to fall in love with." Sighs. "I would love to see him again."

"Your father?"

"Whatever," she says; in another minute she is going to cry.

Michael says what she counts on hearing: "There's a guy out there for you, Shar. Really. All you have to do is wait."

She is getting morose. "If you say so," she says glumly, shifting those big pink sneakers. "But life is hard when you're alone. So hang on to your nice family," she finishes. "It may turn out to be the best love you'll ever get."

"Oh, Shar." Five more minutes and they'll both be crying.

"You want to know something awful?" She stops. "Oh shit, never mind, somebody's coming."

He can hear Eddy Stanko's jacked-up Corvette homing in like a hornet, which means Teah will be rounding the corner of the garage in another minute with neon eyes and her mouth smirched from the uses of the afternoon, and he really does not want to have to deal with both these people in the same breath right now because morose as she is, Shar Masters is not stupid; Teah will say some careless thing and let drop that Mom is gone.

"So, Shar," he says, inspired, "did you leave a note for this guy? He might be over there waiting."

Boy she is depressed. "Nobody waits for me."

"The great Shar Masters? Come on!" Oh shit, here comes Teah, he has to work fast. He can hear the brack of Eddy's Corvette, pulling away. Inspired he says, "Listen, you're worth waiting for."

"Oh kid, you see too many movies." Shar punches him on

the arm so hard it rocks him, but she is grinning. "Oh, hey Teah. Tell your mom I'm sorry I can't stay. My new man is waiting."

EXTERIOR — LATE AFTERNOON — THE HALE HOUSE
Pull back.

Overhead shot: House, backyard, garage. Michael does not know how he knows what this looks like, but he knows. If he could make this into a movie, he could sit back and watch it instead of having to be here, looking at things. SHAR and TEAH pass on the back walk, one leaving, one approaching. TEAH joins MICHAEL on the steps. From this height the Hales look insignificant, two little dots, their faces just blobs without features. Michael shakes his head; he can't just be the camera here. He has to step back into character and play the scene.

They go inside without talking. Even these days, when they rub on each other like dry sticks about to ignite, they are close. What one thinks, the other knows. He doesn't have to ask about Eddy.

"God, Michael, look at this kitchen, smell the garbage, and for God's sake what about dinner?" The homemaking avenger takes out her anger on her brother. "If you don't have the casserole ready for Mom she's going to kill us, and where the hell is Tommy?"

"I think he's having a nap."

She's crashing pots, hasty and furious. In the absence of Clary she is all big sister, intent on running the show. She scolds him in June Cleaver tones. "Don't you know if you let him sleep all day he'll keep us up all night?"

"Oh give me a break," Michael snarls and goes looking for the dog. The best thing about Fang is, he doesn't talk. "Fang?" He expects the Westie to lunge for his ankles as he comes upstairs, gnashing his hightops like a windup toy, but he doesn't. "Fangles?" He finds him finally, nested in quilts in Tommy's bed, right where he left him this morning. "Wake up, asshole," Michael says with a guilty swallow. "Have you been out today? Did I forget to give you water?"

He's half-aware of the phone ringing, Teah talking, but Fang has rolled over and won't speak to him. "So what's the matter, pupper, are you sick? Did you get in somebody's sleeping pills?" Fang nuzzles but won't get up so Michael ends up carrying the dog downstairs with its fuzzy white head bobbing on his shoulder like a baby's. "Something's the matter with Fang," he tells Teah.

She has just put down the phone. "Not now, Michael," she says distractedly. "Just put him to bed and let him sleep it off. There's some stuff we have to talk about."

"What? What is it?"

"Not yet," she says.

"Goddammit, what is it?"

"Put the dog down," she says. "Come in here. Shut the door and I'll tell you."

"Was it Mom?"

"Not exactly." The phone call has pushed Teah into a different mode — not officious, really, but newly important. She is filled to the top and quivering with something, glowing with it, but she seems to be ordering details in her mind and she won't say anything until she has it right. She makes him wait until he's ready to kill her. Then she begins. "That was a call from Naval Intelligence."

Relieved, Michael snaps to. "Naval Intelligence!"

"A Captain Rogers Maynard."

"Was he calling from the base?"

"Not really. Listen. He's a classmate of Daddy's, he says we should look him up in the *Lucky Bag* to confirm it."

The Naval Academy yearbook will check out, Michael knows. He lets all his breath out. "So."

"So." Teah's voice is strong. "We've finally got our orders."

Orders. His taut muscles let go for the first time since morning. *Yes,* he thinks, relaxing into it. In a military family, orders are orders. Orders organize. They save lives. They relieve you of decisions. All his life in the Navy, Michael has been taught that good officers follow orders without stopping to ask for reasons because hesitation can get your ship sunk; you can be blown out of the air while you're still asking the question. Orders. It sounds right. "What are our orders?"

"We're to stay mum and sit tight," she says with certainty. "It's a classified matter."

"Where's Mom?"

"He was calling from a secret installation. Mom's safe, she's fine, but she's part of a sensitive operation . . ." Then Teah's surface shatters and all her hopes come rushing up. "He said he couldn't tell us much, but I think they may be close to finding Dad."

"My God," he says. "Oh, God." He's afraid to breathe. One false move and they will lose this.

"So it's absolutely classified."

"When's she coming back?"

Her voice is tight. "I don't know if they know yet." To Michael's astonishment she grabs his wrists: what one thinks, the other knows. *Oh please believe this.* He doesn't have to assent. Her voice ripples unexpectedly. "To make it work, they have to keep it secret. Us too. We can't let anybody know."

When Dad left, he put his cap on Michael for a minute and took him by the shoulders, saying, "Now you are the man here." He has responsibilities. He has Shar's warning. "We can't let anybody know we're alone here, either."

"We are, aren't we?" In a split second his sister turns a corner. Teah flashes him a sly grin. "I guess that means we get to run the show. So, hey. We can do anything we want here."

But he is not ready to address this. "So OK, Mom's *fine.* And maybe . . ." It would be bad luck even to mention getting Dad back. He changes course. "Maybe we'd better have dinner."

At which point Tommy stumbles in. "Is Mommy home?"

Teah says in an adult tone, "Not yet, Toms."

But his mouth blurs. "I want Mommy."

Michael says, "Not yet, OK?"

Tommy's like a guitar string stretched to snapping. "Then when?"

Michael barks, "I don't know, OK?"

"Where's Mommy?"

Teah says irrationally, "Shut up, Toms, didn't you hear Michael?"

"Where is she?"

And for the moment Teah loses it, shrilling: "I said, shut up!" with such force that Tommy begins to cry. At which point she grabs him and hugs him, murmuring, "Shut up, shut up, OK, OK," while Michael puts the casserole in the oven.

Then he turns to both of them and says, "Let's make brownies, OK? *While we're waiting.*"

Teah blinks. "Sure, why not?"

Therefore they go back to being Michael and Teah, Captain Tom Hale's children who have talked to Naval Intelligence on the phone and are proceeding under orders. Standard Operating Procedure. All they have to do is do their jobs, and the Navy will take care of the rest. They have supper sitting at the kitchen table just like Dagwood and Blondie with Tommy between them, and at nine they put him to bed like ordinary teenagers baby-sitting for an evening. Their mother is fine and they're fine, or they think they are, they manage it perfectly until around midnight when Teah brings down her hair gunk, messing with colored mousse and an Afro comb in front of a *Saturday Night Live* rerun. Then Prince comes on and Michael boogies over and grabs the can from Teah, who shrieks. Giggling, he sprays a mustache on her; they grapple and mousse spurts all over his face and Teah rubs it in his hair, giggling. They are tangled, wrestling and laughing until the laughter loses its breath and turns into an open-throated sound that is neither shriek nor sob, both of them gasping hard or is it giggling helplessly without knowing why. Or being able to stop.

6

OH MY GOD, my children. For the moment, she is lucid. It won't last long.

Is it day? Night? She doesn't know; he has her blindfolded. Where are they? She doesn't know that either. Somewhere. In the car. Relentlessly going.

I thought we were so safe, she thinks bitterly. She wants to howl, strike out, hurt him and get free. But must not stir. Not if she wants this clear moment. She is lucid, but only until he sees and puts her under again.

Careful.

No matter how careful she is, when she wakes, he knows. Something in the air alerts him and like a hawk he swoops down and strikes her with something sharp that numbs her instantly. Each time she wakes it gets harder to collect the flying bits of her consciousness. The most Clary can hope for here is a couple of minutes in which to — what? All she can do is go back inside her head. The one place where he can't follow. It's the only safe place now, she tells herself, but she knows too well that no place is safe. Was ever safe. It's killing her. Here is Clary Hale, nowhere that she knows; there are her children, alone back in the house on Pequod Street — with no immediate family to move in and help, no network of friends to close in around them and protect them.

Nobody to come after her. She is alone in this. He destroyed the note, she knows. Alone here. Clary can feel the wind whistling around her bare bones.

I should have been more careful.

Should have known that with Tom gone they were doubly

vulnerable. Was a fool to think that separating her kids from the base would protect them from the climate of war and the possibility of violent death. Thinks angrily that she should have found a safer place for them, some Navy enclave with guards at the gates, but knows that even armed Marines could not have prevented this. Should have spent her life building character with other women, trying to make them believe she is like them for her kids' sake, so she'd have at least one friend to leave behind to take care of them. Instead of pouring her whole heart into her family, she should have made useful *friends*. Clary is grieving, somewhere deep. *Oh, Tom, I tried so hard.*

Not the first time she has lost everything.

A woman can go all her life trying to do the right thing; she can shore up everything she has against pain and loss and still not protect her family. This makes her groan, but if she wants even a minute before the next needle she has to swallow it, letting pain and rage swell in her throat until she strangles. She must not do anything to draw his attention. If she so much as clenches her fists inside the blankets he'll know it. If she stirs, he'll see and stop the car; if she murmurs, he'll hear and stab her with another needle: terrible stuff that drives her into a dark place where she dreams monstrous dreams.

Even if she holds her breath and plays dead, bumping along on the floor of the car in her cocoon of blankets and wire, she has a limited amount of time because the injections come on a regular schedule. Once she woke to hear his chiming watch. She knows they must have stopped for gas, once for something else, she thinks, heard voices outside the car, thinks . . . doesn't know enough to think. Hates being helpless. God, if she could only strike out. She wants to strain against the wires like some superhero and snap them like rubber bands but she stands five feet four in her shoes, strong but slight, and all her morning workouts put together haven't armed her: *I should have been born bigger. Heavy. Huge.* Armed: Tom's gun, that she refused to touch. Knows nothing would make her proof against him.

Struggling in the middle of Pequod Street at four in the morning he crashed against her, leaving her flattened; in spite of her furious pounding he shoved her in the car and put her out like a spark with the first needle. When she woke and began flailing, he put her out again. The next time she woke up she was like this, swaddled, bound tight. What's she going to do, rolled up like this, with her arms tight to her body? What can she hope to use against him? Silently, she rages: *No matter how strong you get, it isn't strong enough.*

There is a change in the quality of the air in the car. As if the driver is alert to her, and listening.

She has the idea he can hear her thinking.

Even when she lies rigid, pretending to be dead to him, to everything, he knows. *Oh please don't.* But he's slowed the car. *Don't, god damn you.* In another minute he will stop. Will part the blankets and drive the needle into her shoulder. This moment is all she has. To plan. Pray. Or try to. It's hard to think. Whatever. By this time she knows better than to scream. Still as she is in the stifling case of blankets, rigid and motionless, she knows she won't be lucid for long.

7

IT'S GETTING LATE in the week. Clary hasn't been over in days. She hasn't called and she hasn't come. Sarah has something important to tell the girl. If they don't talk soon, she's afraid she'll forget again. As each day passes her memory gets worse and Sarah feels worse about it. If they had only gone underwear shopping last week the way Clary promised, Sarah could have come right out with it, but her underpants are still falling down in spite of the safety pin, so much for Clary's promises to take her out last Saturday.

Lord she is confused. The inside of Sarah's house is a little like the inside of her mind — cluttered with rickety antiques, figured rugs and china ornaments that have piled up over the years; there are so many items that she forgets what they are, but. Move even *one object* and she knows. There's something out of place now, whether in her collection or inside her head she cannot say.

That handsome young man who came the other week, when was it anyway? With the clipboard and the official smile. Did he take something? Did Sarah give it to him because he was handsome and sweet with her or did he steal it before she knew?

Something's gone, she thinks, feeling not violated, exactly, but mournful. He did take something. Took it away from me.

But what?

Restlessly, she roams the house. Unless she can remember what he took, she's never going to get it back.

What was it? One of her frosted animals is missing, she tells herself uneasily, but all her jade temple dogs and ivory and crystal elephants, her china cats and the raffia horses from her and Ivor's honeymoon trip are still ranked on corner shelves in the living room. She likes to move them around like so many children: You go there for now, and you — you will go there. The rest march on every conceivable surface along with thimbles and glass and seashells and owls in all sizes because in lieu of children, which she could not seem to carry in spite of her best efforts, Ivor began a collection of owls for her.

In lieu of children, she has things. She has pillows in profusion: embroidered, quilted, mirrored and painted. Every uncommitted surface is covered with a doily because Sarah crochets. She has footstools and smoking stands; cast-iron doorstops line the stairs. If she wonders whether other people are quite so tied up in possessions, she thinks: Well, parts of my life have escaped me forever. It's important to keep new things coming in.

She also has Clary now, beautiful, lonely Navy wife next door — except for her children, no family that Sarah has seen, and except for Sarah, no real friends. Something sets her apart, but what? Sarah's spent the last four years fishing for details but Clary just gives her a smile that is full of shadows and drops no clues. She keeps to herself and does those paintings, like songs.

Last year Clary gave Sarah a birthday party; she decorated a big sun hat with seashells and dried flowers, because she hopes Sarah will start to enjoy going out. Sarah put it on right there in the dining room and she wore it around the house until she went to bed. Clary photographed her in the hat, blowing out eight plus six candles with a bemused smile.

"You and your children," Sarah said as Clary cleared away the birthday things. Clary's the same age as her daughter, if she'd ever had a daughter. They could adopt each other, Sarah thought, put her heart in her hands and handed it over like a gift, "You four are my family."

Clary's face was a puzzle. "How lovely."

It was getting dark; Clary's children were long gone, playing loud music across the way. Sarah began fishing again. "Unless you think your parents would object."

Clary put dishes back in the corner cabinet. Crash. Crash. Crash. "They're beyond that."

"Your. Ah . . . mother and father are dead?"

"I really don't want to talk about it, Sarah."

"My father stopped speaking to me over something I did when I was eighteen," Sarah offered, expecting something in return. Oh, she ran away with the traveling photographer who made her portrait after the high school May crowning. When she left Harry Devereaux and came back to him, Ivor Ferguson forgave her and loved her all the same but her angry father never forgave. "We were dead to each other." She blinked at Clary. Your turn.

Clary's eyes filled. "I know the feeling."

Sarah trailed the hook. "But at the end we made it up."

Clary turned away, rattling silver to cover the overtones in her voice. "You got a chance to tell him you loved him."

"Before he died." But she never made it up to Ivor, not really, and now Ivor is dead. Near the end of her life now, Sarah measures the remaining days in terms of guilt and expiation — things that need to be fixed before she can rest. Watching Clary move around the dining room like a surgical patient whose stitches are pulling, she tried: "No matter how bad it was or how long these things take, you have to find a way to make them up."

Clary's voice was thick. "It's not that kind of thing."

"Then your parents *are* dead," Sarah said. "Oh, my dear."

Anguished, Clary cut her off. "Don't feel sorry for me. It's my fault."

Yes. It was there, then, what Sarah had always suspected — some story untold, the same lingering sense of guilt clouded Clary's eyes: the loss, the need to make something up to the dead. If only she had Ivor here, she — "Let it go," she said, for Clary, for herself. "You can't help the past."

"I never got to tell them how much I loved them," Clary said. Although she was busy, swiftly covering the cake with plastic wrap and brushing crumbs into her hand, her voice was low, urgent. "Sarah, look. If you care about us, please don't talk about this to Teah or Mike."

Nosy old lady! Couldn't stop. "You don't think they need to know?"

Clary wheeled, eyes crackling. "I wouldn't lay that on them!"

"Lay what . . . What?"

She didn't exactly answer. "When I thought I was over it, Tom and I got married. We were so young — he lost his folks in a plane crash, and mine . . . We were both desperate for family; he was a brand-new ensign and I was barely nineteen. Now he's gone too." She shook herself and started over. "The kids are all I have."

"No," Sarah said greedily. "You have me."

She will never forget Clary's arms around her neck. "Oh Sarah," she said. Now they celebrate holidays together and Clary drops in three or four times a week. They usually talk every day. And they are close, real close. If something has come up that's kept her away, poor Clary must be feeling terrible about it. She may even be on her way over, maybe with some little gift. Sarah's made coffee for her every morning for a week. When Clary pops in Sarah will act surprised. She and Ivor redecorated in the 1940s, pink and green kitchen, with colorful duck and chicken decals on the cabinets and green checkered oilcloth on the little round table, the sun comes in above the pink half shutters; she'd be proud to have anybody come in and sit down. — Well, there you are. I've thawed a little coffee cake.

The way she did for that young man. Handsome in the white shirt, was it last week or last month. So nice, he told her not to say a thing. Something about him: she hasn't told a soul.

That day she'd thawed some blueberry muffins, had the Mr. Coffee on, as good as any ordinary housewife, only a little suspicious when he came to the back door. He had such a nice smile she had to smile back. He showed her that official card with his photo and a seal: "I'm from the Landmarks Committee, you must have had your letter from the city by now."

"I didn't have any . . ." Well in fact there was a whole pile of mail in the front room that she just hadn't quite gotten to, but she couldn't let this nice boy think she was letting things get out of hand so she said, "Oh, of course."

"Then you know why I'm here." He was moving inside too fast, but such a fine-looking young man, and that smile! "And you won't mind filling out our questionnaire . . ."

"I don't know if my husband would want me to . . ."

"All your answers will be held in confidence. Here, let me help you with that tray. What a nice kitchen. And the questions will be confidential too. And for everyone who fills out the questionnaire, the city has a special gift." It was a little silver medal with the town hall pictured on it, and those eyes! From the way he looked at her, you'd think she was still pretty. "But you're pledged to secrecy until we publish our results."

"It sounds very important."

"It is."

So she sat him down right here — whenever it was, so proud of her kitchen, he was so nice, they talked for hours. And the questions: about the house, first, he read the questions off the clipboard, how old, how long, what kind, what about the others in the neighborhood, set up a kind of rhythm:

He asked and she said.

He asked and she said, was proud that she knew so many answers, said so much that she'd forgotten exactly what she *did* say at the end because he had so lulled her that she would have told him anything. At the end she signed the pledge. Until the results were published, she had to not tell anyone.

"Thank you for your cooperation," he said, getting up.

"Oh," she said weakly; had she been crying? Why was she so tired? "Thank you for coming." Followed him to the front door like a lamb. Tired as she was, Sarah could not shake the suspicion that the stranger took something important with him when he left.

At the state university where Ivor taught there was poor Mrs. English, must have been around the age Sarah is now. She turned up in Ivor's classroom like a persistent wraith every spring. When he asked, — Why are you here? the tears rose like the mercury in a thermometer. — Oh, Professor Flenk's senior exam, I missed it and he promised me a retake. Poor Flenk was dead these fifty years, but in the spring Mrs. English used to come back weeping with incompleteness. — Oh please, if I don't take it I will never be finished, she would say, blinded by fresh tears.

Sarah knows exactly how she feels. The trouble is that she can't say what her particular incomplete exam is, and doesn't know why or how she failed it the first time around.

And now. Well, when Clary didn't come over and *didn't* come over, Sarah finally got down to that pile of mail she never quite finishes sorting, uneasy, anxious, nothing *wrong* exactly, but nothing quite right. It took her days, but now she knows. There was no letter from the city. Whoever he was, he lied.

It worried her all last night. She has to tell Clary, but she doesn't come and she hasn't called. Nine-thirty, ten, eleven. Sarah is darned if she'll call. On the other hand, it might be all right to go over if she can think of a *reason*. This Sara Lee coffee cake she's thawed, still warm; put it on a plate: — Clary, I made a little something for you.

Imagines Clary's chagrin: — Oh Sarah, did I forget you? Oh please come in.

Sarah's going to make her beg. — Oh, did you? To tell the truth I'm so busy I never noticed. But if you really want me to come in . . .

But she doesn't like to go out because she only weighs ninety-two pounds and she's afraid of tipping over, and besides. "Tell you what," she tells herself because hurt feelings have made her craven, craven. "I'll give her until six o'clock."

"I wish she'd call, at least." Teah slouches over the breakfast table, singeing the tips of her thick hair with a cigarette. They had Eggo waffles this morning with frozen raspberries and Reddi-wip and the last of the rum raisin ice cream.

"Orders," Michael says with a sour feeling. He wants waiting to be over. "What she has to do to see this mission through. I wish to hell they'd give *us* something to do." He wants the door to open and his mother to come in. *Hey, guys.*

"Our job is to sit on our butts and wait."

Glued in place by orders, he says resentfully, "I hate sitting here. I just wish we could go with her."

"Well we can't." Strands of Teah's dark hair crinkle and turn red as she frizzes them. She squints at him through the singed hair. Then everything about her changes. She says with a sly grin, "So, why don't we enjoy this while it's going on?"

So far today he's done his route, walked Tommy to day care, sat tight, held the fort. He's getting sick of being the responsible one. "What did you have in mind?"

"Ditch school for once. I could have Eddy over."

He snaps, "In hell."

Teah looks at him out of strange, slitted eyes. "You could have somebody over too." Trying to tip him, she taunts. "But you. Probably you wouldn't know what to do."

He can feel his face getting hot. "You don't have an idea in hell what I know how to do."

Yawning, Teah stretches. "We don't even have to get dressed if we don't feel like it."

Michael sleeps in his jeans and T-shirt to save time now; he can sleep ten minutes later and still get up in time to do his route. Since Saturday they've taken on his shape like a protective skin — grungy but not dirty, pliant, practically bulletproof; his lucky clothes. "Right," he says. "Save on wash."

"What wash? You haven't touched the damn wash."

"Well neither have you."

"It's not my job."

"It's not my job either," Michael says.

"And I suppose it isn't your job to clean up the damn kitchen, either." With Mom gone they fight all the time. Teah French-inhales the last drag and drops the butt in her milk. "Shit, who cares whose job it is?"

Michael takes a quick look around the kitchen; it's amazing how a place can go to hell in just five days. The dog is sick and the house smells bad. "Shar is going to freak."

"Not my problem," Teah says.

"Not my problem either." It's not his fault the dishwasher is broken. He knows he ought to call a repairman but Shar's story keeps coming up on him like old scallions, how the state came in and took her. He doesn't want outsiders in here. They've kind of let things go. Dishes started piling up; since Mom's casseroles ran out, he and Teah have been wrangling over whose turn it is to cook and whose to clean. They take things out of the freezer in bizarre combinations and Teah bakes chocolate chip cookies a lot. Besides, no matter how much you do in a kitchen, it never stays done. It's like making beds every morning, what's the point if you just get back in them at night? It's enough trouble, wiping up after poor Fang. He is tired of being practical, can't seem to turn it off, asks worriedly, "How're we going to explain to Shar?"

"That's not till Friday." Teah yawns. "It's still today."

Gross things are drying on the kitchen tablecloth; there are pots standing in the sink. "Somebody's got to clean up."

"It's your turn."

Michael is sick of cleaning up. "I took Tommy to day care." The way Mrs. Weller looked at the food spots on Tommy's shirt, the way she yanked him away from Michael, you'd think he was a neglected child; it was embarrassing. "You didn't even change his shirt."

Teah just extends both arms in a silky gesture, regarding her fists. "What if it's nobody's turn?" Looking at him over matched rows of white knuckles, she says silkily, "What if we just bag everything and watch tapes?"

Watch tapes, make tapes — what the hell, all he wants is to get through the waiting part and finish the damn picture, but he doesn't know what kind of picture he and Teah are in. He wants it to be a high school picture, John Hughes or whatever, cute teens in low-grade trouble, or a war movie, hero comes home at the end, but right now he just doesn't know. "Who's going to write the excuses?"

"You're good at Mom's handwriting." She gets up. "I'll get the tapes. Something that makes *Wild at Heart* look like *Mary Poppins.*"

"One condition. No Eddy," he says.

"Oh that," she says with this proprietary air, you'd think she was this Eddy's personal manager. "He's playing for some record people in Providence. He won't be back until tonight. OK?"

Michael wishes Eddy would never come back. "So, what tapes are we getting?"

"Everything," Teah says, and as he watches ties a scarf

around the waist of her big black T-shirt and throws on a coat; except for the slipper socks, she looks almost dressed. She takes their mother's keys off the hook by the back door. "Trust me."

"Wait. You don't have your license yet. If you get stopped . . ."

"Shut up," she says. "I won't. The best tapes are at the mall."

When she comes back she also has a half gallon of vanilla ice cream and a pound package of M&Ms. Michael rummages in the tape bag. Without the gaudy jackets they wear in the video store, these tapes are anonymous; they could be things he's seen a million times, play-school kiddytoons, they could be stupid, wonderful, forbidden, all the blood and guts and fires and explosions that Mom gets so weird about; porno tapes, things Teah loves and knows he's going to hate. "What'd you get?"

"Everything. You know. Revolting stuff." She goes into the cabinet in the dining room and comes back with a clutch of bottles.

"What's that?"

That grin almost makes him like her. "Trust me."

From the living room, where he is nesting in the sofa and finding it pleasant, Michael hears the blender going. Teah comes back with two huge glasses filled with muddy-looking froth. "What's that?"

"My invention." Like the Mad Professor, she hands him a beaker dotted with floating M&M fragments. "Swamp Things. Magic potion." She can't stop grinning. "Turn you right straight into Mr. Hyde."

"I am tired of being Dr. Jekyll," he says with an evil laugh.

Not exactly making sense, Teah burbles, "Funny you should ask."

The ice cream more or less takes over the flavor of whatever liquor she's put in — Baileys Irish Cream somebody gave his folks one Christmas when Dad was still all right and, he thinks, vodka? Some rum — he can hardly taste it, which means it must be hardly there. The broken M&Ms make it more like candy than a drink; they have several, lounge through three tapes; Michael stops to grill cheese sandwiches in the waffle iron, noting in passing that something has happened to his time sense because some of the sandwiches come out so raw that the cheese doesn't even melt and others are too burnt to eat. Settling back in front of the TV, he starts giggling. "Teah, are we drunk?"

"Hey, I think so," Teah says. She has — what's that on her lap? "Look what I've got."

"Holy fuck." It's Dad's gun. "Where was it?"

"Their dresser. Don't worry, the clip's out." Teah's pulled it out of the neat leather holster, a perfect little Colt automatic Dad bought for Mom to keep in the house while he's out on patrol, in case. My God, in case of what? They've both had the lecture, both been checked out on it, don't you guys ever, *ever* touch this thing and here is crazy Teah aiming it at the floor but going, "Freeze."

He dodges. "Don't be an asshole."

That grin again. Then she says, "The clip's in the back of the closet, no shit." Teah is no dummy. "Plus, the safety's on."

"I don't know," Michael says. But the Swamp Things are sweet in his mouth and his head is filling up with fumes and at the moment he feels so good he can do anything and therefore he lets Teah try this, try that, and then because their folks are gone and this is the last thing in the world Clary and Thomas Hale would want to see their children, or young adults, doing, they take turns with it, this beautiful, heavy, perfectly articulated small object with huge significance, and with drunken gravity put the barrel to their heads, to their own bellies, in their mouths, nudging themselves, feeling its cold nose, but they never once point it at each other or tighten the finger on the trigger even though the clip is safely in the back of their parents' closet, because drunk as they are they will never be gun people, which means it's perfectly all right for Michael to say finally, "This is really dumb." The fog in his head clears for just a minute. "Besides, Tommy."

"Oh my God, Tommy." Teah jumps up. There is no way to sum up the rest. She takes it from him and snaps it back into the holster and looks at Michael worriedly, passing the object from hand to hand. "We can't let him find it."

He just wants not to look at it any more. "Bury it deep."

So he has to put the VCR on pause while she takes the thing down to the basement and hides it somewhere; he doesn't even want to know, just wants it offstage, out of his hands, drowned so deep it won't go off even in the third act. If there is something else they've forgotten, about Tommy, they're weirded out, too buzzed to keep track of the time.

Then in the middle of melted cheese and Swamp Things and this bizarro low-budget soft-core tape about a porno telephone ring, Teah just starts. "So listen, when we run out of money we can start a phone service just like that one," she bubbles with laughter. "You can run your voice up high and pretend to be a girl."

They are holding down opposite ends of the sofa, Teah reclining with one knee raised and her arm draped over the end of the couch like a model in some sleazy magazine while Michael slumps with a pillow in his lap. "I don't know if I can talk girl." Michael tries "Hel-*leow*."

Teah drops her voice to a throaty whisper. "I'm only doing this for the money, sweetheart, we are poor orphan children here."

Michael doesn't even hear what he is saying in that falsetto, the real obscenity: "Orphan children without a penny to our names . . ."

Then Teah says something filthy, filthier than anything they're going to say all day. "Orphans whose mother is never, ever coming back."

"Never coming . . ." back. Even thinking this makes Michael feel dirtier than he felt playing with the gun. They have to play this for a while, shout with laughter about it precisely because it is terrible; they will proceed on the goofy kids' premise that you can fool fate by saying the unspeakable. They both got spanked after some long-ago funeral for singing in the car all the way home from the cemetery, kid magic, singing the protective spell even after they were warned: "The worms crawl in, the worms crawl out."

Teah's into it. "Poor orphans, all alone, what are we going to live on?"

"Porno tapes," Michael says as if rehearsed. "We can make

a fortune." Something's happened, is about to happen, is happening; he feels low, can't stop in spite of the fact that the doorbell may be ringing. "Or we could, like, grow dope in the yard?"

"Or start a whorehouse," Teah says dizzily.

He sprays chocolate bits. "We'll get you a red dress."

The alcohol has left her unguarded. "But I don't know if I want to do that," she says.

Something prurient flickers in him, curiosity like a flame. Michael, who does not even hear the knocking that follows the ringing doorbell, rolls right over his sister's unguarded perimeters. "Not even with Eddy?"

Teah says, "Shut up about Eddy."

But he's so drunk he has to know. He lunges. "Well did you ever?"

She pushes him. "Go to hell."

Aware that his insides are sloshing, he grabs her. What's that? What. Extra light, from the open front door. Yells, "Tell."

"Fuck you, Mikey." Shrieking with laughter, Teah tears loose and leaps over the back of the sofa as he follows.

"Excuse me . . ." It's a new voice.

He's poised on the back of the sofa like a ropewalker and then fired by the moment, Swamp Things, old Errol Flynn, Michael shifts his weight so the sofa rides over backward with him, it is astounding, "Yeeoooo . . . ," pounces on Teah, screaming, "If I go to hell, you're coming after meeee . . ."

Tangling, they roll into squashy ankles, heavy pink legs, neat, squdgy shoes. They look up. The woman's round face is crumpling. "Oh, please!"

"Mrs. Weller!" Michael sits up. Oh shit. "What time is it?"

"Oh dear." There she stands, sweet-faced and horrified, with Tommy, who's jumping up and down about to kill himself laughing, crazy to detach himself and throw himself into the tangle. Upset, Mrs. Weller's trying to find the right face to make; she's blundered in on something she can't begin to understand. "Oh dear."

Michael says foolishly, "Ma'am?" How drunk is he? He wants

to train his camera on this scene, to make it playable, but he's too messed up on Swamp Things.

"I waited with Tommy until four. All the other children have been gone since three o'clock. I'd better talk to your mother."

"I'm sorry, Mrs. Weller, but we lost track of the time." He doesn't know where it comes from but Michael gets himself upright: all those lessons in military bearing, all those years spent learning how to keep a taut ship. His life in the military has informed him; it makes him strong. Manners, he thinks, *manners*. Michael Dealey Hale, son of Thomas Morton Hale, Captain, U.S.N., missing in action but by no means conclusively lost; Michael stands upright, holding his head steady, at attention in spite of all the stuff that's slurging around inside him. Discovered in disarray, Michael reassembles himself in his father's image; he can feel it happening. His shoulders are braced and he speaks with dignity. "I'm sorry, Ma'am."

"Your mother," Mrs. Weller says with less certainty. "Please."

Repel all boarders. His expression makes Mrs. Weller fall back a step. Tommy escapes and hugs Michael's legs. Michael says, with enormous composure, "That won't be possible right now."

Mrs. Weller's craning. She's trying to see past him into the living room. "This — just won't do."

But Teah forms the second row of defense, standing between the outsider and the disaster zone. "Oh Mrs. Weller how nice of you to bring Tom." At her best, beautiful Teah can be imposing. She's learned a few lessons from her own life in the military; how to keep your feet in sticky situations, how to charm people you don't know. "It's my fault, Mrs. Weller, and I can promise you, it will never happen again."

"I — see . . ." The woman is at a loss. "But I'd really like to speak to your mother," she says anyway. "When it's convenient."

"Yes Ma'am." Without looking over his shoulder Michael knows Teah's moved into position close behind his left shoulder to complete the barrier; he can feel her warmth. After all these days of fighting over whose turn it is to clean this, do that, and struggling for control and fanning incipient hatred, he and his tense, nervy sister are basically shoulder to shoulder here. They have a purpose, although it is not specified. Although they may fight every living minute, the Hales will line up foursquare against any intruder. Amazing Teah, sounding responsible, adult, manages to make Mrs. Weller feel guilty for even bringing it up. "The whole thing is my fault, Mrs. Weller. Mom asked me to pick up Tommy today because she has a Naval Relief meeting, but Mike and I have a play at school and we got busy practicing . . ."

Practicing! Brilliant. Michael manages to say, "Right." He's not certain how much longer he can stay on his feet.

With a sharp look of assessment, Teah moves him aside and puts herself in the front rank, building character with Mrs. Weller with an intensity that would melt paint — that touch on the arm, the smile, the way she moves the woman out of the house and onto the front steps. "We hope you'll come and see us in the play."

When Mrs. Weller is truly gone they run from room to room, laughing and pummeling, so wild finally that when Tommy tries to hurl himself into the tangle and falls and bumps his head on an easy chair — not that hard — he howls like a gored warthog in spite of the fact that Teah gets him on her lap and rocks and rocks him while Michael lurches into the bathroom and is completely sick. He feels better immediately afterward, but not Tommy, who just cries and cries and cries. Taking him from Teah, going shh-shh, Michael discovers he's not all that good himself. Although he has never been in any respect certain that there is a God, he finds that he spends a lot of time in private conversation with one; oh God, this, oh God, that. Rocking his baby brother, trying to shush him, Michael lets it out at last: *Oh God please let my mother come home.*

It's late and Clary still hasn't called and she hasn't come. Sarah hates going out, but what else can she do? By the time she reaches the Hales' front door she is exhausted. She has to ring and ring before anybody comes. When the door finally cracks there's something *about* the house, the shadow of encroaching disorder. Clary would never . . . "Oh, Clary, I." But it's Michael who stands there looking at her out of Clary's eyes.

"Oh, it's you. I brought something for your mother."

"Oh Mrs. Ferguson." His hair is sticking up in back and he has big dark circles under his eyes. Hastily, he takes the Sara Lee and makes as if to close the door. "That's great. Thanks a lot."

Used up by her efforts, Sarah leans into the frame. Partly it's holding her up. "I thought, if I could talk to her?"

"She's busy right now, Mrs. Ferguson." From upstairs, Tommy gives an infuriated screech. There's thumping; Teah shouts.

"Just for a minute." Her lips tremble. She wavers like a lone sea oat, about to fall over. "Oh please."

Michael's arms and legs get snarled in his attempt to hold her up and keep her out all at the same time. "Are you all right? I could help you down the steps . . ."

She sways. "Just let me sit down." Reluctantly, he lets her pass. She stumbles on Tommy's toys. The living room is a welter of papers and cookie cartons and strewn coats and mismatched shoes.

"Can I get you some water?"

"Oh no thank you," she says, disturbed. "What's that smell?"

"What smell? Oh, that. The dog's sick. How about this chair?"

"Where's your mother," she says.

His look troubles her. "I'm not sure what time she'll be back."

"She's gone?"

He says quickly, "Not for long!"

Away. Sarah feels her greedy heart lift. "Oh, you poor children shouldn't be here alone. I can come and take care of you."

"Oh no thanks," he says, alarmed. "Shar's taking care of us."

Hurt, she sniffs. "I see. I really need to see your mother."

Upstairs, Teah's voice overrides little Tommy's; Michael says over the racket, which is getting closer, "Yes Ma'am. If you'd like to leave her a note."

"I have something to tell her, Michael. It's important."

Michael is standing over her — dark hair, eyebrows like sable slashes; that Irish skin is so transparent that she can almost see into the boy, what's the matter with him? She has something to tell, and the boy — something shivering just beneath the surface. Maybe he has something to tell . . . But the thumping upstairs has spilled onto the stairs; shrieking Tommy is struggling in Teah's arms as she brings him down, saying angrily, "If I say you have to do it, then you have to do it, Tommy, so you might as well quit."

The pressures of the day mount up; Sarah hears herself: "Cecelia Martin Hale, you stop! Stop talking to your baby brother like that!"

Instead of putting Tommy down the way Sarah would have done if *her* mother had spoken to her that way, Teah grabs the child tighter and, apparently pressed to the limit, says grimly, "I don't know what you're doing here, Mrs. Ferguson, but you'd better . . ."

Teah rumbles, "The fuck . . ."

And explodes. "Butt out."

"How dare you!" She gets up so fast it makes her giddy, shouting, "Apologize." She says, with force, "You. Michael. Make your sister apologize." Yes she has lost her temper; it happens. She quavers, "If you children would just."

He says quietly, "We're not children, Mrs. Ferguson."

"If you don't . . ." In better times, when Sarah shows her temper the earth stops, people scramble to make up. Now Clary would wheedle, Clary would beg Sarah to tell her what's the matter, but Clary's not here. If they'd only apologize she could tell the children. But they're different today. Things are different. "I'll . . ." She's bloating with the unspoken threat. *I'll go home without telling you.* Tilts her head sadly. "Don't you even care?"

They look at her with black-fringed, uncompromising stares. Michael says politely, "Yes Ma'am. Now if you don't mind . . ."

Why, he is . . . He is moving her toward the door! "Listen," she says, dropping breathless fragments. "Tell her it's important. Tell her to call me. Soon as she can. Tell her . . . Oh dear."

But he has closed the door on her.

"Oh dear!" So it piles up inside her in a confusion of urgency. *That young man. No letter from the city. No letter at all,* she thinks, miserably making her way along the boxwood hedge between their houses. Oh God, what did I tell that man about you that

I shouldn't, she wonders, praying that Clary will come back soon and let her confess.

It was the context, she thinks, nice-looking man, nice conversation, questions following so thick on one another that Sarah lost track, so overwhelmed by the will to please this *handsome person* that when the questions became *un*good she followed like a lamb, all those intimate things about Clary and the Hale family. Whose company they kept, what they did, at what hours.

Well at least she has some justification. *Listen, he said the city had money for you.* Then, God, the prurient, ugly confusing questions at the end when she was so tired, oh he made her cry and then made her forget that she had cried. That look of authority, anybody would have . . .

It was like spreading yourself for a doctor. When you're sick for long enough you don't care who looks. Would do anything to please him, she thinks wearily, lurching into the house.

He said he had money for you and God help me I believed him, she will say, and when Clary's forgiven her, Sarah will tell her what bubbles up inside her now, like something undigested that she did not know at the time, but knows now.

By the end I did not like him.

Watch out.

8

"GET OUT OF MY WAY, brother boy."

"Teah doesn't want to see you," Michael says. This is only part of the truth. He's been locked in place here for almost a week, wondering about his mother. *Where is she?* The pressure is intense, but, more: there is this *thing* burning a square in his back pocket, that he barely had a chance to look at before Eddy came; he hid it fast, so he still doesn't know if it's from Mom.

It was on top of the pile when he got home, an outsized postcard from some schlock motel with the name marching across the front in raised foil. The address is hastily printed in block letters, so smeared that he can't be sure it's in her hand; the message space is blank. What does it mean? It's like a note kited into prison from outside, suggesting that maybe there's something going on out there that the inmates don't know about.

He needs some time with it. But first he has to get rid of Eddy Stanko, who's hanging on the doorframe like something out of an evil dream. Teah blew in from school just now, muttering, "Keep Eddy out of my face," and before he could show her the card she stormed up to her room.

Michael is sick of holding the fort. Furthermore he's sick of Eddy. Even though Eddy is bigger, he sets his jaw and in a tone learned from his father, barks, "I told you, she's not here."

Eddy smells of sweet wine. "The hell. She's upstairs now."

He's leaning on Michael, who falters. "Who says?" *Can't do this much longer.*

Behind Eddy, his huge shadow crouches. "I watch the house."

Not alone. "Fuck off or I'll get my mother."

"You and what army?"

Got to do something. His voice shakes. "The cops." *Got to do it soon.*

Eddy studies Michael. "Hey kid. You want something that'll make you feel good?"

"Not really."

Eddy flicks his jacket pocket — does he have a knife? Gun? "Or something that makes you feel bad."

Mom.

Teah's voice comes from upstairs. "I'll be right down."

"Teah, for God's *sake.*"

Eddy just grins that insulting grin.

She calls, "Wait in the car, Eddy. I'll be right out."

When Teah presents herself in the purple T-shirt and Eddy's jacket Michael hisses, "What *was* all that?"

"Nothing," she says breezily; with that hair she looks like the Bride of Frankenstein. "It was nothing."

He can't help sounding bitter. "I thought you broke up."

Exasperated, Teah says, "No I didn't break up with him. I just didn't want to see him while he was still mad."

"The guy is a lowlife."

She lashes back. "He's not what you think."

He and his sister are fighting about Eddy right now because they've shied off fighting about the real issue: what to do about the fact that days have passed and their mother hasn't showed up and she hasn't sent word. Michael knows something's wrong. Teah, the great denier, insists everything's fine. Michael tells her they ought to call Naval Intelligence, talk to somebody at the base, maybe even, oh shit, call in the police. Teah says no way, they're under orders. Say one word and they jeopardize the operation. She has the last word: "Remember, I'm the one who talked to him." Smug Teah. But what can he do? So they simmer and tug over Eddy instead.

He comes in low and strikes. "Eddy. What would Mom say?"

She shoots him an insolent look. "Mom isn't here. You're picking up Tommy, right?"

"Where are you going?"

"Out." Teah turns on him in a flash of rhinestone hoops.·
"You know."

He grabs for her. "Wait, I've got something to show you."
He wants her to sit down with him and confirm his hopes: that
the card really is from Mom.

"Later." She shrugs him off.

"It's important," he says but it's no use.

"Can't. Got to rush." Something in her look tells him she's
not so much running out *to* Eddy as *away* from this: the empty
house, the waiting, all these days they've been stuck in one place.
"OK?"

"I just wanted to . . ." Michael discovers he can't go on. If
he shows Teah now it will throw her into her denial mode.
She'll tell him he's crazy, that isn't Mom's printing — anything
to get away. But the shadows in the house are collecting around
his ankles, rising like smoke, and he shouts after her: "Wait!"

At his tone she wheels and he holds his sister with his eyes,
Michael's dark side all too aware of Teah's dark side. The trouble is they are too close. He already knows she will go anyway,
and that he has the power to make it impossible for her to enjoy
it. He gets in the needle. "Remember what Mom said about
going out on school nights."

And the strangely detached part of him that is always the
camera pulls back for a long shot:

INTERIOR — DAY — THE HALE HOUSE

Brother and sister in opposition, standing in the Hale front
hall. It's interesting, Teah Hale suspended between brother and
boyfriend, inside and out, caught between the dim hallway and
sunlight and a lot of other things — right and wrong, maybe —
Teah hovering.

Then Eddy honks and the tension snaps: "Well you tell *Mom*
good-bye for me." With a thwack she slams the front door on
him.

The shadows in the front hall are knee-high by this time;
pretty soon they'll be up to his chin. He'll have to stand on
tiptoe to breathe. On top of everything else the dog's still sick,
and the stuff the vet gave them isn't doing any good. All he
does is lie on his side and when Michael puts his mouth on the

dog's ear and mutters, "Kill," the Westie just rolls his eyes under the Koosh Ball eyebrows and flaps his flag tail against the rug once, thump, it's terrible. But Teah is a great denier. She says Fang is definitely getting better, all they have to do is wait for the medicine to work. When Michael says they really have to do something, Teah, the master of denial, just fobs him off: "Come on, Mikey, these things take time."

Holding the sick dog, Michael shouts, "Come off it, Teah. Stop pretending nothing's wrong."

Being alone makes him dizzy. The ship's clock chimes. If he's late for Tommy, Mrs. Weller will bring the social workers down on them. It's gotten to the point where he hates to see this coming. With Mom gone, Tommy has started looking seedy for no reason — food in his hair no matter how many times you wash it, rips in his clothes. He cries over nothing and if Michael tries There There, he always says, "I don't want you, I want Mommy. Where's Mommy?" Michael's running out of reassuring lies.

It doesn't help that Sarah Ferguson is on the phone the minute he comes back from day care with Toms. She doesn't even say hello, she just starts quavering about some bad dream, "Is Clary . . . oh dear, I just had to call to make sure everything's all right."

Performative utterance: *It's all right as long as I say it is.* Michael lies. "She's fine."

Sarah's voice crumples like a crushed violet. "You're sure?"

His baby brother is hanging on his arm. "Mi-chull."

"Shut up, Toms." Five minutes' difference in time or a half inch in his mood and Michael might have spilled it all, come out with everything right there. But there's something about the hallway where he takes the call: the sameness of his parents' furniture, the photo of the *Constellation* over the hall table, the carved chow bench and the ginger jars marching in order on the teakwood desk Dad brought back; something about the rectitude of his parents' arrangements that tells him every-thing's OK at least as long as he says it is. And he lies. "She's fine, Mrs. Ferguson, she's tied up with this special project, OK? But she wanted me to tell you she's . . ."

"I want Mommy!"

("Oh, please shh.") For a second there he almost loses it but he finishes strong: "Fine, Mrs. Ferguson. She says tell you as soon as she's finished, she'll call."

But Tommy won't stop yammering, clamoring, working up to a four-alarm tantrum, the kind in which he starts by throwing toys and ends up hurling himself on the floor in a screaming rage. The little kid is near the end, which means it takes all Michael's energy just to see them both through the rest of the afternoon. *Boy, if she doesn't come home soon . . .* Teah doesn't get back in time to fix dinner and she doesn't call, the bitch, so Michael ends up making spaghetti and trying to make a party out of supper; he has to do something because his little brother won't quit, cranking up to that half wheeze, half whine that he can keep up for hours, and Michael is getting increasingly bummed.

On top of which twice the phone rings but when he grabs it, the person on the other end clicks off.

The postcard is still in his pocket and circumstance and superstition keep it there. He can't concentrate on anything until he gets Tommy stashed and besides, Michael has the crazy idea that as long as he doesn't look too closely at it, he can pretend it's news from the front.

With Tommy finally in bed, Michael is nose to nose with good old sleeping Fang, who keeps breathing as Michael buries his face in the white mop. For the moment, he supposes, Fang breathing is going to have to be enough. But he can't stop himself from, he guesses it is praying, *Oh please.*

"Oh please get better, OK?" Michael says finally. He nuzzles the dog one more time and gets up, knuckling gritty eyes. His back is stiff; if he didn't have Tommy, he'd go out running to get his muscles stretched out, but sure as he leaves, Tommy will wake up scared. Even though his baby brother is being a pain in the ass right now, Michael wouldn't want any little kid to wake up to an empty house.

It's time to look at the card. It is one of those complimentary postcards you find in motels, with postage attached. It is postmarked South Carolina. The name of the place is in raised pink foil, with a silly-looking Mexican hat. "South of the Border." Olé. Get it? It is addressed to HALE. Not Tom, not Clary, not Teah or Michael or Tommy, just HALE. It's smeared as if a dozen people had walked over it before somebody finally picked it up and dropped it in the mail. The printing is so blurred he can't tell for sure, but the funny hook on the *H* makes him almost certain it's from Mom.

Desperation makes him bare his teeth. *Got to do something.* But what? They're under orders to hang in here and Mom, Mom is probably under orders too. *You can get in touch, but you can't tell them anything.* It's got to be official business, and you don't get in the way of business. *Military secret.* Right? Is it? Is it right? God, he doesn't know. Part of him would like to bomb on down to the Carolina border and knock on every door in this South of the Border place until he finds Clary Hale, and if it blows the military secret, tough. The other part knows that he is under orders. It is this that's destroying him now, twisting his insides and leaving him tight with frustration. It is the axiom of life in the service.

Hurry up and wait.

Without any word, in the absence of orders to proceed, Michael does what he does every night.

He goes looking for her in the house.

So far he has found some unmailed letters and a snapshot: a nice-looking couple in an old-fashioned snap with a deckled edge that got stuck upside down in the back of a drawer; they are smiling, his hand is around her waist, they look so *nice* and they are standing in front of a solid-looking white frame house. They've got to be his grandparents. They blink pleasantly; good people, a little bit squashy, a little old.

They look like home.

So far in his life, Michael has lived in about ten different places if you count moving to New London twice, and he's gone to six different schools; in fourth grade they moved three times. When your life is in the Navy, you live in so many places that you aren't from anywhere. There's no hometown with its history, no neighbors whose lives with your family go back as far as your grandparents' lives. There is just now. Michael likes it here on Pequod Street, it's the longest he's ever stayed in one place, but he is not rooted anywhere. For a service kid, travel is as rooted as it gets. Family is as close as it gets to home.

What's weighing on him now is the possibility that he might end up with nobody. On the state, like Shar.

He could use some grandparents right now. But Mom never talks about them. What happened between them, that they never call and they never write? Why does Mom keep writing them letters that she doesn't mail? She doesn't think Michael has seen them, but he has.

Her desk is full of them. They are addressed to the Martins on Fessenden Street in Wilmington, he supposes the snapshot was taken in front of their house. He can't find out what the letters say because he's held in place by punctilio: damn military honor anyway. *But I know who you are.*

He doesn't care what happened between them. He wants them here now. If only they would step out of the snapshot and take hold. "Hello, Michael, hello, Teah, oh, Tommy. So sweet. Until your mom gets back, we'll take care of you." He's sick of keeping it together here.

He can't open the letters but there's no law against trying to phone. Wilmington information says there is nobody listed at that address. He tries to march the long-distance operator through every J. Martin in the phone book. "Sir, if you don't have an address . . ."

He groans aloud.

"Oh Fang," he says, because he can't stand to think about the rest. "Are you OK?"

Fang hasn't eaten very much, but he opens his eyes and wags.

Michael fetches up finally in the room he has left until last, turning on the light in his mother's studio. He's up to his nose in shadows now. They're thickest around those dark, repetitive paintings his mother obsesses over and tries to hide. In each one a sagging, tin-roofed house crouches on a windswept point under a single monstrous dead pine. Alone with the huge paintings, Michael sees exactly how disturbing they are. How could he live with her for so long and not see?

In spite of the versatility, the amazing variety of attacks, from super-real to super-fragmented, in spite of the fact that some are acrylics, some oils, some watercolors, these paintings that his mother can't stop doing but never offers for sale are all of the same bleak point. They are like maps of a place in the soul so dark and disturbing that he hopes he will never have to go there. Yet something draws him into the gaping door of the ruined house. Are the paintings about this house or something that happened there? He doesn't know. He only knows that whatever force compels them casts a long shadow over Clary's life. There are no figures in any of the paintings, nobody standing on the sagging porch and nobody hiding in the tufted weeds clinging to the sand outside, but the absent painter commands each one of them. It is as if she is standing right behind him, reconstructing the scene.

It is like being there.

The paintings are beautiful, bottomless. Clary is as nearly present here as she is anywhere.

"Oh, Mom."

Reinforced like this, with his mother's strong hand evident on all sides, he brings out the postcard and looks at it one more time. It hasn't changed. He doesn't know what to do. Feeling the molding dig into his back and the hard floor under his butt, he puts his head on his folded arms.

Which is when the call comes in. Michael answers the phone wearily, thinking this is just another of those aborted calls, but this time instead of the click and dead air he hears an old man's voice, high-pitched with worry. It leaves him bouncing off the walls, waiting for Teah, waiting for morning, anything. Got to *go*, he thinks, but how will he convince his sister the denier, who's so intent on following orders? *Got to get out of here.*

What did the old man say? It was rushed, disjointed. Cut off by somebody or some thing before he could finish. "Son? Oh, son, it's about your mother. I . . ."

"Grandfather?"

". . . just wanted you to know." Something happens and his voice rises. "No!"

Click. Michael is alone again. He keeps shaking the telephone as though this will bring the truth rattling out of it. After it becomes clear that the phone is dead and there's nothing to be gained he finds himself still shouting: "Grandfather?"

It's Friday again. Shar comes in early to clean. She can't help worrying, is Clary avoiding her because she wants to fire her, or is she trying to make her quit? No problem, Shar figures her days around here are numbered anyway, she's bought a string bikini and is losing weight to fit into it, and she has a pretty new silk blouse to wear when her handsome new man comes for her. Lover called her Sunday night after too damn long. She meant to sound pissed and make him beg, but this genius lover wraps his voice around her poor naked body like a silk scarf and pulls her along after him. — You want me to go to the moon with you? Fine.

Of course that was Sunday and she hasn't heard from him since. It is grating on her. She has so much to tell him! She's so glad, and she wants him to be glad.

When she lets herself in, the kitchen is a mess — stuff in the wrong place, cereal everywhere, gunk sticking to the floor. She is scrubbing the kitchen table and muttering fretfully when Michael comes down carrying Tommy.

They say to each other: "What are you doing here?"

He hugs the kid. "We overslept."

Shar takes the offensive. "So where's your mom?"

He sits Tommy down and puts on his bib. "Something came up."

"Seems to me something came up last week too."

Michael is fixing the bib over Tom's dirty pajamas, bending so Shar can't see his face. "Well that was different. Plus." His voice thickens. "Oh shit, Shar. I have — something to tell you?"

"So OK, let's hear it."

"I don't think I can tell you," Michael says.

It's hard to say whether he pushes Tommy off his stool at that moment to change the subject or whether Tommy falls; either way he begins to squall so it's lost for the moment while Michael picks him up and goes There there, he is really nice with Tommy, who Shar frankly believes is spoiled. Lets her stand on one foot waiting while he washes his face with a paper towel and pours juice and cereal. He plops a gob of chocolate ice cream on Tommy's Cheerios.

"Gross." Shar runs the vacuum into the front room so she can think about her man. Sure she was mad at him for standing her up last week, but one word from Lover and she forgets. She's pissed at herself for being so easy, but when he talks to her every word brings him back: lean, strong body, white spot in his right palm like a pale star, that beautiful, beautiful man. Always makes love in a white shirt; she's going to see him naked one day; she loves the heat. *Sweet love*, she thinks. *My baby. Ours.*

But she couldn't tell him when he called. He rolled over all her hints and stroked her with words. Talked that talk. It was like making love over the phone. So what if he asked questions like fishhooks dropped into the sweet flow, what about this with the Hale family, what about that? They snagged her hide, but tough Shar is so crazy in love she would tell him anything.

— Why do you want to know about these Hales?

— Dear one. I want to know everything about you.

— Oh. And so she told him: house a mess, nobody around but those kids. No, no relatives. No, no cops. — Nothing in the papers. Why do you want to know . . . Ask one question and he jerks Shar around with a few more words. — Oh, Lover. Aaaahhh. She can't help it. His talk just pulls her along, she is so blissed out and heated up by their sex, past and present, even though it's only by phone, that she murmurs, mmhmm, mmhmm. She promises. — No, not a word. And you're really coming, right? Phone love is better than no love; she has to make it last until Lover comes for her.

The damn thing is, she hasn't heard from him since. Her heart squashes. *I love this baby, but I don't want to have it alone.*

But Michael lurks in the doorway — the kid has no idea how handsome he is, black hair standing straight up, black eyebrows about to fly right off his face. He's trying to tell her something.

She turns off the vacuum cleaner. "What?"

He shakes his head. "I don't know."

Where is Lover anyway? She wants her love child to have a dad. All the ragged edges in her are flapping. *Love*, she thinks, and she is thinking about both of them: herself, the child. *We need love.* Distracted by the way her legs rub together, Shar is trying hard to get her mind on Michael here. "So, is there a problem?"

"Yeah. Well." His face keeps changing. Finally he comes up with something, but his tone tells her that this isn't really it. "Well for one thing, I don't think we can pay you this week."

"Oh, that. No problem."

Then he blurts, "We have to go to Wilmington."

She whips her head around. "Wilmington?"

He sees her expression and backs off. "I mean, like. Didn't you say you had some major boyfriend in Wilmington?"

"Marlin Winslow," she says with a gooshy look. That she may have plans for, if the other lines she has laid out for herself fail to converge. If she would only hear from Lover, she wouldn't worry, but Shar knows the road of life is paved with broken promises, and she's beginning to lose hope. With two missed periods she has to work fast. Of all her old boyfriends, Marlin looks best. He may have grease under his fingernails, but he is kind. Kind, and he's the only one who's never been to jail. "Sweet guy."

"So. Would you like to go see him?"

Marlin was gentle with her and steady as gold. "I might."

"So," Michael says, carefully. "Maybe you could drive us in our car?" He rushes on. "We'll pay for gas."

"Do what?" *That would show him,* she thinks. *Lover will come back and find me gone.* "Are you OK?"

"Something's come up. Uh. Ah. Our grandparents." With a look that troubles her, Michael explodes. "We've got to see our grandparents."

She takes him by the shoulders. "Is there a problem?"

"Yes. No. I can't say right now." The kid's face is charged with blood; he's upset over something but Shar is so wrecked in love that she can't make it out. "And I was trying to be so cool. Oh look, Shar. We just need to go, OK?"

Teah comes in with her jaw jutting and her fists planted on her hips. "Need to go where?"

"To our grandparents."

The girl rakes her hair with her fingers. "You're out of your fucking mind."

"I told you what happened."

"Asshole, it was a crazy wrong number," Teah snarls. "Some crazy on the phone."

Michael wheels to protest but his sister stomps off; there's enough electricity in the air to jump-start Frankenstein. Shar has walked into the middle of a major fight. "What's going on?"

Michael is abrupt. "So are you going to take us or what?"

"When you won't even tell me what's going on?"

"Oh please. Don't give me a hard time." The kid looks a hundred years old right now. "It's. Look, it's for Mom."

"So, ah. Where is your mother anyway?"

He avoids her eyes. "I told you, something came up. We're supposed to stay with our grandparents until it's done."

Shar already knows he won't answer but she has to ask. "Until what's done?" *Fuck men, they never explain.* And looking at the boy, Shar is surprised by a sudden blow to the heart. *Oh shit, Lover is never coming back.*

But as they tug back and forth, two things are happening.

One: the phone rings. Distracted by argument, Michael crosses the room and picks it up seconds too late to catch the last ring before the answering machine kicks in and broadcasts the call.

Through the speaker Shar hears the Hales' recorded message — ". . . after the beep." — along with Michael's harsh entreaties, "Don't hang up, don't hang up." Then the beep sounds and the thing starts recording. They will play it back again and again. There's Michael's voice followed by a moment of dead air as the caller considers. When the silence is about to become intolerable a man's voice lashes into the room. Harsh and cold, it punctuates the message with a click. "This is your only warning. Stay put."

This is part one of a pair of events so complexly interwoven that even the uncomprehending Shar is thunderstruck. Then —

Two: Teah rushes in sobbing wildly, spinning like a pinwheel in her grief.

"Wait!" Shar yanks Teah out of one of her wide circles, hauls her in and hugs her hard, holding her arms down until the girl stops struggling. "What the fuck is going on?" Holds tight until Teah finds a way, not to stop crying, exactly, but to slow down a little so that she can cough up an answer. For the life of her Shar can't understand why with all the other bad shit coming down this is for Teah the rock-bottom worst.

The kid is heartbroken, sobbing, "It's Fang."

"Oh, God," Michael says so desperately that Shar is mystified. "The dog?"

Bereft, Michael turns on her: *don't you get it?* Whips around and barks at his sister. "I told you he was sick."

"This is about your *dog?*"

But they are progressing in stages to something Shar can almost see, but cannot recognize. Teah turns a swollen, drenched face to her. "He's dead. Oh God. *Mom!*"

Her voice spirals as baffled Shar looks from one of them to the other. They are cut loose from the ordinary and left dangling.

Teah Hale is fixed in the still, hushed moment of realization: "Oh Michael, you were right."

9

EVERYTHING is *now* to him: past, present — it's all the same. The old evil that was done to him, what he has become. What he must do. Is beginning now.

Now that he has the woman he needs it comes back in on him in a confusion of memory and wild visions — his mother's face. Black hair spread on the pillow, when he slipped in his mother's bedcovers and bumped her, tears sprang but she tried to smile; was that dried blood flecking the corner of her mouth? She could not stand up; she was his mother but she never came to help him even when he cried and cried. The last time he saw his mother she was in a box. Daddy held him up so he could look in and see her, they had put a flowered dress on her, beautiful, "This is what death is like." He reached out for her cheek but Daddy jerked him away in disgust, how old was he, three? "She's dead. No more." *But I think death is beautiful.*

He strained at the box, tried to throw himself in; he has been looking for her ever since.

Then they took the box away. Daddy kept hugging him, crying silently. He began probing *while in my belly the tree unfurled.* "No more for me, no more mother for you." And did those things. The hole in his body yawns, terrible. But he will fill it soon. *They* will. Curled tight around the pain, he nursed the tree. Summer and winter all his life since then he has turned inward, tending it. When he grew, it grew. Now it is huge.

He is the tree. It is burning close to the surface now; in some places the design is clear: branches, twigs, the void at the center that he must fill. Together they are everything.

He loves to see it bloom. That first blossom still burns in his brain like a blazing rose — the fire — *in my jammies running in the street in front of the burning house,* can still hear his father's screams. *But they would not let me stay there and listen,* a woman cried: "Look. A miracle. The child escaped." *And tried to take me away.*

I looked up into her face and lifted my arms. Beguiled you and all the while the fire was racing through my brain, my loins, licking at the empty place. — If you could see inside me. But you can't. I can beguile anyone. Have done. Will do. The first death blossomed: understand the rage! "Daddy, I told you not to. I said don't and you still did." *When the roof caved in I howled with joy.* "That will show you." The first stroke in the design.

The woman's voice: "Oh you poor thing, what will happen to you now?" They took him away before the firemen came out with the body so he wouldn't have to look into the charred face. *I want to see.* And thought they were sparing him.

Held him in her arms all the way to the hospital, she did, her tongue flicking over her lips with the childless woman's greed. "Oh you poor fatherless thing." *I have no mother and that is worse.* But — she would not let go! She rocked him like a baby, the fool! Smoke everywhere, his eyes bright with destruction, she didn't see; just held him, piping, "It's going to be all right, baby. We'll find a nice new place for you."

I knew I would need a new place. Secure. Someplace where I can tend the tree. Therefore as they bundled him into the emergency room he lifted his arms to the woman again and, startled, she beamed down on him, keeps on beaming no matter what he does: "Poor baby, look at that sweet smile. You can see he doesn't know what's happening."

My eyes are like lamps. They light up the inside of my head. Headlights glaring.

"Oh look, he's curling up."

Watch out. Everything they touch, they burn.

Silly woman babbling on and on, "Oh, feel his arms around my neck. So little, so sweet."

If they could see into me they would fall down dead.

10

THERE IS SO MUCH RACKET outside this morning that Sarah puts on her quilted wrapper and early as it is she totters out the back door, helping herself along the fence until she reaches the gate where she hangs, trying to look casual, even though the effort has left her gasping. If anybody notices she'll laugh gaily: Oh, hello children. How are you?

There are backpacks and zipper bags heaped on the drive-way and on the walk inside the gate is a wicker basket covered with a checkered cloth; school day or not, the Hales must be going on a picnic, or to the beach. A car door slams inside the garage. An outing! After the way they've been slouching around all week, looking pale and disconnected even at this distance, it will do the poor children good. It's all so festive that it makes Sarah's mouth water; *why wasn't I invited?* If they see her, maybe they . . .

She has no way of knowing the basket contains poor Fang.

What she does see is that Clary's destructive children have ruined the ground under the big copper beech, the lawn is torn up and they've made an ugly hole near the spot where the rope swing hangs. Now they are running back and forth securing storm windows and stowing lawn chairs and telling each other things to do; their voices leap with excitement. Even little Tommy is dragging a lumpy canvas bag along the back walk. Sarah waves and tries to call, but her voice has never been all that strong and caught outside like this, with no walls to contain her voice and make it seem bigger, she can't make him hear.

Their voices are loud enough. Michael comes out of the house with a brown envelope. "I was there when the bank opened. What did you put on the machine?"

"Message saying the family was called away on official business."

Sarah's heart lurches. Called away!

Teah says, "You got the money?"

Oh dear! What money?

"I closed the account. My entire nut." His voice cracks in two. What's the matter with the boy? "My whole goddam camera."

Oh dear, Sarah thinks. Oh dear.

Teah feints: "I'd better take care of it."

"The hell you will."

"It's a lot of money, Mike."

"I fucking earned it . . ."

"Oh shit Mikey, I know."

Sarah thinks: Oh children, your language, your *lives*. She's been worried about them, lights going off and on at odd hours, no groceries coming in, at least none that Sarah, watching from her kitchen window, could see, complete anarchy, children coming and going on no schedule at all and that terrible motorcycle boy hanging around, everything slipping, and now these ugly words.

"So fuck you." How does the boy manage to make this sound fond? What are they doing to each other with these awful words?

And that sweet girl with the minx mouth and the beautiful eyes, that *language*, "Well fuck you too. When this is over I'll buy you a Panasonic. Telephoto lens. Tripod. The works."

By the fence, Sarah flutters. — Don't use that word.

"Forget it. It's my fucking money and I'm holding it."

— I'm not used to hearing that word. Oh children, *please*.

"Oh fuck you, Mikey."

"I love you too." Suddenly aware of the old lady, Michael turns. "Good *morning*, Mrs. Ferguson." It's as if he sees right into her. It's embarrassing. "What are you doing out here?"

"Good morning children." She has to huff and puff just to

make herself heard — if only she could talk as loud as anybody! "Shouldn't you children be in school?"

Teah rushes past, adding a quilt to the pile by the driveway. Says over her shoulder, "Oh it's a kind of holiday."

"Where's your mother?"

The girl avoids her eyes, turns away so fast that her face blurs. "She's not here right now."

"Your mother would want you in school. And that ugly hole . . ." Fishing for Clary, she says, "What would your mother say?"

Michael's dark look makes her falter.

Then she is confused by a new voice. "Don't worry, Ma'am. It's OK." Clary's big old cleaning lady, that common-looking creature, emerges from the garage. "I'm taking care of them."

"Good lord." That Cher or Char or whatever it is, is dressed to kill today in tight pink pants and a strapless top — white eyelet, for heaven's sake, with a cotton lace ruffle; the way the front is swinging, she may not even be wearing a . . . Belligerent Shar catches her staring and pulls her wrap around her, it's tufted with lengths of black yarn like deranged fur. Good heavens. No *lady* would . . . Sarah is upset; has Clary really entrusted her children to this — tramp? She's always been taught that no matter how common people are, a lady must never let them know she knows, so she says politely, "If you're taking care of these children, I'm certain Clarada would want you to have them watch their language."

Shar's hoop earring catches in the yarn fur and she bends her head to disentangle it. "What language?"

"Those — those awful *words*."

"There." Without losing much yarn, Shar has freed the earring. "Got it." Slightly cross-eyed from her efforts, she focuses on Sarah. "What words?"

"If you don't know, I certainly can't tell you."

"No problem." Shar grins cheerily and heads back into the garage. "Nice to talk to you."

"Oh please," Sarah says. "The trip. That ugly hole. Just tell me what's going on."

But nobody answers. The children have gone back into the house for something and Sarah supposes they didn't hear. Oh dear, she thinks. We used to be such good friends. Is it something I've said? Maybe it really is my fault, Sarah thinks, but it's not my place to apologize when it's Clary who's neglecting me.

The children don't even see how hurt she is.

Michael and Cecelia come out carrying a pair of stones — bookends Sarah recognizes — polished pink granite, given to Clary by Tom, what are those heedless children doing with her treasures? Now Teah picks up Clary's best picnic basket and takes it into the shadow of the copper beech while, moving soberly, Michael places the stones next to the hole. Tommy folds in a sitting position the way children do, *flump*, and starts to cry. For children about to go on a picnic, they don't seem to be having a very good time.

By this time that galumphing woman has backed the car out and left it idling with the trunk open, and she's hurrying to the spot where Clary's children have collected under the tree.

Something is beginning.

"Oh please," Sarah tries, "what's going on?"

Then as she blinks and blinks, trying to make it all come into focus, they all kneel under the copper beech.

Troubled as she is, Sarah is excited. Something's happening today. There is an undercurrent, a strangely carnival atmosphere, that makes her want to go over and be part of whatever's going on. No. She wants one of the Hales to come over and apologize and beg her to join them; she wants to kneel and add a daffodil or a spray of lilacs to the little pile of blooms they've made under the tree.

She calls. "Oh children . . ."

But this ceremony under the copper beech has them completely engaged. They don't mean to be unkind, they just wave politely and then go on. Michael says a few words over the picnic basket — it's like a church service — and then Teah nudges the basket into the hole and Michael fills it up and the three of them — little Tommy is bawling, oh dear, is the child sick? — the three children move the branches into place and set the stones while big Shar, that's her name, big Shar Masters makes a funny sign with one hand, it's — oh my goodness it looks like a hasty sign of the cross.

Are they really singing "Amazing Grace"?

The group breaks up, everybody rattling back and forth, packing, locking up and . . . Where are they going? Sarah wrenches open the gate. "Oh children," she says and is thrilled. They hear!

"Oh Mrs. Ferguson," Clary's beautiful daughter says, "we wouldn't leave without telling you good-bye." Although she has been crying, Teah's face blazes with excitement. Dressed like her brother in denims, the girl is clearly in transit, already redolent of the road: we're *going*. Can't wait. But gawky, gracious Cecelia brings Tommy over. "Tommy, say good-bye to Mrs. Ferguson."

His eyes glitter under the bill of a Red Sox cap and he raises his stuffed toy to deflect her kiss. He can hardly wait to be gone. Sarah buries her mouth in his soft neck. "You sweet thing." Whispers into his hair. "Where are you going, child?"

"Going to my gramma's. Now let go."

Troubled, Sarah stiffens. "Wait!"

But Teah bowls her over with a sudden kiss. " 'Bye Sarah, be good."

Something's the matter, Sarah thinks, but what? "Please wait." This is happening too fast!

Rolling down the window, Teah gives Sarah a jaunty wave. She's leaving! Sarah's heart scurries after her. "Child. Oh, child."

Michael's shaking her hand. His outlines shimmer; he too is already in motion, headed out with a face so bright with hope that she must warn him to be careful. The trouble is, she can't say why. He is swift, resolute. " 'Bye Sarah, see you soon."

Something is nudging her hard. Her mouth forms words without sound. *Watch out.* Unless she can remember, they'll think she's a fool.

All four doors slam.

If she can only bring it back. She tries to stall. "Where are you going, *please?*"

In back Michael is busy with Tommy, who mashes his mouth against the closed window: *Good-bye*. Teah salutes with a wave of her map: we're off. It's a brave, foolishly gallant little progress; they could be astronauts, or explorers, setting out. It is that trashy Shar who answers Sarah, rolling down the car window as she backs into the alley in a grand sweep. She's stuck a stuffed Garfield on the back window and she has the radio on high, blaring rock and roll, so she has to shout. "I'm taking these children to Wilmington to their grandparents," she cries, backing into the street with a scrape of tail pipe on cement. "They'll know what to do."

Then she guns the motor and they're gone.

It's as if a part of Sarah is going away. Grieving, she perceives the rest of her life as a logical downhill slide. Sarah will be back inside before she focuses on it, at which point her sense of guilt will overwhelm her because setting out, Clary Hale's children seemed so happy and hopeful when . . .

"I could have saved you the whole trip," she says aloud to her empty room. Part of her wants to run out into the road and shout after them.

She says at last, too late: "Your grandparents are dead."

11

SO THEY ARE HUMMING ALONG; Clary's Tempo
seems like it's taken to Shar like a racer to a new master, rmm
rmm, she loves this feeling of power. The kids started out excited; they had brunch at an International House of Pancakes,
Michael bought Belgian waffles for everyone and then shoveled
them in like a man stoking a furnace; it was strange. Then Teah
made them stop in New London and they went wading. Shar
thought it was like a party, but with something dark and sober
running along underneath. It kept nipping at their heels so
that even in the best times, the kids couldn't rest for long.

At the beach the late spring sun was warm and Teah lay
down on the sand. "Oh, I wish we could stay here and not have
to do it."

And Michael sighed. "Well, we can't."

Tommy had his shoes off and he was trying to drag Michael
back in the water. "Why not?"

The kid didn't even bother to answer. He was staring out
over the water: "I thought we'd be able to see the base from
here."

Then Teah said, "If the *Constellation* was in, you'd know it."

And he said heavily, "I know."

"Besides, the grandparents are expecting us."

Shar thinks she heard Michael muttering, "I hope so," but
she still can't be sure.

What is it with these kids anyway? Is Shar doing what their
mother wants, or what? Now they are in New Jersey and the
vibes are getting to her. Travel always turns on the pilot light
under her burner, long distance breeds possibilities.

She may not get the man she wants, but she's going to get her man. "Good day for a trip," she says. They are somewhere on Route 1 in Jersey, got lost one time too often and she's dead beat. "The least you could do is tell me what's going on."

Michael says patiently, "I'm glad it worked out. Besides, it gives you a chance to look up that guy Murray."

"Marlin." Will he really be glad to see her? She doesn't know.

"Shar!" Teah says. "Watch out!"

"I see it," Shar snaps. She didn't, another close one. Somebody else's kids here, so close; the responsibility is scary.

Teah closes in. "Time for me to drive."

"You don't have a license," Shar says automatically. "You would think your mom would leave me some kind of note," she says. Somewhere in her past some ancestor must have been a bloodhound. She has to keep snuffing around until the answers come out right.

"She lets me drive all the time."

Bloodhound Shar, with dust on her nose: "This trip, I mean."

"She was in kind of a hurry."

"She could of called." Shar's been driving for so long her fingers are sticking to the wheel. "You'd think she'd leave some kind of word."

Michael: "She didn't have much time."

Shape looms in her blurred vision — "Yow, fuck!" Almost runs into this humongous truck. Shaking, she pulls off, surprised at how unsteady she is.

Teah says firmly, "My turn."

The kid isn't a bad driver, at this point her reflexes are better than Shar's and if Shar is a little messed up, well, she happens to have a reason. Shar is, what, Not Herself. The thing she was trying so hard to tell Clary that day. That she has not told Lover yet. Cannot tell these kids here. So what if they are plenty sophisticated, well Shar is not.

She is focused on this baby she's going to have. She thinks. She's so excited! When you've been alone all your life, you want a whole little person you can call your own, that's going to hug you and love you and be glad every single time you come home.

She can't wait to be a mom. The best. Nobody's going to come in and accuse her of not washing her baby's hair. Her baby's going to have such pretty dresses, and she will love Shar better than any man she's ever screwed, Shar's going to give sweet parties on all her birthdays and graduations and they will be together breakfast lunch and Christmas as long as Shar's still walking around.

But she has things to do. Get married, for one. When she phoned Marlin he was surprised, but hey. It will serve Lover right. She will always love him to death but Marlin will be a better father to her child. She can't wait to break the news.

As soon as she hands these kids over to their mom in Wilmington, which — has she been asleep? — they're approaching. She is the grownup here and they're just going along on their own track.

Listen. If Clary herself isn't at the front door waiting, Shar is going to put it to these grandparents. She has to check it out: whether it's OK for her, Shar Masters, to leave these kids with them. Of course she will have to make a good impression. She runs her fingers through her hair and scrubs her teeth with her forefinger. Plus, when they pull up at the house at the address on the envelope Michael has, *39 Fessenden,* she'd better be behind the wheel. Teah's been driving since Metuchen; poor kid will probably be relieved.

She's shocked and hurt when Teah turns off Route 95 in a quick sweep and before Shar can speak, stops abruptly, reaches across her and opens the door. "Is this all right?"

"Say . . . what?"

"Here," Teah says. They are at a fucking Holiday Inn. "You can get a taxi here."

Can't shake the fuzz out of her head. "Did I miss something?"

"Have fun with Marlin, OK?" Michael swings her pack from the backseat into the front; it lands in her lap, thump. "You know where to come to find us in the morning, right?"

"Wait a minute."

Teah says, "In case we have to keep going."

"Why would you want to keep going?"

Michael says evasively, "You know, just in case."

"Wait." Shar's mouth is quivering. They have hurt her fucking feelings. "I thought I would . . ."

Michael reaches over from the back and shoves the door until it swings wide. "So thanks and everything."

"Not this time, OK, Shar? Charlotte?" And then Teah uses against Shar words that Shar herself had coined, in one of their long talks about Shar's love affairs. "When lovers get back together it's like the first time." When surprised Shar blushes, Teah gives her a little push. "You guys need to be alone."

"Wait a minute!"

Unexpectedly, Michael hands her an envelope. There is a fifty inside. "Also Mom sent this, for your, ah, reunion?"

"What about your grandparents?"

"They would say the same thing," clever Teah says. Then she beams at Shar until she gets out. "See you in the morning, right?"

Michael's voice is sharp. "Early. We may have to go south."

"Go south?" Shar blinks; it's like being inside one of those paperweights with fake snow floating around her. She can't get the particles to settle.

"Maybe," Teah says quickly. "Depends. Look, Shar, be good. Have fun. Give Marlin our regards." And scratches off. At the last minute Teah hangs out the window and high school actress that she is, tacks on the old show biz farewell: "Break a leg," she says.

"OK." Teah sags. She's stopped at the corner of Fessenden and Parsons. "I thought we'd never get here. So do we call them Mr. and Mrs. Martin or Gramma and Gramps or what?"

Michael says, "Depends on what they're like."

Her voice is thin; she's almost used up. "What if they aren't here?"

"They've got to be here," Michael says uneasily. "That old man on the phone. It's got to be Grandfather."

"What if it wasn't?"

His sister's face is tight and glossy as a hockey mask. In back, Tommy's still asleep with his rear in the air and his face mashed against his plush Tasmanian devil as if none of this is happening. Michael has never felt so empty. "I don't know. Come on, T., let's go."

Teah temporizes. "I just want to be sure we're doing the right thing."

Michael barks, "Are you going to stay parked here forever?"

"What if she isn't there?"

"If we don't get going, we're never going to find out, OK?"

Teah shakes her head over the steering wheel, dark hair swinging down. She jerks it back and inhales like a diver getting ready for the plunge. "OK." She releases the brake and they start to roll.

It's the right address; Michael checks it against Clary's unmailed letters. He found another snapshot tucked into one of Mom's yearbooks, herself and two girls laughing in front of the house, rosebushes out front, big porch with rocking chairs. It's definitely the right street, old-fashioned frame houses built sometime before people got into ranch-type split-levels. Great, he thinks, Mom's old neighborhood. *When she was little our mother used to play here.* But it's so nice, he thinks, the *houses* are so nice, why won't she talk about it; why doesn't she ever bring us home to her folks? He's rolling past the pleasant-looking houses, panning with the camera as he counts down: "Forty-five Fessenden, forty-three, forty-one." If fate is kind their mom will be standing on the porch. "Thirty-ah. Uh . . ." He gasps. The camera has focused on a vacant lot. "God!"

There is no framing device that will encompass this, or explain it. The house is gone.

The house numbers on either side are clear enough: Forty-one. Blank. Thirty-seven. Thirty-five . . . Where their ancestral home ought to be there's only this lot, overgrown and littered with brick shards and broken cement blocks, like the remains of some vanished civilization.

When he can speak, Michael says, "What happened?"

Teah snaps, "What do you mean, what happened? You got the wrong address."

"No. It's right here on the envelope." He can't let her see to the bottom of his fears. He says with an effort, "This is it."

They get out and look.

Leaving Tommy asleep in the backseat, they walk the margins and comb the deep growth that smothers the lot. Myrtle creeps through the weeds flourishing in the rubble, and violets cling in some places and in front, or what used to be the front, are out-of-control thorny things that might have been rosebushes once. Wading through vines, he stumbles on the cracked front walk, long-abandoned flower beds. "This is where it was."

Teah is furious. "What makes you so sure?"

Hushed by absence, Michael whispers, "I just know."

It's like Pompeii or something, some awful force has swept through here, leaving behind traces only; if he starts digging now he'll probably come up with some broken crockery, or a bent fork. Whatever happened, it happened a long time ago.

Teah's worn thin by the hours they spent lost in rush-hour traffic. They had to ask directions eight times. "You blew it, Michael, admit it." She wants a fight; all he has to do is yell.

Michael keeps his voice level; like a keeper dealing with a mental patient, he has to do this gently: "This is it, OK?"

"No it isn't."

"Really. Listen, Teah." Has to break the news, OK? "It is, but they like, aren't here?" He's afraid to finish: they aren't anywhere. He is distracted by a crunching sound, somebody approaching through the dividing hedge, but Teah's too upset to hear. "And the house isn't here either," he says.

Teah whispers, "What happened to it?"

Behind them, a woman's voice rises. "Are you children looking for something?"

Even though he heard her coming, Michael jumps. "Who are you?"

"Who, me?" Here is a plain, ordinary-looking woman in this flowered cotton dress, ugly apron with pockets made out of potholders, good old American housewife clothes, nondescript glasses with pink plastic frames, everything colorless and normal, *normal;* she could have walked out of one of those commercials where the grandma shows the kid how to nuke microwave brownies, or which detergent to put in the wash. Fat ankles stick up out of fat shoes. "Why, I live here," she says with a bland, meaningless smile.

Teah's voice is thin as skim milk. "Are you my . . . Mrs. Martin?"

"Mrs. Martin?" Everything changes. The woman's voice takes on an edge. "What do you know about Mrs. Martin?"

"She's our . . ."

"Shut *up*," Michael hisses. He says, too loud, "Why, is there a problem?"

"Only if you're looking for a Mrs. Martin." He can't read her eyes behind the glasses. "There aren't any Martins here."

"But they're our . . ."

("Shut *up*, Teah.")

"Nobody lives here," the woman says even though nobody has asked. "It's been a long time since anybody lived here."

"Grandparents," Teah mutters anyway; the woman either does or doesn't hear.

Does her expression change? Michael doesn't know. He says, loud, "But there was a house here."

"A house just like ours," the woman says uncomfortably, because he keeps staring until she answers. "And another family."

"Just like yours?"

"Nothing like ours," she says in a voice that frightens him. "The Martins. It was terrible."

What do you mean? Because the woman is a little overweight there are hardly any wrinkles in her shiny round face; she has user-friendly gray home-permanent curls, but she studies them through flat-looking lenses; when Michael tries to look her in the eyes he sees only reflected glare. Before he can press her, he hears Tommy in the car. He's awake; in a minute he's going to squeal. "Where are they?"

That smile doesn't budge; it could be painted on. "Who?"

"The Martins."

She just says in that plain-as-day voice, "Why, they're gone."

All Teah's breath escapes her in a little grunt.

Michael presses. "What happened to them?"

She goes on as if he hasn't spoken. "They tore it down afterward."

He swallows again, the dust; he can't get it down. Tommy is getting louder; he has to do this fast. "After what?"

"Something terrible happened there," she says without explaining. She has pearly, moist skin with no visible pores. "Why are you looking for the Martins?"

And it becomes important to Michael not to let her know.

Teah does them proud; for the moment, she is as smooth as her mother Clary in tight social corners, skimming over the hard places with grace. She puts on their mom's social voice, saying lightly, "We were in the neighborhood, we just thought we'd drop by."

"They've been gone a long time," the woman says without expression. "It's been years."

In the car, Tommy is getting louder; nothing's going right. "Come on, Teah, let's go."

But Teah is red in the face and shaky; she won't quit. "The least you can do is tell us what happened."

"Oh, that," the woman says, as if she's already explained. She's advancing with her hands spread, trying to move them toward the car so they will get in and go away. "I just told you. They're all dead."

"Dead!" Teah loses it. "But they're all the family we have!"

The glasses wheel on them like twin reflectors. "Family?"

Before Teah can go on, Tommy discovers he's alone and begins to scream with rage. Their interrogator whirls as if pierced by knives. "What's that?"

"Our baby brother."

"A baby." Her aspect changes. "You have a baby in the car?"

"Not exactly a baby."

"I just love babies." It's like adding water and getting instant mother; reflex turns something inside her all squashy; Michael can almost hear it: Awww. Even the woman's voice changes. "That poor thing!"

"He's OK, really," Michael assures her. If the kid would just shut *up*, but he's been a mess ever since Mom left; he's a real pain in the ass now. Hopelessly, he calls: "It's OK, Tom."

"Oh you poor children." She's softened altogether, suddenly mushy and maternal. "Bring him here. He must be starved."

Michael hesitates, considering. Although she is the firstborn and supposed to be responsible, his sister Teah drifts, looking stunned. In the car Tommy is howling. They have run out of places to go. Michael is fresh out of next steps. "OK."

Which is how they find themselves in Elva Morrow's glistening Formica kitchen, lined up at a hygienically scrubbed table under the cold fluorescent glare. Surfaces sparkle and the floor shines; when she opens a cabinet Michael sees rank on rank of cleaning products, everything ever advertised on TV. She has produced name-brand cookies and Cokes for him and Teah and lowfat milk for Tommy, and when he bawls and bawls she opens a can of chocolate syrup and keeps pouring it in until he stops, which does not win Michael over, exactly, but makes him less reluctant to be here, sitting in this clean, clean kitchen with this grandmotherly woman with the gray curls and the dumb smile; when there's nobody here she probably sings along with the commercials on TV.

"It's getting late," Elva Morrow says. "You must be starved. Let me make you some dinner."

Michael stirs uneasily. "We'd better be going."

"It's the least I can do."

Tommy whines, "I want some dinner."

"See?"

Teah turns a transparent, drained face to him. "She's only trying to be nice."

He considers. "If you say so. Right." He's held in place by two things. One: Shar's gone till tomorrow morning, she's supposed to meet them here and if she can't find them she'll be pissed. And, two: as for what's next, he's totally clueless. South of the Border, he supposes; the postcard is the only other lead they have. Even Teah agrees somebody sent them this postcard for a reason.

OK, more than two things.

If he waits long enough, maybe this Elva Morrow will let something drop: what happened to the poor Martins from next door, was it disease or a natural disaster or did God just come down and knock his grandparents flat. He wants to ask this Elva if she knew Clary Hale, used to be called Clary Martin when she was little and lived next door, but something about her, about this *place*, makes him reluctant to bring his mother's name into this obscenely tidy house. Teah is more or less used up now, which means that for the moment he's in charge.

OK, Teah's not the only one who's used up. Forgets when he last ate. He needs time to come up with a new plan.

So it seems OK to him to be lounging in the chrome chair at the table of Elva Morrow's matched kitchen set, watching somebody else's mother cook. Not so bad, seeing her nuke a pork roast and some potatoes and put them in the oven to brown. Boiled lima beans, oh, great, applesauce on the side, with gingersnaps and canned pears for dessert, what his mother laughingly calls Protestant food, all-American, bland, safe. After days of no Mom, even lima beans look good to him. The only un-American thing about the preparation is the glass of sherry Elva Morrow keeps on the counter next to her, filling and refilling as she shreds lettuce and drowns it in Green Goddess dressing.

She works with her back turned, leaving the Hales to let down a little in a sense of security that may even be false, but is all they can manage. Michael's sick of staying one jump ahead; he and Teah have been running on fumes for days. He'd like to hang out and let life happen. It's not such a bad thing to sit here, watching some full-fledged adult cook a square meal and knowing at the end you're going to sit down at somebody else's table and eat too much.

Tommy slips down from his chair and follows Elva around the kitchen asking questions; Michael's lulled by the fact that the woman is endlessly patient with him. When Tommy trips and makes her break the jar of applesauce she says to the horrified Teah, "Never mind. I used to have a little boy just like him."

It turns out she is not alone in the house. When she calls "Dinner," her nice old husband pops up from a paneled basement recreation room, stooped old guy in silver hair and crumpled khakis and lumberjack shirt, one more decor item in this all-American house. When he sees them his head jerks.

"Who?" Everett Morrow can't stop blinking. He too has the bland face and the flat, glinting glasses, but as he gives Michael's hand a tremulous shake, Michael sees flickering just beneath the wrinkled face a glimpse of the captive boy.

"These are the Hale children, Everett. They came looking for the Martins. You remember the Martins," Elva says pointedly.

"Oh, the Martins." The old man slumps. Why does he look so tired? He tries to smile. "That was a long time ago. They've been gone for years. What do you children want with the Martins anyway?"

Teah says foolishly, "We just thought we'd drop by."

"But they're dead," he says wearily. "Didn't anybody tell you?"

Before Michael can stop her, Teah gives them away. "Our mother never said one way or the other," she blurts.

Elva is pink in the face from too much sherry, but that bland, bland smile remains unreadable. She already knows the answer, but she wants to hear it from Teah. "And who might your mother be?"

Uneasily, Michael tries to shush her.

But Teah is beyond shushing. "Why, she's . . ."

As Michael pushes his sister off the dime, growling, "Time to take Tommy to the bathroom," the frail Everett Morrow says forcefully to his unsteady, sherry-scented wife, "That's enough chitchat, Elva. Let's get this dinner on."

Which does not prevent Teah from spilling the rest at dessert-time when Michael is off guard, lulled by the stuffy air in the dining room, the dullness of the beige wall-to-wall carpet and the beige diamond-patterned wallpaper and an overdose of plain Protestant food. The sherry loosens up Elva Morrow just the way it would a loaf of dried-out pound cake. Carving the pork with a reckless hand, slapping fatty slabs on each of the children's plates, she begins to brag. "You kids think you're special and maybe you are, but you don't have a glimmer what special is."

"Shh, Elva . . ."

"Don't shush me. I told you children I had a little boy just like Tommy here." She lifts her head. "Well not exactly. Finer."

Finer. It's a funny, off-key word but Teah's too stultified to answer, so Michael says politely, "Great." He does the math. Any kid this lady had would be old by now.

The old man's hands flutter and his head jerks; it is as if his wife has brought something huge into the room.

"Son."

Everett echoes, "Our Son."

Teah says, "You had a son?"

The old man sighs. "We adopted him."

"Adopted the sun and moon. The stars and planets." She is a little drunk. "So bright."

The old man seems disturbed. "Elva, not now."

"Brilliant." Face shining, she ignores them. "You've never known anybody like Son. From the beginning we could see it. The difference. The doctors told us, this child is so strong and intelligent he can do anything. Anything." Red spots bloom on her cheeks and in this light her lips purse like a movie star's. "He is, what did they say, prodigious."

The old man crumples. "Elva, please."

"Prodigy goes where we're too weak to travel."

"Elva, don't!"

But she overrides him. "It makes its own rules. Listen, children, blood is one thing, but love is everything. There's nothing a birth mother can do that measures up to this. We helped him grow. The greatest thing the two of us ever did together is raising Son."

The old man's voice drops so deep in his chest he may never be able to fish it out. "That at least is true."

They are running along on separate tracks, him grieving, her flushed with memory and excited by the presence of an audience. "I wish you could see his writing. I wish you could hear how well he speaks. He could charm the bears out of their caves."

"And did," the old man says mournfully. "He had *ways* . . ."

Elva's glowing now, is it the sherry or is it pride? "He could take anything apart and show you how it works." The room is warm, the chair's soft; her pork roast and potatoes are layering in Michael's stomach going *there there;* he's too full and drowsy to follow up on anything so he just lets it play.

"Before he was ten he knew four languages, and the things he used to read you wouldn't even understand. Everybody saw it: prodigy. It takes what it needs to grow."

The old man's voice comes out of deep shadows. "I know."

"If it had come down differently, our Son would be famous all over the world." Whatever she is thinking now makes her ugly. "But people hate what they can't understand."

Everett Morrow says, "There were reasons."

"Tried to get in his way," she says bitterly. Her face seems to get bigger as Michael watches. "Well we all know how that ends."

Ashen, the old man reaches for her arm. "Elva, please."

Still giddy with the sherry, Elva turns on her husband, who seems to get older right there in front of them. "Well it's true. And if the neighbors don't . . ."

"Shhh!"

Michael pounces. "What about the neighbors?"

"Nothing!"

"That girl. That foolish, careless girl," the angry mother says, and won't go on. "You don't know what it's like to lose somebody you love."

And before Michael can stop her, Teah says, "Yes we do."

Without knowing why, he knows it is a mistake because the evening changes. Almost before she's finished speaking the couple have swarmed over Teah, those washed-out eyes bright with curiosity, him grasping Teah's arm and the woman cluck-clucking. "You've lost somebody?"

"The Martins," Michael says as a diversionary tactic because the old people are closing on his sister, there-there-ing with sweet concern, trying to pry the rest out of her. If he imagined it would come as a surprise to them, he was wrong.

"The Martins," Everett Morrow says with moist eyes. "So sad."

"Of course," Elva Morrow says. "What a terrible surprise,

what must your mother have been thinking of, sending you down here?"

After almost a week of keeping it together, Teah flies apart. She blurts, "Our mother didn't . . ."

Michael has to cut her off. "So we have to be going. OK?"

But the old people have already exchanged a look that snags at Michael then and later, in the middle of the night. It is as if they've been holding their breath all this time and suddenly have let it out. The old man says gently, "Is there something the matter with your mother, dear?"

"No," Teah says. "I mean yes." She grips the seat of her chair and shudders, apparently reassembling and running a self-check on all her systems. "Oh, shit."

Mrs. Morrow doesn't ask and she doesn't pry. What she does is get all motherly. "Then we certainly can't send you off into the night all by yourselves. Three children alone, like you."

"We're fine," Teah says, recovering. "I — ah — wonder, if you could let us look at a map?"

Elva's like a big frog, watching a fly. "What do you want with a map?"

And before Michael can stop her, Teah just comes out with it. "We have to locate this South of the Border place."

"South of the Border . . ."

"Teah, shut *up*." He hasn't even figured out why they need to keep their mouths shut and here is his sister, flaring angrily:

"Shut up yourself, Michael. You don't know everything." Before he can stop her, she has the goddam postcard out.

Elva Morrow snaps it up. "South of the Border." She could be Naval Intelligence, trying to break the code. Whatever she's looking for, it isn't there. "Why on earth . . ."

So after all Michael's caution, it's Tommy who blows it, just raises his chin from the little glob of dessert that smears the towel the Morrows have put on him for a bib, and spills it all. "Because we have to find Mommy. She's gone."

The old man's breath comes out in a little *pop*. "Your mother is gone?" He's bloated with something he wants to tell.

"Not really," Michael says too fast. "Teah, let's go."

But Elva Morrow goes on smoothly, as if nothing has happened, "I don't think this is a good time to be starting out for anywhere, not you children with this poor baby all alone in the car. What everybody needs here is a good night's sleep."

The old man's voice flutters. "Oh lord."

Michael is staring. *Is there something you have to tell me?*

Everett avoids his eyes.

Elva Morrow is already in motion, like a steamroller that takes a long time to get started and then will not be turned. "We have plenty of beds. But first, let's clean up."

So before Michael can snag the old man and ask the question, plain, motherly Elva has shoved plates into his hands and theirs and routed them. "And after we do the dishes, I'll show you your room. I can't send you off like that, poor children alone . . ."

"We're not children," Michael says with dignity.

She just sweeps them with those marble eyes. "You know what I mean. With nobody in charge. It's much too late."

Even though something about it makes him uncomfortable — he does not like this woman — Michael wavers. Was that this old man's voice on the phone? "I don't know."

By now Tommy is whining. "I'm sleepy."

("Shut up, Tom.") Was it? He has to know.

"You're more than welcome."

"After all," Teah reminds him, "we've got to wait for Shar."

What did he want, anyway? Michael hears himself saying, "OK."

In seconds they're in the kitchen, standing in a little clump. Michael's trying to quiet Tommy when to his astonishment Elva Morrow hooks Teah's arm. Fixing Michael's sister with both hands, she studies her face. "You know, you look just like . . ."

Michael jerks his head around: *like who?*

All she says is, "You look just like a trinket I have upstairs. Wait here."

Thus they end up at the gleaming stainless steel sink, just as sweetly down-home as the Brady Bunch, Teah washing and Michael and the old man drying while Elva Morrow thumps around upstairs, rummaging. Tommy's run out of steam. He sags in a kitchen chair, muttering, while Michael tries to figure out an alternative ending to this day, oh hell to his whole life story.

When she comes back she has something bright winking in a velvet box. "This is for you, sweetheart," she tells Teah. "Hold still." She slips the thing over Teah's bent head. It's a tarnished silver chain with a crystal pendant glittering. "You deserve something special," she says.

Fluorescent light breaks reflected facets into a dozen sparks on her face. Bemused by the glitter, Teah looks both pleased and frightened. "Oh!"

Now the Hales are stacked in a little pyramid at the bottom of the stairs; Teah and Tommy are leaning into Michael, who loops one arm around his little brother and picks him up. In the stairwell is hanging a complete series of group photographs: sports teams, class photos, Boy Scouts, National Guard, and he supposes dizzily that somewhere in each of these pictures is the Morrows' famous Son. The woman moves them along too fast for him to get a good look. *One look into his eyes and you'd see . . .*

Which one, he wonders desperately. Which one? He would like to stop and stare into the pictures, to find the right face and bore into it and try to see exactly what was so special, what the mother saw. He'd like a minute to analyze the smell in the place, of soap and disinfectant and something else — old hopes or sour fear or of the past piled up in the basement in cartons — and he wants a minute to look at the names scrawled in the few books they have in the Fifties Modern living room, but she will not permit it. If there ever was a guy named Son living here with them, the place is empty of him. Instead of the expected shrine in his room, where she has put them to sleep, there are bare dressers and bookshelves, twin beds with white chenille spreads so clean that the tufts have been washed into oblivion.

At the door to the room the old man brushes past Michael: so *close* but they don't speak. "Sleep tight," Elva Morrow says and closes the door on them.

Michael is at rock bottom. "God, Teah. What are we going to do tomorrow?"

"South of the Border," she says. "No problem." For the first time today her face is kind, and for the first time today she says what he has been waiting since yesterday to hear. "After all, that really is Mom's writing on the card."

"I wish we could go now."

"Well we can't. I'm beat." She is fingering the crystal. "And these people are nice."

"I think they're weird." For the first time today, he lets down. "Don't you think they're weird?"

Exhaustion blurs her smile. "Do you want the bathroom first, or shall I go?"

"I don't think we should have told them all that stuff."

She is fingering the amulet, bemused. "Like what?"

Exasperated, he says, "Everything."

Her eyes are as empty as the crystal. "Everything? I didn't tell them anything."

"Don't you think it's weird?"

"Oh go to hell, Mikey." When she turns the crystal, light strikes sparks off it. "I think it's beautiful."

12

IT'S LATE, and although she has managed to get dressed and fix some supper and get started on her special project, Sarah Ferguson is dyspeptic and distracted, lopping around her house in considerable disarray. She is overpowered by the need to make amends. She is going to send the Hales a box of brownies at their grandparents' so they'll know she cares.

The trouble is, she is not in any way sure that she has an address. Besides, although she forgets a lot, Sarah is almost certain Clary's mother and father are dead — some awful story Clary told her about something that happened long ago. And if she does manage to get the package fixed, how is she going to get out to the post office without Clary's help?

Oh my, she thinks, and wonders why the uses of the day have left her so weepy. Weighed down by the heavy sum of scores unsettled, she tells herself the brownies may help. Melting the chocolate, she perks up when she lets herself lick the spoon.

By the time she finally finishes baking it is after ten. The phone has rung a couple of times but Sarah is much too busy to answer. And she does feel better. The brownies are fine. In spite of her age and confusion they came out of the oven looking as good as any she's ever made. Success leaves her short of breath.

It's possible that there's something stirring outside, sound of a window frame snapping in the house next door, glass breaking in the back door, but her own exertions have left blood roaring in Sarah's ears; the sounds inside her head are all she hears.

It takes her a long time to get them turned out of the pan

and cut and put into a little carton, and even longer to find the necessaries to wrap them: brown paper, scissors, tape. She keeps wandering into rooms and forgetting why she's there, just hangs in place as time stretches. When she has everything, she has to make herself a cup of tea so she can begin. The tape turns out to be Scotch tape printed in a poinsettia pattern and left over from some long-ago Christmas when Sarah was still young and mailing presents to Ivor's family, which means it sticks and therefore it takes her forever to get enough unpeeled to secure the messy package she has made. The arthritis in her hands makes it even harder and by the time she finishes, her fingers and hands and forearms are aching and it's later than she ever stays up, and if there are footsteps outside, if there is an unaccustomed low-keyed rattle or scratching on the fabric of the house, as if of somebody testing locks or trying windows, Sarah is too preoccupied and exhausted to hear.

Now that she has finished the package she is stymied; where in God's name does she think she's going to send it? She paddles around for a long time, trying to find her address book, before she remembers that the people she wants aren't going to be listed in it. What to do? All she really knows is the name of the city. The rest will have to wait for tomorrow.

Cecelia Hale, she prints, Michael Hale and. And, she thinks and then, delighted that she remembers, Master Tommy Hale. Adds with a flourish, Junior.

If she is observed, Sarah is too involved in her project to be aware of the shape outside her window. After all, in a small town like this one, at this hour all decent people are asleep. Oblivious, she finishes, smiling. She leaves a space for the street address and as something alien either does or does not stir in the next room, Sarah prints the last thing she knows for certain about the Hale children. Wilmington, Delaware.

She will figure out the rest tomorrow.

If it isn't too late. Her breath comes and goes in no particular rhythm.

Marooned in her kitchen, she does not know what to do next. She has no idea where the children are tonight. Or what it is exactly that worries her. If their grandparents are *dead*, she thinks. Oh God, yes. Dead. Why does she keep forgetting? If they are dead, will there be uncles and aunts in the family home waiting to receive them? Clary?

What if they've gone all that way and there's nobody?

Oh dear, she thinks, disturbed by forces that are not entirely within her; oh dear, what can I. Silvery slide of soft shoes on the Kazak in the dining room. What. What's that . . . Soft, decisive smack of a flat palm on the swinging door, intake of breath as he prepares to push; serve me right, she thinks, without knowing why.

Oh, she thinks because without knowing, she expects it. At least it will be over.

She is almost glad to see him.

"Oh," she says without surprise, "you've come back."

"Where are they?"

He is standing in her kitchen, *her kitchen*, how did he get in, cellar into the dining room, open parlor window, or did she forget to shoot the dead bolt; even now, when she knows he means her harm, she is struck by the brilliant glare, the vitality, yes she has been thinking about him; in this light he shimmers just like Harry Devereaux, my love, my doom — Sarah, pull yourself together. Her speckled hands reach for his and at the last minute fly up: "What are you doing here?"

His expression is pleasant enough, his voice is neutral. "I said, where are they?"

"Who?" In her secret heart she is thinking: I'm too old for love, but maybe at least I can get him to take the package. With the instinct for survival that fuels and informs the old and makes them clever about getting tasks done for them, Sarah thinks not of what the intruder may do to her but ways in which she can use him: won't mind stopping at the post office, nice young man, so well dressed, will only take a minute.

"You know who," he says and turns on that smile.

"Why, I." She likes him, doesn't like him, loves him, knows only what her mother taught her, ladies don't tell strangers other people's business. "I don't think I ought to tell you."

"You have to. It's important."

She wants to please him, but. "Oh dear, I'm sorry, I . . ."

He is still neutral, quiet, patient. "Listen. They're in danger."

"Danger!"

"Danger," the fine-looking young man says, so forcefully that she knows that this at least is true. "Only I can help them."

Sarah blinks uncontrollably; he is too fast, this is all too fast; it's hard for her to concentrate and even harder to know what to say. She stalls dumbly, "Help who?"

His expression changes; he is getting impatient; now something else shows in his face: "You know who."

Instinctively, Sarah moves back a step. Oh my goodness, she thinks, but does not say. You don't want to help them at all. Thus Sarah Ferguson, aging, addled, valiant and feeling a little foolish. "I don't," she says. "I don't know."

"Cecelia." He advances. "Michael." He closes on her. "Tommy. I'm a friend of their father's."

She does not believe him, she doesn't! What will happen if she thwarts him now? But she has to protect them; she does. "I don't know where they are." In her blind need to make restitution, Sarah rushes on. "And if I did know, I wouldn't tell you."

"That would be a mistake," he says. "Now where are they?"

A brave little giggle escapes her. "Gone," she says. "Who knows where?"

He clamps iron fingers on her arm. "I warned you."

"It doesn't matter," she says, squinting to keep the tears in. "Do what you want. I really can't tell you."

"But you will," he says.

And begins.

As he bears down on her with questions, as the questions become more insistent and, unanswered, devolve into threats which are delivered and made good on, Sarah will go off somewhere inside herself to hide. In some part she welcomes angry fingers digging into her arm and instead of weeping accepts the pain as a form of expiation, because God knows she isn't much of a person, and this is her chance to do something bigger than she is. He twists her wrist in both hands; dear God! But she can bear it. Stony, careful, newly clever, Sarah Ferguson understands now that her interrogator wants her to tell him where Clary Hale's children are because he intends to kill them, and foolish, gallant Sarah thinks she can win back their love — Clary's love! — by protecting them.

"You will tell me." He gives her a final shake and lets go.

She staggers and regains her precarious balance.

"Where." He raises his arm; when it comes down this time the fist will smash into her.

She shuffles backward.

"They." He closes the distance between them, advancing with the fist raised, fixing the old lady with his eyes as if he can nail her in place with his glare and smash her skull before she can shake his eyes.

But terrified as she is, Sarah won't stay fixed. Fear gives her speed. She is astounded. This energy! Where is it coming from? She scuttles away and the fist lands on nothing.

The last word lands like a whiplash; he lunges. "*Are*."

Leaves her backing into the hall with her left wrist hanging limply; amazingly, she doesn't feel the break.

Still hoping to prevaricate and so protect and defend, she says weakly, "Who?"

His eyes are pale as marble and so dense she cannot see into them. If he was gentle last time he is savage now, intent. They are beyond questions and answers. He came here to find the children and if he has to kill her he will do this, he will do it in spite of her best efforts to keep their secret and he will give no quarter. "Stop that or I'll kill you." The fist staggers her.

She understands that he is going to kill her anyway.

She's backed into her corner cabinet; it shudders, rattling a dozen of her carved animals. God, he is about to hit her again; "Wait," she cries, and in an astonishing fit of bravery she gropes in the cabinet behind her back and seizes her best elephant, the biggest, beautiful Belial carved in malachite with diamond eyes and tusks in ivory, her dearest Belial, so heavy she can hardly lift him, "Take *that*," she cries and flings it as hard as she can, only to see it glance off the raised arm of the intruder.

Oh God, she prays, *accept me*, bowing to this huge, murderous blow with a whimper; redeemed by her silence, Sarah accepts whatever pain may follow. She is satisfied, blessedly unaware that she's left everything her attacker needs to know printed on that undeliverable package of brownies. *I deserve it*, she thinks. *But at least I didn't tell him.*

When it lands, the intruder's blow sends Sarah not back inside her failing body but somewhere else altogether, into a dimension where age and physical frailty and all those old, sad sins of omission no longer figure, where his shattering kicks will rattle what's left of her without affect. So much for regret, for guilt and a lifetime of missed chances. She is light and free. Released.

13

MISERABLE, Michael drifts through the next hour stashed
with Tommy on a twin bed. Dodging his prickly little brother's
elbows and knees, he broods, while on the other bed, Teah
tosses once and goes directly to sleep without passing Go. He
wants not to be stuck here in the dark thinking, but he can't
stop until he's studied his footage on the events of the day,
rerunning it in his head. Now he can't stop; it's on a loop,
running on perpetual fast forward while Tommy squirms.
When Michael hisses, "*Hold still*," Tommy gives him a poke. He
nudges back and is startled when his brother's hand closes on
his flank in a mean little pinch. "Stop that," he whispers, but
Tommy doesn't hear; with his fingers still digging into Michael,
he plummets into sleep.

Alone in the dark, Michael peels off his baby brother and
flees the bed. He rolls himself in the comforter on the floor,
where a long stripe from the hall light falls on the rug. The
floor carries vibrations; he can hear the whole house: the Morrows droning, the slamming of a door. Footsteps. Somebody is
still up.

Sometime later the bedroom door opens. Has he been asleep
or what? Feeling drugged, he struggles to consciousness.
"What!"

A familiar shape fills the door. "Took a while to find you
guys," says a voice he's too sleepy to identify.

He's paddling through fog. "Who?"

"You gave me the wrong house number. Good thing I saw
the light. Good thing the lady was still up." She stumbles around

grumpily, bumping into things. "You guys got yourselves into the wrong house."

"Who is it?"

"Shush, Mike. It's Shar."

So damn *glad.* "Yo, Shar!"

"Who did you think it was?"

"So, great." He can't focus. "But what are you doing here?"

"Nothing," she growls, blundering around in the dark until she collides with one of the twin beds.

"But what about Marlin?"

"Go back to sleep."

He says sleepily, "What happened to your boyfriend Marlin?"

She falls like a tree next to Tommy, who gives a little squeak as the bed shakes, and then subsides. "Yeah, well," she says. "It didn't work out."

The floor is so uncomfortable that Michael thumps and thrashes, trying to make a nest for himself. The foam-rubber pillow died and ossified years before he got to it. His comforter is full of lumps. He is awake for so long that even the old folks have settled down. Then in the dark hall downstairs the phone begins to ring. He hears the old woman stumbling down the stairs and the sound cuts off in mid ring as she jerks it off the hook. He can hear her whispering. The conversation goes on for a long time. As he crashes into sleep, where he will lie like the undead, Michael is aware of the old lady's voice still droning like the motor of a small appliance buzzing long after the owner has forgotten it.

It is morning.

To Michael's surprise, Everett Morrow wakes him. He opens his eyes to find the old man's face close to his, as if he's about to tell Michael a secret; he's leaning so close that Michael half expects him to lose his balance and topple. "What do you want?"

"Time for you to get going," the old man says urgently.

But when they stumble down to the kitchen the old lady raises a whisk from a bowl of batter, surprised. "Where do you think you're going?"

"South," Michael says. He's caught the old man's urgency, rushed everybody to get dressed, gotten them this far and here she is, trying to keep them here with more food.

"Oh no you're not. Look what I've made for you."

They have to hurry; he's not sure how he knows, but he knows. "I'm sorry, we . . ." But she is moving to intercept them.

The old man says, "Elva, let them go."

She seems upset. "But I'm making pancakes."

Tommy starts: "I want pancakes."

"See? You have to stay. You poor children can't go out on an empty stomach." She stands over them in her checkered housedress, huge and glowering. "It won't take long."

But the old man is disturbed. He takes her arm. "Elva . . ."

She tries to shake him off. "Let go!"

Distressed, he pulls her into the next room; Michael can hear them wrangling. When they return the old man's face is wet, but he seems to have won. She tells them, "OK, OK. Ev'rit's right. But at least let me pack the nice lunch I fixed for you. I got up early to cook." She throws a box of powdered doughnuts at Michael, a mixed bag from the supermarket dated last March. They've been jumbled in the box for so long that all the jimmies and frosting have worn off. "And while you're waiting, eat these."

Takes her time about it, too, while Teah and the others munch on the doughnuts and Michael paces and the old man stews.

Finally the Hales are marshaled on the front walk: Michael and Tommy and Teah, with her face flushed with sleep and sunlight flashing off the crystal pendant, and — it cheers him up to see this — standing with her feet wide and that big freckled jaw set, good old Shar. She's put away that pink thing she had on for the big meeting with Marlin and she looks as tough as Michael in a sleeveless sweatshirt and faded jeans: You want me to drive to hell for you? Bash your enemies? Find South of the Border? Sure, you bet. OK, fine. Shar isn't very smart, but she's loyal; she's blunt and predictable, where there's no guessing what romantic Teah will do. He doesn't know what it's going

to take to find his mother, but he feels better about it, having
Shar along.

He can't wait to be off. Michael is carrying Tommy while
Shar lugs her backpack and Teah accepts the food the old lady
has packed for them. In a grandmotherly fit Elva Morrow has
prepared a picnic basket with fried chicken, carrot sticks, a pie
in one of those disposable aluminum pans. There's even a
checkered napkin spread over it. "I couldn't send you off
empty," she says; the scene is so wholesome it makes Michael's
skin prickle.

"Oh let the children go," her husband says.

"I will, I will," she says, but she doesn't. She glares until he
fades into the bushes. When Michael looks for him he's gone.

Michael says dutifully, "So thank you very much and good-
bye."

Teah gives him a look: is that the best you can do? Advancing
on stocky Elva with her unnaturally smooth face, Teah gives
her a hug that makes her blush. "Oh thank you for everything."

"It's nothing." The sunlight flashes off her glasses so they
can't see her eyes. "You deserve a good start."

Michael loses track for a minute. He's distracted by Shar,
who has drifted away. She's slipped around the hedge that
separates the Morrows' house from the overgrown foundation
of the Martins' place, and from here he can see her wading
through the deep grass to the spot where his grandparents'
front door used to be. As Elva Morrow spreads a road map for
Teah, Shar paces the floor plan of the vanished house with her
head down like a junior scientist on an archaeological dig, soberly turning over stones with her rubber-toed driving shoes.
Crazily, Michael thinks Shar is searching for Clary; at the first
sight or sound of anything unusual, she'll drop to her hands
and knees and begin to dig.

Elva Morrow drones on and on. "Now, if you children take
the route I've marked in our atlas and stop for the night outside
Richmond, you'll make South of the Border by tomorrow afternoon easy."

Last night she seemed anxious to keep them; now she's trying
to string this departure out, so deliberate and tedious that

Michael wants to grab Teah and flee. Wild to get away, Michael yanks his sister's hand. "Yes Ma'am. Say good-bye to Mr. Morrow for us."

"Wait. I have to put you on the right track."

"Teah, come *on*." He calls, "Yo, Shar. We're leaving now."

Teah yips, "Wait a *minute!*"

Implacable Elva continues. "Be sure you take this road. That'll keep you on the right track. Young man, you just be patient. Your sister and I are not quite through with the map."

Shar lopes up empty-handed; like Michael, she has found nothing. "Are we leaving or what?"

"Take care of Tommy," Michael mutters, handing him to Shar. "I'll stick your pack in the trunk."

While the women mull over the map, he moves to a place of safety behind the car, where he can look up at the Morrows' house without being seen. He can't say what he's looking for: some detail that will help explain what happened to his grandparents, some trace of his mother, maybe, or at least the ghost of their house, or is he looking for the legendary Son? What does he expect to see up there? Son scratching at one of the attic windows, contained and huge, and crazy as a trapped gibbon? Mom? With an effort he shakes off a sudden chill. Whatever he's afraid of, it is not here. The Morrow house gives back a face as bland and blank as that of Elva Morrow herself. And his mother's old house, where he thought against reason, or was it hoped against hope, his grandparents would be waiting for him? Completely gone.

All they have left now is the postcard from South of the Border. Maybe they will get there and Mom will be waiting. If she isn't, he doesn't know what he will do. Die, maybe.

With a sigh, he opens the car trunk.

As he does so, wispy Everett Morrow materializes unexpectedly, flat and insubstantial as a picture in a pop-up book.

Michael whirls. "Where . . ."

The old man murmurs, "Shh."

Snaps his mouth shut. . . . *did you come from?* So he really does have a secret to tell here. Stepping back so they are shielded by the raised trunk lid, Michael nods in complicity. But a long minute passes in which the old man says nothing and Michael tries to figure out how to get him to begin. "Did you. Ah." Pressed, he finally manages to get the rest of it out, squeaking, "Phone our house the other night?"

The old man doesn't answer. When he does speak, his voice is fragile as a newspaper out of the last century; he's gone so pale that the age spots stand out on his face. "If you want to find your mother, try Tarpon Springs."

Distressed, he says, "She sent this card . . ."

"In Florida," Everett says without moving his lips.

". . . from South of the Border." Troubled, Michael says more for himself than for the old man, "She's got to be there."

The old man mumbles, "Don't count on it. Try Tarpon Springs . . ." He can't stop looking over his shoulder, but Elva seems to be wrapped up in Tommy, putting a sailor cap on his head while he giggles and salutes. Then she looks at him over the child's head, nailing him with her glare. And abruptly he tips into uncertainty, finishing, "I think."

Michael hisses, "What do you mean, you *think*? Don't you know?"

Everett puts two fingers over Michael's mouth, but Michael has to know; he whispers anyway: "I have to know."

His face twists. "I'm not sure."

It is disturbing; everything is slipping around. Until he can get it straight, he can't tell Teah. "Just tell me what you said."

"Who, me?" Elva Morrow is headed their way. The old man shrivels as she approaches, like the Wicked Witch just about to melt. His gray eyes are bland, empty as the sky. "I didn't say anything."

Michael reaches out, urging, "Please." But the old man dwindles as he watches; it's terrible. Shar and his sister Teah are coming around the car on the other side, Shar saying, "Wait a minute, I need my shades. They're in the pack."

Teah closes on him, impatient and self-important. "Come on, Mikey, give Shar the keys."

So in the clamor of departure he cannot be positively certain what he's just heard, the old man's final words to him, which Michael thought — thinks — is almost certain — frame not a warning but an entreaty. The diminished Everett Morrow has just gripped his arm and in a voice so strangled by emotion that the words are blurred, has said, at least Michael thinks he's said:

"Somebody has got to stop him."

Poor little people, he thinks as he stalks through Clary Hale's silent house. He can get them to do anything he wants. He is like the emperor's son, given to peasants to hide: sees subservience written in their bodies. The gods that took his mother left him with a powerful instrument — a deadly charm. He can make it work anywhere. Has. All those teachers, pushing him forward. Employers, mentors, great enablers, one word and he has them competing to do him favors — he can see it in any mirror, the face of a fallen angel, a smile that blazes without having to be rehearsed.

Comprehended it the night of the fire. Sat up on the table in the hospital with his feet dangling and in that sweet child's voice convinced them of everything. The woman standing beside him, beaming, beaming: "If no one comes forward, Doctor, we'd love to give the child a home." So glad to have a child at all that she never asked questions. Old couple, beautiful boy, "you sweet *thing.*" *If you love me, give me this. Get me that.* They always did. Kept him like a diamond in a velvet box, thinking he would go forth and make them notable. *I can take anything I want from you and make you thank me.* He will redeem their dull lives, but not the way they think. All his life he has used them. Move here. Get me this. Conceal — that. *And thank me for using you, because you think I love you.*

But the empty place inside him burns. *Mother.* He has her now, locked away like a diamond waiting to be put into its setting. And he's a thousand miles away.

There are things he must do.

He pauses in the bedroom, smashing the glass in a dozen family pictures. The husband. Those children. He memorizes the fixed faces in the photographs, thinking coldly: *This is taking too long.*

The design burns close to the surface now: the tree.

He opens his hand and turns the palm so he can look at the tree in miniature. At its center is a white scar, where the palm was gored and healed. He can look into it and see the injury his father did him, *the hole at the center of everything.*

That he must fill. *But first, the obstacles.*

Around the hole in his palm the tree spreads, carved in flesh, with the design sealed under the skin in red ink. He did it to show lovely little Clary Martin, next door. Before. To prove his right. But she didn't see. Well, now she will.

The star at its center is leached of color as if by lightning. *What it's like inside of me.* And in the empty place he thinks he can see her dark cloud of hair spreading on the pillow, the fleck of blood at the corner of the mouth. He must fill the void with a woman — Mother, Clary, he cannot say but writhes with urgency. In his continuum, they are one.

He strips the spread and sinks his palm into Clary's pillow, as if to burn the design into the spot where she rests her face.

The tree grew so big it took him over, demanding to be expressed. If he stays, it tugs him back. Too powerful.

At first he wanted to leave the design behind. Imagined he could carve it into somebody else and walk away free. When he was, how old, twelve? Pretty little Daria, that smoky hair. Meant to carve it in her belly. Lie here, he said and she did. Hold still. Let me do this. That charm, she loved him! *I can make them do anything for me.* But she started wailing at the first cut and they came: *what are you two doing up there in the attic?* Her angry father ripped him away; *nothing, I was just* and weeping Daria — child loved him so much she lied, *nothing, he was just.* But the father *would have* the police. So he and the old couple had to leave that place in a hurry, cover it up, start in a new place, they do what he asks because he knows how to bore into their hearts and pull out what he needs: ordinary people. Fools.

Then there was the next place, the loving teacher, who . . .

And then the next. The next. Driven to fill the place in himself, he tried this, tried that. Thought he had found the way.

In Wilmington. That beautiful girl with his mother's face.

Clarada Martin raised her hands to him; she could have been reaching for the sun. So close. He thought he could fill it in love.

Until he made the mistake.

In the years that have fallen in between he has changed.

The tree burns brighter, demanding: *I will be completed.* The spot in his belly incandesces. *Here.*

They are the same now. He is the tree. *And we are close.*

But first, the obstacles.

He must begin.

He quits the house. Turning back to the closed face of Clary Hale's house, the blank windows, he could be looking at a corpse.

Oh my God, my children. She tries to pull herself to the surface of consciousness but she's been under for so long that it's like trying to come back from the bottom of the ocean, straining up and up to reflected light. *What.* How long has she been out? She can't tell. *Where.* Clary knows only that for the first time since he took her, she's completely alone. There is a difference in the sound quality, something about the air. No shot today, without the shots, she can . . . *Where is he?* Gone. Thunderstruck by dread, she can't, oh my God, she can't remember. *Where?* Tries to get up but can't. *What is he doing, what.* Can't bring it back. The children. What? The children! Thinks, just before she sinks back into unfathomable depths, *Oh my God.* It is like being drowned.

14

YOU WOULDN'T KNOW IT to look at her and there's no
reason for it, but Shar is like a parade today, Shar Masters with
her straw hair in springy curls and her bracelets jangling, coming into South of the Border, South Carolina, in the Hale car
with Clary's kids. They feel fine and they're all singing, now
that they're almost here. Shar's eyes are bright and her earrings
shiver, silver chandeliers she's put on because they have driven
out of late spring in New England straight into summer. It's
like riding into hope. If she was all business yesterday, leaving
that clean, creepy all-American house in Wilmington, she's brilliant today, in her red sandals with her name picked out in
rhinestones on her red T-shirt.

"Hey wuoww," she says as they ride in, "South of the Border."
Verses, dancing sombreros, a little Day-Glo ink to lift the heart;
the signs have been pointing the way for miles.

The kids should be happy they've made it to this gaudy para-
dise but Mike's voice sounds a little thin. "I guess this is it."

She knows the kids have something in mind, she heard them
up in the night discussing it, but they haven't clued her in. She
says brightly, "So wow, man. Can't wait to get into that pool."

Mike is so hung up he doesn't even notice. "What pool?"

"That one, dummy." It is in front of the motel, glittering at
them. Shar woke up in Richmond this morning and found out
she needed to put on a lot of color, so, what for? In hopes. She
put on her bikini underneath because life is a beach, today at
least. They are going to meet up with Clary here, the kids
haven't said so, but what else would be the point? Nice Clary
will come out of the motel in one of those T-shirts with the

legend and the Day-Glo sombrero and she'll be like: "What took you so long?"

High time. A family needs to be together, and even if it's somebody else's family so does Shar, especially at a time like this, knocked up like this, and fresh out of men. Clary will tell her what to do. She'll go, Oh, Shar. There there.

"So. Where are you guys supposed to meet your mom?"

Michael says unexpectedly, "I don't know."

"In the motel, dummy," Teah says to him. "It's on the card."

Shar's surprised. "What card?"

"You can let us out here."

No problem, Teah says it's on the card. But, South of the Border? It's a riot, but not exactly a Clary Hale kind of place, total nightmare theme park with the bumper stickers and the T-shirts and the Day-Glo buildings and the carnival rides. But when Shar asks, Teah fobs her off, and Michael gives back this desperate grin, mouth tight over the teeth, black rings around the eyes. Well the trip serves her purposes, this South of the Border looks like a party on wheels, may not be Clary's kind of place but it's definitely Shar's. These look like her kind of people, good things could happen here.

Except when she pulls up in front of the festive, ticky-tacky motel, the kids do not explain and they don't get out, either. They just hang here in silence, ba-dum, ba-dum, breathing in and out.

Another car comes up behind them, crowding her. Shar says, "So, are you guys going in to get your mom, or is she coming out?"

Why is Michael's voice so heavy? "Um. Ah."

Shar is getting mad at them. "OK, people, what's the deal?"

They avoid her eyes. Michael says, "Why don't you go park?"

At this rate she's never going to get in that pool. "Why don't I pull up here and wait?"

"Better go park," he says, getting out. "It may be a while."

"Go ahead." Teah gets out. "We'll come find you in the lot."

They passed the parking lot coming in, hundreds of cars wedged in, thicker than the Goofy lot at Disney World. It's a million miles from the pool. "How're you going to find the car?"

"Oh, here." Teah pulls a red hanky out of her back pocket.

"Just tie this on the antenna." She picks up Tommy. " 'Bye Shar."

Shar wants to see them go inside; she'd like to wait until they come out with their mother, after all she's supposed to be in charge, but the driver behind her is honking and the kids have made it clear that they won't go into the motel until she leaves. "OK," she says grudgingly, pissed because she feels left out. "OK."

Smiling, Teah gives her a brave little wave. "O-ka-ay."

Then, to remind them that she's the adult here, Shar says, "But don't go in the water without me. You're only kids. You need somebody to take care."

Drives into the parking lot and parks the car. And waits. And waits; time goes by, the late-afternoon sun is turning the place into one big heat mirage; even sitting in the shadow of the car, she's about to melt. Her makeup has already started to run down, soon to be followed by parts of her face. Pissed and anxious, she decides to go look for them, sticks a note on the windshield and takes off, legging it between the rows of parked cars, looking back every now and then at the red square she's tied to the antenna to be certain she can still find her way back to it.

Which is how she happens to be looking over her shoulder so at the exact moment she bumps smack into him before she even sees him, WHUMP. That *warmth*. Her heart staggers. Lover! "Oh lord, it's you."

That voice makes her gasp. "Charlotte."

"What are you doing here?"

"I told you I loved you."

"Oh, Lover, I thought that was just horseshit."

"You know it's true." His hands fit on her upper arms as if drawn by magnets and he turns her around. "Now let me look at you."

She ducks her head; one look in those white-green eyes with the shrinking pupils and she's a goner. "No."

"You know you want it."

She tries to pull away; it is breaking her heart. "Don't."

He lifts her chin. "Beautiful."

She's trying to stay mad at him but it escapes her like a long sigh: "You too." He is. She's supposed to be mad at him but she can't help it, gave him up forever when he didn't show and now here he is right back in her life. He gave her a baby, which ought to be enough, but now he's found her, kind of like the prince. Her voice ripples over tears as she says helplessly, "How did you find me?"

Her one true man says, "I just knew."

And before she can look into his eyes or glance around for the Hale kids, are they all right, he's pulled her to him and once again there is that CLANK of body on body, her lover drawn, Shar drawn, metal to magnet, arrow to quiver, heart to home, close, God help her, and straining to get closer. "Now," he says, in an urgent murmur with no beginning and no identifiable end, "I want to be with you."

"I'm supposed to be taking care of these kids . . ."

"You," he says. He doesn't even hear. "Just now, just you."

Never to separate, Shar thinks, if indeed she is thinking now; her mind says, the children, what about the . . . but her lover has come all this long way to find her, there must be a reason for it; although her head says, *careful,* her body cries, "Oh Lover, when?"

"Forever," he says. "Now."

"Oh God, we can't, not now." This is a lie; she would do anything he asked, she always has, one reason she has got this extra passenger in her belly. She can already feel him between her legs. Her voice almost fails her. "Not in front of all these . . ."

He draws her along as if she hasn't spoken. "I have a room."

Why she has this extra *thing* to tell him. Oh shit, wait a minute, Shar. *The kids,* she thinks, or tries to, but his hands are quick underneath her T-shirt, feels them sliding up on her, up, oh, *there* and although when her Lover did not come back to her single room back in Rhode Island on that particular Saturday even though he promised, the newly pregnant Shar made herself certain promises, her resolutions are forgotten now as are the children, as her unused body tells her this won't take long; she needs! If they get back to the car before she does, why they can wait. More, another sly part of herself remembers that Teah and Mike have in no way been straight with her about their mom, this is just tit for tat. Therefore as she says to him "Yes. Oh Lover. Yes," that secret part raps out a cross but reassuring little message: So what if they have to wait a few minutes, Shar sliding into delicious guilt and all that follows; let 'em wait. Fobbing me off like that; it serves them right.

In the room, they are everything to each other, naked Shar, her Lover, beautiful tanned face and throat, brown hands standing out against the white: when we are married maybe he will take off the white shirt. In the middle, her wonderful new man says, as if he's known from the first moment, "You're going to have my baby," and a shiver runs right straight through her belly, where the baby waits. "Oh, Oh, Oh," she cries, and lets those powerful brown hands, that sweet mouth slide along her body, erasing everything from her mind and tired bones except his touch, and she arches, frantic to meet him, *don't even have to tell him,* oh! Shar wide awake and singing, "Yes!"

She will do anything. *Anything you say.*

And when they're done, he begins again. As they close in on each other, slower this time, as if fated, her Lover sings her a little love song about the three of them at home down in sunny Florida, him, Shar and their baby going to live forever in the sunny, sandy sweet place: *what if he's lying,* she thinks back in there somewhere but his promise has a place to go to live in, and the place has a name; running his fingers along Shar's soft places while she fumbles at his shirt buttons like Pandora, Lover murmurs:

". . . so we'll go down there and live forever in my little house, lie under a tree and watch the sponge fishermen go by," the blood in her ears echoes: forever, but she murmurs, "Oh where, Lover, where," he is humming in her ear, "and watch the Greek boys go down in the harbor and dive for the crucifix," she has responsibilities but it sounds so beautiful, "If I could only . . . ," now they are humming together, "so all you have to do is this one little thing," the details, it seems so real! "Yes," Shar says, or hears somebody that sounds just like her say, "And we will be naked together . . ."

And then he finishes, Lover pushes aside her avid hands and reels her in, "Just go and tell the kids you can't go with them."

She tries to say, "But I'm supposed to be . . . ," but when he runs those lips over her again, murmuring, "You have me to look after now," she thinks it must be the right thing to do, the kids have probably found their own mom by this time anyway — oh wow, that touch, yes that one — or are just about to find her — there! — they'll be so happy with their real mother that they won't even need old Shar, oh! — and besides, the hands, the mouth; his love makes her beautiful, he even makes her feel thin . . .

When she can stop gasping and trembling at least enough to make herself get out of the bed and stand up well enough to walk, she goes to the bathroom mirror and while his reflection sprawls, lean and easy in the reflected bed, Shar pulls herself together, tremulously patting powder over the red flush that spreads on her breast and throat above the neck of the rhinestone-studded T-shirt she put on this morning in hopes. Her Lover loves her after all; he wants her to go with him and stay with him forever; the knowledge pounds in her belly and tingling snatch and crowds her throat, but Shar has responsibilities; she has to go and find the kids now, and break the news . . . Lover. He stretches and rolls toward her, letting his fingers trail along her thigh. Oh, God. She turns, drawn back to the bed but he lifts one expressive hand; he knows she will do anything he says and right now he says, "Later."

Her heart yearns: later. He will take off the shirt. "You go and tell them now," he says. "We don't want them waiting for you."

Anything you say.

Then she swallows hard and, leaving her entire future waiting in the dim, cool motel bedroom, Shar walks out and across the road, looking for the bandana that marks the Hales' car. As it turns out, the kids are sitting under a tree just outside the entrance to the parking lot. They look pretty much played out. Tommy is in the tightly manicured Bermuda grass with his legs spread, marching that goofy stuffed toy across the space between his knees while Teah leans against the tree trunk, staring at nothing, and Michael looks into his hands until Shar clears her throat and they look up. When she sees their expressions, she almost weakens.

"So," she says. Got to start somewhere. "Did you guys find your mom?"

Michael's mouth makes a wavery line; he just shrugs.

Teah sighs. "Not yet."

"So, ah," she says, with her heart sinking; Lover! What am I going to . . . "So. What are you guys going to do?"

"Wait," Michael says. Shar would like him to rip off a list of their next steps, A, B and C, but nothing comes.

"Are you all right?"

"What the hell do you think?" He glares. "We're fine."

"You sure?"

He looks older than he is, big, tough; the look challenges her to dare to contradict. "I told you, we're fine."

"Oh. I. Ah." Shar knows what she has to do, but her heart's pulling her in the opposite direction. In spite of her best intentions she hands Teah the keys to the car. "Oh, look. Here."

Teah jumps. "What's this?"

"The keys. So. Well," she begins in a guilty, upbeat tone. "Keep them in case. Oh hell, look guys." She chokes on false cheer. "I bet you guys will never guess what's happened."

The way Shar is right now she can't tolerate a silence. She's like a kindergarten teacher trying to jump-start her class. "I mean, like, what's happened to me?"

When nobody bites she has to prompt. "Remember my new man that I told you about, from home?" In the darkened car last night she confided, so she doesn't have to say: the guy who got me like this.

"Oh, you mean your boyfriend," Teah says without spirit; the kid looks all played out.

Mike says, "That rat."

"Yeah, well." Shar can't stop grinning. "Turns out he isn't a rat after all. He's here."

"You're kidding."

"No shit." The grin is about to split her face; it felt so *good.* "Imagine that, he came after me." Her voice is thinning out, but she goes on. "All the way down here."

Teah says, "That's great."

"He wants us to get married."

"So, congratulations." Michael manages a weary smile.

Teah says, "Really."

"But I can't," Shar says. She knows now this is wrong; resolution cools her. "Not until you guys get back with your mom."

Teah's eyes fill. "Listen, you're a mom now yourself, Shar, you've got responsibilities."

Responsibilities. Shar is surprised to find her hands on her belly. "Well yeah," she says slowly, so maybe what happens is her fault; pregnancy makes her all squashy.

"We're not messing up your wedding, no way," Michael says, as grandly as the Father of the Bride.

"I know," Shar says without conviction, "but first."

Teah hugs her. "Oh Shar."

"I don't know what to do," Shar says with her heart breaking. She can't desert the kids, but she needs him so *much*. Oh shit. Good Shar pushes bad Shar back into a corner and slams the door on her. She has to go back and tell Lover that these kids are counting on her and she can't be his until they find their mom so she can get shut of them. He loves her, so he'll have to see it, right? If he loves her, he'll understand. If he loves her, he'll wait.

Teah sees her face. "Oh Shar, be cool."

"I'm trying!"

"Go for it," Mike says.

"You guys!" Got to do what you have to, got to do what's right, Shar tells herself firmly and goes on in a leaden voice. "So. Ah. You guys hang in here, OK?"

So she has either told the kids she'll be right back or else bad Shar has snuck out and tripped her up so she hasn't told them anything. She thinks she's said it all, she's really coming back to them, and, choked with love and miserable and desperately confused, she finishes: "So, OK. OK?"

"Sure," Teah says bright. " 'Bye, Shar."

Michael calls after her: "Good luck."

Behind her they are grouped like, what — Spirit of '76 in her first-grade history book. *How can I leave these kids?* Tommy waves. She can't bear to see their faces so she runs. As she hurries back into the motel she worries: has she done it right?

In her pain and confusion she thinks so, but she's running too fast to know.

Going back down the dim, carpeted hallway to the room, she's upset, excited because this is either a wedding or a christening she's returning to, the thing in her is so small she can't even feel it but she knows: This is my baby, and I am running right into its father's arms. This feels so good that it can't be true; at the last minute she breaks into a run because she's afraid she'll find him gone. She's scared to death she'll find him there: *How can I leave these kids?* She's scared that the minute she starts trying to tell him about the baby he'll whirl up and vanish; she's scared to death that she'll open her mouth to tell Lover and the words won't come out, she's scared that, God she is scared . . .

Her heart leaps up because he is there.

Lean and graceful in the bed, completely relaxed and perhaps even half-asleep, confident that she'll do everything he tells her, her lover sees her coming and stirs, spreading his arms to her.

"Lover."

"Did you find them?"

In her confusion she blurts, "Oh-Lover-I-found-them-and I . . ."

"You told them they were on their own from here on."

"I . . ." Tries to tell him and can't because she doesn't *know*, thinks maybe she can slip into it through lovemaking, glove over hand, both one, thinks when they are engaged she'll break the news, takes off her shirt and jeans and slides into the bed, where once they are bonded in love she'll just come out with it, thinks, oh! That silky body, Lover! Thinks . . . Stops thinking. "Mmmm . . ."

"Good," he says and as she slides back into bed with him with her arms spread and her loving face raised to his, he brings both fists down on her head with such force that it makes no difference what Shar thinks, thought, was thinking, because the swift, vicious blow brings with it only darkness, darkness and silence, obliterating words, thought, light.

15

WHEN THEY DITCHED SHAR in front of the motel an hour ago, they really thought they were going to find their mother at South of the Border. "After all," Michael said. "This really is her writing."

Teah said, "What if it isn't?"

"Come on. It has to be."

"What if she isn't here?"

Michael chewed his knuckles. Was it time to tell her? Not yet, he thought. He wasn't ready; the old man might be crazy. No. He was carrying the old man's advice like a talisman. Bring it out too soon and it loses its power.

But Teah was edgy. "Well what if she isn't?"

"We'll think of something."

Tommy started up again. "Can we take Mommy home?"

"Yes." Remembering that Naval Intelligence was somehow in the picture Michael amended. "At least I think we can."

The building looked like the one on the card. She could be right up there in one of those motel rooms, or sitting in the coffee shop, waiting to explain; when they walked in the first thing they saw would be Mom smiling that great Mom smile, her face split open and love shining: *Oh, guys!* She seemed so close; Michael was ready to promise anything. "Sure we can, Toms."

Teah checked guest registers and showed Mom's snapshot to the desk clerks in several different buildings while Michael scoped the eating places, from coffee shops and refreshment stands to the four-alarm restaurant, where one of the waitresses finally brought him down. "Kid, we got so many people in and out of here we don't even look at their faces."

Daunted, he sneaked into motel units, cornering the maids: "Did you, like, after somebody checked out, did you find this card and mail it for them?" He had to do all this without looking like somebody looking for a missing person, thought he was doing fine until one of the maids propped her fists on her hips and studied him, saying as he spun in place, trying to think of a way to disappear, "Son, if you got so much trouble, how come you don't call the police?" To which he said, "I can't talk about it now," and fled.

He fetched up back here at the car, where Teah was already sitting with Toms on her lap. "Nothing I could find," she said. "Nobody saw her, she never signed in here."

"God, we." Needed this. "Maybe they checked her in under a different name."

The reproaches began, Teah first. "Oh Mikey, what are we doing here?"

"You said we would find Mommy."

"Shut up, here comes Shar."

"She looks . . ." What did she look? Ruddy and distracted. Shar's face turned to rubber as he watched, contorting itself into one expression after another without ever hitting on the right one.

Teah didn't have to ask what he meant. "You're right. Look."

Approaching, Shar couldn't have known she was already stamped with the badge of her intentions: that purple love bite at her throat.

So much for their first hour here. So much for Shar.

Ten minutes ago Shar loped off to meet her man. She might as well have disappeared. Tracking her departure with his camera eye, Michael imagined that if he watched her through a Steadicam, he could follow her into the motel and talk her out of going with this Lover, but this was private. Everything about Shar was private now. FADE OUT.

With Shar gone, they are marooned here. South of the Border is south of nowhere. They've come all this way and tried everything and their mother isn't here. There's no sign that Clary's here or has ever been here, nothing left behind, no note at the message center, nothing scrawled on a paper napkin for a waitress to pass on, no telltale earring or abandoned scarf looped on a plaster cactus to point the way, and not one clerk or attendant who's seen or heard of a lost mom with dark hair and a face like Teah's, no trace of the most important person in their world. Michael feels hollow. "Do you think she'll be back?"

"Mike, she's in *love*."

"No, not Shar," Michael says. They have to talk over Tommy's head. He says heavily, "You know."

Teah's empty hands fall open. "I don't know."

They are the only still objects in a swiftly changing scene. On all sides of the big tree where Shar told them good-bye, the paths are crosshatched with happy tourists, all going somewhere. Overnighters in dismal pastels head off for an early dinner, towing scrubbed kids in fresh T-shirts with their heads still wet from the pool, while sweating day-trippers in crumpled clothes make one last run on the souvenir shop before they slap on the bumper sticker and head home. Everyone who leaves is immediately replaced. Entire families in South of the Border hats and black T-shirts with the sombrero lope toward the theme park; if they don't ride all the rides tonight no problem; they come from Canada, Oregon, Manhattan Kansas, Tokyo, prepared to stay for days. Tourists here travel in constellations; parents, grandparents in some cases, every kid with at least one adult attached — perky mom, divorced dad. Everybody has somebody to be with; everybody has someplace to go.

Everybody else.

Michael's stuck under this tree; his tapes zip by so fast nothing makes sense. Cross-eyed with concentration, Teah's squinting at the postcard as if she thinks if she just looks close enough she'll see their mother waving an infinitesimal hand from one of the tiny windows pictured on the front, while Tommy grumbles and tramps around the trunk in decreasing concentric circles, with a tantrum like a storm center forming over his head.

"I want Mommy." Late afternoon is not Tommy's best time

of day. At home Mom would stick him in bed with his stuffed Taz and a book, but here they are. His circles are getting tighter. They take him over Teah's sandals and Michael's Nikes; the next round will bring him crunching over their laps. "I want Shar."

Teah snaps at him. "You can damn well forget about Shar."

Snap. Crack. It's like a Punch and Judy. "I want Mommy." Teah has yelled at Tommy, so his heel comes down hard in her lap. Tears of pain fill her eyes. "Ow!"

Tommy stamps across her and crunches over Michael: "Mommy. Mommy." Thud.

"Ow!" Michael grabs an ankle, bringing him down in mid flight.

He starts to scream. Tourists stop in their tracks; attendants stare as Tommy roars. "I want my mommy."

Mike locks his arms around him and starts rocking. "Sh sh Tommy it's OK, kid, OK really, OK," hugging and rocking, muttering nice things until Tommy's sobs slow down and, satisfied that this is a family matter, the horrified onlookers drift away. He holds the kid, going "therethere" into his soft, soap-smelling hair, and in a voice so low that only Tommy can hear, he whispers, "I want my mommy too," hugs him so tight that the bawling finally subsides and the sobs play out into sporadic sniffs. "Be cool and I'll get you some candy." Tommy snuggles, starting to feel better; sighs.

Now Teah starts. "What are we going to do?"

Michael thinks he knows, he knows; he doesn't know. He says over Tommy's head, "Maybe we should wait for Shar."

Teah says bitterly, "Don't hold your breath."

"She didn't exactly say good-bye."

"You know Shar in love." Sitting here under the tree with her dark hair falling in deep waves, Teah looks like one of those fools on the front of the trashy romances Shar reads, waiting for storybook love. If the right guy comes along even Teah could blow off looking for Mom and go away with him, just like Shar. She gives him an unnecessarily sharp look. "But of course you don't know anything about love."

You don't have any idea what I know about.

He lashes out. "Well neither do you!" This is bad. He keeps seeing Teah coming in late with her cheeks burning and her face smeared, out of her mind with Eddy Stanko, but he hears Shar: "I am sick of being led around by my pussy." He is stone sick with anxiety, can't let Teah see it, begins to wonder if anybody in the world comes out the other side of love unhurt. Then Michael trips over the next thought, falls and lands with his face in it:

If you didn't love people, life would be a lot easier. No love, no problems anywhere.

If nobody loved anybody it wouldn't matter about Capt. Thomas Hale, U.S.N., trapped out there under layers of mysterious black ocean, Michael's father either dead or not. Old as this misery is, it stays fresh. It saws in his throat like a rusty razor blade — if only he *knew*. In a world without love it wouldn't even matter about their mom being gone God knows where, leaving no word except a secondhand phone call from Naval Intelligence, and this rotten postcard, which turns out to mean nothing.

They've come too far on stupid hopes.

It was crazy to think Clary would be down here waiting for them just because she probably sent this card, and he can't help wondering, would it be crazy to plow on to Tarpon Springs just because the old man told him to? Hell, he thinks, no crazier than sitting around that empty house doing their homework while everything went to pieces around them. No crazier than staking everything on one phone call because this official-sounding guy told Teah he was in Dad's class at the Academy. So what if the name did check out? People lie. They even mess with records. It was crazy to believe it was Naval Intelligence, and dumb to keep the whole thing secret just because this guy said they were under orders. Trouble is, you say "Orders" to a military person, even a kid, and you can make them twitch.

Orders. Even officers' children have to question orders at some time. The whole thing could be a lie. What if there isn't any secret Navy operation, and their mother is in no respect involved? Then there's no hope for their father. Michael hasn't wanted to admit this, but he misses Tom Hale so much that for a while there, he held his nose and swallowed the story whole. It promised certain things he needed: the *Constellation* safe somewhere after all, awaiting orders to reveal itself, Dad too — *I wanted to tell you, Mike, but orders . . .* Michael imagined his whole life waiting out there somewhere just the way he used to have it, Mom, Dad, happy endings, everything restored.

He knows better now. Or thinks he does.

His mother isn't even here.

It's too much.

"How the hell could she do this to us?" Rage rises in him; he's like a thermometer, mercury hitting the top with a splat. "Why didn't she leave word?"

At his tone Tommy twists and wriggles out of his arms.

The skin around Teah's eyes crumples. "What if she couldn't help it?"

"She didn't even try." He is raging. "Who does she think she is anyway, who the hell does she think she is?"

"Oh shut up, Mike."

He loses it altogether, saying bitterly, "She doesn't care about us." Entertains the unspeakable. "She doesn't give a shit."

Instead of arguing this point, beating him back into an acceptable position with reasons, A, B, C, which is at bottom all he's really asking for here, Teah caves in and begins to cry.

It sticks like a cleaver in his chest. *Thock.* This is the most terrible single thing he's ever said. He rushes away from it, saying to Teah, to God, "I take it back. I didn't mean it, OK?"

He's afraid. The hand that gives also takes away: the threat on the answering machine, the card. No Mom. Something bad is happening, has happened. There is no good anywhere. "She would never walk out on us." The rest follows, coming in like a note on a flaming arrow: *Not without a fight.* "They'd have to drag her."

Fear drives him to his feet — too late to escape the swarming dread that gnaws him from the toes up, like rats. He has to get moving or there won't be anything left of him but naked bones.

Teah looks up. "Where are you going?"

He thinks he knows what to do; he knows what to do, doesn't know what to do. Tarpon Springs; he doesn't know what he knows, or how to tell his sister. "I'll be back."

Clearing the shadow of the tree, he starts to run. He makes two neat circuits of the parking lot before he peels off and circles the motel, thudding around the fake adobe buildings with such concentration that he doesn't even see the windows he's passing, or know he's being watched.

His next circuit takes him around the outbuildings and through the filling station, where he stops to make a couple of purchases. Stuffing them in his jeans pockets, he trots away, heading into one more circuit of the grounds, trying to slow the racing images in his head to keep pace with the regular thudding of his feet.

Now he has to figure out how to tell Teah. How to explain why he didn't tell her about Tarpon Springs, when he doesn't know. *I was saving it, OK?* He can see Teah tearing him apart: "What do you mean, saving it?" What can they do when they get there anyway, two high school kids and a little boy? He still doesn't know how to start. Teah will say he's crazy. Well maybe he is.

He's breathing hard. Sweat slides down inside his T-shirt like blood in a Band-Aid, sticking it to him, but he has to keep running until he figures this out. He would like to just go on running, strong, free, without a plan, but it's hot, he's getting winded and it's late, time to begin the approach to the runway and set down in their little encampment under the tree.

Michael squares his shoulders and homes in at a smart, businesslike clip. "Candy bars." He tosses them into Teah's lap.

She cracks one and bites into it, trying not to let him see how relieved she is to see him back; OK this is hard for her too. "Where the hell did you go?"

"Reconnaissance." He tries for a commanding-officer voice. "Come on, it's time."

She pushes her hair back with her knuckles and yawns. "Oh sure. What did you have in mind?"

"Restaurant," he says with brusque, military confidence; he

has to hit the right tone so he can move her along. "First dinner, then Phase Two."

"Who put you in charge?" Teah protests automatically, but she seems cheered by his certainty.

He doesn't exactly answer. "Come on, hurry. Look, I bought a map. Georgia and Florida."

"Florida!"

"We have to go there. It's hard to explain. Come on, let's eat. There's something I haven't told you," he says.

The restaurant is cool, the food is good and Michael waits until they've finished their platters with fried everything to spread the map on the table and explain. He expects an argument but his sister surprises him with a what-the-hell shrug. "Why not?"

So instead of numbering his reasons, one, two, three, he goes over the route to this Florida town Mr. Morrow told him about just one more time, irritated because Tommy's dropped off and Teah's stopped listening. Instead of following the map as he traces their route with one finger, she's lifted her eyes to something or somebody over his left shoulder. Her eyes have glazed and she's fixed on something he can't see.

Unnerved, Michael turns and for the first time sees him.

The stranger regards them from the table in the corner, a tall, lean man with a military set to the shoulders and a military squint to those pale, level eyes. He is looking at Teah, who is looking at him. Something about the man — the set of the head on the strong shoulders or the good looks — sets him apart. It may be the air of ease that gives him a distinctive sheen; for whatever reasons he stands out in this commonplace dining room cluttered with ordinary people, clumps of tourists from nowhere; it's like looking at a star.

But this singularity is not what has drawn Michael's sister, nor is it what holds her now. It's the eyes. Forgetting Michael, the map, the plan, his sister looks at the stranger with the same heated concentration she wasted on worthless Eddy Stanko. If they were at a high school dance, he'd say they were falling in love. She seems not to know that she has her fingers curled around the crystal pendant ordinary-looking old Elva Morrow put around her neck in Wilmington, the old lady probably got it on the shopping channel but she laid it on Teah like buried treasure and you would think she had given Teah the moon — Elva Morrow, whom Michael understands he never liked. There is Teah, transfixed.

Then all the air in the room stops still. There is no breeze, nothing in his chest, nothing left to breathe. Michael himself is fixed here like a specimen in a killing jar, rocked by fear so powerful that he may never take another breath. *Have to get out of this place;* what is it? He doesn't know.

He finds the breath somewhere to gasp, "Teah!"

Bemused, she turns. "What's the matter?"

He squeezes the words out. "We've got to get out of here."

Now she is looking at him. "But I haven't finished my . . ."

He slaps his hand on the table. "Out. We have to get out."

"What's the hurry?"

"I can't *be* here," he says. *Hurry,* he thinks, without knowing why it's so important. Has to escape this place, the three of them contained in this bright room with that *person.* Is he running toward, or is he running away? He doesn't know. Maybe he's spooked into trying to outrun his feelings, which are mostly bad; it could be his sister's rapt stare that has lit the fire under him; if they clear out now he can keep her from disappearing into the eyes of that stranger. Something about their locked gazes, what, how *fast* this kind of thing can happen frightens him, but that isn't it either.

He's not sure what's the matter with him; he only knows he has to get up and get out of here while he still can.

How much shows in his face? Teah says crossly, "OK, OK!"

Getting up, Michael dips his chin in his left shoulder, trying to sneak one more look at the stranger at the corner table without letting him know he's being watched. The table is empty. The stranger with the military eyes is gone. "Come on," he says irrationally. "Let's get out of here while we still can."

16

WHEN THEY DO STOP they're halfway to Georgia, and they stumble into a motel without noting who sees them leave the road or who follows. Too tired to speak, they lug Tommy into a featureless motel room, generic, could be anywhere. Putting him to sleep on the sofa, they drop like felled trees on the identical double beds.

In the night Teah wakes him. She can't stop screaming. Drugged with sleep, Michael lurches. Whatever he's been afraid of for so long is finally here. He struggles out of bed and grabs her shoulders and pins her down. Still heavy with sleep, alarmed, he cries, "What's the matter, what's the matter?" and in the half-light from the bathroom sees her shirtfront part and the fall of beautiful, pink-tipped breasts — his *sister* — and in pain and confusion he shakes his sister hard, growling, "For God's sake, what's the matter with you?"

But locked in the dream, Teah can only mumble "Out, watch out watchout," and when frightened Michael begs her to come back from sleep and explain she wakes finally, indignant. "What do you want?"

Shaken and sweating, Michael cries, "What, Teah, for God's sake, watch out for what?"

Sleepy Teah says gruffly, "Don't bother me" and stamps off to the bathroom. When she comes back she turns her back to him, escaping his questions. Before he can stop her, she flees into sleep.

In the morning they wake up to ordinary daylight, morning sounds. Michael says in hushed tones, "What *was* that?"

It's as if it never happened. "Nightmare, what nightmare?"

"You were screaming."

Teah answers so indifferently that he has no idea whether she really remembers. "Oh that, it was nothing."

"You kept yelling to watch out."

"Watch out . . . Oh yeah, right," she says, but her mind is absolutely on something else. "It was only a dream." She finishes putting on eyeliner and, looking at him in the mirror, tosses off the next detail. Unwitting Teah says absently, "I think this motel was on fire."

Oh, is that all. "Teah, for God's sake!"

"Well, *sorry*."

He turns away. "C'mon, Toms. Let's get dressed and load the car." He stuffs the child's dirty things into his pack.

But now that he's brought it up, Teah keeps worrying it. She finishes with the blusher and as he gets ready to take things to the car, says unexpectedly, "Or maybe it was something else."

"That what?"

"That got into my dream. This thing I heard, when Mom thought I was asleep?" Trying to recover it, she gives herself a little shake. "At least I think I did. It was late, we were coming back from somewhere in the car. I was in the back and they were talking? Oh never mind. No. Wait. Something she told Sarah?"

"You mean Mom?"

"Yeah. Mom." Spreading her hands on the dresser, his sister leans forward, staring into her reflected eyes. "Oh shit, I don't know. At least I think she told her. I suppose I should have asked Sarah, but she's too old to remember anything. I think I heard Mom say . . ." Her head jerks. "Oh!" She looks up into his reflected face. "It didn't make any sense at the time, but from what she said . . . — I think Mom's parents got wiped out in a fire."

In two jumps Michael spins her around. "You knew that and you didn't tell me?"

"I don't know that," she says. "Not really." Pulling away, Teah shakes her head so hard it rattles; then she dips it so all her hair flops and looks at him through it. "I didn't really know until now." Her voice drops to a whisper. "What do you think?"

In the hush that follows, he thinks he doesn't know. It puts him right back in Wilmington, staring into the crumbled foundation. Instead of his mother's house, he's looking into a void. So there is that. There is more about Wilmington, what else; Michael isn't ready to sort it out.

"Mike?"

He wants to answer but he can't. "I guess we'd better head out," he says finally. Teah nods. Tommy comes out of the bathroom in clean clothes and Michael turns to details he knows he can handle. "You pay the bill and I'll load the car. Where are the keys?"

"Here's the trunk key." She separates it from the others on the ring. Good old Teah, trying to put herself back in command.

"What are you afraid of, I'm going to drive away?"

"Give me a break, Mike." If they can't go any deeper now, they're going to have to go ahead. Teah returns him to the ordinary, saying crossly, "It's all you need."

Don't even need this key, he thinks but does not say. Reaching deep in his pockets, he closes his hand on his father's keys. He has carried his father's key ring for three years, ever since it came home in a carton of Dad's things they packed up and sent back from the base. Clary was unpacking Dad's stuff and in the bright faith that has always been her hallmark putting it away in the closet, because at that point maybe even she thought the *Constellation* would be found. Unless she was doing it for his and Teah's sakes, putting Dad's stuff away against his return so they wouldn't lose heart, while they sat on the bedroom floor and watched her closely for signs. As Clary was hanging up his uniform trousers, something fell out of one of the pockets and slid down the bedspread, landing next to Michael on the rug. His father's key ring, with the miniature flashlight Michael had put in Dad's stocking one Christmas still attached; he can still feel the thank-you hug. It was restored to him like a relic. Like a relic it has powers that leave Michael thinking, then and now: *He didn't take it to sea. That must mean he's coming back.* Yes Michael needed it, he wanted it; he had to have it. He is carrying it now.

His fingers feel the notches in the keys. It's crazy — how much of his present is made up of things left behind by people who are gone.

Teah isn't listening but he says anyway, "See you in the restaurant. Right now I have something to take care of."

Tommy wants to follow him but when they get outside Michael plants his little brother on the grassy patch in front of their motel room. "You have to wait here. Promise?"

Tommy looks at him over the head of his stuffed toy. "OK."

"Good man. When I get back I'll buy you some saltwater taffy," he says carelessly, because he is intent on what he's about to do. "You and Taz play here."

As he comes down the little hill into the parking lot he thinks he sees a figure slipping back into the building at the far end, and crazy as it is, Michael can't shake the idea that this person was messing with Clary's car. Impossible. Who would bother their old car out here in broad daylight with a dozen other shiny late models crammed with luggage? *Be cool, it could never happen. All this uncertainty is making me weird.* Still he checks all the locks and finds them secure. Tells himself not to get carried away but walks around the car one more time anyway.

Once he has everything stowed he gets into the car. Alone, he does what he's intended all along. He gets into the driver's seat and takes out his father's keys, struck in the heart all over again at the sight of the little silver flash. Shrugs and puts the key in the ignition so he can try everything: gearshift, brakes, wipers, lights. Good, OK, fine. If he has to, he can push his sister out of the way and take the wheel.

He locks the car and goes back to retrieve Tommy.

Who turns out to be gone.

Asshole, who said losing one person made you proof against losing any more? Tommy's the last person he expected to lose. The spot in the grass is empty. There is nobody around.

"Tommy!" He begins to run. "Tommy! Toms!"

Then he's jerked out of his tracks by a stranger's voice. "Forget something?"

"Tommy!" The sight freezes him where he stands.

Across the way, in front of the restaurant, his baby brother plays in the lap of a stranger as happily as if they're old friends. Idiot Tommy sits, happy and ignorant, in the circle of this new and completely unknown person's arms. *I left him alone. Anything could have happened to him. Anything.*

Tommy's turned his cartoon-kid face up so he can look into the stranger's eyes and he's laughing, my God, playing with this kidnapper, could be molester, could be murderer, this stranger. Could be anything. Here are his brother, so small you could break him with one hand and this unknown, chattering like old friends.

Fear gives way to anger. Didn't I tell you never to talk to . . . "You bastard, you put him down!"

The man does not drop Tommy or jump up guiltily. Instead he gives Michael a careless wave. He does this so naturally that for a second even Michael is taken in by the ease, the authority with which this stranger summons him, must be an officer: the white shirt and dark tie, the aspect: neat head with its trim, military look. His hopes trick him. At this distance the man holding Tommy looks not unlike Captain Tom Hale, and if not Tom then maybe a friend or classmate, or somebody from the sub but, crazy. No. Who? Who is he? Michael's heart gets so big it chokes him. Who?

"Tommy," he shouts, and when the kid doesn't even look up, he starts to run. "You come here you little bastard," he shouts angrily, yanking Tommy away to a safe distance, where he stands trembling while the stranger sits quietly as if nothing has happened, silently regarding him. "You little asshole," he says to his little brother. "You don't ever, ever talk to strangers and you don't ever, ever go with them, you hear? Dummy, you . . ."

"*Don't,* Mikey." Squirming, Tommy starts pounding on him. "Cut it out."

"You don't ever, ever talk to . . ."

"Mikey, stop," Tommy squeaks indignantly, struggling to get down. "He's not a . . ."

Furious, Michael shakes him hard. "Thomas Morton Hale Junior, you know damn well you're not supposed to talk to . . ."

And stops cold because the unknown has just spoken his name.

"Michael Hale," the stranger says, getting up in a fluid blur of arms, legs, extended hand, which he expects Michael to shake. He advances as if they are already friends. Michael saw those eyes at a distance last night in the restaurant and felt faintly threatened. Up close like this, he begins to see what Teah saw. They are the color of white jade his grandfather Hale brought from Singapore, pale and dense, and what Teah saw becomes clear to him. The eyes draw him; they command. The eyes are holding him right now; the owner will not let go until Michael has thoroughly studied them and is satisfied. There is another element that draws him here; Michael recognizes it with some measure of relief — that officer's presence, Michael thinks, even as he falls back a step to keep the distance between them. The stranger is bigger than this place somehow, and although he's in street clothes instead of the uniform he has the neat, crisp look Michael recognizes from his dad, the contained air of a man who has worn a uniform every day of his adult life. The white shirt and dark trousers look authentic and so does the pencil holder in the white shirt pocket; he holds Michael's eyes with a familiar, authoritative calm. "Michael Dealey Hale, son of Thomas Morton Hale, Captain, U.S.N., and Clarada Martin Hale."

"How do you know?" Michael backs, avoiding the extended hand.

"It's my business. And that's Thomas Morton Hale Junior." Tommy braces with the dumbest little salute; for all he knows, this could be Dad. "Cecelia Martin Hale is waiting for us in the restaurant. Come on. It's time for you to come along."

Michael backs away, but he can't shake the eyes. "Wait a minute. Wait."

Pale, steady eyes. "There's something you need to know."

"You can't just . . ." Distressed, Michael breaks off. "*Know!*"

"Come along. Official business." Pale, seagoing eyes. Pale eyes, with that even, Navy stare as if with vision stretched by looking long distances on round-the-clock watches; these same eyes look out of his father's face even in his photographs; Michael has seen these eyes in the faces of his father's shipmates, but drawn as he is by the eyes of this man he doesn't know, he thinks — cannot be sure, but thinks he sees something else flickering there.

"Official business." Michael is not easily bought; there is a part of him that has to keep asking questions until it is satisfied. "You're the guy that called? You're Captain Rogers Maynard?"

The stranger shakes his head. "No. But I am from Intelligence. Captain Maynard asked me to come."

"What do you want?"

"It's OK, son. Let's go inside." He fixes Michael with those level Navy eyes. "I have news for you."

"News!" Michael cuts to the chase. "Where's Mom?"

The eyes are like magnets. "Quiet. Not here."

Even so, Michael can't stop mulling it. "If you have news, why didn't you stop us last night at the restaurant?"

"Too crowded."

He says stubbornly, "I saw you watching us."

"I had to be careful." The newcomer says significantly, "There are lives at stake."

"Lives!" He thinks: *Mom.* Can't help thinking: *Dad.*

"This is a sensitive matter." The stranger lowers his voice, drawing a circle and pulling Michael into it. "Understand. I had to wait until I was sure you could handle this. I had to be certain I could count on you."

It crosses Michael's mind that if anything goes wrong with his mother now it may turn out to be his fault, for not going along with this officer, who has not introduced himself but is clearly in command. Pulled into the next-to-last move in this part of the game, he teeters on the verge of trust. "Why did you wait so long?"

"An officer has to know who he can trust."

There. Michael says automatically, "Yes Sir."

"Come on, son. The Navy is counting on you." Completing the transaction, the stranger moves Michael the last few steps as he says without explanation, "It's time."

As the three of them come into the restaurant, Teah outrages Michael by leaping into the role of responsible adult, saying to the stranger, as if they've been old friends for years, "Oh Commander, thanks for rounding them up."

"My pleasure." He gives her this *smile*.

"Wait a minute, Teah. Wait."

Erasing everything that's happened so far, including her own helpless tears and screaming in the night and all the times she fell back and left Michael in charge, his faithless sister goes on carelessly, as if it's Michael who's the baby brother here. "I hope these kids didn't give you any trouble."

"Natural caution," the commander says easily, and he and Teah exchange looks. "It's a quality we look for in an officer."

But his dad left him in charge and he's trying hard to do a decent job of it. "Who exactly is WE?"

"Oh, Mike," says Teah and he understands from her condescending insider's tone that his sister already knows. Without a second thought she completes her betrayal. "Michael, this is Commander Cleve Marshall, from Naval Intelligence? Cleve, this is my little brother, Mike Hale. Now Michael, apologize."

So here is Michael Hale, a Navy junior who tries to do a good job of taking care of the family his father left behind, Michael sitting with his brother Tommy and his older sister at a corner table in a motel restaurant somewhere in deepest South Carolina, fixed, almost hypnotized by the tall, quiet man who holds their eyes with such authority that there's no escape.

"It's natural for you to be suspicious," he says quietly. "Of course you're worried about your mother in spite of our assurances, but the first thing you need to know is that she is alive and well. And safe." He sweeps their faces with those pale, seagoing eyes that give back endless horizons; the deep tan looks right but this is clearly not a submariner like their father; this man has spent months, years outside; he says, "Naturally our operation is a secret, which is why I was so cautious about getting in touch, but with your departure and certain other elements, events converged."

Michael says carefully, "Maybe you'd better tell us about the operation."

Commander Marshall is swift. "I'm sorry, that's classified. But if you want to ask about your mother . . ."

"Yes."

". . . I'm free to talk. Your mother is perfectly safe."

Mom! "You know where she is?"

"Of course I do. We put her there."

Anger flares. "And you're just now telling us?"

"For her own safety." He gives them a significant look. "And yours."

At the fringes of this conversation a complete vision of his mother flickers, Clary with her face turned so he can't see her expression, receding as he tries to advance on her, his mother hopelessly out of reach. "Who *says*?"

"Michael, don't."

"It's all right, Teah," the commander says. "Understand, I had to wait until the time was right."

"You could have trusted us," Michael says bitterly. He wants his mother back; he wants her now. "You could have shown yourself." The weight of the past few days piles up on him, compounded by the insult — all this secrecy, them not knowing, when of all people they should have been told, and he bears down. "All those days at home, all that in Wilmington, you had us right there at South of the Border and you wouldn't show yourself?"

"Michael, stop!"

The man says simply, "It was too soon. Listen, son. In this business you can't be too careful." He extends lean, strong hands across the table and puts them on Michael's, fixing him with those eyes. "Now, son, don't be like this." To his own surprise, Michael doesn't struggle; this Commander Marshall holds him with such conviction that all he can do is wait.

"I had to have you where nobody could hear."

He echoes, "Where . . . Nobody . . . Could hear." With this detail the encounter becomes real.

"I had to wait until we could sit down, eye to eye."

Still Michael hangs back. "What class is my father's ship?"

"SSBN. Trident." He makes a half salute. "Good man."

Michael gauges him. "How much does she weigh?"

"Eighteen thousand, seven hundred fifty tons." He grins. "Give or take."

It is exact. That look: it makes Michael feel strong, adult, sure. "OK," he says carefully. "OK."

"OK." Then, with disarming ease, the commander puts the next link in place. "Naturally I can't expect you to believe me right off, but . . . ," he leans close so that nobody outside the circle can hear and even so, he drops his voice, ". . . if you want to see your dad again . . ."

Hope makes Michael's voice leap. "Dad!"

"You have to trust me anyway. Now, your mother is a different story. She's . . ."

Teah's voice is husky. "Where is she?"

"It's for her own safety. She's . . ."

Where? Somewhere? Nearby? Michael can't breathe. In the long pause before the man goes on, he can hear the insides of his head boiling over. Michael's voice seems to come in on long distance. "Sir?"

"She's at a location not far from here. Now that we know each other I'm prepared to let you see her," the commander says finally. "But you have to be willing to go along with me, no questions."

Wait a minute. Michael is Tom Hale's son. He knows how these things are supposed to march. He wants more than anything to see Clary, but he has to be careful. "Before we go anywhere, you'd better show us some ID." Teah hisses angrily. The silence that follows is so long that Michael thinks: Oh my God, what have I done?

He holds his breath.

But after an extended moment that fills from the bottom up with Michael's fears, the officer pulls out a black wallet and with a grin unfolds it. "Of course. S.O.P."

Dizzied by the confrontation, Michael stares at the card behind the plastic window without really seeing; the seal looks familiar, that's this guy's picture, all right: Commander Cleve Marshall, U.S.N.; lord, he *wants* to believe. His voice is shaky. "Looks OK to me." He hands it back.

"Very well." The commander looks around to be certain there is nobody within earshot. Then he leans forward across the table and says in a voice so low that only they can hear, "It's a secret installation off Sea Island, Georgia. We have to use extreme care about how we proceed." Studying Teah's face, then Michael's, he says directly to Michael, "But I wouldn't ask you to begin this without showing you some kind of proof. Your mother said I might have trouble convincing you . . ."

There is another long pause during which Michael holds his breath again and the commander reaches into his pocket, coming up with an object which he puts into Michael's hand, closing his fingers over it. Astonished, Michael feels the weight and bite of something he knows. It is like holding the keys. Afraid to look at it and know for sure, he puts the closed hand in his lap.

The commander ends the silence. "So she sent this."

Slowly, Michael opens his fingers and looks down. He is holding his mother's dolphins that Dad gave to her right after they were married, that Clary puts on every morning no matter what she's wearing, this is a significant sign, symbol, emblem, everything, glittering in his hand. He is holding the submariner's emblem, dolphins bumping noses on a heavy gold pin: hers.

17

HER CONSCIOUSNESS is too clouded to admit clear memories; something in this place is fogging her — drugs, she knows, but no injections since he left — thinks it must be in the food, because in spite of her desperate situation she can't stop sleeping, half wakes weakened by inertia, struggling through thick clouds that roll in without stopping, obscuring her vision. Each time she wakes, she wades through fog to the little shelf of food he has left and tries to guess: How is he poisoning me?

Tried not eating, but all it did was make her weak. If she's going to escape him, she has to eat so she can get strong. Tries avoiding first this food, then that one, but Clary's mind stays misted, like a windshield in filthy weather; lord it must be in the water. Gallon jugs lined up along the heavily insulated wall, probably it, but what to do? Salt water dribbles out of the taps at the little sink and although she would do anything to clear the murk out of her head she needs water to survive, can't do without it, although she's tried. Failed. Has sunk into the ocean of sleep, keeps sinking. When she manages to surface, splintered memories confuse her: *up periscope,* bright foam breaking over the bow . . . No. There is only this sealed room, a.c. humming, and for the rest the occasional nightmare fragment of memory delivered to her whole. Eyes. His face!

Lean, unforgettable. Brilliant, cruel.

You. What do you want with me?

In Pequod Street she begged, argued, struggled, fought him but after the first — what — chloroform there was the needle, hands so skillful he could have been a nurse, did they send him to a, stop it, Clary. What is he giving her? Head almost cleared once; they stopped so he could sleep; he took a minute too long to wake and Clary, still tied but working in the dark, printed her home address on the gaudy postcard like a desperate tourist, would have added: CALL THE POLICE, but no time. He woke and she cast it to the winds, no stamp, worse than floating a message in a bottle.

In Carolina he rolled her in blankets and threw her in the back of the car, raging and weeping, every time she struggled the needle zinged in and put her out. God why didn't she guess that their terrible progress would end here? They rode in by night and dear God she knew it: the tin roof, the cupola, that sagging porch under the dying Australian pine, the vision that replicates itself in all her paintings and seeps into her dreams, casting a long shadow over her adult life.

"Our place." He fixed her on the spot and made her look. "Remember?"

She trembled in a fury of denial: "No!"

It was the same, but not.

What he had done inside. That beautiful room! In the doorway she staggered, confounded by plush carpeting instead of splintered floors, soft lighting, gleaming furniture. The outside of the house was nothing like the inside. As it is with him. He dragged her inside and with that terrifyingly casual gesture, made it clear he intended to keep her here forever: "— over here your studio."

"Studio!"

"Oils. Sable brushes. Everything you will ever want."

Stunned as she was by drugs, she was raging, furious: *Don't presume to know what I want,* but when she tried to talk her tongue betrayed her and her breath came out in a useless little whir.

"Aren't you glad? Say you're glad, so I can let go of you."

Damn fool Clary was never any good at hiding what she felt; instead of dissembling, she threw herself backward so violently that his fingers dug long gouges in the soft skin of her wrists. As if nothing had happened, he readjusted his grip and pulled her back in place. With steely grace, he spun her around.

"But I did it all for you."

Muddled, she looked up. Saw. The far wall by the fireplace

was covered with draperies except for one space that had been stripped to the plaster and worked, reworked, worked over one more time so that, spreading on the white surface, studding the wall in infernal beauty, she saw . . .

"Oh my God." She jerked away so fiercely that she almost fell. Emblazoned on the pale surface, it assailed her, the same design she had seen drawn, no, carved and stained into his hand, how long ago? In another life. Before the fire. She groaned.

His voice lifted in triumph. "The tree."

He had set it out on the wall in oils and studded it with bone and brush and bits of glass, a design as brilliant and complex as a tapestry. The emblem of her destruction.

She whispered, "The tree."

His eyes were fixed points that could not be turned or changed. Nothing she could say or do to him would cause even a flicker. She could shoot him in the face and not extinguish them. "Remember? Remember how I showed you the place?"

She couldn't stop shaking her head. "No." She did remember. But never understood.

"Now it's time for you to take your place." His eyes were so pale and mad that God help her, she could not know whether he intended to rape or murder her or chain her there in the middle of the design. His knuckles burned her scalp.

She ripped free and wheeled, screaming, hurling herself at the sliding glass doors as if she could crash through and escape. They wavered and almost buckled and then hurtled her back into the room. With staggering force he brought her down, making it clear that as long as he was watching she would never escape.

He dragged her back to the design. "But it's for you. This is all for you. I would do anything for you."

Inexorable, he yanked her closer to the exposed wall and the spreading tree; she thought he was going to smash her head into the blank spot at its heart. Instead he pushed a switch plate in the wall and a door opened. "But I fixed this room for you. In case."

He threw her into this place. This *place*. Black hole he has thrust her into, where she has lost all sense of time. Stifling, unlovely, utilitarian, it is like a meat locker in the middle of this carefully finished house, and even in sleep Clary is aware that on the wall just outside the door there burns the tree, heavy with his intentions. If she had only herself to think about, she would tear her sweats into strips and make a noose; she'd run at the wall again and again until there was nothing left inside her head. But there are people she loves, that she can't desert.

She was wild when she was a kid, and after the fire completely alone — nobody to turn to, nobody to tie her down, but then she married Tom, who turned her into a mother, which raised the stakes in her life; now her life is knotted in all those other lives. They hold each other in place and she loves them so much, she . . . Jerks back to consciousness, alarmed. *Are you all right?* And starts pounding on the door.

There's no way out, she's tried: the windows are boarded and baffled, door padded and unbudgeable; there's no way up, no way down, no way to be heard through insulated walls, she's his for as long as he chooses, Clary Hale trapped with her fingers bleeding from clawing for openings, her shoulders and fists aching from pounding, her throat tattered from screams, threats, entreaties, apparently unheard, or heard but not marked.

When he came back into the padded room her first day here, he said coldly, "Don't even try to escape me."

Clary had to pretend he could be reasoned with, he might even have fallen down in a deep sleep on the night of the fire all those years ago and waked up whole. The alternatives were intolerable. Raising herself on one elbow she tried to make her tongue behave but could hear her voice slurring: "What do you want with me?"

His voice came up from somewhere too deep to identify. "You know what I want."

Dear God, she thought she did. "I'd rather die."

He turned those eyes on her. "I can wait."

He kept coming back as she slept and woke and slept and woke again, each time a little weaker from whatever she is being given, each time she wakes she is a little stupider but she *will* find some way out, has to get out and get back to her children. Trapped, she has tried everything — lies, reason, threats. She has even begged. Until yesterday their exchanges never varied because nothing she said would budge him and she would not yield. There was no reaching him. Frustration drove her to tears in these encounters, sometimes to violence, sometimes to humiliation as her demon captor ignored her blows, subduing her with infuriating ease.

God, she thought angrily, *why didn't you make me a man?* She hated being smaller, slight, hated knowing that fit and strong as she was, she could never hold her own with her captor, who is strong enough to smash her with the flat of his hand.

Sometimes she raged at God for making her a woman and therefore vulnerable, to physical attack, to love: Tom was so beautiful that she never saw the folly: marrying a man who went to sea, whose job took him out to places so dangerous that he might never come back. *You give yourself to love, but all the time you're marrying loss,* she thought, choking on grief, *Oh, Tom!*

At others she cursed her own stupidity — imagining she could start over, get married and raise a family just like anybody else. Couldn't she see how precarious it was? After the fire, after everything, how could she ever be safe? Thinks bitterly:

A woman is never safe.

God, she had spent even the best days of her life in terrible peril. She had been in danger even when she thought she had put the past behind her for good. In all her life she has never felt so weak or been so powerless.

Now her captor has stopped coming.

She is alone here.

He is gone. To do. What?

It will be worse than anything he's done to her so far. Now that he is gone their exchanges fill her head, rewind and replay again and again, Clary ruined by every turn of the wheel: if only . . . If only. She is crazy with second-guessing. Is there anything she could have done? Might as well try to reshape a diamond, or demolish an ice palace with a match.

Her captor glittered with resolution. *The tree,* he said, as if it justified everything. She is here because of it.

But yesterday changed everything. What did she do? What did she say that sent him out of here, terrible as an armed chariot with knives lashed to the wheels?

My fault, she thinks now. I was a fool.

They began as before, with the struggle. "God damn you, let me go."

Holding her in the air like a pretty ornament, he watched her writhe, powerless and running in place. "You know I can't do that."

"If it's money you want I can get you money." She knew it wasn't, but she had to temporize.

"Money is nothing."

She could hear her teeth clashing. "What if I give you what you want?" Furious, she spread her arms. They both know that's not all he wants. He could easily overpower her but this is a complex, subtle captivity. There is the weird business of the tree. What does he expect from her?

"Sex isn't enough. You have to want it."

"God!"

Then: that *face*. It blazed with madness. "If you don't, you will."

She shook her head. "You don't know me."

The pale eyes remained fixed on something she could not see. "I've known you longer than anyone."

"Then you know you might as well kill me now."

"But Clarada. I love you."

She understands that in time she may beg him to kill her. Trapped, fuddled and desperate, Clary tried: "I'm married."

"Not any more."

It was as swift as a blow to the head. In one sweep he had wiped out her hopes of ever seeing Tom again. She cried out. "No!"

Then in a moment of terrifying calculation, he confirmed it: "Don't you think I knew enough to wait until I knew he was dead?" Watching the pain flicker across her face, he twisted the iron in that agonizing wound that stayed fresh; did he think he could cauterize the place in her where Tom was ripped out? "He's gone."

"You don't know that."

"I have proof. You know it too. Even if you won't admit it, you know. Did you think I would rush in before it was time?"

Desolate, Clary wept. "I don't know what I thought."

"I waited, Clary. You knew I would."

"I didn't even know they'd let you out."

"I waited. I take what I want but I waited, Clary, I watched until I was sure Thomas Hale wouldn't be back would *not* be back would never come back, and when I knew this for certain it was time. Then I came. Understand, I have been watching you."

"Watching!"

"Watching and you didn't even know."

"Please don't — this is so terrible."

The voice was low, hypnotic. "I watched you, Clary, just the way I used to watch you back then. In Wilmington."

My parents. The fire. Terrorized, robbed of Tom one more time, Clary cried out in the guilt of the victim, "You were watching all those times."

"I watched your lights go on when you got up in the morning and go off when you went to bed at night and I watched your house when you were gone and saw those kids of his come and go; I watched you when you didn't even know I was watching, Clarada, I watched until it was time . . ."

"Time!"

"Understand, Clarada, time for us, time for you and me to . . ."

"It will never . . ."

". . . become one."

". . . be time."

Thus he overrode her in that low, hypnotic tone, "And when it was time, Clarada, then, Clarada, I came into your house."

"Impossible."

"I came into your house, Clarada, I saw your paintings, Clarada, and I know you remember, the waterfront, the shack, I saw where you sleep, Clarada. I looked at your things."

She twisted in a spasm of denial. "I keep it locked."

He smiled. "It wasn't always empty when you were gone."

"The children would never let anyone in."

"Maybe not, but the woman did."

This almost felled her. "Shar!"

"All she wanted was a little love. Ugly thing, she trusted me, you remember, Clarada, how I can make people do anything."

For the first time he let her see into him; somewhere deep inside the man there flickered the light she had seen the first time she ever looked at him, the furnace he harbored, the glow that hypnotized, and drew . . .

"You know the way of women alone."

Grief took her breath. "If only I didn't!"

"It was such a simple little thing, my hands and voice, you know how I am with women, Clarada, don't try to tell me you have forgotten, and she was lonely, big homely woman, poor Shar cleaning your house . . ."

"You didn't."

His eerie dignity: "I use what I have to. To get what I want."

She lowered her head. "I know."

"She let me in, would have done anything for me, still will, didn't want to let me in, but wanted me, I can make them do anything. Anything."

Understanding exactly how he had broached her best defenses, tricked the temple guards, sneaked *in*, Clary murmured, "Poor Shar."

". . . showed me the house, and your baby . . ."

This shook her where she stood. "You. Talked — to — Tommy."

"I held him in my lap."

"You. Held — my son." Shuddering, she could not stop.

"You know I can have anybody I want to. I always could." It burned behind his eyes, what he believes: the imperative.

"— You!"

"I held your son in my lap and made him promise not to tell you I was ever there. Your own little boy, Clary. I get what I want. Nobody will deny me. Nobody. Understand, I can come into your life and rip out your heart and you'll never even know it, I can slip in and take anything. Anything." He had pulled something out of his pocket and flashed it at her. "Look."

Tom's photograph, from the little frame on her desk, how did he . . . It is a violation. Breath fled her in a rush, leaving her voice thin. "Tom."

"Understand, I can take anything I want. I can walk into a person's body and rip out their guts and have them thank me, I can steal their soul and they'll never even know."

"Stop!" She lowered her head. "Tell me what you want."

His voice was cold and still, as if echoing from a great depth. "I want us to go back."

She cried, "It was never what you thought."

He bore down on her. "I want to get back what we had."

Backing, she shouted, "It was never what you thought."

But he was so close his eyes scorched her face. "I just want to make it the same."

"Well you can't." Then, driven to the wall, Clary rose up, she did; she tried to turn the thing around, to snap the loop he had created like so much magnetic tape; she had to, she would say anything to prove her point, and therefore launched herself at him like a projectile, shouting, "Everything is different."

Silenced, he turned.

Like a fool she rushed on. "I'm different. Listen," she said desperately. What did she think she could do, turn him with reason? "Years have passed. Years. I'm different and it can never be the same."

His fists were so tight that cords twitched in his arms, shoulders, his jaw; she should have been warned. But Clary was gathered and bunched for this final assault, convinced it would change him; collected and bent on it, she fixed on those pale eyes and stared directly into the pupils. She looked into those pale eyes with the black lashes, trying to reason with her demon captor who was both beautiful and terrible because implacable and even more terrible because his pale eyes locked with hers in an unwavering glare that should have warned her, should have . . . He said, too quietly, "Then I will have to make some changes."

"No. Look." Her voice shook with pride as she produced the

proof: "That's impossible. I can never be that person again. I have children now."

"Children." Oh, so that's all. That indifferent *tone:* God, she should have been warned. "Children are nothing."

Fool, she just rushed on, the brave little tailor prompting her own destruction. "Children are everything."

Like a machine, he took in the information, making adjustments. "The children. I see."

Oh, no!

Without releasing her eyes her captor quite simply withdrew. The pale irises clicked shut while he went back inside himself to think. When he emerged he was monstrous. His head snapped up.

"Well then, I'll just have to take care of them."

Thunderstruck, Clary covered her mouth. "Oh my God."

It was already too late. Silent, steely, he moved her to the iron cot and sat her down and jabbed the needle in her arm. Deliberately, he checked the level in the water cooler, tested the seals on the windows and numbered the supplies. Then in the doorway, he turned and spoke.

"Understand, I take what I need."

"What are you . . ."

"And the rest . . ."

"Going to do." And it struck her. "Oh my God. My children!"

"The rest is nothing," he said.

With one sweep of the hand he dismissed the fire, the kidnapping, all the terror and misery that came before this and will follow, slamming the door on her high, pure, unpunctuated scream.

18

IN THE MOTEL PARKING LOT, Commander Cleve Marshall lowers his voice, drawing the three remaining Hales close. He has, after all, promised to take them to their mother; she seems so near! "You understand we're going to have to proceed with extreme caution."

Without question, Teah moves into his shadow, looking up at him the way she used to look up at Dad. Tommy clings to one of his neatly pressed trouser legs. He has an ease, an air of power that draws Michael as surely as it does the others. The commander moves with the certainty of foregone conclusions: he is after all the adult here, and an officer, whom they can trust. With a bridge officer's squint, Marshall scans the parking lot. There is the usual collection of overloaded cars and pick-ups — apparently empty, but you can never tell. He could be looking for a surveillance team, a tail, anything that would compromise this mission. "We'll go in my car. It's less conspicuous."

Suspicious Michael whirls, looking for a dome light, U.S.N. stencil, anything. He could not have said what's touched a wire inside him and pulled it tight, but it has.

The commander acknowledges his caution with a curt nod. "Unmarked. Necessary precaution. — All set?"

The weakest part of Michael wants to bundle up all the pain and worry and hand it over, but something holds him back, echoes from bedrock Mike Hale who has been left in charge of his family by his father. *Not so fast.* He is waiting for the commander to make one false move.

"We haven't said we're coming," Michael says.

It is as if he hasn't spoken. "I'll help you get your things out of the trunk," the commander says to Teah, who nods and starts around the back of the car.

Michael snags his sister's arm in one of those unspoken communications that pass between siblings who have been living together for so long that each knows what the other means. One more test: he has found a place to make a definitive stand. "No."

Teah tries to jerk away; he won't let go. "OK, Michael," she snarls, because she knows he's right: this is too fast. "I'm sorry."

"Is there a problem?"

"I'm afraid we can't do that Sir," she explains regretfully. "We can't just leave our car." What she means is: we can't just pick up and go with you.

Alone out here in the deep sticks, cast adrift in the parking lot of a chain motel on an interstate in a place he's never even considered coming to and is in a hurry to get out of; uneasy, unprepared and more or less unsupported — Dad gone, Mom lost; even Shar has bugged out on them — Michael thinks: This is the only way I can think of to test him. "Orders, Sir."

One way or the other, it will settle things.

The commander says quietly, "Well I am under orders too."

Michael blurts: "So what are we going to do?"

He half expects Marshall to order them into his car or pull a gun and force them in. Or he may threaten: "Or else you can forget about seeing your mother."

But there isn't any face-off. The commander backs off with a disarming grin. "OK, no problem. We'll go in your car."

"Great," Teah says. "Let's go, Mike. OK?"

Michael doesn't know why he's still uneasy or why distrust makes him feel guilty and ungrateful, but he digs in. "Not yet."

Impatient Teah hisses, "Are you crazy?"

The commander remains unruffled. "No?"

"No." Michael says: "Two cars." He stands with feet set wide and his chin jutting, prepared to hold his ground. He is aware of families and commercial travelers straggling out of the motel and into the parking lot with their belongings, road-weary drivers gearing up for one more day on the interstate. He is still waiting for that one false move.

But there aren't any. Marshall stands there with this unwavering smile that leaves Michael feeling like a damn fool for even questioning. The eyes that regard him are clear and untroubled, the expression as direct as sunlight. Michael blinks. In this light, if he squints only a little bit, the commander's outline shimmers. Something about him: the height, the clean jawline, the military bearing, make him look all of a piece with Michael's father. Even without the uniform to identify or is it define him, he has that authoritative stillness, the kind of calm that can afford to wait. "I admire your caution, son. Your father would be proud."

Dad. *And in this light.* One. "You know my dad?"

"Only by reputation, son. But I'm a good friend of his exec."

Two. "What's his name?"

"Executive officer of the *Constellation* is Commander Wally Watson. They were classmates but Wally got passed over for captain when your dad was promoted."

In spite of which he asks: Three. "How long can my dad's ship stay submerged?"

"At least a hundred days. Son, you know I can't tell you anything beyond that. The information is classified." That smile! "You'd made a good officer."

"Yes Sir." Thus Michael falls into his hands.

"Understand. All I'm trying to do here is help you find your mother. Listen," Marshall says abruptly, changing direction. "If you people aren't easy with this, I can just . . ." He makes as if to turn and leave them.

Teah cries, "Oh, no!"

"Wait!" Helplessly, Michael grabs for his arm. "Please wait."

"We *need* you," Teah says.

"Oh, so you do want me to help you. Tell you what," the commander says easily, "if you're still having a problem with this, we can take two cars."

"Oh wait, I didn't mean to . . ." Now that he has what he wants, Michael is abashed. "Look, I'm sorry if."

But the commander simply goes about his business, remaking the plan as if the most important thing here is accommodating them. "I'll lead and you can follow, but you're going to have to stick close and be ready to turn when I turn. My car is over there, the blue number, unmarked of course. We even have car rental plates to throw people off."

"Throw people off!"

"It's OK kid, be cool. Nobody that will worry you."

"God," Michael says. "I'm sorry."

"No problem. Natural caution." Marshall gives him a man-to-man slap on the shoulder. "Good man."

"Yes Sir."

"Understand, from here on you're under orders."

Teah echoes Michael with a half salute. "Yes Sir." Under orders, they get in their car. As he backs into the lot and heads for the access road, Teah pulls up behind, following the commander's car like a heat-seeking missile that can't be shaken and will not be turned. Her fingers lock on the wheel so tightly that they turn white.

As she zigzags anxiously, terrified of losing the blue car, her tone brings back every fight they've ever had. "Two cars. God, Michael, you really blew it. You and your stupid suspicions."

"Dad would want us to be careful."

"Dad." Her sigh spans the hard years that have fallen between them and Dad. She is yearning after the commander. "What about Mom? What do you think Mom wants? Don't you think she wants us to hurry?"

"Oh shut up," he says wearily. He's leaning forward as if he and not Teah is the driver, tightly focused on the blue sedan; through the back windshield he can see the commander's neat head, the military set of the shoulders, the assurance with which he holds the road; he thinks he can see the clear jade gaze flickering from highway to rearview mirror, good commander keeping them framed in the rearview mirror.

After all these days without Clary, all these years without Dad, it's a relief to be going along in the world with an officer in charge. Therefore when Teah puts the cap on her reproaches, his response comes so quickly that he's certain it's right.

When she says, "I just want you to remember that I said this, Michael, if this slows us down and anything happens to Mom because of you dragging your damn feet, it's on your head."

Michael responds for his own sake more than hers, "Shut up, Teah, the commander knows what he's doing."

"Mommy," Tommy says, "where is Mommy?"

"We're going to get her," Teah says happily.

Michael's heart lifts. "The commander is taking us." It sounds right.

Teah's voice hits a note that surprises him. "Amazing eyes."

"What!"

"His. Like white jade," Teah says, and then becomes herself again. "Do you think they'll let her come home now?"

"Depends on the nature of the operation," he says, repeating the commander's words. For the first time, he lets himself open the door on his hopes, so Teah can see. "How it affects Dad."

"Dad!" Superstitious Teah knows better than to spell it out because she knows you only get what you want if you're careful not to name it.

They both fall silent, fixed on it.

At the moment they're on the straightaway, hard on the tail of the blue car; everything seems so near. Mom seems so near. When the blue car cuts away from the interstate, Teah takes the curve too fast, following him onto a state road that rambles along in deep shade, under arched branches of live oaks heavy with Spanish moss. In time they emerge on a series of sun-blasted causeways that rip along over marsh country that is not exactly solid ground but is not exactly water, either; in this territory there is no way of telling which is which.

EXTERIOR — DAY — CAROLINA

All Michael can manage is a montage — saw grass, trees, the commander's car. It is dizzying. The saw grass whips by with a mesmerizing sameness and as they drive the water keeps chang-ing position — sometimes it's on their right, sometimes on the left and sometimes on both sides as the road shimmers with heat mirages and the air gets thick with a swampy, industrial stink; even when there is no water in sight, the smell and texture of the air tell them it is nearby; it is as if the land is floating between water and sky and in places, chunks fall through.

Although he's bad at maps, the family has always counted on Michael to find their way back from places. He has a sense of how buildings lie in the land around him, how the roads spread out and exactly where he is on them. They count on his uncanny ability to locate himself in any landscape.

He's trying; he is, but it's hard. The roads Marshall has chosen double and twist so often that Michael can no longer tell whether they are going away from a given point or toward it; he assumes the commander is doubling back to confuse whatever enemies are tailing them, and is content to let him lead. As they ride into early afternoon Teah drives grimly, intent on keeping the blue car in sight. People keep getting in the way, farmers in pickups pulling out of side roads, trucks of produce going somewhere. All the muscles in her jaw and neck are rigid; her eyes have begun to glaze and her fingers are clamped on the steering wheel. Frantic when a truck overloaded with bales of hay turns onto the road right in front of her, she veers around it and swerves wildly to keep from being hit head-on. The oncoming driver leans on his horn until they're out of sight.

Michael says, "My turn." In the back, Tommy drums his heels on the seat and begins to whine.

"You don't drive."

"That's all you know. Now pull over, you're going to kill us."

Teah's voice rises. "If we stop we'll lose him."

"Just flash your lights and he'll pull over."

Her infuriated little shriek lets Michael know how far gone she really is. "I don't want to pull over!"

"I don't want to pull over," Tommy bawls into the back of Michael's neck.

Teah clamps tight fingers on the wheel, growling, "Shut up, Toms."

Then, miraculously, Marshall pulls into a gas station in a small town that's no more than a collection of shops, a fruit stand and a grocery. Teah unfolds, one joint at a time, and wobbles toward the ladies' room, rolling on the outsides of her shoes like a cowboy who's spent too long in the saddle.

The commander leans in the car window. "Everything OK?"

"My sister's pretty used up. How much farther?"

The commander squints into the middle distance. "We're almost there. It's only a matter of minutes."

Almost there. Michael slides out of the car. If he stands where the commander is, will he see their destination? Their mother? Tommy's hanging on his arm, a dead weight that he'd like to hand over to Mom. His mouth floods and he gulps. "Then why don't we just go?"

"It's not that easy." Marshall seems preoccupied. "I have a couple of things to take care of."

"Sir?"

"Before I take you in there."

Close. They are close. "I'll help."

"Negative." He shakes his head. "This is official business."

When Michael comes back from the men's toilets and the vending machines with his baby brother, he finds Marshall loading sacks into his car — food, soft drinks, a bag of ice. "What's that?"

"Supplies. When your sister comes back, fall in behind me. I know a place down by the water."

"I thought we were going to . . ." Michael wavers; food.

"Everybody's got to eat somewhere."

"I thought we were practically there."

"We are," Marshall says; his eyes are so clear and cloudless that Michael is embarrassed for having asked. "But we're under tight security. I'm sorry, son, I can't just plain take you straight to your mother. There's too much involved. Now remember the tail and stick close."

Because they have no choice they follow the commander onto a side road that brings them out on a little bluff where a stand of Australian pines shades both land and water; because the land and water in this part of the country make unfamiliar patterns, Michael has no way of knowing whether this is a bay or a river he is looking at, or just one more shifting scrap of tidal water. He's brought them to a local park. It's late in the day for lunch and too early in the year for school vacations and the place is deserted except, it turns out, for two old ladies in polyester shorts and pastel eyeshades eating at one of the picnic tables. As they get out of their cars, the old ladies wave at them. With a curt nod in their direction, the commander picks up his sacks of groceries and heads the other way. They stop at the far end of the cleared area, at a table on the lip of the bluff. Nearby is a bathhouse; below there is a float anchored a few yards out in the channel. Wooden steps lead down. The current below is slow, gentle, the air is warm and there's a slight breeze; they've come so far south that it's like summer, and Michael would like nothing better than to slide down into the water, but it's a strange color and even here in the shallows, the bottom is obscured.

Teah says, "It's beautiful. Are you bringing Mom here?"

"It's not that easy."

Tommy says, "I want Mommy."

"Not yet, sweetie." Teah turns to the commander for reassurance. "Cleve?" She uses his name so easily!

The commander puts down the sacks. "Soon, Teah. This looks like as good a place as any to wait it out."

Michael says carefully, "To wait what out?"

Cleve Marshall's eyes reflect the moving shadows of the trees above them. "I'm sorry, I'm not at liberty to tell you," he says, silencing them with food. He has bought grinders for them, he's brought soft drinks and chips and fruit and cookies, and in a little insulated bag, ice cream sticks, all this *stuff*. Now he drops in a detail, like dessert. "But don't worry. Your mom wanted me to give you this message. She said to tell you, she's deep into painting these skies."

Michael looks out: the sky here off the point is eight shades of silver, nothing like the skies at home, he can almost see her at it, eyes narrowed to fix the colors, black cloud of hair pulled back; the commander knows her, all right. It's real, she's really here. "OK." Something inside Michael lets go a little. "Cleve."

When he looks at Teah he is startled by her eyes. She is following the commander with the look she used to save for Eddy Stanko; he sees her reach out as if to touch him and at the last minute, draw back.

It's like a party. Murmuring, Teah and the commander spread the food on one of the picnic tables while Michael, who is giddy from hours of not eating, cracks open a package of plastic glasses and pours drinks for everybody. Tension and exhaustion have made them so hungry that they eat until they've had enough and keep on eating until they're stuffed and sleepy, readily accepting everything their new ally has to offer, and when he rolls up the trash and stows it and sprawls in the grass, they follow without question, content for the moment to lie here in the shade while Tommy plays nearby — lazy, tired Michael and dreamy Teah looking up at trees that shift in the breezes, listening to the whispering moss.

Michael says, "This isn't bad."

Teah rolls on her back, losing herself in the pattern of moving branches. "It's beautiful."

"It seemed like the right place to me," Marshall says.

Michael says lazily, "How did you find it?"

"Oh, that. I used to live around here."

"Right," Michael says. It seems completely logical.

"Cleve." Breathless from lying in the grass with him like this, this *close*, Teah stirs, rolling on her side so she can look at the commander. "You really used to live here?"

He says even though nobody has asked him, "It's convenient to the installation."

Lulled, Michael repeats: "Installation?" It's strange out today; him and Teah on the loose here in the soft breeze when the rest of the world is still in school is strange. This picnic is strange and Cleve Marshall's sense of ease is strange, considering his cautions about security, about the sensitive nature of the operation and the possibility of people following; the man is lounging here in the sparse grass with his tie loosened and collar open as if they have all the time in the world. Strange. Warm as it is, he keeps the shirt cuffs down and buttoned but the white shirt conforms to the body; strong forearms, well-defined biceps make Michael strongly aware of something running underneath: heat or energy humming close to the surface. The stranger is lying close to Michael's sister, just lying on his belly in the grass making whistles out of weeds when the Hales have come all this long hard way to find their mother, who has been gone it seems like forever and who they have been told is only minutes away.

"The secret installation," Cleve reminds him. "It's right near here."

Michael stirs. "Then why are we sitting here?"

"Because it isn't time to go yet."

"You, ah, want to make sure we're not being watched?" Michael is trying hard to reassure himself.

But the commander isn't looking at Michael; he is fixed on the fall of hair on Teah's neck. "Hmmm?"

"The tail, remember? You said we were being tailed."

"Oh, that," the commander says absently. "We shook them a long time ago."

"Then how come we're all lying here?"

"I told you, we're in a sensitive situation. We can't just rush in."

Michael is so full it's made him lazy and stupid; lulled, he's going, Right, yes, yes, right, thinks he's perfectly relaxed, sprawling here in the grass with his hands in his pockets, except he isn't. He flexes his hands: Ow. He's had them clenched so tight the fingers are stiff and dented by these pieces of his parents, that he has been gripping without even knowing it — he's had his father's keys in one hand and in the other, his mother's dolphins are biting into him. Even though it hurts he can't let go because prickling close to the surface of this pretty day is a clutch of unanswered questions. Abruptly, he sits up. As he does so Marshall sits too, and after a brief glance at Michael, turns his gaze on the water. Shifting uncomfortably, Michael clears his throat. "Hey, wait a minute."

"Look!" Cleve Marshall says, swiftly raising his arm to draw their eyes. His voice is quick with excitement. "Way out there. Somebody sailing."

Next to him, Teah sits up, leaning in close as if to see where he is pointing; she is looking not at the water, but at the speaker. "Where?"

"Out there. Look over there."

Obediently, she turns her head, and while Michael sits in the dirt, choking on unasked questions, his sister follows Cleve Marshall's gaze out over the water; leaning close she lifts her arm and they sway together, moving as one. "I don't see it."

His voice lifts. "Look at it. Beautiful!"

"I still don't . . ." Teah slides even closer.

"Right there. Just sight along my arm and you'll see it."

Michael sees her cheek rubbing his sleeve, can almost feel what she feels, warm muscles moving under thin fabric. And understands what else it is about this man that draws them, that makes him squirm. The force is strong, sexual.

It draws Teah, who leans even closer.

"Cecelia, see?"

"Oh." Teah's voice slides up in delight. "I see it. Oh Mike, Tommy, do you see?"

They don't, of course; Tommy runs to the edge of the bluff and stares out, but Michael is watching his sister and this stranger, for he sees now that the commander is in fact a stranger, nobody he remembers and not like anyone he knows, not really an officer, what is he, what is his power? He sees Teah half-hypnotized and drawn to the stranger in a moment of perfect synchronization, his arm lifting, her body stretching to follow, both beautiful heads turned at the identical angle; Michael can feel the magnetism — this is nothing like Eddy Stanko. *Be careful of my sister* — fear flows into knowledge: *He makes people fall in love with him.* And what frightens him most now is not the strong current between them, the potential, but the understanding that anything can happen with this person, anything can happen to them here, because except for this Cleve Marshall, whom they have just now met and cannot possibly know, they are all alone in this empty park.

Teah's voice is slow, dreamy. "Oh Cleve, it is so lovely."

Because all his life since he can remember he has used the camera to make sense of life, Michael pulls back now. He needs to fix his camera eye on the close group they make, the trees, the isolated park, the water beyond. But he can't get far enough away to frame the scene; he has to find some way to stand off before he can make sense of it, and right now he is in the middle. For the moment, he has no idea what kind of story they are living or what kind of pattern they make.

He will spend his best energies trying to pull all the elements into a narrative framework that he can make sense of, because until he can understand this story, that they are plunged into the middle of, he can't even hope to control the outcome.

He is dimly aware of a distant sound — car doors slamming, the pastel-looking old lady picnickers leaving. Michael supposes he could run after them but would never do it, not with Marshall here, not when they are so close; makes another mental note, you are not in love with him, not that way, but he has hold of you too. They are all three paralyzed now, transfixed in the moment. Michael wants to speak but there is nothing he can do or say here, nothing.

The next thing is sudden. "Enough."

What?

It happens with a palpable *snap*.

Michael shakes his head. Who spoke? What's just happened?

It is Marshall; commander or not, he is in command. He stands abruptly, ending this. He just pulls away from Michael's dazzled sister, leaving her bemused and cooling, rubbing the warm spot on her face where it had been resting on her commander's arm. He says, "Time to get moving."

Michael's sigh of relief explodes into speech. "Let's go!"

But Marshall wheels. "Not you two. Not yet."

"Wait a minute." This time it's Teah who says it for them, dreamy Teah betrayed by the suddenness with which the man, no, the magnet has let go, shattering the moment. She scrambles to her feet. "We're coming."

His voice is sharp. "You can't."

"Why not?"

"Do you want to see your mother?"

Teah persists in a tone which Michael recognizes where the commander does not. "What's the matter, don't you trust us?"

"You have to do your part here." His tone brooks no discussion.

But Michael knows this mood. Teah is too much like him; pushed too far, she can turn to iron. She follows Marshall to the parking lot; Michael falls in behind her, knows his sister well enough to know she's usually the only one left at the end of one of her last stands. The moment — whatever it was — with the boat, the physical closeness, shared warmth, have somehow left her feeling entitled. As the man who is going to take them to their mother unlocks his car, she reaches for his arm. "If you trust us, why can't we come?"

For the first time he shows a flicker of exasperation. "Because this is a complicated operation. To be perfectly honest, we're not the only people involved in this. I have to go and check out the environs. I have to make a preliminary sweep before we go in."

Teah digs in. That tone! "How do I know you're not going to just leave us here?"

But the commander won't engage in the kind of scene Teah is framing; he is used to being followed without question. Now he turns his head slowly, raking her with a look so heated that it makes Michael squirm; it is complicated and full of promises that stop his passionate, angry sister in mid flight; without even trying this man can just bring her down. He takes both her hands and lifts them, holding Teah with those pale eyes until her eyes get lost in them; there is something going on here that Michael understands and is only now beginning to credit —

He can make anybody fall in love with him.

"Cecelia Martin Hale, I didn't bring you all this way just to abandon you. In no way am I going to leave you here."

Forgetting Michael, Tommy, everything, she falls into his eyes. "Then let me go with you."

He says quietly, "Do you want to see your mother?"

She lets him let go of her hands. "Yes Cleve."

"Then wait here."

"You're coming right back?"

"Inside an hour."

She sighs. "Inside an hour."

They stand in the road, watching him go. Teah cries, "An hour!"

"He told us to wait, so be cool." Michael goes on slowly, thinking it through because he too is drawn, pulled in, tied to the commander like a tin can to a car, hope bouncing after him. He says at last, "This may be some kind of test. We need to wait and see what he does."

19

THIS is taking too long.

He is in the next-to-last phase.

With the children gone, Clary will have nobody but me.

And I will have everything. What his father took, love and the mother, self and manhood, everything. *But first I will make her want it.* Then he will take Clary and when he does, he will put her into the empty place inside him; he knows how.

In the beginning he thought their love would fill the void, but what should have ended in fusion ended in fire.

To fill it now, he will have to kill her.

He had made the old people leave a dozen cities by the time they reached Wilmington, where the beautiful girl with his mother's face waited; "Son, what you did . . ." *Don't you love me?* "We would do anything for you, Son." They grieved but he walked out of all those places like so many abandoned rooms. For reasons he brushes away like flies. Not his fault, the things he did. Daria. The girl in Pittsburgh, never mind what he did to that one; they guessed he was the one who did it but nobody could prove anything. The others. "We can't just keep moving, Son." "But you have to. I *need*." In each new place he was insatiable. He swooped down on one city after another and sucked it dry — of women he needed for whatever purposes, people he could use, things he could do: college degree at twenty, might as well get that over with. All those earnest educators begged him to study medicine or law or history in some dead hall of graduate studies where things happen only in dusty books. "Son, with your intelligence, you owe it to yourself."

Why bother? He already knew how to charm birds from the

trees, charm money out of your pockets and have you thank him for it; I'm sorry this investment didn't work out, but believe me, the next . . . put it in a dozen different banks and while he was put away, it grew. *Why should I want more schooling? School is for fools and children. I have a man's needs.* Man's things to do: the tree. It is the cost of his survival and the design for his future. He is the tree — strong, supple, clever in the shelter of its leaves, I can cut out your liver or take your money without your even noticing and have you thank me for it afterward, and *they could not stop him;* the more money he found, took, kept and put away where it would make more money, the more he wanted; the more he had, the hotter the empty place inside him burned.

He slipped into Wilmington, Delaware, with the foolish old people pulled around him like a clever disguise; let the weak people of the world think he was ordinary too. See, you can trust me, I'm just like everybody else. He let the girl's parents see only the ordinary, concealing the storm, the flame.

He knew her at once: tangled black hair, face shimmering with his mother's light; *looks just like her.* So close. He could hear her sweet voice. He was a dark shadow, sliding swiftly over the moon. When their outlines were matched he would have it. She was perfect. Everything in him was rushing toward completion. But he had to make her see! Secretly, he made the design in microcosm in his hand: carved branches in the skin of the palm and fingers, twin trunks in the soft underside of his wrist; gored the palm to make the empty place to show her what needed filling: the hole. It is as close as he has ever come to seeing inside without splitting his belly with a knife and pulling everything away to expose the place.

I will put you — here. The agony: he could have accomplished this in love but need made him reckless. He burned too bright. The empty place at the center of him burned; he would drive her like a stake into his heart. *Clary!* She screamed and lunged away.

Just when everything was going so well.

She pulled away so wildly that his nails raked gouges in her arm. The shock was cataclysmic. It was like interrupting a lunar eclipse.

And everything went bad.

The earth cracked. The sky turned black. Lightning scorched the tree. Torn open, he spun in rage that grew and branched out to overshadow the world. And he did what he did. What should have ended in fusion ended in fire.

It has cost him years. He thinks they put him in state prison at first. Raging, he lost track. In the dark he did something — he does not even remember what. Something to someone — kid in the holding cell? Guard? A nurse? He thinks there was blood. They swarmed over him with hypodermics and locked canvas sleeves across his chest and then moved him out fast. They whipped over highways to another place and put him in a cube. The windows were covered. So was the peephole in the door. He was alone with an open toilet and a bed. He could feel his way from one to the other. No light.

What am I doing in this dark place?

Her fault. *Just when we were so close.* She didn't see!

Well she is going to see now.

Oh my God my children. Clary is trying to do without water because that's where the poison is. She will do anything to outrun the terror, to outwit it, find some way to run ahead and forestall it, Clary Hale still drugged but with the murk in her head gradually beginning to clear. Her throat, no, body, no, *brain* is parched with thirst but functioning better; her thoughts are perhaps a little more consecutive. She has to get back into her right mind so she can find a way out of this place he has made for her.

She is weak; her body drags her down. This is like a long convalescence; she doesn't know what parts of her are still broken, only that she wants to be whole. She will do anything — eat bad food, run in place to build her strength. She's drained all the juice from the cans of fruit he left for her along with food he left, loaded with salt to keep her thirsty; she eats to get strong. The last fruit cans are open, juice gone and the contents rotting; the place is beginning to smell. She's battered the door with the chair and scrabbled at the covers on the windows; what can she do here besides pray?

She has to find a way out, but how?

Clary fumbles; her thoughts are jumbled and useless; instead of plans, wild memories clutter her consciousness, one piling on the other in such profusion that she thinks the drugs have robbed her of control of certain muscles, emotions, thoughts. Withdrawal symptoms, she thinks: pains in the joints; her mouth pulls to one side now in a rictus she can't correct, and the thirst! But she can't drink that water again, must not — what is he giving her — stirred, she succumbs to the clattering whirl of images of the past. Memories catch and stutter into a sequence that appalls because it is so vivid, spinning her back.

Helpless, she is returned, whole, to the awful, buried moment that she has spent her life trying to outrun. When Cleve opened his hand to her. What happened afterward. Thus Clary is brought face-to-face with the fact that she can barely credit now, after all the years of terror, misery and devastation; dear God!

It is this.

In the rosy beginning before the fire was ever even imagined, she and her fierce, mad captor were — Oh, God! She was in love with him. *Forgive me.*

That was a world ago. She was a different person.

And he has always been the same. *I didn't know!*

Ripped out of her life and thrust bodily into the past she has spent her life trying to forget, she is staggered by guilt. He has forced her back to it: the fact that ignorant, long-lost Clary Martin had in her astounding innocence sought him out — Cleve Morrow, the strange, dazzling young man with the unearthly eyes. Unwitting, loving, young, she had courted her own destruction. Now he is forcing her back. He will put her at the center of his dreadful design.

When Cleve threw her into this place he has made for her his eyes were terrible. "I will make you want it. The tree. Everything."

She had flung herself against him, shouting, "No."

"The way you used to want me."

All her life since then she's tried to bury what happened, to bury him: "I don't remember anything."

They both know this is a lie. "Your eyes tell the truth even when you don't." He was merciless. "And you remember what I wanted from you then."

"That life is over," she said bitterly. "I never wanted you."

His eyes flashed with arctic light. "You loved me, Clary."

Tears filled her mouth. "I'm not the same person."

The silence that surrounded what he said next was chilling. "We are what we are."

"Then, dear God, I didn't see what you were!"

"Now we are going to be together," he said.

"After everything!"

"Because of everything. And you will want it too."

She said, with dignity, "Well I don't think I can do that." Clary Martin Hale, who is through begging.

"You may not want it right away." Her captor was gauging her, sizing her up like a stolen jewel. "But sooner or later you will."

They were through talking. He shut her up in *this place,* Clary Hale, mother, painter, an ordinary woman who is a lifetime away from any dimension in which she could possibly have loved him, even in his terrible beauty, Clary shouting through the closed door: "In hell."

He either heard or he didn't; his voice dropped into the darkness, so still and sure that she can't shake the memory. "As before. And you'll be happy here."

Weak as she is after numberless days in this dim, closed room, alone and frightened but beginning to regain some control over her thinking, Clary is poleaxed by memory and dragged into the lost world of her past. She is a helpless observer, with no power to warn the ignorant, passionate, sixteen-year-old Clarada Martin, who thought she was in love with the stranger next door. All she can do is watch as that pretty, ignorant girl is struck by love, bemused and swept away. She sees that former self drawn by a dark, inexorable force. All she can do is watch it unfold. It's like looking at a foreign object. Grieving, she thinks: *Idiot. Poor child!*

Lived at home, Clary did, safe with her mother and father in a nice old frame house embraced by porches, they used to sit outside in the swing on summer nights and eat ice cream together, she and her mother and father, until a new family moved in next door, plain-looking, slightly off-center but pleasant, quiet people with their astonishingly handsome son. They never quite said why they'd moved away from the last place or where they came from. Decent working people, her parents thought, ordinary, ordinary except for the son. The son. Clary watched him from the upstairs window, going in and out like the king of the world. Graceful, sure, how could he have come from them? Adopted, they said. Of course. He was light-years beyond ordinary, the gifted son of some exiled king, given to peasants to raise. His outlines shimmered with passion, promise, with — what? He was tall, lean, older; Clary couldn't even guess by how much, all through with school, he did something in the world, what did she care about details? He moved silently with animal grace and there was something in the clear, pale eyes that drew her, a hypnotic steadiness, brilliance, the suggestion of the incomplete. What did they promise? She didn't know; yet the face seemed shadowed — something lying underneath — just beneath the visible ran fierce currents of the unknown.

The eyes: *he could touch me without even being near.* No wonder she was struck blind, no, deaf. No. Stupid. The air between them vibrated with unspoken promises. Crazy with love, she put a red scarf around her dark hair and spun in and out of the house, looking for him; she glued herself to all the windows in hopes; she thought she would die before he noticed her, and little Clary Martin — not much older than Teah is now, poor *kid,* she thinks, sobbing — she really was in love with him. Whoever she thought he was. In that life without knowledge of the future, pretty, foolish, ignorant Clary Martin fluttered close to Cleve Morrow, who carried about him the hint of great mysteries; she yearned, waited, prayed for him to notice her.

When he did it was like flying into a nova.

Sometimes getting what you want is worse than never having anything.

God he was beautiful.

The touch, the voice: she would have followed him anywhere. She almost did. Cleve Morrow, so brilliant; his center flamed so bright that there was no way to see into him. Now that she had his attention the eyes turned like the beam on a lighthouse and fixed on her. *For some of us hell is getting what we want.* Her love! He was powerful, obsessive and demanding, more: he compelled. She might just as well have been sucked into the whirlwind or drawn like a toy boat to a giant magnet, pulled into his orbit so that they would be together forever, circling endlessly.

When she and Cleve were together there was nothing but the enclosure. Clary was caught as surely as a butterfly in a killing jar. *If you love me come with me now. Sit there. Do this.* Did I have any idea what we were doing, or what he was? He promised so *much,* wanted even more, and she did love him. Who wouldn't love him, who was too young and still ignorant of the mad, dark side of certain kinds of love? Who, that didn't know, could fail to love — *that?*

In those days he could make anything seem right; forget your life, he said, forget everything except my love for you, I want us to be together forever. High school girl no different from anybody else and his attention transformed her. "You look just like . . ." "Like who, like who?" Marine lights glittered in his eyes as he answered but did not answer. "Like love, Clarada. Like love. Come with me to a place as beautiful as you are." "But school." "You don't need school, I'll talk to your parents." He could have sold them anything. Had already sold her; he lied. Told them his parents would be there, told them it was only for the week, those pale eyes so clear that even her father trusted him, that good man who would do anything to keep his daughter safe. ("She's still in school." "I'd never ask you if my own parents weren't going." "Take good care of her." "The best.")

Clary watched with excitement, afraid they'd let her go,

afraid they wouldn't let her go, frightened by his intensity, idiot girl too much in love to say no but half hoping her sweet, conscientious parents would do it for her. But her father called Mrs. Morrow, who promised, "Sweet child, I'll be just like a mother to her," and they believed. Well, she lied. *She would do anything for him.* (He could pull anyone into the pictures he drew: *What I need, I use.* "I wish you could come too . . ." And, "I would never do anything to hurt your daughter, Mr. and Mrs. Martin. I love her." Clary's heart opened like a flower. "Very well," sweet Dad said so formally that it might have been a betrothal. "Take good care of her.")

This is how we give ourselves away. Just hand them over — so carelessly!

"What happened to your hand," I said, when we were on the plane, sitting so close it was like being in bed. There was white gauze wrapped around and around it and on up the wrist. "Oh nothing —" he jerked away; would not let me turn it over. "Doesn't it hurt?" "Nothing hurts me," he said and those pale irises opened, pulling me in. "Oh my God, Clary, I do love you."

And I heard myself! "And I love you Cleve." God forgive me, I think I said, "Forever." Kids don't know how long that is.

He brought me to this place — this place! As it was twenty years ago. "Oh Cleve," I said, "it's beautiful, but where are your parents?" "Coming on a later flight," he said, and dazzled by Florida, I just went along humming, fine, yes yes, oh fine.

Clary shakes herself. She is in Florida again. Trapped. Her belly clenches.

The moss hanging from the trees, me with Cleve's arms around me . . . "It's ours for now," he said, and it was like landing in a dream with all old debts canceled and all rules suspended, a handful of hours in that beautiful, sunny place with Cleve so fond, slow and so gentle that I didn't even know what he was about.

"We're alone for now," he said and she could feel warmth growing in her when he went on in that low voice that suggested everything, "let's take advantage of it." Then he led her into the front room of — *this place!* It was sun-shot, beautiful.

Look at it now.

"Bend your head," he said, and put his gift around her neck:

a chain, with a crystal pendant flashing. "The light is my love for you. I want you to wear this for me." The sunlight threw reflected color on her face and she laughed, besotted by love, little Clary Martin, so pleased.

God forgive me, I thought I was in love with him — not quite ready to let the rest happen. Hard to explain how you can almost make love at that age, go so far, arrive at the brink without a fool's idea of where your lover's body is trying to take you; why. should. it. matter. It did. I think because at some level even then, I — no, that poor little Clary girl — knew that I was in no way ready for what he brought — too much. Beautiful as he was, there was something terribly the matter with him. Cleve was brilliant, and false, like a flawed diamond, sharp and, as it turned out, cruel.

But how could I see all that, fooling along through the long afternoon; he was patient, kissed me here, there, he waited; when we looked up again it was dark. I said, "Where are your parents?"

"Oh that," he said so smoothly that it meant nothing. "I guess they couldn't make it after all," and he tried to pull me down again.

When you are a girl and waiting to be sure, there is that one buffer you keep between yourself and the last moment — I thought it would be the parents coming, and, wait! He and I were here alone.

"I can't."

"Shh-shh, this is only part of what we came for," he began to move faster, hands so fierce, strange words coming out, "Just like her, like her."

It frightened me; I pulled against him. "No!"

He seemed surprised and when I started to fight; he grabbed my wrists and held me in place with the strangest look. "Please."

I was struggling, sobbing hard. "Don't!"

"Wait. I have something to show you," he said, and then, lord, he pulled back the shirt cuff and undid the bandages.

I was afraid.

"Hold still! You have to see."

The sick smell of injured flesh, what he was trying to show me. It was like looking into a disease. "Oh, God!"

"Look and you can see it written here," he said, "look and you'll see your place in it," he held out the seeping hand and arm in a cosmic There.

It was hideous. The pattern was fresh, rubbed into the skin; he had carved it into his hand — branches in the fingers, trunk cut into the wrist, how long had it taken him, how badly had it hurt? It looked like — it looked like a tree, but with something terribly the matter, the dreadful design was broken, or interrupted, by this bloody hole that lay at the center — the pit into which everything disappears. "Now," he said, "now you can see how much I love you."

I died.

"The tree! My fortune is at these points: law, finance, politics, power, anything I want," he numbered them on his fingers.

"Oh don't," I said, crying because he was insane and I couldn't stop him. "Oh God, oh please."

"As soon as I am whole." He flexed the hand and it bled. "Look closer, and you'll see." His voice was harsh and his breath scorched me. "It's the same with me. Inside," he said again and forced my face into the hole struck at the middle; it was fresh, and welling with blood: "And — I — will — put — you — there," he said. As if it was already accomplished. And I knew I was in terrible danger.

"And I will keep you forever," he said and the irises flexed for a second right before the pupils disappeared. "And be whole." God help me, he was shouting, all gnashing jaws and spit and madness, "And we will do it in love, Clarada, understand?"

I heard myself screaming, "We will never do anything in love," so terrified, but I struck out with the blade of my hand, bringing it down into the injured palm; he doubled over, "No!" And then Oh my God he said the worst thing, "Mmmmamama. . . ." he didn't even hear himself, just fell hard on me, howling like an angry child; I don't know what he would have done then — the two of us grappling with nails dragging and teeth gnashing — but we were stopped by a confusion of noise and light: fluorescents turned on and the sound of something big smashing — a chair on the floor next to his head.

The old man's voice. "Son!"

He let go and whirled to confront them. Father, mother, two old people clinging in the doorway, but the mother had this look; *before he could do anything the old man pulled me away and put me behind them; I don't know what was between the three of them, only that I could feel blood in my hair: the place where his teeth had closed on my scalp.*

They put little Clary on the bus home to Wilmington. She

wept for days, terrified that he would come after her; she would never understand what drove him, but after everything, she saw he was mad. When he did come, her parents guarded the door. "No, Cleve, she doesn't want to see you," sweet Dad so patient, firm as if Cleve was just anyone — she could hear him that night, hammering and raging, howling in the dark. Finally she went to the door herself with Father at her elbow, lying in an attempt to keep them safe. "I'm sorry, my parents don't want me to see you any more." She gave him back the crystal. His glare drove her back inside; she couldn't bear to see into the center of his rage.

Then there were the calls, the letters, the terror every time the doorbell rang. Her dad went to Cleve's parents; they were angry at the intrusion, how did Clary's parents dare, but there was fear running along underneath the old people's righteous expressions and they made impossible promises. The sin of complicity.

Cleve would not stop calling, sending notes, handwriting on the envelope so beautiful that it almost made you forget who it came from, until you opened it and saw the drawing of the tree; there were entreaties, half-threats, half-promises; trembling, she burned them in an ashtray without reading them, one day dear God he sent his mother over to plead for him, embarrassed plain-looking woman with tears in her eyes, Elva Morrow down on her knees in front of that stupid girl, so humiliating: *she would do anything for him,* the gifts! There was no end to it — Cleve in love, violent and driven, Cleve determined, bent on it, and when it was clear to him that there was no turning her, there followed the succession of twisted gifts, like threats: a snapshot of Clary torn in half, a Dresden shepherdess beheaded, dead roses wrapped in silver paper with a black ribbon and at the end, a gold pin — little heart, she thinks — twisted and smashed, destroyed with such violence that it left her sobbing and shaking. Dad went to the police, Clary saw the lieutenant going to his door, quietly reasoning, laying out the parameters, while the girl sweated and trembled behind the living room curtains, was that what did it, what toppled him?

What he did next was terrible.

So maybe that was Clary's mistake, not falling in love with a whirlwind, but imagining she could turn the force once she had let it loose; her fault for thinking that there was any way to protect herself once the giant began to move. He was like a force of nature. Unreasoning. Inexorable.

We should have packed up everything and fled him, gone to another city and changed our names; anything to escape. Should have hidden in South America, even Iceland might not have been far enough; they should have done anything they had to, to elude him, or maybe — Clary is sobbing now. Even though a lifetime has passed, the loss scrapes her raw; the grief is still fresh. Mother. Dad.

If I'd killed myself, maybe they'd still be here.

Or maybe she should have bought their lives by going out front when he stood on the walk and roared her name, or simply given in, sacrificing herself to him to get her parents out of his path. She might be dead, or worse, but her mother and father whom she loves so much would still be alive. It would be only fair; after all, who brought this down on them? Whose fault was it anyway? His, for what he did, or hers for thinking he would give up and go away?

"It's OK now," Dad said. "We have the police."

Helpless, trapped, she realizes how sadly wrong children are when they believe their parents can truly protect, and defend. But she had to believe because they were the powerful parents, and she was only the child. She even believed in the police, when in fact no power on earth could help her: little Clarada Martin, in her folly. He slacked off — no more calls, no notes. Foolishly, they began to relax their vigilance.

So probably what happened next was her fault, for imagining any power on earth could protect them. There was Clary growing careless, tired of the house and desperate to be free and just like all the other kids for at least one night — school baseball game, she thinks now, appalled by her stupidity. It had been so hard for so long. She didn't want much, only for once, just once, *not to have to think about him.* Left home in a car full of friends, she did, stayed on for the party after the game, lord she was so happy she almost forgot him for a minute until cops broke into the gym, "You'd better come with us, Miss Martin."

The return! Her parents' beautiful old frame house lit up the night sky like a mystic's vision of the inferno. Lost in flames. Cleve Morrow's hair glinting white above his tanned face and his mouth like a furnace, Cleve roaring: "Clary, see it, the tree!"

Oh my God, my parents. Both dead. Fire! The loss is still fresh. It never goes away. She has spun out her life since then in guilt and grief.

When she was called to testify at the hearing she was afraid to face him; the monster who had been Cleve looked at her with those pale eyes, murderer stood in open court and confronted her and against all expectations, spoke. "They were coming between us, Clarada. Now we can begin." *They were coming between us.* Those incandescent eyes, fixed and terrible, her loving destroyer warning Clary that no matter where they put him, she would never be safe.

His voice followed her out of the courtroom and down the corridors: "First, love, Clarada. Then fire. Next, blood."

She heard the prosecutor's charge to the jury: Bury him deep.

She can still see the fire. Hear him raging with loss: "Why couldn't you let it stop at love?"

My God, my children; she is on her feet in the stifling room he fixed for her, Clary Hale, who can't stop pounding on the door.

"My God, my children." *The fire.*

20

IMPATIENCE has moved into Michael's head and set up its infernal equipment; he's operating at a high hum, like overheated machinery. What if they're stuck here? What if Cleve never comes back? It's been more than an hour. He keeps walking up the road away from the park, in hopes. Staring at the point where the road emerges from the live oaks, he sees nothing. Says, just to drown out the noise in his head, "Maybe he's coming back by boat."

"Boat, yay!" Tommy runs back and forth along the edge of the bluff, yelling and waving. "I see him, I see him, no I don't see him." He is frantic. "Look Teah, isn't that a boat?"

Teah groans. "Oh don't, Mike. This is hard enough!"

"Be cool. It's a possibility."

It's been more than an hour. If Mom is so close, where the hell is she and why can't they just go see her? Why is he making them wait? What if he never comes back? In the time since the commander left them here they've waited and paced, paced and watched; they've tried to answer Tommy's hundred thousand questions when they can't even answer their own. Told to wait, they are waiting; they're jittering, edgy and wild with it, but they have no choice. They've policed the area and taken the wooden steps down to the water a half-dozen times, telling themselves it's like the Zen archer, if they can just think about something else he'll come, but they can't think about anything else. They've run out of things to do and are sitting here letting misgivings pile on misgivings.

After a while Teah says, "This is awful." Her look begs

Michael to tell her that isn't true. "All this time and he still isn't back."

"I know," Michael says instead. Can't stop himself.

"What if he isn't coming?"

He tries, "Of course he's coming, he told us to wait."

"Right. Besides," Teah says for both of them, "he wouldn't buy us all this stuff and bring us all this way for no reason. I don't think," she goes on uneasily. It is as if she's had dense dreams and has just waked up and asked him to interpret them. She squints at Michael. "What do you think?"

His breath pops: hah. "I think we've got to start somewhere."

Teah says, "I mean, about this guy."

"I think we've got to find Mom somehow." Michael has his own needs; dammit, it's Teah's turn to reassure him. The hum in his head is deafening. "What about you?"

"I don't know." Teah is neither here nor there. "What if he ditches us? What if we're just stuck out here?"

So he ends up reassuring her. "Why would he pick us up in the first place? What would be the point?"

She sighs. "Right. He would never bring us all this way just to ditch us."

"He's not the kind of guy to waste his time."

Teah says, "After all, he's an officer."

The dolphins. For the first time Michael is uncomfortable with this. What if he got them some other way? This is too horrible to think about so he says doggedly, "Besides, he brought us the dolphins from Mom."

"Right." Teah brightens, and this cheers him. "So I guess we'd better wait." She is sitting again, looking out over the water, and Michael is struck by something in her expression. It brings back that moment on the bluff with the commander; they looked almost like people in love. When she turns her head that way, dark hair swinging over the collar of the pink man's shirt she is wearing, his feisty sister shimmers at the brink of beautiful.

This as much as anything makes Michael uncomfortable. "We don't have a whole lot of choice."

At the sound of an approaching motor, they both jump up. Teah's breath shudders. "Cleve!"

But it isn't. Michael's mouth fills with spit. He's like a starving person with a steak just out of reach. "It's a patrol car."

It's a park policeman in olive drab, boots, with the drill sergeant's hat and a genial look that makes Michael disproportionately glad to see him. "Can I help you people?"

Oh hell yes, Michael thinks, but doesn't know how to begin. Can't. "Oh no, Officer, we're just waiting for somebody."

He says pleasantly enough, "Out here on a school day?"

It's been a long time since home; if Marshall is right, Mom is close, but it's been an hour plus since he left them here. He isn't back. He hasn't even sent word. Pushed to the limit, angry Michael is tempted to spill everything. But they are under orders. His life in the Navy makes him prudent. "We're down here on vacation."

"I see by your tags that you've come a long way to get here."

Michael and Teah exchange looks. "We came down to . . . visit relatives?"

Teah adds, "Our uncle is taking care of us." She goes on too fast, saying foolishly, "He's from around here."

"And who's your uncle?"

Michael gives her wrist a warning squeeze: Orders. The secret operation.

"Oh, he'll be right back," Teah says.

The park policeman seems satisfied; he's stopped paying attention. He says absently, "Anybody I know?"

Once again Michael is swayed; is strange, powerful Cleve Marshall, who says he is a commander, really OK? What if he just runs the name and description past this officer, like, a reality check? Marshall doesn't look or sound like a good old boy from down here in spite of the long-distance squint and the deep-water eyes; if the Navy is down here, this state cop would know about it and if Cleve is Navy this man may know. Checking would make Michael feel better really, but he is afraid. What if this state cop turns out not to be a state cop after all? Anything he says now may jeopardize the operation. He is sworn to secrecy. "I don't think so."

The policeman asks kindly, "Anything I can do?"

"Well, I . . ." Michael's close to the end of his string now, but, perfect officer material, he has to override his misgivings and keep silent. The commander is their only link to Mom; if he turns out not to be what he says he is, what else do they have? He can't let go of the hope. He has to sit tight and hang in there as ordered, but in spite of all his strictures and resolutions the hum in his head won't quit. It separates itself into words that plop like stones into his already troubled consciousness: *what if there isn't any secret operation?* At the last minute he opens his mouth to speak but circumstance cuts him off: the sound of a car.

"Oh look!" Teah's voice is loud, glad. "That's him in the blue car. Right there. He's coming."

Michael's flattened. *Sir. Thank God you're here.* He can't believe how close he's come.

"Now," Marshall says when he and the park policeman have exchanged pleasantries: us officers together, and this local representative of the law has driven away. "It's time for me to take over. From here on, we go in one car. Your car, I think." He holds out one hand and when Teah looks up at him, says, "I drive."

She gives him the keys without question and Michael does not protest. They will do anything to end the wait.

Tommy's voice is huge. "Can we see Mommy now?"

The whole thing is so precarious that Teah whirls with tears in her eyes. "Oh Tommy, *please.*"

In the car, they give themselves to the ride, going along in almost complete silence. Only Tommy makes any noise, droning, "Mmmmommymmmmommmymmm . . ." Michael and Teah fix on the sound while the commander drives with fierce concentration that forestalls conversation. Now that they are getting close there's nothing more to say, nothing more to do here but put their heads down and forge on through to the secret installation where Naval Intelligence is supposed to be keeping their mother safe. From — what? It isn't safe to try to figure it out.

Now that they are actually under way, Michael's suspicions have abated; he is neither hopeful nor excited. Mom's been gone for so long that he's afraid to let any part of him go running ahead. Marshall has complete command now; he's at the wheel of the Hales' car, intent on a track only he knows; there's no room in the car for questions. They've run out of options. All they can do is go along with him. They are so deep in the sticks by this time that without wanting to Michael remembers all those grisly fairy tales about children lost in the forest by people bent on getting rid of them. Intently, he numbers roadside stores and signposts, weathered shacks, distinctive trees, because no map in the world can show them how to find their way back from wherever he is taking them.

Secret installation is right. They drive for an hour but nothing they do convinces Michael that they aren't essentially describing a large circle. They loop and turn, doubling back again and again so that anxious Michael has to tell himself, OK OK, maybe we're still being followed. He has to believe because his mind is in overdrive by this time. His heart gives a little skip as the line disappears from the center of the asphalt, but he tells himself: secret installation, has to be isolated, naturally it's stuck out here in hell . . . essentially helpless, he's desperate for reasons to attach to everything that's happening to him. He's reached the point when the need to make everything make sense has overpowered every other form of logic. Almost there, he thinks as asphalt gives way to oystershell, and sees from the way she is leaning forward that Teah is thinking some of the same things.

But they aren't there, wherever *there* is. Instead the countryside keeps whipping by like special effects from a movie Michael can't classify — fields, clumps of thick, gray-bearded trees, dead pines clutching air like skeletons in a horror picture and over all the silvery sky clamped down on them like a dome from which there is no escape. After a time the road tapers into a track through land so swampy that in some places they are driving over boards thrown across mud. They come out onto a spit surrounded by channel with nothing on the far side but faceless marshland.

The car stops. The road has stopped. They are at the end. It looks like the end of the world.

Marshall reverses the car and gets it pointed back the way they came. Then he turns off the motor. "OK. Get out."

Michael stiffens. A tall, ramshackle frame building, old barn, he thinks, juts out of the blasted landscape at the tip of the point. It's nothing but a stack of dry, naked wood that has never been painted any color, listing like a child's house of cards about to topple. Michael sees no flag, no office buildings, this doesn't look like a . . . "This isn't it."

He opens the door. "But it is."

Michael's heart thuds. Oh God. "It can't be."

Teah begins, "Mom isn't . . ."

"Come on," Marshall says, cutting her off. He pockets the keys. "From here, we walk."

As Teah and Michael unfold slowly, stretching, they exchange looks. What one thinks, the other knows; it has always been this way: *This is wrong.*

Is she here? There is no indication and no way for them to know. What should they do? Run ahead calling her name, or dig in and make a stand here? Maybe they should stop cold and make him bring her out. But — lord! Marshall has taken Tommy on his shoulder. Carrying their baby brother, he has struck out along a path through tall dead grass at such a pace that it whips at his trouser legs. The dry little swish is the only sound except for the thud-thud of his quick footsteps. He is heading for the weathered barn. They have no choice but to follow.

Teah calls in a thin voice, "This doesn't look like a . . ."

Marshall turns, flashing that grin. "Sure doesn't. It's an underground installation. Be cool." Then he strides on as if he doesn't care whether or not they follow.

Of course. "Listen," Michael parrots, "it's an underground installation. Be cool," but he gives Teah a look that lets her know that whatever misgivings she has, he shares.

"I don't care," Teah mutters, "it doesn't look right to me."

"It looks like nothing from the outside," Marshall says. "One of our specifications is concealment."

She murmurs to Michael, "Do you really think Mom is here?"
He shrugs.

"I don't know if I like this."

They talk without moving their lips, the way they used to when they were little and fooling the grownups. "If we don't like it, we can always leave."

"He's got the keys."

Michael drops back so he can tell Teah through clenched teeth, "I've got Dad's."

"Dad's keys!" Words hiss out of Teah like escaping air. "You bastard, you know I wanted them."

Marshall turns. "Are you guys coming?"

"Yes Sir." Michael looks at Teah. "Maybe we should just."

But they can't. "He's got Tommy."

"Right." They run to catch up with the commander. An outsider could not see it, but everything is different now. Without words, they have considered it. Something has been decided.

"Oh wow," Teah says in a voice only Michael would know is phony. "This is really it then."

"I told you it was." They're almost at the door. "Our most secret installation." Before he bends to lift the bolt, he stops and faces them with Tommy in his arms. "But before I let you in."

They wait in silence.

"You haven't told anyone about this."

Michael rocks on his heels, studying him. "Who would we tell?"

"Nobody at school, nobody at home."

"Nobody," Teah assures him.

"Then nobody knows."

"Nobody. Not even Shar Masters," Michael says as the commander, who they think is no commander, puts Tommy down to remove the bolt.

"Shar Masters is dead," Marshall says automatically, so intent on what he's doing that he doesn't even hear himself.

No.

Teah seizes Tommy, yanking him back even as the heavy

wooden door slides open a narrow half yard and Michael shudders as the smell of gasoline assails him, Marshall must have spent the last hour preparing this does he really think we; he gasps, "Your dream!" Does not have to say anything more to Teah, that knowledge each has of what the other is thinking; he can see from her eyes as she backs away with Tommy clutched to her that it has come back whole to Teah, the nightmare that woke her, screaming, was it only this morning? *I think our grandparents were killed in a fire.*

But now that the commander, who they know is no commander, is close to the end of his efforts here, impatience makes him overconfident. After all, haven't they followed him on faith so far, and haven't they demonstrated trust by letting him have the keys to their car? Of course they will follow. Without turning to make certain they are still behind him, he starts inside. After all, they've followed him all this way on blind faith, isn't he about to reunite them with their mother? Is half-inside when Michael rushes him from behind, pushing hard. He falls, shrieks in pain, a ragged, guttural sound without words — oh shit he must have landed on a . . . there's no telling what he has landed on nor will they stop to find out. Teah puts Tommy down and slams the bolt in place, shutting him in for as long as the thing holds. Michael grabs Tommy and they flee, stumble in their haste and fall over each other, get up and run again, Michael terrified and jiggling the bawling Tommy, hearing Teah's breath sobbing in her chest. They are halfway to the car when the stranger, God knows who he is really, the stranger inside the barn collects himself and begins talking in a loud, official voice.

"Of course, Skipper, just as you say, Sir, and Mrs. Hale, Ma'am, you'd better say a word to your kids out there, your children, after I brought them all this way. That's it, Clary, just let them know how foolish they are being . . ."

In that second there is a slight hitch in the Hales' progress, no more than the shadow of an instant because Michael and Teah know as well as the man inside the barn does that there is nobody else locked in there with him. They all know he is lying, but what if Mom . . . Tommy: "Mommy!" There is no answer. This was never Mom. Therefore to his astonishment even though he holds the car keys their enemy will hear their footsteps pounding as they retreat, in another minute he'll hear the motor start and they'll be out of here. Michael and Teah know he's going to find his way out of the barn in minutes and no matter how fast they get away or far they go, they know he will come after them. Their pursuer is taller, faster — they don't have much time — and in spite of the fact that he keeps up this false patter, "That's it, Mrs. Hale, just stand over there and we'll get them to open the door . . . ," they put doubt behind them and keep on going, are almost at the car when they hear the first violent battering noises as he attacks the door and with them, his shouts of rage, the beginning threats. Cleve Marshall or Cleve whoever-he-is will kill them as soon as he escapes from this fragile temporary prison, he will have them arrested, have them court-martialed, he will come after them and get them, he'll . . .

Words devolve into sickening crashes as this raging, deadly stranger takes some farm tool to the barn door, bent on destroying it, and as they reach the car they understand that the man locked in the barn is no longer talking or pretending to talk, no longer making veiled threats or open ones, is no longer shouting after Clary Hale's fleeing children; he is not even addressing them directly now because the rumble of anger collecting in his throat has swelled; it is tremendous, all speech and semblance of speech fused by fury into a single, riveting sound.

What they hear as they slam the car doors and sobbing Teah fumbles with the ignition is pure noise, everything that threatens them joined and blended, expressed in that single, riveting scream, the naked, open-throated howl of nemesis.

21

JUST WHEN EVERYTHING was going so well. He is trapped.

Listen, then, to what I will do to you. I will have you and then — delicately — I will lift your face and set it in the place I have made for it. But first your children will die for this. First I have to . . . He crashes to the straw; rage screeches into his head and sets up a howling that obliterates thought. Blinded by fury, he gropes through a veil of blood. Present collapses into past.

What am I doing in this dark place?

After the fire they put him away. Trapped in a black cube, he snapped into a ball and went inside to think. Unrealized, the unborn tree writhed like a knot of snakes, troubling his days and electrifying his dreams.

Yet the face he turned to the doctors was smooth and calm.

He spun out the first year there. They told him the state had put him in one of those prisons, or was it hospitals, locked places that were both or neither: a forensic institute. It was intended for cases like his, that defied labels.

Are you ready to be reasonable?

I could kill you right here. I could light your hair and burn you to the ground. He smiled. — Yes, Doctor.

You won't attack me if I come in.

— I've never been violent.

That's not what it says here.

— That. That was a misunderstanding. You look like an intelligent person. I can explain it to you.

Has always been good at telling people what they want to hear.

— So that's it, Doctor. You can see how it was.

It's a shame to see your talents going to waste.

— I was going to medical school. To be a doctor. Like you. Flattered them. *With your potential . . .*

— Whatever you say, Doctor. Whatever you want me to do.

And all the time the tree burned close to the surface, lighting up the dark. Its fire made him brilliant.

You know more than some of our psychiatrists.

— Then give me a little light in here, so I can read. I need something to write with.

Here's a brush, you can use ink.

— I am no painter.

Sorry, nothing sharp.

With the brush, he wrote letters to Clary and then tore them to bits and watched them disappear down the drain in the floor of his room. And all the time the tree burned.

This is taking too long.

He couldn't do what he wanted with a brush. The silverware was plastic; it bent under pressure and snapped. Scouring the tight little room, he finally found what he needed: a bolt from the metal bedstead, because the tree was coming clearer now; he had to see it. He made the first cut in a place nobody would notice, rubbed in talcum to make it scar over. Ahhh. It was exquisite. He worked slowly, in the dark.

In the daytime he taught himself Chinese and read anatomy and criminal law; the doctors reasoned that he couldn't hurt anybody with books. He was designing a plan for getting out. It would take years, but he had years.

At every juncture the tree twisted inside him; it sprouted a hundred blooms. At the center of each he thought he saw the girl's face, Clary was it. The girl. Well he could wait for her. And she had better be waiting for him. When the old couple came to visit each year at Christmas he told them where to put his money: invest here. Take it out of that and put it there. Like the tree, his money grows. Enough to build a world on. He got a mail order degree in criminal law. Model patient. Paving the way out.

If you could see inside me . . .

The tree: This is taking too long.

To the doctors, he was intelligent, tractable. He knew what they wanted to hear, knew ahead what were the right answers in the psychological tests they brought in like children trying to trick a puppy. He said and did everything they wanted for as long as it took him to convince them to let him out of the locked room and into the locked ward: Model patient, progress is amazing. Yes. He charmed doctors here, counseled patients there, spun out their trust and because he was so deft and skillful, he ended by assisting his therapist, I could take your soul and have you thank me for it. And have. While the tree etched its way through his muscles, flesh, burning him from the inside out.

This is taking too long.

Driven, seared and distracted, he thought he saw the tree in the body of a woman, nobody special, but for what he needed, she would do. Thought he knew how to stop the fire. If he could only do this to her he would be able to bring the tree to the surface and let out some of the heat. If he couldn't have Clary yet, and so finish it, he could at least ease the pressure. He wanted to make the tree spring out of her belly in blood. Easy enough to confound the orderly who collected the razors after the morning shave, easy enough to set the stolen blade in a toothbrush handle, easy enough to get their confidence and easy enough to plan.

You've come a long way. You're very perceptive. If you want to work with Marla, you can.

For the tree and its host murder is nothing and nothing is for long. Marla was new in the hospital. He made her love him, always easy. With him, it is a prerequisite.

— I want us to be alone together. Fool woman loved him; she would have done anything. Love is essential in these cases even in stopgap measures like that one. Struggle ruins everything.

She blushed. — I'll sneak out. After lights-out, she did.

When he put his arms around Marla he felt Clary; this wasn't Clary but he had to go ahead. — Lie down. She loved him; she did. — With me next to you. They did. — Now let me touch you. Here. She loved him so she lay quietly; he was so deft that she didn't even feel the first cut.

But an orderly blundered in: — Did I hear something?

He held her close. She loved him! She covered herself, the tiny mark on her belly, blood starting: — It's nothing. Nothing.

I thought I heard . . . Ma'am, are you all right?

One word and she could have him sent back through all those locked doors into the locked room. But Marla loved him. She did. The tree put his hands on her shoulders and looked deep into her center. — Nothing, she said, with a mad, loving grin.

It didn't matter that he couldn't finish. He would talk his way out of this place and begin again. He would represent himself at his own hearing; with his talents and his clean record it was going to happen this year or the next and if not the next year, then the next.

With every year that passed the design became clearer. And the tree burned.

Meanwhile, he prepared. The first cut in him was ragged and healed badly: a raised welt that looked nothing like it should. He sharpened the bolt on the cement floor and while he was waiting to get out, he worked on the tree and while he worked on the tree, he planned. He knew what he had to do, but he would use up as many women as he had to, perfecting it. When he got out he would not go right to her, but when he got to Clary, he would make her love him again and when she loved him, he would fulfill the tree.

Gets up from the straw. This time he will do it in blood.

Oh my God, my children.
They're all I have left.

In the end, she emptied the gallon water bottles into the toilet to keep from drinking any more, so Clary is weak but lucid now. This place! She knows there is still bright water glittering outside, Florida sun burning a hole in empty skies; in the old life she thought it was beautiful. She remembers the sun-shot room, light flashing off the crystal Cleve gave her. Mother, Dad!

Maybe if I'd kept the crystal they would still be alive.

When he torched her house like an avenging angel Cleve destroyed her life. Mother, father only ashes flying upward in a whirl of fire, *I loved them so much;* she can no longer see their faces. Clary is afraid of losing Tom the same way; you can look at a photo and look at a photo and still lose the person. And now her children are in danger, all because she believed the judge who promised to bury him deep.

She was a fool not to know! Even though Tom had brought her back to life and she had rebuilt herself — almost an ordinary person — she should have known. *The monster who loves me will dig his way out of whatever hole they made for him and come back.* At some level, maybe she did know.

A dark force she didn't comprehend put her on the edge of her chair those last few days at home on Pequod Street; anxiety jabbed her soft flanks and dragged its fingernails up and down her spine in a relentless sawing. For no apparent reason, some dark engine inside her began whirring at tremendous speeds. Driven back to the Florida paintings, frightened because she didn't know what spurred her or why it was so important, Clary found herself slashing at them. *I have to finish.* All her brushes were thick with black and purple. She worked long days and got up in the night to paint. Maybe she thought if she could only do it right, she'd have a way to ward him off: a protective charm. She thinks she flared up at Shar, sent her home to get her out of the way. She can hardly remember; it was light-years ago, before Cleve Morrow plummeted back into her life.

The signs. How could she have been so stupid as to ignore the signs? How could she shake and sweat in the grip of premonition and pass it off as just one of those things? Tom said, *You can't spend the rest of your life afraid,* but still. Not the first time she'd waked in the night rigid and jittering; it took Clary years to learn how to put aside her fears.

But there was something more going on those last few days, little differences in her arrangements that she could not identify — perhaps papers moved in her studio, aborted calls on the answering machine. She must have been crazy; instead of barricading the house and arming herself, she turned her back and tried to ward off danger by weaving spells. If I can keep Shar away long enough to do this, if she tells me her troubles it will break my concentration, if I can just finish this painting. If I can just. Driven, obsessed and struggling to keep what she had, Clary turned her back on the devil, building charms she had the power to complete: If I can make four sales at Fenton's gallery nothing bad will happen, if I can just. She spent the week racing an unspecified deadline: If I can just.

Friday she hugged her kids and relaxed, thinking, Home free. It was nothing. Safely through another week. With the bravado of kids whistling their way past a graveyard, she rented a horror movie; needed to exorcise her fears with a little imaginary gore. She made popcorn to celebrate, kissed Tommy and put him to bed with Fang for company. Teah was home on a Friday night for once, instead of out with Eddy Stanko, whom Clary is too clever a mother to forbid; good Mike was home, he is maybe her best friend. She and her big kids stayed up late watching *Return to Horror High,* making a party as they have done so many times for each other's sake. They sprawled on television pillows, giggling and crunching popcorn as if Tom was fine somewhere and on his way back to them, taking comfort from being together until the movie ended and Michael and Teah went to bed. They were dead asleep, like everybody else in the neighborhood except Clary Hale. Next door, Sarah Ferguson's window was dark. Outside on Pequod Street everything was quiet and Clary stood there in the stillness that mothers in particular are starved for, listening to the sound of absolutely nothing. In the silence she could stand in her bedroom and imagine Tom Hale miraculously returned to her; he would be in the front hall, waiting for her to come down to him, they would sneak away from their own children like a pair of randy teenagers, making love in her studio with the hook-and-eye latch hooked in case one of their young woke and came looking for them. Clary lingered, dreaming. But it was time to check the locks and go to bed and so, distracted by love remembered or imagined, disarmed and unprepared for anything out of the ordinary, she wandered into her kitchen.

He was standing by the stairs that came up from the cellar.

I should have known.

They were twenty-some years and hundreds of miles from Florida, in a world she had remade, and still Clary was not safe from him. She had lost everything and survived, and gone on, and now he was here, proof that even though she thought her loving destroyer had already stripped her of everything she cared about, she had still more to lose. Orphaned by the fire, Clary had found Tom and saved herself and surrounded them both with the next generation for protection. She had put bolts on the doors and double locks on the windows. She had survived and grown strong and still she could not arm herself. Nothing she did or tried could protect or prepare her.

"I'm back."

He must have broken a basement window, cut out a panel with a glass cutter because there was no sound to alert her and snaked in through the hole he made. In spite of all her precautions, he had gotten in. She could die tonight and bury herself deep and still not be safe against him: Cleve Morrow, lean and graceful as before but somehow huge, this powerful image of her past life returned to the present and standing — no, lounging — easily in her kitchen.

In spite of all her precautions, in spite of a lifetime spent in fear of just this, she was stunned. "My God!"

More than twenty years. The gorgeous monster shimmered with that same terrible power. "It's me. Don't you know me?"

"Murderer." Recognition made her tremble. For in that first second in her silent kitchen Clary saw the deep flickering just beneath the surface — the part of Cleve Morrow she had once imagined she loved. In the next it was obliterated by everything that had fallen in between. She could still feel the marks of his teeth in her skull. "I never knew you," she said.

"It's Cleve!" God help her he smiled.

How long has he been out of the forensic institute, free to swoop down and demolish her? Why didn't the state let her know he'd been released? He had a deep tan; he stood easy in his clothes and he moved like a man at ease in open spaces. *Dear lord he could have been on the streets all this time, could have been right here in town without me even knowing.*

She thought bitterly: *They let me think he was out of the way and I was safe. Don't they even notify the victims, doesn't anybody care? I should have been warned. He cracked open my world and spilled out the people I loved best; he smashed us all like eggshells and yet here he is.* She raged at him, shouting. "Get out."

"You are still beautiful." His tone was sweet. His white-blond hair fell in the same old way.

"Don't!"

He advanced, all grace and ease. "Clarada. Please. We used to be so close. And we will be again."

Behind the smile there was that flash of the forgotten boy; in spite of what he was — is, the face had not changed that much; monstrous as it is, no foul thing Cleve Morrow has done since Clary thought she loved him is written there. The face stays the same, lean and chiseled as an archangel's, and whatever the man thinks and is and has done is locked tight behind the jade eyes. Those pale eyes shone as if they were brand-new, no trace of past erasures; each time he met you with that compelling, freshly minted smile. What he presented all those years ago — presents now — is a face unmarked by the dark, ugly forces that drive him.

She hissed, "After what you did?"

"I only did what I had to." Shrugging it off, he advanced as if none of it had ever happened. He tried to reach into her with those eyes; unless she could stop him he was going to pull out the most secret parts of her and make them his again. "You know I did it for you."

Flames, shooting up. She thought she could hear her parents' screams. *My God, my children* . . . If she couldn't do anything else she had to protect them, furious Clary Hale already backing along the kitchen counter, fumbling behind her as though she could plunge her hand into a drawer without his seeing and come up with a gun, a knife, anything to erase Cleve Morrow from this picture, efface his image forever, where did Tom keep his gun . . .

"Everything I've done I did for you."

She said quietly, "No you didn't. Now get out."

"How can I leave now?" He was so easy, familiar that she

wanted to kill him. "Now, when we're so close? Admit it, Clarada. You knew I would come for you."

"*No!*" Reaching behind her, she groped in a drawer and connected with the cleaver, foolish, furious Clary Hale, barely five four at a hundred twenty pounds. Who did she think she was that she could overcome her attacker, and what did she imagine she could do? Anger roared through her like a flash fire. "Get out. If you don't go, I'll . . ."

He was on her before she even saw him move. In one easy sweep he had pinned her against the counter. He'd taken the cleaver away from her before she could even get it out from behind her back. Now he held her wrists, not forcing himself but making it clear that he would not let go. "When I get what I came for."

She thought desperately, If only Tom. But Tom is long gone. She was alone. "The police are coming," she said wildly. "I called them from upstairs."

He was laughing. "No you didn't."

"They're on their way."

"No they aren't." He indicated the kitchen wall phone; the receiver was dangling.

The pressure of his hands on her wrists maddened her and because she didn't know what to do next she went on anyway. "They'll send you back where you came from. They'll keep you away from us."

Abruptly, he let go. "Sure they will. Just like last time."

"Oh God."

He said, "Clarada, it was dark in there, where they kept me. I missed the sunlight. I missed you." He said, "I thought about you every day." The next thing he said rose from a place so deep inside him that it came up black and dripping; his tone made it repulsive. He called her, "Woman."

I wish I was a goddam tiger. "What do you want?"

"I want you to come with me." The smile made it obscene.

"I'd rather die." The minute she said it, she knew this was wrong. She had children to protect. With Tom gone, she was in the front ranks; slight as she was, unarmed, she was the only thing standing between her attacker and her beautiful daughter, sleeping upstairs in the room immediately above their heads; alone as she was, only Clary could keep him from hurting her sons.

"No you wouldn't." Smiling, he twisted her wrists, turning her so they were facing. "Let's go."

What happened next surprised both of them. She wheeled on him, all whites of the eyes and teeth flashing, and closed her teeth on his hand. Then she wrenched free and darted away. She had to find some way to lead him out of the house and then lock the doors on him. Then maybe she could . . . She didn't know what maybe-she-could. There wasn't time.

He was on her heels. The desperate, wordless chase took place in silence, punctuated only by the rattle of her own breath tearing her throat and the pounding of their feet. If she threw anything or screamed for help it would rouse her children and bring them down, Teah screeching and hitting, and grim Michael trying to protect her, Tommy wailing in his vulnerability. They were nothing against him. God only knew what he would do to them.

She had to get him out of the house. She dodged into her studio, but it was a trap. Ducking under the arm he swept over her like a scythe, she ran into the hall and when he stampeded her, veered into the living room, leading him into the center of the room. Then with the agility that comes out of desperation, Clary leapt the sofa that stood between her and the hall, thinking wildly, *If I had Tom's gun,* but the gun was in their bedroom, *can't let him get upstairs* . . . Instead — her plan! — she backed into the front door and without being able to see what she was doing, struggled with the latch.

To her astonishment he stopped. "If you want to, go on out."

"What!"

"Have it your way. You go on out, I'll just go on up here." Without even looking to see what effect this had on her, he turned and headed up the stairs. "Oh, kids . . ." At her gasp he turned with careless grace, raking her with pale, opaque eyes that did not see the same things ordinary people did. "You think I don't know you have kids up there?"

He hardly noticed that he was holding the knife. It moved

easily, like an extension of his hand. He didn't have to threaten or beg. All he said was, "Go ahead. Go on outside. I'll take care of things in here."

And so without having to hit her or throw his knife or lunge and snag her by the ankle and pull her down, without having to bind Clary Hale or handcuff her or even threaten violence, the graceful marauder bent her to his will. Threatened as she was, outraged and embattled, Clary understood as she understood nothing else that Cleve Morrow had always known about the children, and if she failed to do what he wanted from this second on, he would go upstairs and murder all three of them.

She would go with him to save her children's lives.

Spent, she said in a low voice, "All right, Cleve."

"Understand, this is for all time." He added, without having to explain, "If anything goes wrong, you know what I will do."

She knew. No matter how far they went from here or how much time she let go by before she tried to escape him; whether or not she managed it, he would make good on his threat. Anything she did now, if she struck him down or eluded him and got away or found help and had him arrested and buried deep in a prison on the far side of the world, he would get out and come back. He would escape and hunt her children down like rabbits. He would gut them like rabbits or smash their skulls. If she fled him to the ends of the earth this Cleve Morrow, who had killed before, would find her. He would track her down no matter how far she took her children or how cleverly they managed to hide. He would sniff them out and when he did, no power on earth would protect them, not police nor federal agents, nobody. He would find them and murder all of them. All her muscles went slack; her head drooped: Clary, at the end of the trail. "I want you dead."

"I know." He gleamed with the dreadful inner light of madness. "But that will change . . ."

"No it won't."

". . . when I am completed. When it is realized."

"What? What are you talking about?" In her terror she thought she knew, looked into his eyes and saw that she couldn't even imagine.

What drives him is more dark and violent than even she can guess: what he will do to her. The scheme.

That night she groaned. "Oh, God!"

"No matter how long it takes." Then he said quietly, "You know where we are going."

When she looked in his eyes, she did. She shook her head so violently that her hair flew and her mouth dried out.

"I know you want it as much as I do," he said. He jerked her around so that they were both facing one of her big, disturbing paintings. "The past. The place. I saw you painting it."

Her belly shuddered. "I can't stop painting it."

The eyes glinted. "See?"

She said raggedly, "Let's get it over with."

"I knew you would see it," he said.

Resigned, the desperate Clary tried to play for time. "If the place looks torn up, they're going to come after us." He raised his head. "You want it to look normal here. Normal. You'd better let me go." She began a hopeless little patter about things she had to do to make the house look the way it looked every day. She went on and on until he agreed, anything to get her moving. And then didn't Clary keep him there an hour or two longer, as with the concentration of a woman about to plunge into childbirth, she made everything ready, thinking if she could just stall him long enough maybe something would change. She baked that for her children, prepared this, cleaned that, stacked paintings and folded the wash, lulling him with her activities until his attention wavered. He had taken a silver letter opener from the living room and he seemed preoccupied by the play of the light on the blade. Crazily, she began drying pots and pans she had washed unnecessarily and putting them away. With her back still to him, she bent over the counter and scrawled a note, but she could feel his eyes on her and under the cover of her activities, she slipped it in her pocket, hoping she could find some way to drop it on the way out to the car. If only the bastard would *look away*. She kept herself going on the outside possibility of a cavalry charge — somebody from the base dropping by to give her news of the *Constellation,* strong old unexpected Shar at the door: I saw your light. Maybe Sarah Ferguson would call to find out whether everything was all right. Or, dear heaven, the car with out-of-state plates might attract police, oh God if only she *did* this for long enough he would realize she wasn't pretty little Clary any more. Maybe she could make herself so ugly he would flee. She stalled and fidgeted until the darkness outside the window began to pale and she understood that no matter what she did here, or how desperately she tried to put it off, they had come to the moment.

Basilisk eyes stripped her to the bone. "Let's go."

"All right," she said miserably and in the next second saw Tommy in the doorway in his bunny-feet pajamas, blinking into the light. There were things she wanted to do, nothing she could do except will him: *Tommy, go back,* too late.

Cleve caught her eyes and looked around unsurprised, saying easily, "Hello kid."

And to her horror Tommy, *her baby,* rubbed his eyes and said, "Hi Cleve."

How did you know his name?

Cleve's triumphant glare almost killed her. *If things had come down differently, he would be mine.* Then he said as quietly as Tom on any evening, "Now make the kid some cocoa." And he handed her a packet, just slipped it out of his pocket so quickly that she knew he had come prepared for everything, even this. "With this stuff. It's harmless. Then we'll put him back to bed."

There were so many fears battling for space inside Clary's head that she didn't try to sort them out. Instead she did as he told her; she would do anything to keep Tommy safe. Therefore she dropped the powder he gave her in the cocoa and left some in Fang's dish. Then she gave her little boy the toys and food Cleve produced from a carton he had left planted just inside the cellar door, *bastard, monster, how did you get into my house, and when?* And then she told her Tommy exactly what Cleve Morrow told her to say — how long had he planned this? The obscenity!

As she closed the door on Tommy he said, "It's time."

Gripped by silent, dry sobs, Clary Hale closed the door on her sleeping children and left the house.

As he bent to unlock the car, she slipped the note out of her pocket and as quickly as she'd done this he pounced, crumpling the paper and throwing it down. It was then that the enormity overcame her and Clary lost control, hurling herself at him, sobbing and pounding with her fists. She was frantic, powerless, raging because strong as she was, this man outweighed her and his steely power outstripped hers; he was a storm, a fury. When she struggled he brought out something on a rag — what was it; she recognized the smell. So all that time she was fighting her losing battle; all the time she was scheming, trying to stall until she could manage an escape, the unremittingly clever and willful Cleve Morrow had been playing his own game. Even before he clamped the pungent cone on her face like a choirboy snuffing a candle and she lost consciousness, she understood that her enemy, her captor, could have done this at any time. He could have done it as soon as she came down into her kitchen and found him standing there. He could have overpowered her without any of this, that they had just been through; he could have done this and tied her up and dragged her away.

In one of her few waking moments, near noon in some nameless Virginia town, in one of the motels where they spun out the days on their trip south, waiting for the sun to go down because he chose to travel by night, Clary charged him with it. Fuzzy, weak and hallucinating, she gagged in the aftermath of whatever injection he was giving her and said, "The chloroform. Why didn't you use it in the first place?" Sick by that time, leached of strength and plagued by nightmare images that made it impossible for her to know which things happened when she was asleep and which when she was half-awake this way, she had an immediate and clear knowledge of the answer: Even a spider prefers a living victim.

"I wanted you to know what we were doing," he said.

Dear God, she does. Days have passed since she last saw him, she doesn't know how many. In her attempts to escape this place, to outthink her captor and get away, she's tried this, done that; in spite of her best efforts she is trapped here as surely as if he'd had her chained to the wall and the place hermetically sealed. She may be trapped here until she dies. If she kills herself to escape him, he will murder her children. If he has not already murdered them. She is at the end of her strength now; she can pray, but that's all. Despairing, she buries her face in the mattress.

If only I could die.

Then the door opens. It is like judgment day.

The light crashing in from the sunny room beyond is so strong that it makes her shrink and hide her face. He's back. No. There is a difference in the atmosphere — the sound and smell of somebody smaller and less confident. Different. She uncovers her face. There is a woman standing there; Clary can read the outline but a trick of the light makes it impossible for her to see the face. Astounded, she blinks and forces the words out; she's surprised at how weak they sound. "Who is it?"

Squinting into the dimness, the intruder says in a hick twang, "Are you OK?"

"Who are you?" Clary has bunched herself up at the head of the bed in an irrational attempt at escape; she's scrambling to wedge herself into the corner, drawing her knees up as if she can disappear.

"Beetrice. You can call me Beetie. Boy, it smells in here." She pushes the door wider to let more light into the room. Now Clary can see her face. She is a plain little cracker girl with tiny teeth and a sweet grin; her hair spouts in silly twin tails that are anchored with plaid bows set too high on her head and loose hair frizzes around her face. She sounds so matter-of-fact, so, what, *harmless* that Clary's muscles stop spasming. Cautiously, she slides to the edge of the bed where she sits quietly, getting used to the light. Weak as she is, she is already wondering, can she jump this person? If she pushed her out of the way would she be able to keep running or would she collapse, completely winded, at the end of the drive?

"What do you want?"

"Who, me?" Beetie's wearing cutoffs and an incongruously frilly-looking top. When she puts her fists on her hips and regards Clary, her many bracelets clatter down her arms. "He sent me in to clean. Don't try anything, he left me a gun."

Clary cranes to see past her. "Where is . . ."

"Who, Clevie?" The girl tosses off the pet name as if she's talking about a puppy, something you could tame and lead around on a string. "He's gone away."

Gone. Clary's heart rushes out, after her children. "Gone where?"

The girl says, offhand, "Beats me. He said he would be back by today, but in case he got, you know, held up, he said I should come in here and check on you? I'm supposed to see the a.c. is OK and the toilet isn't backing up. But the stink! I think we ought to air this place out. And the bed, boy, you're sure ready for clean sheets."

"Back from where?" Clary says carefully.

"Oh, that. I guess it's OK for you to know. He went about the money."

This is not what she expected. "Money?"

"The, ah. You know." Beetie knuckles her breasts in embarrassment. "The — ah, I guess, ransom?"

Also not what she expected. "He told you this was about ransom?"

Beetie is straightening by this time, dumping all the cans of rotting fruit into a garbage bag. Keeping one eye on Clary she rummages busily, talking as she works. "He told me your folks ripped him off with fake stocks, and this was the only way he knew to, get his money back?"

"That isn't true!"

"Fuck that shit, lady. He told me to watch out for you. He said everything that comes out of your mouth is a lie."

Clary is flattened, like a popped balloon. "I see."

"But don't you sweat it, Ma'am, OK? You won't be here much longer anyway."

Clary focuses on walls, ceiling, the door, the girl, but she can't stop the room from whirling. "I won't?"

"Shit no, no way. As soon as we get the money, you're out of here, and we are too."

Her voice is as thin as a strand of saliva. "How do you know?"

"Because he says so, OK? Shit, it's so damp in here everything's started to mildew." Beetie takes the towels out of the shower enclosure and throws them out into the sunny living room. "So he's up north now, getting his money back? Enough to keep us in hotels and big cars for the rest of our lives, and when he gets it, man, you're out of here and we're out of here too. Here's what, he's taking me to all the best places — Rio, and Paris, I think, I'll go out every night in all new clothes." Her eyes glitter with reflections of a dozen TV shows in which women swank around in jewels and furs. "So when he comes back, we split for parts unknown."

Clary begins. "You really believe that?"

Beetie says simply, "We're in love."

"Oh, Beetie!"

Disturbed by Clary's tone, the girl turns. "Ma'am?"

She says carefully, "He's not what you think he is."

Now Beetie fixes Clary with an angry squint. "Don't you be saying anything bad about him."

"And this," Clary begins.

"I mean it."

But Clary shakes her head. Her spread hands indicate the room, the setup, her captivity. "And this isn't what you think."

For a minute, Beetie falters but her face hardens in a visible effort to recover. "Oh sure," she says bitterly. "Lady, he warned me about you, so you'd better just shut up. He told me you lied."

Clary's voice is deep. "I'm not the liar here."

"Just shut up, OK?" Threatened, Beetie advances on the bed. "Get up. Get your ass over there, with your hands on the sink where I can see you're not up to anything, while I change your damn sheets."

Clary discovers that it's difficult to stand. "It's all lies."

"He don't lie to me, he loves me."

"Or so he says."

"I don't have no truck with no liars," Beetie says; does she mean Clary? Cleve? Uncertainty makes her brusque. "Just do like I told you."

Swaying, Clary says, "Please listen. For your own sake."

"Oh, Ma'am, don't make me have to bash you, OK?" By this time the plain girl with the bobbing pigtails is bundling the sheets and stuffing them into a pillowcase stiffened by Clary's tears. Beetie hurls the dirty linen into the other room and turns back to Clary with a blind smile that to her despair Clary recognizes. "Nobody puts anything over on Beetie. Please?" Her eyes are glistening with visions Clary can't see. "Listen, we're engaged."

"Oh you poor kid!"

Beetie doesn't even hear. She just keeps working with that blunt, blissful grin. "When this is all done, we're getting married."

Clary groans.

"You can get back on the bed now, while I . . . Geez, what happened to all your water?"

"It's gone."

"So. You spilled it all or threw it away or what?" Beetie says matter-of-factly, "If you totally drank all that, you'd be dead by now." She studies Clary's shaky progress across her prison. "Are you OK?"

"I'm fine." Clary goes hand over hand along the wall. She's finding it hard to make it back to the bed; any hopes she had of jumping this girl and overpowering her so she can escape are gone now. She can't even walk without help. "It all leaked out. I'm so thirsty, I . . ."

"Well, shit, I guess we'll have to get you some more. So if you'll just get your ass on the bed, I'll be letting myself out."

Clary says in a low voice, "Don't go."

"Oh don't cry Ma'am, I'll be back in no time."

Brave as she is Clary sinks on the bed and begins weeping helplessly. "Oh please." Now that she's started she can't stop.

Concerned, Beetie turns anxiously. "Oh, Ma'am, what is it?"

"Please don't close the door."

"I said I'd be right back."

By this time loss and grief and weakness have pushed her to the limit, Clary Hale pleading. "I can't stand it if you close the door."

"I have to, Ma'am, so you might as well stop crying, OK?"

"I *can't*," Clary cries in grief, by no means certain that she can ever stop crying; she is caught up in it and sobbing for all her losses, beginning with her dead parents and the lost Tom, weeping for her children in danger and for herself, at the end of hope now and about to be locked up again, shut into the lonely dark. At rock bottom now, Clary is shaking with it, sobbing and so breathless that the words come out in a little huh-huh-huh that softens stringy little Beetie, who in spite of the gun is, after all, no more than a girl.

"Oh come on, honey, please?"

So after all this, without even trying, Clary turns her heart. "Can't," she gasps helplessly, "I just can't be here any more."

"Oh shit, please stop," Beetie says and comes over to sit down next to Clary as if she thinks she can reason with her prisoner, or at least steady her until the sobbing stops. But it does not. "Oh, Ma'am," Beetie says, because by this time she is ready to do anything to quiet Clary, "Oh, Ma'am," begging, promising, persisting in her kindness until some of her words reach Clary, whose sobbing slows. "I'll do anything if you'll just stop."

Still rocking in misery, Clary looks down at herself — the purple sweats she was wearing the night he came for her — and even though she is still racked by grief her mind is running along ahead. In seconds she identifies the light at the end of the tunnel and sets out for it. "You will?"

"Really."

Clary considers her audience. Her breath quivers as she says carefully, "If only I could get out of these awful clothes. I've had them on ever since he took me away from my kids."

"Kids!" Beetie's head whips around. "He never took you from no children," she says suspiciously. "He would of told me."

So Clary sees her opening. "Teah. Michael. Tommy."

This rattles her. "Shit. Kids."

"I've been trying to tell you, he lies."

"Kids." Beetie falls back. Says uncertainly, "He don't lie."

Clary's voice is low. "He lied about me. Just think about it," she says. She sees she has Beetie now; using the lever of suspicion, she can move her where she wants. "What else is he lying about? Oh Beetie, please, I'm not asking for much." Cleverly, she adds, "Unless you're his creature."

She flares. "What do you mean, creature?"

Clary fans the spark. "You know, that does whatever he wants."

The girl's face slips through a spectrum of changes. "I ain't nobody's creature, I'm just in love."

"It wouldn't hurt anything."

"I don't know," Beetie says slowly. "I don't think so." Grimacing with concentration, she considers. Clary has touched her pride. She looks up. "But that would show him, I guess."

22

"WHEN SON WAS TWELVE years old," the hospital visitor begins, "there was this teacher, in one of the places we lived?" He peers into the face of the woman in the bed. Without knowing whether or not she hears, he goes on. "This is something I have never told anyone. This teacher? Thought there was something the matter with him. She came to us. She said, 'Don't feel bad, it isn't your fault, I know he's adopted.' I told her, 'Be careful. He knows everything,' but she wouldn't listen. 'Wherever you go, our Son is there ahead of you. Whatever you think, he already knows.' Well, I tried to warn her." He drops his voice. "He did something to her. Don't ask what, it's awful. Charm the birds out of the trees, Son could. And kill them. But of course you don't know him."

Of course she does. *Lover.* Whom this old man calls Son. Somewhere deep inside her battered body, Shar sits weeping. She is grieving over what he did to her, but there is more; a memory she cannot make come clear. She is turned in on herself in a fury of concentration. What else is the matter with her? What is it?

The old man stays by her bed, grasping her hand and talking. They are alone, the room is too bright; she doesn't have a clam's idea what's really wrong or how long the two of them have been like this, her in the bed, feeling stuffed with fuzz but *stronger than you think;* she gets off on her own toughness, right. It may be the only thing she can count on.

She's lying here in the bed with him butted right up next to it in the visitor's chair. She hears him let his breath out in a long, uneven sigh. She needs to think but she feels so bad even the littlest things elude her. *Please.* The old man goes on talking as if she's in here for appendicitis or something, and it's his job to entertain her. Or make her hear his confession. *Please shut up and let me think.*

But he goes on in an old man's voice, woody and uncertain. "After it happened, we had to move. So what if it wasn't the first time? Never mind how we knew what to do, Elva and I. We have spent our lives covering his traces. We can back out of a place in no time and leave no tracks. Elva always found us a new house. I always got another job. We had each other, wasn't that enough? Listen, we were never closer than at those times, riding out of trouble and into some new place, us three against the world, Elva and me and this amazing gift that had been given us to treasure and take care of. Son.

"We would do anything for him." Leaning closer, her hospital friend peers into Shar's face; she can smell his musty breath coming and going, alleviated by the sweet smell of wintergreen breath mints. "I know you're in there," he says, "and I'm not letting go until you come on out and tell me you're all right."

Oh fuck off, Shar thinks; if she cries it's going to wreck her busted eye; would you please just please fuck off?

But the old man hangs on as if he has her on a leash and as long as he holds tight he can keep her from slipping away. "And the next time, and the next — oh lord, if only we had known how to stop these things. How can you tell people to watch out for somebody when you love him more than anyone? You can't turn off the sun."

Too many things to remember. It's hard. Without opening her eyes she shifts slightly, trying to remove her hand from his, but he won't let go. That pain in the crook of her arm — I.V.? She thinks she can feel the tube rattling, something cool going into her, glug glug. But how did she get here, and what did the doctors say to her that's left her grieving so?

"Besides, we were trying to start over. Oh please, until you've had a child of your own you can't know how a parent feels."

Child. Oh, that. Thud. Oh, right. Shar manages not to groan. Something about the baby.

"This is our *life* we're talking about, Elva's and mine, our past present and future. We *believed* in him. Then it was too late. We were afraid of him."

If the poor old guy would just stop sighing, she thinks. She knows who it is, wringing his hands at her bedside, but she doesn't know where Everett Morrow came from or what the two of them are doing here, her with a knot on the back of her head and pain in a hundred places, she feels too bummed, too rotten to care.

The words make painful little explosions of light behind her eyes. "I know, I know, we should have stopped him, we should have seen the signs! But Son never did the way others do, so how could we see? It was like a miracle. We were so old to have a child, he was perfect. Given to us, understand? Elva found him in the street after the fire. Put his little arms up and looked at her with those huge green eyes, all our hopes in the flesh, our Son. When he smiled at us, it was like a gift from God. Who wouldn't overlook the things he did?"

Even now the old man's face is filmed with the sheen of memory, Shar sees through her one good eye, which she has slitted just enough to make sure he is who she thinks he is and they are where she thinks they are. Sure, she thinks angrily. I know who you are, but how the fuck did you get here?

". . . even after the things he did turned out to be bigger than we thought." He leans even closer and says in a confidential whisper, "He would do anything to get what he wanted, and what he can't have — another child's white puppy, terrible! — he kills."

And how the fuck did I get here. Lover! What in blood-soaked creation has happened to him? She knows; doesn't want to know. Wrecked and suffering as she is, she turns in on the one thing she has left to console her: *his baby.* Then she understands. *There is something about the baby.*

The old man's voice is hushed; you'd think he was in church. It is like a litany, every new line followed by the same response: "What he can't have, he kills."

She tries to speak but no sound comes out: "Lover." After what he did, does she really want anything of his? Her heart flutters. *But it's mine.* Shar is all over bruises, like somebody who has had the shit kicked out of them, but that isn't it. She can't get to the source of her grief. *I think.* Shar needs to go somewhere quiet so she can ask herself some questions and yet this sweet old guy won't let go of her hand and he won't stop maundering, either, he is taking on like a Gold Star father, grieving over some hero that's just been blown up in the war.

"We knew from the beginning Son was different. We felt so *honored.* It was like having something special given to you, to love and preserve? Like some ancient race from another planet has singled you out, to take care of their next leader, you know?"

The hell of it is that she does know, Shar thinks now, filled up to drowning with memory. She knows exactly.

"We could tell it at once. The brains." Here is Shar battered and hung out to dry and the old man is so *reverent.* "Understand, whoever you are, he's always one jump ahead of you. What we thought, Son already knew. What he wanted, he took, and God help the person that stood in his way."

That means me. He was a rat, she thinks mournfully. He was not what I thought.

"So everything that's happened is probably our fault," the old man says. Shar wishes he would just stop trying to explain, but the words come down as relentlessly as rain. "For not stopping him when he was little, or turning him in when he got big, but we have our reasons. Son is his own country. We couldn't break the rules."

He does that to you, she thinks, but feels too punk to say. Her mouth is so sore that she's afraid to open it; they're giving her I.V. and stuff to drink through a bent straw. It turns out she doesn't have to say anything. It probably doesn't much matter whether she even stays awake; now that he is into it, there is no stopping the mournful Everett Morrow. I stayed in his *house* in Wilmington and never guessed he was Lover's father because Lover lied about his name . . . Oh Shar, you stupid, lovelorn jerk.

"But then he burned that house and killed those people." This yanks her around all right. *What?* "And now this. I don't know what to do."

Burned what house? Hey, Shar thinks. Is there something going on that I don't know about?

"But I'm really sorry about what he did to you," the old man finishes. "You look terrible."

Starting at the toes, she flexes and relaxes all the muscles in her legs. *It isn't so bad,* she thinks grimly, but she tries to keep drifting. She'd like to stay out here in semiconsciousness, safe from the truth and beyond reason. If she wakes up, she'll have to find out.

"So you'll have to forgive us for not warning you. Son is so strong he makes you doubt yourself." His breath escapes him in a harsh little sigh. "You lose track of where to draw the line."

Slitting her good eye, she sees the old man is regarding her; she is supposed to say oh fine and forgive him for everything, for this Son and the way he led Shar along and then betrayed and hurt her, but the old fool and his Son can rot in hell before that happens, she thinks miserably. She aches in every dimension. Let them all rot in hell.

If the old man guesses what Shar is thinking he can't afford to reflect on it. "Whatever Son wanted, he knew how to get." That sigh: he can't stop sighing; the sighs are coming so thick and fast now that they threaten to turn into uncontrollable sobs. In another minute she's going to slip into tears right after him. Damn him anyway, for coming out with the saddest of all truths. "After a while we lose power over our own lives."

So that Shar has to come out of hiding after all. "Oh please, don't cry." She gives the hand holding hers a little squeeze. "Cut it out," she says; talking hurts her throat. What did Lover do to her, anyway? After he bashed her in the head, did he really try to strangle her? Choking, she manages, "There there."

"Oh, thank God." Relieved at the sound of her voice he pulls himself together and leans over her. "It's you!"

"I guess so."

"You're back." He catches her peeking and bathes her in a watery-looking smile. "Thank God you're all right."

The last thing she is here is all right. By the time they brought her around she was wrecked and dehydrated, angry and aching and confused: "Don't move," the doctors said, "it's going to be a few days before it's safe for you to move."

Oh, shit! Unbidden, the rest comes back to her. Shar in the emergency room right after they brought her here, surrounded by doctors and stupidly croaking: "What about my baby?"

Well they were puzzled right enough. "Baby? What baby?"

"Goddammit, the one I'm going to have."

So. Ah. Uh. She remembers doctors conferring, shaking their heads, the baffled resident pushed out in front to break the news, young and clumsy, saying, "Ma'am, I don't know what you thought happened to you, but don't worry, in no way is this a pregnancy situation, OK?"

Then the older doctor bent over her and said gently, "I'm sorry, Ma'am. You've still got the playpen but the cradle doesn't look so good."

And before Shar could focus on what he was trying to tell her, they gave her a shot that put her out.

Now the grieving part of Shar returns to inform her and jerk her back to full consciousness. *All this, and I don't even have the baby.* She hears herself sob.

Unwitting, the old man makes it even worse. "You know, all this is an accident."

There was never any baby. It's too goddam much. Outraged, Shar struggles to raise herself on one elbow. "What do you mean, an accident!"

"Me finding you. I just came down here on happenstance."

She doesn't know who to hate — Lover, herself. "My whole fucking life is an accident."

Everett Morrow pushes her down. "Be still. You'd better lay back." After all this time sitting by her bed, he has reached his patient, he has brought her back to life; giddy with relief, the old man smiles. Maybe he's just glad there won't be a murder charge. Seeing her good eye open has perked him up. "I was worried about you and those poor kids."

She moves so abruptly that the I.V. tree clatters. "What about the kids?"

"Easy. Easy! Here, take some of this." He gives her something sweet through a bent straw and resumes:

"I didn't find out what was going on until you were halfway out of Wilmington, I said something to Elva about this South of the Border place, and out of nowhere the wife got all upset and started to cry."

Bitch, Shar thinks. That woman is a stone bitch.

Then he says something that makes no sense to Shar. "It turns out he was after them. Well I got on top of it then." He looks like a person who's never been on top of anything but his voice flutters with pride. "Do you know what that woman said? She had been keeping this — secret from me? My wife. My wife and she said, 'I was keeping it for Son.' I said, 'Elva, not after everything. Not after everything he's done,' and even though she was crying she said, 'Everett, he's still our Son.' " He studies Shar for a moment. "You're starting to look a little better. I can see some color in your face."

She croaks, "What secret?"

He shakes his head and sighs. "You know. Every time one of these things comes up we vow this is the end, we're through helping him. I was ready to put him away for life but you know how mothers are. Crazy blind with love."

The story of my life.

"After all," he says, "she is a mother, and you women know what mothers are like."

Not really, Shar thinks, and is relieved to discover that this makes her sad and angry instead of only sad. "What secret?"

"It took me a while to get it out of her, it turns out she'd gone back on everything we'd promised each other. Son called in the night while you and I and those poor kids were sleeping, and Elva told him everything. I don't know what he did to the old lady up north but he found out you were all in Wilmington and he called. I would of lied to him, but Elva. No. Try to understand."

He is having a hard time going on. Bereft as she is, Shar puts one hand on his arm in an attempt to make him feel better. "It's OK. Be cool."

"So she told him everything. Where you were going, you know, to look for their mom." His face darkens. "It was terrible. She knows what he's like, but Elva? She was just going to let him take out after you. She was going to put you all in danger and never say a word." He shudders. "Understand what he is."

"And I loved him." She hates him.

"He can fool anybody."

No, she hates herself. "I was so stupid!"

"No, you're just a woman."

She says angrily, "What do you mean just a woman? I can take any two guys."

"Women, he can make them do anything."

She brings her free hand down on the mattress so hard they both jump. "Then he has to pay!"

"Don't try to talk. Take it easy there. Easy. Down." He gentles her with his hands until she is quiet and then resumes, talking softly in an attempt to lull her. "Listen, you're not the first one to be fooled. I had to lock Elva in the closet, back home, so she wouldn't try to warn him. Elva, who knows the whole story and knows how he is. I never should have let you leave Wilmington like that. I should have called the cops, called out the guard, anything to protect you. Oh my God, I could have at least told you to watch out."

"It wouldn't have done any good." The drugs have filled Shar's mouth with cotton balls so that her angry words come out in an indecipherable mumble.

"Lord only knows what would have happened if I hadn't come down to this South of the Border place and marched into that motel and demanded a passkey, you'd be dead by now."

"I wish I was." But she isn't.

"Do Not Disturb sign like that, motel room paid up through the week, I feel so awful. Honey, you could still be lying there."

She is in no way certain he has done her a favor, Shar Masters, who's gone dizzy in love and gotten herself fucked over one more time, but shit old man if you are blaming yourself here, you are blaming the wrong one.

"The thing is, I'm the only one who could have found you. Not everybody would know his two dozen names." He is looking at her like a child waiting to be praised. "So maybe that makes up for it at least a little bit?"

Instead of praising, Shar charges him. "Why the fuck didn't you stop him?"

"I couldn't." He is looking at her through tears. "I can't."

"You could've at least called the cops."

Then he looks into her eyes out of a face so fragile and threatened and filled with love that it frightens her and says as if it explains everything: "But he's my son!" He's twisting his hands so hard she expects to see dirty water dripping from them. "And now those poor kids?"

Shar starts jangling like a fire alarm. "*What about the kids?*"

"Oh it isn't you he's after," he says worriedly. "It's those kids."

"Oh my God, the kids!" *That's all he wanted.*

He is close to tears. "I thought you knew!"

It's what he wanted all the time. She sits up so fast the I.V. stand teeters. "Fuck no I didn't know. Get out of the way."

"Oh lie down, please."

"Is that your raincoat?"

"Oh lord, this is so terrible."

"Give it here!"

"Her children," he says miserably. "Oh, God, I don't know what he's going to do." Like a baby playing peekaboo the old man tries to hide from the future by covering his face.

"Where is he?"

He shrugs but his manner tells her he knows.

At the crash of the I.V. and the thud her feet make, hitting the floor, Everett Morrow looks up, alarmed. With his hands flying, he jumps to his feet. "Stop," he begs Shar, who has ripped out the needles without regard for what she's doing to the skin and is staggering to the door. "Stop," he cries, rushing to support her. "Please wait! You need your I.V."

She says grimly, "Where's the car?"

"Oh please don't."

"Come on, asshole, where's your goddam car?"

"Wait, oh wait, please." He tries but cannot stop her and so Everett Morrow finds himself swept up in Shar's desperate progress, crying, "Wait, oh, *nurse!*"

23

IT'S HOT OUT, it's beautiful, it's bright blue above and unremittingly cloudless, it's past noon on Route 19, it's Florida. It's almost Tarpon Springs. With a better map they might have gotten here sooner although, looking at the profusion of chain stores and fast food pit stops lining the road, bigger-than-life plaster oranges, humongous plastic American flags whipping over shopping centers, sequined glits on strings revolving over used-car lots and on top of one fake Moroccan palace an enormous plaster cow, Michael is beginning to wonder whether sooner would have made any difference. His mother is just as gone; anyone could get lost in this place.

Florida is not anything like he expected. The little he knows is from his mother's thunderous-looking paintings of that isolated, windswept place on the deserted point, and from what he is learning firsthand right now, going along Route 19. The two images don't match. The garish sprawl is so unreal he isn't sure it's Florida. Someday he will come back and make a major picture here.

EXTERIOR — DAY — FLORIDA

At the wheel and driving without a license, MICHAEL searches the road. The camera pans a cluttered commercial landscape.

He leans out the window, trying to take in everything at once. Except for palm trees springing out of cement islands in the middle of the dozens of parking lots, there's not much indication of *where* this is, much less what it's really like. Yet it's festive, festive, almost unbroken roadside mallscape done up like a football homecoming float with reflective this or Day-Glo that to draw the eye to businesses jammed in and jostling for attention, with blinking or revolving this and shining that; it's blinding. Light is everywhere, bouncing off cars and glinting in hundreds of reflective surfaces; the road itself is shimmering in the bright sunlight although it's only the middle of May, heat mirages filling from the bottom up with the exhaust fumes of a thousand cars, half of them loaded with water skis, Windsurfers and power boats, towheaded locals in jams and muscle shirts all hell-bent on somewhere, and giddy outsiders surprised and excited by all this unalleviated sunlight, tearing off in eight directions because they've been dropped into rental cars and delivered into brilliant, perfumed panoramic four-alarm vacation landscape in living color. Still there is that white sun, that sky, certain trees in blossom; although Michael is having a hard time reconciling this Disney World vision with the ragged beauty of his mother's paintings, this really is Florida.

On any ordinary day he would be excited, but after yesterday, after all the terror and grief and misery and betrayal, it's like being at a movie shot by some alien filmmaker who doesn't care what Michael expects. He has the idea he's watching a completely unrelated life unfold on the screen with no way into it, or looking at a traveling scene in an early talkie, watching people trudging along in front of a projected, changing landscape and knowing as well as the actors do that there's no way in hell they can leave the path and go off into the projected trees or dive into the projected lake because they are doomed to play out the whole thing trapped on a treadmill.

Urgency drives him. *We've got to get to her before he does.*

Did they slow down the monster? Hurt him? Disable him? Nothing? What? He does not know.

Have to get there. Sweat glues his fingers to the wheel. *What if we can't?*

This is too much for him to think about. They have to, that's all he knows. Maybe it's because he's alone now, with his brother and sister lost in sleep and returned to a safer, more familiar world, or maybe it's crashing exhaustion that threatens Michael and makes him falter. In the blurred underworld of unremitting travel he has lost track of breakfast, lunch and dinner, morning and night, bedtime and the morning alarm clock; since they escaped the commander or whatever he was — clever, murderous Cleve, who may even now be on their tail — they have been on the road, eating on the fly and sleeping in shifts. Relieved as he is to be this close to Tarpon Springs, Michael is disoriented by the lack of normal *times* for things, driven and crazed. Fixed on the road, he drifts between hallucination and unquenchable wish.

It is so *wild* here; anything can happen. In another minute Dad could actually pull alongside in a Navy car and he and Michael will rescue Mom together. Or else Michael will come out on the waterfront and see the *Constellation* surfacing in the Gulf, listen, crazier things have happened. There was this battleship moored in the middle of what looked like dry land in Wilmington, North Carolina, ghostly masts and radar scanner rising out of the middle of the pine trees, why not Dad's sub out there off the beach somewhere, part of some bigger Navy operation after all? *After all, we are all under orders.* In his life in the Navy Dad has done plenty of things his kids don't know about. He could be down here somewhere, waiting. Oh God, couldn't he?

Or else Shar will turn up; Michael swallows that hope with a guilty shudder because she's dead and they don't know what happened; he hasn't even had time to grieve for her. If there's nobody else coming to the rescue, if they do indeed have to do this alone, Michael thinks maybe some miracle will bring him to the right turnoff and he'll accidentally *find* the road leading to the house on the point that he has memorized from his mother's obsessive paintings; he'll just walk into the picture that has been like wallpaper running behind life for as long as he can remember; he'll go up on the porch and she will come to the door.

Scanning the mall parking lots and the fruit stands and the steaming asphalt aprons outside Wendy Friendly Howard Johnson Taco Bell Bennigan's McDonald's Frisch's Big Boy Roy Rogers Burger Chef looking for his mother, he is not so certain. Florida seemed like a good idea when they set out — it was all they had! Running close to used up and fresh out of last resorts, he managed to keep going on the outside possibility, but confronted by the reality, Michael is beginning to despair.

How in God's name is he going to locate her out here on Route 19, in between the IHOP and the Jalapēna Terrace Cantina and the Publix and the Kash'n'Karry and the Bonanza Outlet Mall; how is he going to find one lost person with half of America spilled onto the sunny highway, bombing along in cars plastered with bumper stickers bearing everything from South of the Border legends to "WELCOME TO FLORIDA/ NOW GO HOME," and the rest of America bent on commerce and lining both sides of the roadway in a relentless, neon-studded, carefully planted American-flag-flying Day-Glo-pennanted blur?

He's going along in this strange new world like a displaced Martian with no map. The sparkling, sun-shot world is laid out on all sides like a theme park and he can't find the way in.

Teah jogs him with a little shriek. "God, Mikey, watch out!"

He swerves. "Don't do that!"

"It's the turnoff. You're just about to miss the turnoff."

"I saw it," he says untruthfully.

TARPON SPRINGS

They make the turn and suddenly the place falls open.

He supposes he should thank her.

The minute they leave the main road, the landscape changes; asphalt gives way to blasted-looking grass clinging to dirt too sandy to support anything that grows and the spaces between buildings yield glimpses of low-slung heavily mossed trees and scrub palms clinging to the sand like stubborn animals. New buildings alternate with tin-roofed shacks left over from the old days, suggesting that there is still some unclaimed land left in the middle of all this glitter. As they cross the next road the place starts to look more like the Florida of his mother's paintings. The highway intersects a tired, dusty-looking small-town street.

Teah grips his arm. "Turn here."

They are in downtown Tarpon Springs, at the head of a narrow old-fashioned street that curves around a harbor. To the right, they can see the bobbing masts of fishing boats. So they have found the water after all. He can't know that the town is built on a nick in a coastline so riddled with coves and inlets that it may take the next hundred years to find the one they're looking for. Michael thinks his mother may not be in this place, but for the first time since they started this hard trip three, four — he's lost track of how many days — ago, she seems near.

Teah says in a hushed voice, "I guess this is it."

Whether or not it is, he can't go any farther.

"Yeah." He pulls into the nearest parking lot.

"What are we going to do?"

He opens empty hands to her and withdraws them quickly so she won't see that they're shaking. Ahead the dusty-looking town waits. Is his mother here? Can they find her before Cleve finds them? He can't wait to get out of the car. He steps into heat mirages shimmering like ghosts of the past.

It is instant 1929.

Except for the stucco gift shop here at the head of the main drag and the glossy new Greek restaurant just across the way, the street looks quiet and old-timey, as reassuring as a TV grandmother's lap. He imagines for a minute that if he wants to find his mother, all he has to do is ask. The town is like the set for an early black-and-white movie, in which the locals are friendly and anxious to help.

Diagonally across from them is the Spongeorama, museum with a guide on a bullhorn offering sponge boat cruises on Anclote Key. Does the guide trumpet something about a giant squid? Just beyond the boats a screen of mangroves rises, glossy-leaved, bushy-looking things flanked by spiky trees. The far side of the harbor is so close it looks as though the ships are wedged in a slit in the land. It's a little like finding the marooned battleship in North Carolina, stacks and radar apparatus rising above the pines. The Hales have been lifted out of ordinary life and put down in a dream. The street is flanked by one- and two-story buildings, jumbled souvenir and gift shops with fly-specked windows filled with sponges, coral, generations of plastic toys, stores interspersed with Greek restaurants where locals sit at sidewalk tables, eating in the shade of the overhang.

Forget supermarkets and discount stores, this is downtown Tarpon Springs. Probably there are computers and faxes in the
backs of those buildings but there is some local chamber of
commerce fighting to keep it as it used to be, and to Michael it
looks like a free ticket to a simpler past.

So here they are. Now what? Fuddled, Michael finds he.
Can't. Pull. His. Feet. Off the ground.

Teah sees and jerks his arm. "Hey! It says we can't park here
unless we're going to that restaurant."

"We don't have that kind of time," Michael says doggedly,
but he is startled to find his legs wobbling. He hangs on the car
door, flexing one knee and then the other. What next?

Frantic Tommy hurtles into Michael, shoving him off balance. "I want my breakfast."

"Tommy, it's past lunchtime."

He's had enough; he's snarling, like Fang. "I want my lunch."

"Maybe we'd just better get back in the car."

Teah says firmly, "Not before we eat."

God he feels bad. "We have to keep going."

Tommy bops him with Taz. "I'm tired of riding."

"Like, where?"

Michael snaps, "I don't know where!"

"We don't even have a goddam map."

They are ganging up on him. "I *hate* the car."

Teah says, "We've got to eat."

"I hate the car and I'm hungry."

"Let's go," Michael says.

"Aren't you even going to ask if somebody's seen her?"

He's surprised by how hard it is to squeeze the words out.
And how close he is to used up. "I don't know."

Besides, his sister is looking at him out of their mother's eyes.
"Come on. We have to eat."

His lungs collapse in a sigh. "Right."

It's Greek food, fine, they eat at a hole-in-the-wall across
from the big restaurant, stuffing their mouths without much
conversation, because they've done the last thing they know
how to do. They are up against it. Lost in space without a plan.
Clueless. It's almost overwhelming. Teah, who has napped and

is more or less fresh, keeps answering Tommy mechanically while Michael broods. Looking out the flyspecked front window at the tourists spilling out of the Spongeorama, the master of next steps is trying desperately to think of one. Then as Tommy mainlines baklava and makes guggling noises with his straw in the bottom of the glass and gets Teah to take him one more time to the bathroom, Michael begins a crude sketch on the scalloped paper table mat. It's the house his mother always paints — oh shit, *painted* when they still had her — what is he going to do, show people this drawing and ask them if they've seen this house? Or is he supposed to put it in the want ads in the papers, or post it at the police station, along with the Wanted posters? He doesn't even know where the station is. And besides, how are people supposed to get in touch with him anyway, call this restaurant and ask for Michael no-last-name?

Police, he thinks uneasily. He and Teah have too much to explain — down here all by themselves — and what would they say? They can't even prove there's been a crime. He doesn't even know where to start. Except for one or two tourists bopping along in visors and sun hats, the street outside is empty. Closed up against the heat, the old-fashioned main street is like a ghost town, blank glass fronts glaring at other glass fronts, all perfectly preserved. Shaken, he thinks: *What do we think we're doing here, three kids?* This is like everything the Hales do. They have to do it alone.

Teah comes back from the bathroom with Tommy and Michael pays the check, noting as he does so that he's running short on cash, but by this time he is so low on everything — energy, hope — that it seems like no big deal, perfectly logical and to be expected.

He is near the end now. Fresh out of next things.

He knows it and looking at Teah, he knows Teah knows it. He snags a Mounds bar and stuffs it in his pocket like a losing general desperate to provision his army.

Then they blunder out into the sunlight, bumping like billiard balls in a bad split, blinking at the brilliant Florida light. If they are looking into store windows it is to put off the moment when they get back into the car. Used up, miserable and lost, they come to the window of the next-to-last gift shop on this side. And they see her. See. Her.

Michael grabs Teah's elbow: *zap*. Electricity fuses them.

Mom.

It is Clary.

She is standing among tables and counters loaded with plastic souvenirs and shell lamps and bleached coral and bizarre natural-state sponges, trapped in a wonderland of hanging fishnet and crepe paper streamers, their mother Clary Hale blinking down at herself with a strangely concentrated expression.

Mom. Michael clamps his mouth shut with his teeth.

She's supposed to be considering the dress she's trying on but she has that look that lets them know her mind is on something else. She seems surprised by what the store owner and the stringy, scowling girl who seems to be in charge have picked out for her. Clary feints for the mirror in the back but the tough-looking girl she's with — *girl she's with* — has her hand in the pocket of a windbreaker, wait, it's too hot for a jacket, and nudges to keep her in place, muttering something only Clary hears. With a shrug, their mother spreads her hands and without a mirror, tries to gauge the fit of the dress.

"I don't care if you don't like it," the girl growls. "This is all they've got."

It is white, like a wedding dress, with heavy lace cutting a line across her shoulders, exposing the bra straps; although she seems confused and less than steady on her feet, Clary turns and in the unconscious grace of any woman in a new dress, looks up at the inside of the store window to catch her reflection.

Instead she sees Michael and Teah.

Teah whispers, "Look."

Forever marooned at waist height, Tommy tugs. "What is it?"

Teah's lips move. *A gun.*

"Shh, Toms," Michael whispers; it's important to whisper. "It's just this old boat in the window." Even though Tommy stands on his tiptoes and cranes, he won't be able to see beyond the dusty little boat with the paper flag and heaps of miniature sponges. They can't let him know what's going on. They are not supposed to be in this scene. Something's the matter here.

The girl's voice drifts out. "I'll show him who gives the orders around here." When Clary does not respond, she says, louder, "Now do you want the damn dress or what?"

In the next second she catches Clary staring out the front window and swivels to see what her captive is looking at —

"Shh." Michael clamps his hand on Tommy's head, fixing him in place. Helpless, they wait.

Clary's expression does not change.

After a minute the girl twitches her hand in her jacket pocket and turns away: oh, it's only some kids. "So what about the dress?"

They see their mother nod.

And her stringy guardian goes back to negotiating with the store owner, wadding Clary's old clothes into a paper sack with one hand, paying without ever taking the other out of her pocket.

Mom. She sees us.

From here they can see their mother's eyes have filled but Clary does not acknowledge them and they don't call out.

Everything in Michael rushes out to meet her but he doesn't move and Teah doesn't move because there's something wrong; Mom sees them, the contents of her heart are written all over her face, but she is shaking her head. She is telling them to go away.

Teah's fingers close on his arm. "What are we going to do?"

Michael says, "Police. I have to find the police."

"Hurry!"

But he revolves in place. In this street with stores like closed faces, there's no knowing where to go.

Then Teah hisses, "They're *leaving*."

"Stop them."

"Asshole. The gun! Michael, hurry."

Shoving the paper bag at Clary and nudging her with the blunt shape in her pocket, the grim little guardian pushes Clary toward the door.

"Too late."

"What are we going to do?"

Michael's breath comes out in a desperate rasp. "I'm not losing her now."

And because this current does run between them and she and Michael have never needed to discuss anything that really mattered, they rivet themselves to the window outside the store. Michael puts his hand on Tommy's head, pushing him down as Clary and her guardian come out. "Oh look," Teah says falsely, "look at the little baby sponge nets," and Michael says, "Yeah, Toms, look!" Thus they keep their baby brother's attention fastened on the dusty boat model in the window, while with her eyes blinded by tears but her shoulders as high and her back as straight as their father's, their mother comes out, passing *this close,* and goes on down the street with her companion, leaving her children behind in the quiet, sandy street in the oldest part of Tarpon Springs, Florida.

24

IF CLARY IS AFRAID her children will make themselves known and blow the game, she doesn't have to worry. It turns out they are stuck to the sidewalk. Electrified, brother and sister are clinging in front of the cluttered window of the dusty souvenir store on the main street in downtown Tarpon Springs, Michael and Teah fused like melting plastic soldiers while Tommy clutches his stuffed Tasmanian devil and fidgets because everything of any importance in the world goes on over his head.

"I want the boat," Tommy says.

"Shut up, Toms."

Louder. "But I want the boat!"

Michael says through his teeth, "Shut up, I'm warning you."

Before he can move he has to pry Teah's fingers off his arm; she seems surprised to see them still digging in. By the time their mother recedes to a safe distance and he does move out, Michael goes cautiously, as if the world is made of toothpicks and a misstep will dislodge one and shatter the entire structure.

Finally their mother's intent, grim-looking guardian hustles her around a corner; keeping her shoulders high and her back straight with military control, Clary goes without even a twitch of her trailing fingers.

"Hurry or we'll lose them," Teah says.

"I know." Michael is already running.

They bolt for the car. Now that they've lost sight of her and broken the connection, they're terrified Clary will evaporate, as fleeting as a holographic image that blinks out the second it's separated from the power source. They have Tommy between

them, half dragging, half carrying their struggling brother to
the car while he drones on about the boat, grumbling into Taz's
plush fur.

In the awkward little flurry in which they can't decide who's
driving, their mother almost gets away from them. A rusty white
pickup truck shoots out of the side street, Clary no more than
a smear of white in the passenger's window, and Teah barely
manages to get going and insert their car in the stream of traffic
in time. Michael hangs out of the car, straining to keep track
of them. When the pickup turns off the main road Teah turns
too, but they're frustrated by a changing traffic light; Michael
is wild by this time, ready to run lights and risk arrest, anything
to keep their target in sight, but there's no way to leapfrog the
Brillo-curled old lady in the shiny old sedan in front of them,
who jerked to a stop as soon as the light turned yellow. As the
rusty pickup rattles away, distanced by the cars that have cut
in behind it and just about to make a quick turn and lose them
altogether, Michael thinks he can see their mother's pale face
bobbing in the back window. *Oh, Mom!* he thinks. *Good-bye.*

They are left behind, marooned on a road into the unknown.
It takes them over a series of bridges onto causeways, over
causeways into an area so beautifully manicured that Michael's
heart sinks. It's nothing like the territory he imagined. This is
different from all the Floridas he's seen so far. They are back
in the late twentieth century. There is a lot of money here.
There's no place in this picture for an old-fashioned house with
a tin roof like the one his mother paints so obsessively. Nothing
like the rugged-looking, isolated point where it sat. He and his
sister can go from house to house ringing doorbells and raise
only security guards who, kids or not, will run them off the
property. Everything is airtight, meticulously groomed and
sealed against the heat; closed to outsiders.

Without maps, Michael can locate himself anywhere, found
their way back from the point where Cleve Marshall tried to
trap them, but today, for the first time since he can remember,
he's lost all sense of the lay of the land. All the roads lead to
circular drives studded by gateposts and ornate mailboxes; the
place seems to be made up of cul-de-sacs and dead ends. He

doesn't know whether they're going from island to island here or only over fingers of artificial land that guarantee every house a dock and a place to moor a boat, and he can't even guess how many veins and arteries of water lie between them and open water. He doesn't even know for certain what is their relationship to the mainland.

Oh shit, he thinks with sinking heart as Teah turns into yet another cul-de-sac. This can't be it. If this isn't it, we're never going to find her.

Then at the far end of the loop he sees overgrown trees crouched over the entrance to an overgrown drive. They are completely unlike the manicured palms that flank the other neat, plastic-looking lawns; the sandy road leading in suggests a place as different as the surface of the moon.

"There!" he shouts. "Right there. Turn!" and Teah does.

Instead of ending at an expensive house like all the others, the road goes on. The property is bigger than the others and they ride on through scrub pines and palmettos, sandspurs and Florida holly bushes, coming out into a clearing that gives onto the water.

The point.

Even though there are more manicured houses with neat docks across the water, close enough to swim but too far to shout, it is wild here. The last bend brings them out to the end, where an oystershell road leads past a ramshackle garage to a frame house with long porches and a tin roof.

"Mom's place!"

It is. Where it stands alone in all his mother's paintings, here the house is surrounded by palmettos and hibiscus and oleanders, old plantings that must have gone wild over the years. Live oaks and Australian pines hang over the road, strung with Spanish moss like skeletons draped for Halloween. The big tree that his mother always paints at an angle, as if whipped by hurricane gales, is straight and quiet, sheltering the shabby-looking house with the tin roof and the tin-roofed cupola. Somebody has extended the porch to meet a cypress deck that wraps around the side of the house. To their right is a dock with a boat tied at the end.

Teah's voice drops. "Oh Mikey. The house."

Tommy says, "Are we there yet?"

Michael says in a hushed tone, "Shh, Toms. I think so."

Instead of going forward, Teah turns off the motor and coasts to a stop next to the garage.

Quietly, they get out. They aren't sneaking up, exactly, but they have fallen silent. Even Tommy hushes.

I can just go right up there on the porch, Michael thinks. I can just open the door and walk right in.

Instead they go around to the side of the house and without knowing what they're going to encounter, start spooking along the deck. They are practically in the living room.

Somebody has spent some money here. The whole side wall has been replaced with an expanse of glass overlooking the inlet, all that weather coming and going, whatever the owner needs to see, like, anyone approaching, and inside, the spare, elegant blue and green living room is — but wait.

Inches away, the stringy, muscular woman who dragged their mother out of the gift shop is standing with her back to them. She has both arms raised, holding a. What? She's flailing intently at the draperies on either side of the fireplace, so fixed on what she is doing that she doesn't see the three Hales clumped outside on the deck watching. She's working in long strokes, raking away with a vacuum cleaner wand, cleaning angrily, as if there's something more than dirt that she has to get rid of, routing out the enemy with an angry scowl that deepens as Michael slides the glass door open — it's so easy — and simply confronts her. "Ma'am?"

At first she doesn't hear him because of the vacuum; she's just thwapping away at the fabric while the cleaner hums.

He raises his voice. "Ma'am!"

She starts and whirls, furious. "What!"

"Ma'am?"

Brandishing the vacuum attachment like a shotgun, she feints. The tough country-looking woman — no, girl — seems to be alone here. "Who are you, go away!"

Pretending not to hear, Michael pulls the others in behind him. "I have to talk to you."

"I'm not supposed to," she shouts over the whirring motor, but Michael just smiles. In a fit of frustration she loops the cord around her toes and with a jerk of her foot yanks it out of the wall so she can make herself heard. "You have to get out," she yells into the sudden silence and then blushes and drops to an ordinary tone. "Look," she says, advancing on him with the vacuum nozzle, "get out and I'm not kidding, you've got to get out of here."

Teah and Tommy have moved in to flank Michael, who stands firm. "I'm sorry, but no."

"He could come back at any minute. He could . . ."

"Look, I'm Michael Hale and this is Teah and that's our little brother, Tommy?" In spite of the fact that the woman has raised the cleaner extension against him and is trying to use it like a Watusi assegai, he advances, drawing the others close so that they make a grave little mass confronting her: The Hale family.

She falters. "Kids!" Recovering, she feints with the cleaning wand. "Listen," she says, "you have to go away."

"We can't."

"I don't know what he'll do."

"We're not leaving," Michael says.

In the uncomfortable pause that follows he studies her and sees that tough as she looks, this person is not too certain of herself and furthermore, unless she's got it stashed in the pocket of the zipper jacket she has hung on a chair at the other end of the room, she doesn't have a gun; there's no room in the cutoffs or the pink muscle shirt to hide even a switchblade. He takes a step forward and as he does so she takes a step back. "Where is she?"

Upset, she rubs her free hand across her eyes, accidentally dislodging the scarf tied like a headband around her forehead; the grim mask drops as she gives them a quizzical little look that reminds Michael of poor Shar. Up close like this, it's clear that this grim-looking little guardian is not all that much older than they are and that she has more on her mind than whether to let them in. "Could you just go away?"

"Our mom. We came to get her," Michael says.

He might as well have hit her over the head with a rubber

mallet; she is blinking hard. "I was hoping it wouldn't come to this." She's backed until she can't back any more; Michael has her up against the draperies that flank the fireplace. "Your mom. I was hoping she was lying to me."

With the natural guilt of kids, who expect to be proved wrong by people in charge because they are adults, he thinks, what if I'm wrong and she kicks us out? He says uncertainly, "We know she's in here."

"And if she isn't lying . . ." She has been going hand over hand along a chain he can't see. Her breath pops: Hah! The information seems to be reaching her in stages. "That bastard," she says. Now their adversary is at a loss, backed into the draperies that cover the fireplace wall with no place to go, half-kid-half-woman with the Hales bearing down on her. They are so close her eyes cross; with the frizzy hair around the ears and that Smurf expression, she looks less comic than miserable. She's spread her arms as if there's something behind her that she has to protect. The fabric at her back hangs unevenly, and as she backs into it, Michael sees the arrangement covers a doorframe; there's a little bulge where the knob protrudes. The thing is so nearly concealed by the fabric that an outsider might come into the room and never notice it.

"So where is she?"

She shakes her head miserably. "Leave me alone." She's so flushed that freckles and zits stand out like chicken pox.

Michael bears down. "Is she in there?"

Her mouth is working. "Go away, I have to think."

Jittery Michael presses her. "Let us in!"

"I can't." Her eyes glaze over with tears. "I promised him." She can't make her voice behave. "We're supposed to be in love."

By this time their adversary looks so dizzy and pained that he and Teah could probably knock her right over. Teah sees it too; he can feel it in the way her muscles tighten. Shifting his weight, he bunches himself as if to lunge but to his astonishment the frazzled guardian just drops her arms and stands aside. "OK," she says, "OK. She's in here."

She pushes a button set into the fireplace molding and the

drapes slide back. There is in fact a door, but there's more. Emblazoned on the surrounding wall there is a bizarre design, disjointed branches and tendrils studded with silver and gold and bits of broken glass. It crackles with savage energy, so complex that for the first second, Michael can't make it out. It is a tree. It is a tree, but a tree designed by a madman, twin trunks with huge branches rising above, heavy with leaves and velvet blooms. But at the center, there is nothing. At the heart of the tree the mad creator has gouged a hole in the wall.

Michael's breath stops. Teah grips his arm. He speaks with an effort. "What's that?"

Uneasy, the girl glances over her shoulder. "Nothing. Just something of his. Please hurry, OK?"

Teah murmurs, "Mikey, this is awful."

"I know." They understand who made this. It is like looking into his mind.

The girl bends to the lock, saying hurriedly, "Look, the stuff she's been taking has left her a little weird, plus also, it's kind of dark in there? Like, if you're going to start with her, you'd better start slow. So I'll just let you in, and then I'll go?"

"You had a gun." Michael accuses her: "I saw you with her downtown."

"Listen, I had to. He left me in charge. But, this *place*." She lifts her hands in apology. "I didn't know."

Michael says angrily, "You had the gun on her."

"I had to." She is close to tears. Her face won't hold still. "You don't know what it's like." Backed into the tree like that, all jiggling hands and jerking elbows, the confused girl gropes behind her, colliding with one of the embedded flowers, and in a startlingly sensual gesture, strokes it. "You don't know him."

He can make anybody fall in love with him.

Then she says brokenly, "I thought he was telling the truth."

Teah's voice comes out with a little thud. "Right." Unaccountably, she goes on. "You had to *think* he was telling the truth."

At this Michael thinks, *My God. That moment on the bluff.* But there's no time to examine it because their mother's tough little guardian has pushed the door open a crack. "Whatever you do, hurry. When he comes back God knows what he'll do."

"Mom. Mom!" Teah peers in. "She isn't answering."

They are so close that it frightens Michael; what if something goes wrong now? What if he comes back? Thinking fast, he calls after the girl, who has seized her zipper jacket with the — is it really a gun — with whatever she is hiding in the pocket, and she's backing out. "Hey, wait."

"I can't."

"We need your help."

She wails, "I've already done enough!"

"Just this one thing, OK?"

She hesitates.

"Call the cops for us?"

Astonishingly, she says, "Who, me? No way. I can't."

"But . . ." There's no way to express it. Michael tries to sum it up. "This *tree*."

The Smurf face is compressed in pain. "I can't do anything more for you. Listen," she groans. "We were in love."

And he is frightened, not for what may happen to them and their mother, but for what the monster who made this may have already done to her. He lingers in the bright room. "That's terrible."

As the girl flees her voice trails behind her. "I know." Struck by conscience, she turns in the doorway. "OK," she says. "OK." Says explosively, "The keys are in the boat." And is gone.

Behind him Teah says, "Mike, come on!" She blunders into the dim hole with Tommy close behind. Stale air rushes out. "Mom," Teah cries, leaving Michael alone in the bright living room with his own preoccupations, calling, "Mom, it's us! We're here!"

And for the first time in what seems like weeks he hears his mother's voice, low and rich, coming to him out of the depths, filled with everything that has happened to them since she saw them last but using the same plain, strong, deeply loving words she would on any ordinary day. "Oh, guys!"

25

THE ROOM he has left their mother in smells terrible, like rotting fruit. It is cramped, anybody pacing could cross it in three steps. Running across the wall by the door is a set of appliances laid on a board supported by cement blocks — microwave, pocket refrigerator, electric can opener. There are stacks of plastic plates and cups but no cutlery. He has left her no tools she could use to hurt him or try to pry her way out. In the far corner are a shower stall, a little sink and a toilet, and running along the wall opposite the door is the metal bunk where his mother and Teah and Tommy cluster. The rest of the space is occupied by ranks and ranks of neatly stacked food cartons — enough supplies to keep her for months, Michael realizes with a sick shudder. There is no daylight. Boards are bolted over the windows and far overhead, a flickering fluorescent strip lights the room. Even the sound quality is different, everything muffled by the heavy padding he has laid over the walls. He has even padded the ceiling. This is worse than jail. When he sees the rips in the padding he understands everything. Oh God, he thinks. Oh, Mom. This is so awful.

She is with Teah and Tommy. They are clumped on the bed, hugging and sobbing, Clary in the white dress with her hair still wet. She is pale and weak. The smile she turns to him shines, but being so near to his mother after all this time — all this emotion — makes Michael strangely diffident.

There are too many things holding him back. He doesn't want her to see him crying is one; another is that he's scared she's hurt; but the real thing is the questions. What he cannot put out of his mind is the image of Teah and the commander on the bluff in Georgia, lifting twinned arms to point at the boat; *he is a magnet.* That wild, unfinished tree on the wall outside this room. How does she fit into the design? *He could make anybody fall in love with him.* Clary has been gone all this time, yanked out of her life and dragged down here, what does he want with her? Michael shakes with grief. Used up, wrung out, without even a quarter inch of himself left to draw on, he finds himself bound hand and foot by questions. Therefore he stands at a slight remove.

Clary smiles at him over the others' heads. She sees his distress, but because they are so much alike she holds back too, respecting his dignity.

His voice shakes. "Mom?" He would like to sound manly, in control, but he does not. Dad left him in charge, and now look. "Mom!"

"Hey, Mike!" she says over Teah's head. Kissing Tommy, she gently disengages him so she can stand.

"It looks like we didn't take too good care of you."

"Oh Michael, it's OK!"

His feet come unglued from the floor. "Mom!"

"Come on, Toms," Teah says gently because in the lexicon of love and rivalry, she knows it is Michael's turn. "Climb on and I'll carry you."

When Clary stands she lurches slightly and then recovers herself. "I'm so glad it's you."

He knows better than to help her. Overwhelmed, he falls back on the dumb things people say to each other at times like this, when there are no words to measure up. "Oh Mom, we missed you."

"Oh Michael, I'm so happy you came."

They raise their arms and advance at the same time; when they collide they hug as if it's been years, no, centuries, but just before Clary and her son connect — she's so *skinny* — she says, "Oh guys, you." Emotion beggars her; she finishes, "Guys!"

When they cling, he understands how weak she is. "Are you OK?"

"I wasn't, but I am." She moves back a step so she can see him. "I love you guys so *much.*"

Restless Teah is prowling the room, opening the microwave, flushing the little toilet, and every object she touches prompts a thousand questions that begin buzzing in the room like oversized mosquitoes, troubling all of them.

"This room. All this." He's choking on it. "Mom, what *happened?*"

She just gives him a beautiful smile and says simply, "Our lives got hit by a train."

There is a little pause in which he stands with his face wide open, waiting for more. Then Clary looks directly into him and lets him look directly into her as she says so clearly that there are no more questions and none needed, "The engineer is crazy."

Rage is compounded by memory and self-blame, heavy freight barreling down on him like a runaway eighteen-wheeler. "Marshall."

"No. Morrow." That smile does not waver. "He has a lot of names."

"Oh, Mom. I was so stupid. I . . ." *I'm going to kill him.* If they don't start moving she is going to catch him crying after all. Michael retreats into the Dad role, saying, "Can you walk OK?"

She nods. "I think so."

"We've got the car."

"Don't you think we ought to talk to the police?" She is studying him. "They're here, aren't they?"

Michael ducks so she can't see his face.

Her voice drops. "Didn't they bring you?"

He shakes his head. "I think we'd better get out of here."

She hits a stern Mom tone. "But they *are* coming."

He won't answer. "Come on, Mom."

"You mean the police aren't . . ."

"It's just us," he says shakily.

"Oh, dear God."

"But we have the car."

For the first time his mother looks frightened but she keeps her voice level, taking his elbow, moving Teah and Tommy too. Intent now, wired and rushed, Clary says in that even tone she uses only when things are at their worst, "Then we'd better hurry."

Fools, idiots he supposes, they form up and go out through the front door with Michael supporting Clary. Instead of sneaking they take the direct route, heading for the car as if it's an ordinary day and they are really going somewhere.

Until they see what's happened to the car.

Even from the front porch Michael can see the car is useless. The hood is up. Wires, hoses, pipes stand out in all directions like the guts of a farm animal eviscerated by a tiger. Disassembling the motor, he was quiet and skillful and the destruction is disproportionately vicious and thorough. Behind their car is a shiny new Tempo with a rental sticker on the bumper and next to it the muscular little girl-woman who gave them the key to their mother's prison stands, regarding the Hales with such an agonized look that they don't even have to ask.

Clary says, "Beetie?"

Misery has altered her expression so her mouth wobbles and her eyes are red smears in her face. She barely squeezes out the next words. "I tried."

He comes out of the garage. Something is different. He has an almost imperceptible limp — the barn, that scream, what did he fall on — but there is more; he comes out of the garage with a strangely altered smile.

The liar they thought they trusted is transformed.

He advances, regarding them with a bright, cloudless glare. A shotgun rests on one arm as carelessly as if it has grown there. He is supremely graceful, comfortable in his skin. After a thing like this, Michael thinks, you should be monstrous; after a thing like this you should contort with guilt and shrivel and turn hideous colors, but there he is with a soft Gulf breeze lifting the silver-blond hair and the pale eyes picking up the color of the water, with a look of chilling serenity on the lean, tanned face, Cleve or the Commander or Marshall, whom they trusted. No. Morrow. Those creepy old folks! Son of a bitch, they put him on to us. Morrow, not at all angry at this escape attempt, just cool about it and as magazine-ad handsome as ever. "Well, Clarada."

His mother's voice is dark. "We're leaving now."

"Not yet."

"You can't keep us," Clary says.

"Wait. I have to show you something."

Puzzled, Beetie looks around.

His mother is determined; she has her shoulders braced but Michael can feel her trembling.

Her captor lifts his head. "Something special, that will show you the way. Come and you'll see how much I love you."

Michael mutters foolishly, "It's OK Mom, we'll protect you."

"No." She is swift, urgent. "Stay behind me," she says in a low voice. "It's worse than you think."

Michael mutters, "I know."

"In there," Morrow says. "Let me show you." He gestures toward the garage. Beetie turns as if to look inside but he jerks her back, fixing Clary with his eyes. "I want you to see."

"Guys, stay behind me." She says, louder, "Stand back, Cleve, we're leaving. We've called the police. They're coming."

"If you'd tried the phone, you'd know nobody is coming." He is standing in the clear now, still easy with this and completely comfortable, taking his time with her, with them. The gun sways idly, smoothly, aimed nowhere in particular but definitely connected. "Come on. I want you to see. This is only a first passage, I need to perfect the method, but you'll see."

"Let me go, Cleve."

With the shotgun still cradled, he spreads his hands. "It will explain everything."

Michael gasps. There is blood on the cuffs of the starched white shirt and there is blood in a delicate arc on one of his thighs.

"She was scarred, so it isn't perfect, but it's a start."

Clary cries, "Beetie!"

"Here, Clarada. In the garage."

Next to the car, Beetie stands paralyzed. Her expression makes it clear that she doesn't know what he has in the garage.

Clary does. She is rigid, clenched. Everything in her shrinks as he advances with his left hand extended. "I'm not leaving the children, Cleve."

"I never wanted the children." He lies. "If you want me to, I'll let them go right now. Just stand away."

She charges him: "You think you can do anything you want."

"If you love me, I can."

"I can never love you." Clary's voice shakes with hatred.

"Not yet, but you will in time. They all love me in time." He gestures toward the garage. "She did. Whoever she was. It's one of the essentials."

"Then why me?"

"You know why. *You have her face.*" He raises the gun. "I knew as soon as I saw you. You're the key to everything."

Every part of Michael clenches as he gauges: their relative sizes, his, the craggy enemy's, no, he is really calculating distances — between them and the gun, them and the boat; it's not that far but he knows how quickly the destroyer's hand will follow his eye if they make a run for it. Only Beetie stands beyond his glare.

"Together we will own the world."

Michael wills Beetie: *Do something.* But Beetie is paralyzed.

"The garage. I want you to see what's inside."

"You can't show me anything."

"You don't understand." His smile is bright enough to sear. "I can show you your place in the tree!"

Clary's hands fly up like stars. Grief rips the words right out of her. "Oh my God!"

"I want you to see how beautiful it is. Now. In the garage."

Clary groans. "At least let my children go."

"Not until I have you for certain." His voice is still light, his face shines, but as they watch a shadow rushes across it like a winter cloud. "We have to complete this. The last time — we came so *close* . . ."

Beetie: "The *last time!*"

Clary says bitterly, "We were never close."

". . . but you have to want it," he finishes, so fixed on his quarry that he doesn't notice as Beetie starts to move.

By this time Clary is shaking so hard that Michael's afraid the vibration will rip her bones out of their sockets and her skeleton will disassemble; in a minute all that glue or whatever it is that holds his mother together will let go and she'll fall in a clatter. But ashen and determined, she defies her kidnapper, her captor. "Then you might as well go ahead and blow a hole in me."

It's as if she hasn't even spoken. "Not fire," he says wildly. "Fusion. Forever. Come with me and you'll see." He advances, not so fast as to make them bolt, but a half step, just enough to let Clary and her children know that once he starts coming, he will roll right over them: Teah clutching Tommy, who is clutching his stuffed Taz, Michael, who wishes he could whirl like a Tasmanian devil and bore into the man like a power drill, destroying him. Morrow is murmuring again, spinning another spell in that practiced verbal wizardry that Michael knows now for what it is. His voice is vibrant as he says, "I just want you to see what's inside me, Clarada. Just come, I have it all prepared. When you see what's inside me you'll see where you belong, Clarada. Understand that together we will be one in love, Clarada," going on in a hypnotic monotone, "together we will be love," he goes on and on, so caught up in the music of the spell he is creating that he is not aware that behind him, Beetie's brought the gun out of her jacket pocket.

Michael: *Shoot, Beetie.*

Then Clary says, "You are nothing to me."

The look he gives her then almost levels them. He drops the words one by one into the hush that follows. "I am your future."

Teah moans.

Beetie, Michael thinks. *Shoot!*

But his voice has woven its spell there too; the girl has raised the gun in both hands like a TV cop but her resolution is diffused by remembered love and fresh pain. The barrel wobbles as she stands there wavering.

Now Morrow has his left hand at the neck of his white shirt. "It's all here, my love. Come here and I'll show you. Beautiful, perfect. Except for you. My only love. Come and take your place in it."

Because he will not release Clary's eyes even for a moment, Cleve won't see the volley of changes rattling across Beetie's stubby little features or see her shift her grip on the pistol in an agony of indecision, trying desperately to steady the barrel, which she has more or less aimed at the back of his head.

"No," he says suddenly. A shadow crosses his face and the hand drops from the buttons at his throat. He advances on Clary.

Clary cries, "No."

"It's too soon for you to see. First, you have to come into the garage with me."

She says quietly, "No."

"My only love."

Michael grips his mother's arm. Teah and Tommy move in even closer. Nobody is breathing. The air stops moving. Time stops. Everything stops except his voice. They are all in danger. Still as Beetie's face twists and her arms waver and Clary stands transfixed and shivering with revulsion, the handsome, graceful killer advances.

The silence cracks open. "Son of a bitch!"

They whirl as Beetie pulls the trigger, missing her lover's vital spots either accidentally or on purpose but blowing a nick out of his upper arm; Michael can see blood fly. The jolt makes Morrow pull the trigger reflexively and the shotgun goes off, spraying the air. The kick throws their captor off balance for no more than a couple of seconds, during which Clary and her children start moving out of the frame and away, sprinting for the boat. Before Morrow can right himself, Beetie hooks him under both arms from behind, and because he's been thrown off center manages to wrestle her lover, the liar, her adversary and onetime love in a half turn away from the water so that Morrow won't see the Hales spilling into the boat and working away at the motor.

Staggering to his feet, he whirls, with all his words blurring together in a guttural growl. Like an avenging spirit Beetie clings, hanging on as the still-handsome, bleeding murderer bangs her against trees, trying to scrape her off and then lurches and bucks, intent on throwing her. Snarling, she sticks to his back like a spiny sea creature until he breaks free finally and twirls Beetie around so they are facing, locked in a short, nasty struggle filled with blood and spit and violence that goes on just long enough for the Hales to get the boat started, Cleve Morrow and the heartbroken Beetie shouting and tearing at each other in such a tangle of rage and betrayal that they may not even hear the motor catch and turn over; they are still grappling as desperate Michael gets it started and Clary heads the boat out of the channel; the Hales hear another shot as they make a hairpin zigzag from that channel and into another, blindly broaching the labyrinthine network that stands between them and open water.

26

ALL HIS THINKING LIFE Michael has used the camera to deal with reality when it gets too big for him to handle directly. Now all the careful strategies he has constructed to protect himself dissolve and he is brought up against it: the profusion of nature.

This is not a movie. This is huge.

The shore is overgrown with plants he has never seen before, the air crosshatched with birds he cannot name. Snowy egrets he knows, his mother paints them, but the rest — common terns and oystercatchers and great flying sickle shapes that will have to land before he can identify them as pelicans; cormorants, skimmers, at least a dozen others — light and take off from the mangroves and scrub palms behind them and the sandbars ahead in such variety that it's a relief to spot a pair of gulls. Compared to the subtle, civilized blue-gray skies at home, the three-hundred-and-sixty-five-degree expanse here is beautiful and monstrous. Huge, crazy cloud formations go crashing across the horizon. To his right, a distant storm sends lightning cracking into the Gulf yet to his left the sky is brilliant and in front of them the white sun descends serenely, as if nothing else is happening; it is too much.

And they are alone here.

At home he is protected by the continuity of house, car, New England streets, the geometry of the malls, people who know him. At home he is another Navy junior, *poor kid his father* . . . never mind, he's handling it, but out here in this small boat, under terrifyingly beautiful coastal skies, he is nobody.

And for all he knows, their kidnapper is about to catch up with them.

With Clary in the stern beside him, Michael has followed his mother's instructions and nosed the boat straight out, into the Gulf of Mexico. In the bow, Teah's chin bobs on top of Tommy's round little skull. Michael's sister is hunched and stiff with anxiety, digging in with her chin until Tommy yips because she's trying hard to keep her whole head from trembling. For a few minutes they skim along, but then their speed seems to diminish. Michael can't tell if it's a trick the skyline is playing on them or whether the motor is failing.

"Mom." The wind takes his voice. He can almost see it trailing out behind him like the sleeves of his mother's white dress.

But she hears. Freed after this long, hard time in that tiny dark prison, stretching and blinking in the unaccustomed light, Clary shades her eyes and scans the shoreline, trying to get her bearings. She studies the sky — all those years sailing with Dad; she seems to know. "This is far enough out. Now head south."

"Mom, I think there's something the matter with the motor."

Fixed on something Michael can't see, she says urgently, "We have to keep going."

"I think there's a problem with the . . ."

She cuts him off. "Not yet! He could be following."

". . . motor." He twists to look behind. "I don't see anything."

Impatient, she chops the air with the blade of her hand. "You're not necessarily going to know."

He doesn't mean to sound plaintive, but he does. "We can't just keep going."

"We have to." Haunted, terrorized, she grips his wrist. "You don't know him."

In places the shore looks completely wild, in others, populated, but driven as he is, panting and threatened, fleeing Tarpon Springs without a map, Michael isn't clear about their choices. All he knows is that they are heading south as fast as the stuttering motor will take them. At this distance the notched shoreline is too complex to read. Behind them is a receding morass of mazelike inlets like the one they just escaped from.

Farther north, Anclote Key leads back into Tarpon Springs, where for all they know, Cleve Morrow is already down at the local docks telling lies about them. Is the killer setting out in a borrowed boat? Or is he tracking them by car, speeding along unseen roads that parallel the water? Terrified and running flat out, Michael sees their pursuer crouched behind every mangrove, hidden in the undergrowth at the head of every dock they pass.

As they head south, the changing shoreline gives way to a deserted beach, tin-roofed beach shelters visible from here: the sign.

"Honeymoon Island," Clary reads; her face is all eyes and teeth. Is this where she wants to go ashore? But her whole body is angled forward in the boat, urging it along toward some point Michael cannot see; she is fixed on it, so intent he is afraid to ask her. They are paralleling the beach now; the day is on the wane, and Michael sees the last stragglers leaving with umbrellas and coolers. Reefs and sandbars lie between them and the shore. There's no place to dock. If they turn inland here they will have to slip over the side and swim in until it's shallow enough for them to wade, three people and a little kid, like sitting targets for Cleve Morrow, who is from around here and who knows these waters. Who probably has friends here. He could be anywhere. If they find help, who's going to believe them anyway?

They are up against the prince of lies.

He can make anybody fall in love with him.

They need time to plan.

South of the island beach, Michael sees another strand of beaches — another island. Beyond, the land curves slightly, and in the middle distance he sees a vision of civilization. Rooted there in the haze of encroaching twilight like a mirage are high rises stacked like Domino sugar boxes in the middle of all this nature; Michael thinks: crazy. A town. It is in plain sight but as remote as the moon.

He grips the tiller and studies his mother. Clary is steadier than she was when they first broke out: drugs wearing off, he supposes, because he understands now that the only way Morrow could have taken her away was by doping her. Her eyes are clear now, but the days alone in that dark sealed room have changed her. She's Mom, she's OK, but she is not yet acclimated to all this light. All she wants to do now is outrun what happened to her, but the boat is running light, riding too high in the water; they're almost out of fuel. Michael has to broach it, does not know how. He roots in his pocket and hands Clary half the Mounds bar, which she unwraps with a grin and eats, watching his face. In the bow Tommy sees and before he can start fussing Michael throws the other half to his baby brother.

He waits until she finishes and then tries again. "Mom, we have to land somewhere."

"Not yet," Clary says. Putting her hands over his, she changes their course slightly, sighting by the high rises ranked like travelers' beacons, steady but unreachable. He moves aside and she takes the tiller. She is fixed on the remote city.

"Listen." It isn't only the fuel supply. He's trying to tell her something there's no way of explaining. "We're running out of everything."

"We have to be careful," Clary shouts, over the sound of the motor. Urgency blurs her voice. "He could be anywhere."

Pushed to the limit, he wheels: "Cut it out, Mom. You don't know everything!"

This sobers her. "Maybe not." Clary throttles down so her voice will reach the bow, where Teah is brooding. "Teah, what do you think we should do?"

In the bow his sister turns, left out of the deliberations: *you take care of Tommy,* shouting "What do you care what I think?" but as she does so, reflected light flashes off the thing hanging at her throat. Clary makes a sound Michael does not recognize.

They are barely moving; Michael is squirming with impatience. They're all equally anxious to get away, but in the middle of all this peril and haste, everything just. Stops.

"Cecelia!" Clary's voice is sharp. "Where did you get that?"

This is so sudden and the use of the proper name so grave that Teah starts. "What?"

Michael is looking from one to the other; they're using gas but getting nowhere; should he yell at Clary to get her going again? Should he push her hands off the tiller? But something is going on here that he doesn't know about. Clary hands him the tiller and advances to the middle seat so she can talk directly to his sister; twinned heads bend close and he sees that his sister has grown into his mother's outlines — clear features, dark hair, military carriage — and that his mother is fixed on something, riveted by questions he can't even identify. "That," Clary says.

His sister's voice is deeper than he remembered. "Mother?"

Clary touches the thing sparkling at Teah's throat. "The crystal. Did he give that to you?"

His mother's tone, the remembered flash of twinned arms, his sister's body echoing the monster's; in the strange hush that surrounds the two — yes, *women* — he understands that whatever it is that's going on between mother and daughter here in the boat as he watches is as important to his mother as anything else that's happening to them.

"Oh, this. No." Teah touches the crystal at her neck. "The old lady did."

"Then he never . . ." Clary's voice drops. "Are you sure he didn't . . ."

"Oh, Mother. No." Teah's face changes. She reaches out for her mother's hand, squeezing hard. "He didn't anything."

Clary says, "If he had, I couldn't stand it."

"I couldn't stand it either," Teah says. She and Clary exchange a look Michael can't read as his sister responds to information that has delivered itself to her whole. *We women* . . . Yanking at the crystal, she snaps the chain and tears it off with a murderous look. "I'd like to kill him."

Clary says, "So would I."

"Oh God, Mom, I'm so sorry."

"It wasn't your fault, Teah." Clary lifts her head. "I suppose it was mine."

Teah's lips curl back over her teeth. "It's his fault," she says with force. She throws the crystal over the side. Light flares off it as it turns over once and drops to the bottom. Then Teah turns to her brother as though none of this has been discussed.

But her face is altered by whatever has just passed between the two women, familiar Teah, suddenly grim. "Mike, Mom's right. We can't stop for anything."

Clary takes Michael's hand for a moment. "Please. We have to try and make it."

He shrugs and goes ahead full throttle.

For a while it looks as though they are in fact going to make it. The high rises seem closer. They are skimming along just offshore. The motor misses every once in a while but they're still going, everybody leaning forward as if they can honestly cheat the wind and keep the boat moving until they're there, fine, OK, OK fine, all they have to do is get past these two little islands and the next big one and . . .

"Oh shit," Michael says.

The motor sputters.

Clary murmurs, "Come on, come *on.*"

It's almost over.

They are paralleling the smaller of the two islands, gliding on fumes: come on baby, come on, come on.

Clary calls to Teah in an even tone. "Teah, that life jacket? Will you put it on Tommy?"

Tommy hasn't learned to swim; squirming to look past Teah and back at his mother, he's frightened. "Mommy, what's the matter?"

"I just want you nice and snug in case we have to get wet, baby," she says calmly. "Teah, you be sure and buckle Taz in too."

"Right, Mom." They all know what's happening.

"Mommy . . ."

"Honey, we can't stay with the boat after it stops working."

"Mommy I don't want to get wet."

"Shh honey, don't worry, I'll take care of you."

The motor sputters and quits not far from the little island; the shore presents what looks like a solid mass of roots and glossy leaves — thick, shiny-looking mangroves dropping tendrils that meet things that look like spiky upside-down roots reaching up out of the muddy sand, or is it sandy mud, sharp instruments waiting to stab intruders. The clutter of jagged roots and shoots is interwoven so thickly that it's hard to see whether the plants are really clinging to dirt, that people can walk on, or whether this is only a closely knit island of floating vegetation. Poling with the oar, Michael brings them closer. Now he sees the glossy leaves shade a sandy mud base. If they can break into the solid front of interlocking plants, they can probably cross the little island.

Except for the birds that start and fly up in clumps as they approach, the place is completely still. The mud is crosshatched with what look like fleeing grains of sand — thousands of fiddler crabs washing back and forth over the mud in restless little waves. There are egrets here, sandpipers and crows and over there, a heron. An osprey regards them from a low branch and as they approach, takes off. The mangroves are forbidding. Michael thinks if they go ashore here, maybe they can just camp on this scrap of sand and hope some boater will come along before it gets too dark for anybody to see them. Maybe somebody will rescue them before the tide comes in and takes the ground right out from under them.

"It doesn't look so good," Teah says.

Clary says, "We're going to have to deal with it."

Michael is angry. "Why doesn't this asshole boat have a radio?"

"We still couldn't explain where we are," Teah says.

"Mom, what are we going to do?"

"We're going to have to go ashore," Clary says finally.

Tommy whines, "I don't want to go anywhere. I'm hungry."

Michael is wary. "We have to be careful."

But Clary's kicked off her shoes and stuck them under the heavy cotton lace that bands the neck of the dress. She already has one foot over the edge. "If we stay with the boat, he's going to find us. Teah, when I get steady, hand over Tommy."

"Mom, stop!"

But with a splash she is in the water. As it turns out, she is standing on the bottom. The water hits her at chin level. "See if there's anything in there we can use."

There isn't much. They find a boning knife in a rusty tackle box. With a savage look, Teah elbows Michael out and picks it up. There's nothing left for him but a fire extinguisher which he hefts and then discards because it's unexpectedly light: whatever it was armed with has evaporated to crumbs. Angry at his sister for claiming the monopoly on revenge, for being first and grabbing the knife, Michael stands with his thumbs hooked in his pockets, looking into the empty tackle box.

Tommy is muttering into his mother's neck. With strained cheer, Clary says brightly, "Any food?"

They shake their heads. Then they take off their shoes and slip over the side. Hungry now, tired and shaky, Michael says, "So OK, it's not too great, but at least we're someplace else."

"It's a start," Clary says. For the moment they stay where they are, hugging their knees on the unyielding verge of the mangrove cluster, Clary and her children moored in the sandy mud, looking back at their boat. It bobs, dead in the water.

Everyone is quiet. Sitting like this, looking out at the Gulf, heartsick Michael wishes for his father. The Gulf feeds into the ocean. The ocean is big. Listen, he tells himself desperately, anything is possible. Something could still happen. Couldn't it? He can't bear to think about the answer.

Except for the sound of small things crackling in the mud and a distant hum, the place is silent. Teah murmurs, "It's so pretty here."

The distant hum of . . .

Michael hisses, "Shh."

Approaching hum of . . .

"OK." Abruptly, Clary stands. She's heard it too. "Let's go."

Michael says, "Where do you think we are?"

"Close," she says, parting the mangroves. "And so is he."

If from the moment of their escape a camera eye recorded the Hale family's progress along the coastline; if it could mark the progress of the motorboat and pinpoint the place where they have come ashore, it would also pick up the outline of the land and their current position in the land. The island flows through Gulf waters like a living creature smoothly coursing south, with irregular dots of land like bits of foam trailing behind, separated from the main body by shallow water. The Hales have landed on one of the overgrown dots. On the Gulf side of the island, the smooth beaches curve like a spine, but along the belly of the island beast, the outline is more complex. Notches and grooves and inlets lead into its belly. It is as if the great organism is opening in places to absorb and digest whatever approaches through St. Joseph Sound. If nature is terrifying, this is terrifying; if nature is beautiful, this is beautiful.

Of itself the island is in no way threatening. Except to those who proceed with no way of knowing who or what else may be lurking there.

For there is more going on in the living Florida landscape, that no camera can record.

He already knows where they are.

If only you could see inside me.

It burns.

The tree is electric; current whips through him and he contorts in an ecstasy of pain: This is taking too long.

Almost before his quarry has cleared the inlet, he begins to change. Alerted as his boat buzzes away — Clarada, free! — he struggles to rid himself of the enemy — who is she — somebody clawing at his back. He is whirling in an attempt to shake the snarling little woman who's clinging like an angry crab, who is she, not important, just something he's used. And is trying to throw away.

That should be her lying dead in the garage. But the useless creature clings. He can't shake her and he can't scrape her off. Outraged, he rises up like a statue of the Creator parting the waters and then in an acrobatic stroke flattens the girl by throwing his arms above his head and hurling himself flat on his back. He drops like a tree on top of the furious Beetie, squashing her flat. As he falls she lets go and the gun discharges as it spins away, leaving a profound silence in his ears. All he can hear now is the electric hum of the tree that empowers and compels him; that is close to completion now and will not let him rest until the transformation is made. He has to go.

This is taking too long.

"Cleve."

The stupid girl: has she spoken? He rolls over and considers her. Tears stand in her eyes and she is gasping, entreating him to do — what? Beat her for getting in his way? Reproach her? Kill her? Carve the tree in her body and watch her die? There isn't time. She doesn't signify. Whoever she was, she's nothing to him now. He gets up.

The girl on the ground is writhing; her whole body contorts. But she is nothing: a tool that has stopped working, no more. Stepping over her, ignoring the bloody nick in his arm, the pursuing lover, or is it avenger, gets into the rented car. Behind him Beetie claws her way to her knees. If he looked back, he would see her getting up but he's too far away to hear what she's shouting as she stands back there in the road behind him, shaking her fist. He is fixed on the road like a homing missile drawn to his quarry, an engine of destruction intent on completing itself.

Beetie's head droops and she watches him go with her fists clenched. Troubled, she turns as if to go into the garage and at the last minute shakes her head. She isn't strong enough to face what he's left inside the tin garage. Not yet. Instead she limps toward the house and carefully lowers herself onto the bottom step. Counting her injuries, she begins to brood. She will still be sitting there when the old man rolls into the clearing in the vintage car with the sleeping woman in the back. She is gathering herself for what comes next.

In the harbor in Anclote Key, the hunter pulls up next to the docks and in short order he has a boat; do not ask what he had to do to the owner to get a boat. There's no time for transactions now. He doesn't even have time to lie. He chooses according to weight and class and speed. Although the boat Clarada fled him in is slow, they have an appreciable lead. But he knows these waters. He will close the distance between them before they even know he is following; he will follow them to the death.

He has his imperatives. First he must kill the boy. Then he will make the tree in the belly of the girl so he can show Clary. When she sees it she will understand and then he will show her the prototype; dazzled, she will understand how much he loves her. Of course they will make love. Then he will take the knife he carries hooked inside his belt so it presses into the bare flesh of his flank, and he will begin. It will be complete.

This is taking too long.

The tree twists inside him like a living thing; frustration fuels it and burning branches whip him on.

This is taking too long.

He shouts to no one, "Soon!"

Shooting into the open water, he does not have to consider which way to turn. He knows.

He gives himself to pursuit. He whips along scanning the coastline and soon enough he spots the boat: Yes! Abandoned there. Which means they must be: Yes. Exactly where he thought.

All the urgency ebbs out of him. The flames recede. They are his. In time, he thinks. In time.

They expect him to approach from the water. Fine. Everything drains away except an enormous sense of leisure; it is so simple. He knows exactly what their choices are. If they came ashore here, they will come out of the mangroves — down there. And he will approach them from: yes. In time. He has nothing but time. Lazily he cuts into the channel that separates the islands here and noses his sleek boat into the sound. As the last ferry of the day clears the island and heads for the mainland he makes a sharp turn into the channel that penetrates the belly of the island and leads to the dock. Except for one or two living inconveniences — obstacles easily disposed of — the place is his.

The narrow strip they're on is barely wide enough for them to creep along it. In some sections the sand has succumbed to the mangroves and leached away so they have to wade. In others they seem to be going along well until they come to a place where there's no sand at all and the bottom drops off unexpectedly, yielding to a deep channel; there is no margin here. They are caught between the mangroves and open water. They have no choice but to fight their way through the thickly linked branches of the plants. Teah goes first because she has the knife, and making sure Tommy has hold of the tail of her dress, Clary follows. Empty-handed, Michael hesitates, thinking angrily that if he'd gotten the knife before Teah found it, he would be first. If they run into Morrow what does Michael have, really, that he can bring to the accounting? Who in hell is he, anyway? He casts around for something to gouge, strike, claw his way with, even if it's only a broken shell. He can hear his mother and sister crunching ahead. The idea of being separated from them in this hideously beautiful place is so much worse than plunging in unarmed that he launches himself. They are surrounded by plants here, covered and embraced and threatened from below, where things growing up from the mangrove roots stab and snag them, and in a slippery, miserable struggle over slimy mud, they begin to make their way through the almost impenetrable wall the interlocked plants have woven between them and wherever they think they are going.

Where are they going?

He doesn't know.

Thinking about it later, trying to reorganize what's happened to them so he can look at it directly and then maybe begin to put it away, Michael will realize that some things are so horrible while they're going on that you can't afford to think about them — the heat once they get away from the water; mosquitoes, nameless insects slithering out from under their fingers, the roots and tendrils and treacherous shoots tearing at them as they go along in a crouch in some places, on their knees in others and in others, facedown in the mud, wriggling through tight places on their bellies. They emerge to discover that they are nowhere; to get anywhere at all they have to wade to the next piece of land and force themselves to plunge back into the mangroves. They are driven, grunting with pain and anger at the insult, but nobody, not even Tommy, little, sturdy, *the skipper's kid,* nobody speaks and nobody cries. Tough as Tommy seems, Michael sees he is about to crumble, and scoops him up.

Then unexpectedly the mangroves thin out to almost nothing and they can stand upright, threading their way between bushes and palmettos under overhanging trees in changing terrain in a place so wild and apparently deserted that they might as well be nowhere. Emerging from the mangroves into waning sunlight, they hurry along without regard for what they are coming out of — or walking into. The bushes give way to long grass. Teah shouts and, running to catch up, the others stumble upon something completely unexpected, a framework of bleached wood running along over dunes at waist height — astonishing in this wilderness.

It is a boardwalk. Civilization.

It is like walking into a jungle clearing to find cars pulled up outside a K mart.

Spent, Clary gasps. "We're here."

Teah laughs. "Wherever this is."

"Somewhere," she says, lifting Tommy and setting him on the boardwalk. "Somewhere civilized."

"There," Michael says. The sign on the far side of the boardwalk reads:

STATE BEACH
CALADESI ISLAND

"State beach." His mother grins like a kid walking into a party — almost herself again after this long, hard time. "That means there are going to be state cops."

"All we have to do is find them," Michael says.

Exhausted, Clary considers. "They probably have regular patrols. We'll let them find us."

"All *right*." He is on the verge of feeling better. Then he sees his mother's face. "Is there a problem?"

She's looking around uneasily; what's the matter, does she think he's going to sneak up on them? "I just think we ought to stay out in the open."

When they turn, daylight is fading and the beachscape has turned black: sea oats, sea grapes and sandspur plants march in a silhouetted ridge on the low dune between them and the vivid evening sky. Their mother scrambles up on the boardwalk and leads them across the last dune to the open sand. They are too far gone to run; instead they walk in silence, heading for the light.

The rim of the sun is standing at the end of the walk like a white-hot doorway into heaven. In a few yards the boardwalk spills them out on a strand so pale and beautiful that Michael sees the words flashing behind his lids: HAPPY ENDING. Roll the end credits. We're going home as soon as they bring up the houselights and the ushers come in to sweep the place. He does not know how long their progress to this point has taken, only that now that they're out in the open with nothing standing between them and the water, the sun is just about to set. They belly flop into the soft warm ripples, and when most of the mangrove ick has washed away in the gentle tide they pull themselves out and sit in a little cluster on the beach to wait. The sun drops into the Gulf in an orange smear and then disappears altogether.

On both sides the afterflow is brilliant — silvery on one side, rose and mauve on the other, the sky going to a dusky blue as they watch and in the next minute — thump, it is night.

Nobody comes.

They sit for a long time without speaking while Tommy drowses. After a while Clary says, "I thought there would be a beach patrol."

Teah sighs. "I guess the island is closed for the night."

"It's OK," Clary says and Michael is disturbed to realize that his mother's voice is getting thin. "When they open up tomorrow, the rangers will find us. All we have to do is . . ." She clears her throat and begins again. "All we have to do is hang in here."

Then before they can identify or assimilate the sound, they see a pair of headlights bouncing down the beach from a distance. It's a state truck on balloon wheels, and as it gets closer and separates itself from the surrounding shadows Michael is glad it's too dark for his mother and sister to see that his eyes have just stupidly filled up; shit yes he is crying: relief, he guesses, or too much no food or where is his dad now that they all need him or whatever. It is the park patrol.

Teah says: "The rangers."

They wave. The driver toots. Clary murmurs, "Thank God."

The truck approaches. Pulling Tommy along, the three of them get to their feet and prepare to meet it, relieved and joyful because they are almost at the end now, then can just take everything — pain, loss, fear, hunger — and hand it over to the rangers. There are two of them. They can see the driver's Smokey the Bear hat, the best sign they've seen since they left home; another head bobs on the passenger's side. Michael's heart lifts. *Oh, wow!*

The driver is in such a hurry to help them that even before the truck comes to a halt he opens the door so he can jump out as soon as it stops. The light in the cab goes on. Michael's mind is already running ahead to the brightly lighted rangers' headquarters where they will tell their story, the gun the state police will strap on him when the posse or SWAT team or whatever starts out after his mother's kidnapper because Michael is the man here. He alone knows the bastard's habits, he alone can lead the chase.

Except that the ranger slouched in the passenger's seat doesn't move. He slumps with his bare head lolling against the side window and the neck tilted at a bad angle; the head bumps cruelly as the truck pulls to a stop and the lolling ranger does nothing to recover. His only movement is the movement of the truck, in fact he seems so careless of what is happening to him that he might as well be — lord, he might as well be dead, and the other — God, there is something about the way the stolen hat sits on that handsome head, the familiar grace with which the driver opens the truck door and the assurance with which he leaps down that makes it clear that this was never a ranger. It is somebody they know. The real park ranger, crudely propped on the seat like a badly made decoy, is dead.

27

ISLAND, MICHAEL THINKS. Oh shit. Nobody comes and nobody goes.

There is not much moon.

They are lying under the boardwalk in some unidentifiable part of Caladesi Island, clinging as they listen to the sometimes close, sometimes distant *thock* of Cleve Morrow's heels on the wooden walkway that runs in several directions on the island.

Before he even got out of the truck they fled him. As he strode toward them, calling, "I'm here to help," they fled, running for the boardwalk that led into the heart of the island. They heard his voice raised, thick with menace, their pursuer making wild promises as they thudded along the wooden walk. Then as the boardwalk framework shuddered under his first footfall they slipped under the rail into the weed-laced sand and rolled underneath. Like God, their unholy pursuer seemed to see what they were doing. They heard the footsteps of Cleve Marshall, no, Morrow: Cleve Morrow, lover and arsonist and murderer — more, that they were afraid to guess at — thundering directly over them in the first movement of a dangerous dance that would occupy the rest of the night.

Near and far they could hear him shouting:

"It's all right, I won't hurt you."

He put the next words into the silence carefully, one at a time. "Understand, I love you. I love you all. I'm here to help."

His voice probed the darkness like a medical instrument, delicate and sure. "I love you. Let me show you how much."

Then after too long had passed they heard him say in a light voice, "Understand, I'm not going to beg," and after that his tone shifted completely. "Don't make me look for you."

The voice came out of a hush, so still that it struck them cold. "When I find you it will be even worse."

Clary Hale and her children wriggled together like threatened animals and dug into the sand without regard for the debris left behind by workmen or the sandspurs that bit into their bodies through their clothes or the passage of insects they could feel but not see. Angry because he was unarmed and therefore completely helpless, Michael rolled away from the others. With his face pressed into the sand, he lay on his belly fanning the perimeter with his fingers, reaching — for what? His fingertips brushed empty paint cans, collided with plastic, what was it, a stinking bucket abandoned by workmen, sloshing with traces of leftover — what? Fine, he thought bitterly, I can just bop him to death with the bucket, sure, the plastic wouldn't even make a dent. He wanted to kick, rage, attack the bastard with his fists but knew he couldn't make a sound. Even Tommy was quiet as Morrow's footsteps shook the walk nearby and came to a halt.

If they were trapped here, there was nothing they could do about it but lie quietly in the sand, trying not to breathe and praying their pursuer did not see them and couldn't hear them holding their breath. They knew he was listening intently, waiting for them to betray themselves. Even Tommy had to be still for as long as it took. They had to be quiet even if something found its way out of the sand and crawled over them, whether it was a snake or scorpion or something worse. Some night creature slid through the dry brush nearby and at the sound, Morrow wheeled sharply; they could hear the scrape of his heels. He was directly overhead.

He spoke into the silence that followed. "The longer this goes on, the worse it will be for you."

They heard him pacing in a tight circle. "Don't make me wait.

"I have a gun." This was either true or it was not.

"I have a knife." Of this they were all certain.

They had no way of knowing whether this next was the truth: "I have a light."

Next: "I have food for you. Food and something to drink."

They heard him waiting.

Then they heard him walk away.

Now he has been silent for some time — gone? Waiting? He may have doubled back so furtively that they couldn't hear; he could be crouched nearby, waiting for them to betray themselves. They wait. But the stillness is complete, and they understand that he is truly gone. He isn't here. He's somewhere else altogether. They are relatively safe for some minutes, during which Michael rolls over and knots into a sitting position, examining his options: the useless empty cans, the bucket — bilge in the bottom of it, some oily smell he can't identify, a rich chemical stink.

There is a thud overhead. He freezes. Morrow is back.

The next words drop into the stillness. "I have a light."

This is true. Morrow has been to some other part of the island — to the ranger station? To the truck? — and now he's back; from far down the walk they can see the sand underneath the boards slashed by approaching slices of light. It's only a matter of seconds before he shines it through the slats directly overhead and picks out their huddled shapes.

What will he do? Poke a shotgun through the slits in the boards and fire? They are like fish in a barrel here. In the last minute before the light catches them and they are discovered, they slide out from under the protection of the boards. They have to believe they can do this without his knowing and escape into the dark, but as they emerge they hear a light *schtt!* as he slides off the boardwalk and a thud as their pursuer, their enemy, their nemesis lands in front of them, pinning them with the light.

"So there you are." They can't see him for the glare.

Clary tries to put her children behind her but angry Michael won't be left. He shoulders his way to her side with the goddam bucket; it's all he has.

But their enemy sees only his quarry. He shifts the beam until it is full on Clary; the light glints wildly off the torn white dress and then travels slowly over her scratched and bleeding legs. Abruptly, he fixes it on their mother's face.

Michael watches Clary turn to marble. She says coldly, "You might as well go, Cleve. It's over. Whatever you thought you had with me has been over for twenty years."

"No." His tone matches hers. "Almost over. There's only one thing left to do."

"If you want to kill me, go ahead and get it over with."

"You know that's not what I want." His voice is low, vibrant. "I've waited so long." If he is aware of Michael and Teah he gives no sign. Instead he plays the beam over their mother's hair, her body in the damp, filthy dress and says quietly, "Now step away from them."

She shakes her head.

"I'm not going to hurt them. I only want you."

"Then let them go."

It is as if he doesn't even hear. "I have a gun."

Fury rocks Michael: *I don't care.*

Clary cries, "Please!"

"I need them to keep you," he says. "Give up. Come along."

Michael's teeth clash. *Rather die.*

Sobbing, Clary bunches herself to fight. The light bobs as the destroyer reaches for his gun, and as he does so, the outraged, fumbling, desperate Michael lifts the stupid bucket and just as Morrow raises the gun he lets the bastard have it in the face.

For a second, nothing happens.

It is like watching a death in slow motion.

Michael hangs like a fool in an accidental freeze frame, thinking *God, oh God.* He can hear his mother's breath.

And in the next second Morrow's flashlight drops and begins to roll slowly into a dent in the sand where Michael can pick it up. Now he can see their enemy standing rigid, with his fists boring into his eyes.

The Hales begin to back away slowly, to escape his notice.

He can't see.

His jaws click open in the long breath that stands for an agonized scream, hissing out of him in a wheeze of pain.

Outraged, he shrieks and rushes past them, blundering down to plunge his burning face in the Gulf.

There, Michael tells himself foolishly, but he knows better. In horror movies, he knows by heart that just when you think the monster is dead, it always gets up again. Again. You have to keep killing it. The corpse rising out of the water. The hand reaching upward out of the grave. The bloody, impaled figure pulling out the stake and coming after you. The possibilities almost disassemble him. He will keep it together by telling himself, *This is not a movie;* God how he wishes it was.

Shaken and hopeful, they will misinterpret the hideous scream: "*It burns.*"

Clary whispers, "We'd better go while we can."

He doesn't have the heart to ask her where.

They turn off the telltale flashlight and throw the batteries into the woods. Paralleling the boardwalk for a few minutes, they see that it expands to surround a fair-sized building — a bathhouse. Civilization. To Michael, it is like a fortress. In a place like that, they could hold off armies. "Mom!"

Cautiously, they hoist themselves onto the deck long enough to drink from the water fountain. Michael spooks along until Teah yanks his elbow, murmuring, "Come on, Mike, we can't stay here."

Michael says, "We could dig in."

"This is the worst place."

"You think you know everything." He turns. "Mom?"

But his mother's voice stops him in his tracks: what the women already know. "Wood can burn."

It hits him in the belly — that empty hole where her house used to be — deaths by fire, terrible, more certain than loss at sea. "OK," he says, and discovers that he is built on a fault. The ground under his feet is tearing apart and everything inside him starts shuddering at once. "OK, Mom."

Going to the edge of the walk, Michael drops back into the sand. Shivering, Clary hands Tommy down to Michael and she and Teah follow. He goes along with his brother's warm body clamped to him like a poultice, drawing out the anger, and Tommy's chin digging into his shoulder. Although the child is half-asleep, the stuffed toy dangles from Tommy's hand. Driven beyond exhaustion, they plunge away from the boardwalk without any idea what they are going to find, without a plan except to try and make it through to morning when even though this is not a movie, the park will open for the day and the first boat from the mainland will come in.

There comes a time in the lexicon of exhaustion when you hit the wall. They crumple, more or less, in the first sheltered place they find. They've crawled into the shadow of a wooden utility shed, a silly little structure too low to look like any kind of shelter at all. They are essentially hidden in the middle of this comparatively open space with no surrounding bushes to hide an approaching enemy. If he calls, they will hear him. If he comes along the boardwalk, they will hear the boards give under his weight. A broken stick will alert them. They can be out of here before he zeroes in on the spot. Michael imagines he'll keep watch; Clary promises to watch and so does Teah, but they are strung out to nothing now, and one by one they give out, bushwhacked by sleep.

His voice wakes them.

When they hear him this time, he has slipped into a new tone that invades sleep so stealthily that at first it seems right at home in Michael's dream of Tom Hale on some lost afternoon when the two of them were out in the backyard together, father and son who wants to be just like him, raking dead leaves out of Clary's flower beds. The voice seems so *right* at first, even and friendly like the voices of his father's shipmates, military men. Thank God it's you. Then recognition hurtles him out of sleep and leaves him unshelled and naked, skinless and unprotected in the Florida night.

The thing speaks in an ordinary seaman's voice: "Right, Skipper, I had it set up, but they swerved and spun out on me, and fouled up the works."

The next voice sounds like their father's. "Clary. Kids!"

Clary sits up with a little sob.

It is as if he's speaking in tongues.

"This way, Skipper, if we line up here maybe we can get them to come out."

That other voice again: "Mike, listen. Teah, darling. Toms."

Michael doesn't have to look to see whether the others are awake; Teah grips him on one side and on the other, his mother's fingers and thumb almost meet in the soft part of his arm.

Teah murmurs, "Guys, it's Dad."

Tommy, who has never heard him, stirs, turning a face that opens like a flower. Before he can say: Daddy, Michael covers his mouth.

"Come on out kids, it's your father."

But it isn't. Michael knows. He has known it all the time, has spent all his life until now trying to maintain faith in the illusion, but pressed to the wall by hardship, fresh out of happy endings and beginning to understand there may never be any, he is brought up against it. *Not this time. Or ever. Ever. No.*

"Clarada, it's me."

Oh, Daddy!

Michael can see tears sliding down his mother's face.

"Come on out, your father is here."

Good-bye.

Weeping, Clary shakes her head.

And Michael finds himself crying too, not so much mourning as relinquishing that which he has hung on to for so long. *This is not a movie.* The camera stops rolling for good. *My father is dead.*

In time the concert of voices stops. They wait for a long time. Finally they hear the footsteps of one man moving away. In a matter of minutes they will hear the voices resuming at some distance, Cleve Morrow trying to reinvent their father in some other part of the night.

Although they don't know where on the island Clary's suitor, murderer, patholog, sociopath, is at any particular moment, they know where he isn't right now. Slowly, they get up. The darkness is thinning slightly, threatening to turn into day. The shadow where they've been hiding is going to disappear with the night, leaving them ridiculously exposed. Clary stirs cautiously, stretching and shaking her legs and arms to make sure they're still working. She moves out. "Let's go."

Crouching like troops in some elaborate wartime maneuver,

they parallel the boardwalk now, following it away from the beach in hopes that it will lead them to some point where they can strike out for the mainland, although where they'll get a boat they don't know. They go cautiously, stopping when the angry voice stops, moving again only when they hear it echoing even farther away.

"My darling," they hear once, words filtering through the underbrush, "these are the things you and I will do together," Cleve Morrow's velvety voice coming and going as he paces the boardwalk, circling the bathhouse like a mad sea captain, assailing the night with a catalogue of acts of love strung out in an obscene incantation that rolls out on one long, unbroken breath. It is crazy; the words come faster and faster, full of passion and without sense in a wild recital that impales Clary and makes her squirm. Then he starts on Teah, and Michael sees his sister writhe as if she's been stabbed and back away, lowering her head like a boxer as the stalker tries to lure her with words. ". . . you, Cecelia, come on out soft girl, so beautiful, let it all out, let down, and then you'll let me draw it into you, you will see it in blood on your belly and along your arms and legs, the branches, the twigs, the beautiful leaves . . ." It goes on and on while Michael's nails rip his palms and the inside of his mouth starts to bleed where he has bitten it through. Clary buries Tommy's head in her skirts as if she can keep him from hearing.

And the obscenity trails off into a seductive chant without words, intimations of something they can't make out, and then it dies and everything is silent. They know better than to move.

When he begins again it is in his own voice, bluff and hearty, calculated to make them so angry that it will flush them out: "Well, Tom, Tom Hale! I've been waiting for you. Let me tell you what your wife has been doing with me while you were gone. Let me tell you what I am doing to her, let me do it to her here, where you can see," spewing on and on as if certain that the right note will catch Michael or Teah or Clary in the flank and detonate.

Bowed under the assault, they cluster at a slight remove because their pursuer has not yet located them. It's just as well because by this time Michael is about to shake apart and when he does, he will risk discovery — everything — if he can only hurt the attacker, shove his gun into his mouth and stop that talk. Blood pounds in his head and floods behind his eyes and only his mother's hand on his arm keeps him in line, moving along slowly behind her and the others in agonizing half-inch steps forward.

Thus they advance in stages, pursuer and prey, the mad hunter fanning the island, now on the walk, now in the sand, now silent, now ranting, while Clary and her children creep and then crouch motionless and then move out again in a tortuous progress toward the side of the island closest to the mainland. If they can only get there maybe they can find something, anything, that will give them hope — a place to hide in, somebody to help, a boat to get away in.

As they break out of the bushes they can hear his feet thudding on the walk behind them. They have emerged amid a little cluster of buildings — the rangers' office! Rangers. The rangers will have a radio, a telephone; they will have guns. And food. It's almost over. Michael's mouth floods. On the porch next to the office is the door to the gift shop and lunch counter and at a little distance they can see a wooden ticket booth on the slope leading down to the docks. Spurred by hope, Michael squints into the harbor, trying to pick out boats tied up to the docks but there's nothing there, not even a canoe to slip away in. There is only a blunt lip marking the place where the first ferry of the morning will land in a few hours, and at the head of the dock beyond, the ticket shack.

They are at the end. *All we have to do is hold out,* Michael thinks. *But how?*

"There," Clary says, pointing at the main building. "Maybe we can phone."

"Maybe we can even eat," Teah says.

"I'm hungry."

"Shh, Toms."

But Michael hangs back. "Something's wrong."

Teah: "He's *coming.*"

Clary's voice is low, vibrant. "What's the matter?"

He whispers: "I don't know." He's taut and jittery; as they advance Michael sees two things: the door to the rangers' office standing open and in the doorway litter spreading, shifting papers lifting and sliding in the morning breeze, nothing more than trash lighted by a shaft from the door.

Behind him, Teah whispers, "Hurry!"

But Michael stops the others. "He's been here."

Clary's face changes. "Don't go in."

They don't have to go inside to see. They know what they're going to find. Phone line cut and radio smashed, trail of destruction leading to something even worse. From here they can see the feet of the other park ranger lying askew, legs sprawled so carelessly that they don't have to see the rest of him propped in his chair with his throat slit, gaping at the ceiling. As they back away from the building Teah whispers, "Mom! That smell."

The sky behind them changes abruptly as smoke and boiling light crash through the ceiling of the distant bathhouse, fire struggling up and up, into the receding night.

"Wood can burn," Michael says.

Footsteps crash toward them.

"He's coming!"

"What are we going to do?"

"Hurry," Clary says.

"Where?"

"We have to hide." Pressed, she darts here, there. They can hear him breaching the underbrush, howling; they have to hurry, but they might as well be at the edge of the world; except for the main building there's no place left for them to go. Unless they can make it to the boathouses — way over there! — or plunge into the water before he comes out of the woods and spots them, they have run out of places to hide.

Michael cries, "Where?"

"Anywhere. Fast."

They can hear Morrow roaring down on them like an express train. Desperate, Clary judges distances — boathouses, too far; water, folly! Thus they are driven into the only place.

With Tommy under one arm like a puppy, Clary darts for

the ticket shack; without looking back to see whether the others are following, she dives inside and as Michael and Teah plunge in behind her, shuts the door just as the crashing stops and they hear sharp footsteps begin on the boardwalk as their pursuer clears the woods. The roaring stops.

Everything stops.

It's like a little coffin. Clumped inside, they are aware of several things at once: the heat in this narrow place, mosquitoes and chiggers and sand fleas coming alive with the dawn and gnawing at them, but this is nothing to them. They are dead empty, running on fumes. Maybe Morrow didn't see them. Maybe he's already searched here, maybe he'll think nobody's foolish enough to pick this place. If they can hold out here, maybe mainland police will spot the fire and come for them. Oh shit, Michael thinks, and maybe I can fly. The park rangers are dead and the police onshore are probably still asleep. The island is so remote they may not even see the smoke. The Hales are forgotten here, outsiders in an unfamiliar landscape, and the hell of it is that their pursuer could probably talk even the police into helping him: handsome local man with that unearthly charm. Wife, Officer, gone completely mad, Officer, you know how women are. She's kidnapped the children. Yes, Officer, they're out here.

And nobody left to tell them this is a lie.

Michael's sense of loss and isolation is complete. He has lost his place in the land for good and all.

Then as his muscles begin to knot and he and the others settle on the floor of the booth, stashed like folding chairs put away for the long haul, he tells himself maybe it won't be long until the sun comes up. Soon they will crack the door and if they don't see anybody, they can sneak out. Even if they do see him, they're so close to the dock that they can make a break for it; they'll beat their pursuer down to the end and throw themselves on the first incoming boat.

For a long time they don't hear him and then they do hear him. He is like a mad ventriloquist creating a swarm, a crowd: "Yes Officer, they were last seen somewhere around here."

Another voice: "Terrible thing."

Another and another. It doesn't stop; how many people can he be? The voices go on and on in a concatenation that keeps the family trapped in the ticket booth, rapt and breathless and completely silent, mesmerized. He is a quartet, a quintet, a troop, a regiment, and if during this passage a boat cuts its motor and approaches, sliding into the cove under cover of overhanging mangrove branches, they are too rapt — killer and victims, performer and audience — to mark it; he has filled the dawn with so many voices that none of them, speakers or listeners, will know.

A freshly minted voice assails the shack. It is cold, cruel, direct. It may even be the true voice of the speaker. "You know it's only a matter of time."

Words can't hurt us, Michael tells himself, but he is shaken. Into the bottomless space between hope and what's happening, the next words drop.

They come out of nowhere in that hushed actor's tone that can be heard all the way to the back of the hall. "You might as well come out. I know you're in the ticket shack."

When they don't answer and they don't come out the hunter begins pacing. They hear footsteps sounding as regularly as the parts meshing in some large but intricate machine. Then the pacing stops.

Silence is worse.

All Michael can hear is the unnatural sound of Teah, sliding her molars back and forth, back and forth.

Tommy sniffs.

Michael can feel something crawling on his face.

The world splits open with a crash.

Something shatters the window above their heads and thumps Michael on the shoulder. It is like being shot. When he reaches down and picks it up he realizes that it's a chunk of metal. Armed at last, he grips it so hard his fingers freeze on it.

Outside, Morrow says quietly, "See how easy that is?" He is that close.

They wait.

"Did you really think you could hide from me?"

Clary covers her mouth.

"I want you to come out on your own," he says.

"And if you don't . . .

"I have other means."

They can hear something sloshing; even before their pursuer, captor, lover, murderer opens the gasoline can, Michael catches the smell.

Before he can stop or put himself in front of his mother to protect her, Clary gets up. She's so stiff she can barely stand but her voice is clear. "All right," she says. "I'm coming out."

His tone is disproportionately mild. "I knew you would."

Standing in front of the narrow door, Clary keeps grinding her fists along her flanks, scrubbing with her knuckles as if she can make her skin fit right.

"On your promise that nobody gets hurt."

"I never wanted to hurt anyone."

"Back away," she says. "I won't come out until I see you out in the open."

"Here. You can see me."

"Not there."

"Open the door."

But now that she is forced to capitulate, Clary is hard and sharp as glass. "Not here. I want to see you out there. At the end of the dock. Where you can't reach my children."

"I don't want your children, Clarada."

"Then go."

"I never did."

"Then let me see you go."

"If that's what you want." His voice drops an octave, warning. "You know I have a gun."

They are all standing now; through the broken window, they can see him go, tall and swift, striding along with a raincoat billowing after him like a superhero's cape. At the end of the dock, he turns and waits.

Clary's voice is shaky with foolish bravery. "Guys." She means: *darlings*. "Stay here. Maybe I can talk to him."

"Now," he says. "You can come out now."

Clary straightens her shoulders and lifts her head. "All right."

They follow her to the place where sand and oystershell give way to the wooden dock. But Morrow raises the right hand with the ranger's pistol and levels it at Michael and his sister. They have to stop and pull Tommy to a stop while their mother advances in a progress so agonizing to Michael that he wants to run ahead, throw himself in front of her, lunge at their enemy and take a bullet if he has to, anything to end this; he's enormous with it, about to implode. Next to him Teah is jiggling but they are only kids and this was never a movie and so they stand at the invisible barrier, spitting and simmering with wild plans, watching as their mother closes the distance to meet her enemy at the end of the dock, and if hidden in deep shadows cast by the rising sun a small boat clears the inlet and glides in under protection of the overhanging mangroves, they are too fixed on what's happening to see.

They are watching Clary now, with her back straight and her shoulders back in the stained white cotton wedding dress, walking out to the end of the dock.

With that handsome head raised and his shoulders set, the enemy waits. The only sign that their best efforts have even touched him is the stain around the eyes — traces of the caustic that sent him screaming into the Gulf. While they are drained now, unsteady and frail because they haven't eaten, he looks refreshed. As she draws closer to him, the vicious, weirdly beautiful destroyer spreads his arms as if in surrender. Then in a swift gesture that shatters hope, he rips open the white shirt so violently that the buttons rip loose and he pulls it off and lets it drop.

The voice is strange, reedy. He pulls the confession out of a lifetime of silence. "It burns."

In the next second he has stripped the trousers so quickly that it's as if he hasn't moved. He is beyond speech.

He is naked, brilliant and monstrous.

Clary's voice is so deep Michael hardly knows it; she is staggered by recognition. "Oh God!"

It is the tree.

How many years did it take him to carve this design into his body, and at the cost of how much pain? What could he have been thinking, and is he thinking now or is he only the agent of some dark power that expresses itself on the surface of his living flesh? Twin trunks and body, arms and branches, the tree rises in a series of livid welts from his feet, beginning with fresh marks at the ankles that he must have made in the reaches of the night, bloody new gouges dug so that they join the older scars, those livid ridges that bloom and rise from the groin.

The tree swarms over the body of their pursuer, captor, murderer, gorgeous monster, and spreading along his arms it creeps up his throat in a vivid mantle of disfigurement, branches and twigs and growing leaves carved into living flesh and rubbed into raised scars that are both splendid and terrible, sign and emblem of where he has come from and what he intends, for blazing white in the belly is a heart-stopping vacancy: the place in his body where the carved design stops.

Clary stops cold as he raises his arms as if to cup her head in his hands and pull her into him.

"I — will — put — you — here."

The tree is in his body. His body is the tree.

Marked with the tree, the visible map or design of his intentions, he is almost complete now. He has become what he is.

Almost as an afterthought, he picks up the gun.

Clary shudders.

Because the people she loves best, her allies, are only children and she must protect them, she is one woman alone here. She has to do this by herself. Trembling, she touches her children in what may be a farewell and leaves them behind, moving out to confront her enemy. She will meet him at the end of the dock. Pushed beyond endurance, she is still on her feet here, able to keep on going because she has managed it so far, which means she must be tougher than she thought. She is tougher than anybody knows, she feels it, tough enough to get up the next morning and smile at her children and begin what she knows will be the rest of her life without her husband, goes on even though she has lost the one man who is everything to her. She has managed to face the loss and keep going without Tom and without any hope of Tom, which means that she is not about to crumble now and no matter how much she fears him, she is not about to capitulate and go anywhere with this monstrously beautiful creature who is bigger than she is, bigger than Michael or Tom, big enough to best her in any struggle. She may not yet know how she is going to end this, but she thinks she can buy time by bargaining.

If Cleve had been the woman we would not be here, Clary thinks angrily, and it is the age-old injustice of unequal size and unfair allotment of physical strength that infuriates her now, and she is doubly angered by the guilt that seemed to come with vulnerability — that in this world somehow the victim is always blamed. *What is it about me that made him do what he did,* she wonders. *Is it my fault, for looking like his mother, or is it his?* The question has haunted her ever since the beginning. From the beginning guilt has hounded her. *What did I do to bring him down on me?* Since he picked her out at sixteen and fell on her like a hawk the guilt of the victim has paralyzed Clary Hale and cut her off at the knees.

In one blow this creature ruined her, casting bright, quick, enduring Clary who wants only to *live* now, into the role of helpless prey. Swamped her in guilt. My God, he killed my parents, *over me.* With Tom's death she was further diminished in spite of her strengths: widowed; but, God, she hasn't changed! Can't all those people who feel sorry for her see she isn't changed? It is Tom who is gone, not her, but it's as if she's disappeared along with him, Clary Hale detached from the circle of Navy life, poor girl lost her husband, poor thing. Angry, disgusted Clary, still whole but unable to prove it to the world because widowhood has left her disenfranchised, her children unprotected. Except for her.

But now he is stepping close.

And she sees the tree in detail.

"Your face," he says. "I will put it here."

"Oh, God!"

It was never me, she thinks, looking into his pale, mad eyes. It was this. This.

Those hands, ready to close on the side of her head: "And — we — will — be — it."

She is making a sound she's never heard before: *The fire, all the pain, and just for this.*

And without regard for her position or his strength or the gun, Clary hurtles into her pursuer with the force of her whole body, all butting head and teeth and battering fists, hammering and shouting, "No more!"

Her head hits his gut so hard that he staggers. His hand flies open and the gun spins away and hits the dock.

Before Michael can take in what's happening, Teah lights out with her knife pointed like a spear, screaming without words, with spit trailing behind her, "No!"

Startled, the madman turns and Michael, who is trying to put his brother aside so he can go after Teah, is the only one who sees the lean, handsome, seared face begin to change. In that unguarded second, tears of regret fill the killer's eyes; it is astounding.

"But I love you!"

Wild with it, Clary attacks him. "No!"

In the next his arms fly like scythes and that face becomes a tribal mask with great gnashing teeth as the women close in on him. He lashes out so surely and with such force that it's clear he can and will throw them off and overcome them. He will level them.

But Michael has set Tommy on a tall piling where he will stay, howling, until he figures out how to wriggle down. Running hard, Michael closes the distance that separates him from his mother, throwing himself into the tangle at the end of the dock. Furious, he climbs the murderer like a tree. Gouging with the shard of metal, he finds himself caught in the knot of struggling flesh. Caught up now, trapped in battle, they are unable to subdue the enemy and afraid to stop.

Terrified, desperate and driven, they tangle, destroyer and victims, man and woman, beloved and lover, hunter and prey, and then abruptly separate at the sound of a shot.

He freezes.

They freeze.

They hear a man's voice quavering. "This is mine to do."

And the murderer is momentarily distracted.

Poised at the end of the dock, with the tree burning blood-red in his body, and the splotch in his belly glaring white, he stands back to see who has fired. He makes a half turn and in that instant sees what the Hales see. Unseen in the struggle, the boat has come out from the shadow of the mangroves. It drifts just off the dock. It carries three people, one at the tiller, one slumped amidships and one in the stern. Now the woman at the tiller is backing water, waiting for the old man standing in the stern to raise his rifle and take aim.

Clary whispers: "Look!"

Morrow, who has never really been Morrow, strikes his fore-head with both fists.

He is something else now.

An eerie, high-pitched cry comes from the heart of the tree: "Oh Daddy, don't."

Stricken, the old man falters and lowers the rifle: "I can't."

Michael is dimly aware of his mother backing away, stooping so her fingers sweep the dock and collide with something, pick-ing it up . . . what; tree branches flail like whirling blades, and facing their adversary Michael renews his grip on the scrap iron, thinking, *What are we going to do?* Next to him, Teah bunches her shoulders and waits.

His last cry splits the air. "Don't!"

And in the next second, they are riveted by a shot. Blood blooms in the white center of the emblazoned belly, and tee-tering at the end of the dock the monster whirls one last time, spreading arms wide with fingers like leafless branches scraping the sky. His lean, perfect body is altered now, the tree design smirched and diffused by the uses of the past few days. Mi-chael's metal shard has made an ugly slash in the design that crosses the tightly wrought shoulder and the design is scored by cuts and the marks of their mother's nails. There are scratches in his wrists from the long night of pursuit through the brush and his seared face is smudged with blood. The nick

Beetie's shot put in his arm has begun to bleed again and on his leg the puncture wound from the fall in the barn in Georgia has begun to fester and turn dark. Still, in this last moment of confrontation, the mad light in his face flares. He is like an incandescent bulb in the second before it blows out. He is beyond speech. And in the snowy vacancy of the unscarred belly, the blank spot that he has stalked and pillaged and contrived and murdered and mutilated in an attempt to fill, blood wells. He looks down, incredulous. Then he looks up at Clary and those pale, extraordinarily beautiful eyes fix on her until the pupils widen to exploding, driving out the color in the terrifying fragment of an instant before she raises his pistol in both hands and fires again and the sockets fill with blood. He is everything and nothing in that moment: monster and victim, lover, destroyer, all; his lips come together in a silent *Mm.*

And her third shot blows him off the dock.

Astounded, her children cling, spreading their arms to embrace Tommy, who hurtles into them.

"That's it," Clary says; her face is glossy, shut tight as the visor on a knight's helmet. She puts her arms around all three of them at once, gathering them tight. "That's it."

Spent, the Hales cluster on the dock, silent and frightened, because even though this is not a movie they know that the monster always gets up and sleeping or waking, in dreams or in memory, in fears or in actual fact, they will have to confront him again. Again. Again. The Hales clump tightly, with pinched, spiky faces turned outward, prepared to meet the enemy. But only bubbles come out of the water below and in time the bubbles stop and he floats up. They are aware of the boat beaching in the sand, three people getting out — Beetie, the old man, who can't stop sobbing, and . . . And the third is Shar — Shar! Tommy stops howling and grabs his mother's knees with a little *whump* of escaping breath. And still Michael and Teah stand with Clary, back to back to back, what's the matter with them really; he doesn't know. They can't seem to untie the knot.

Shar is coming out on the dock to greet them; she sees Clary's face and takes her by the arms. "It's all right," she says quietly, trying to disengage her fingers from the pistol. "It's all right. It's all right. It's all right."

But Clary and her children remain shaky, clinging for strength. Triumphant as they are, relieved and hopeful, they are forever changed. Together, they will move into the future with great care because for the rest of their lives a certain part of each of them will stand guard.

Shar is hugging all three of Clary's children at once; they have their backs to the water so they won't have to look at the body. At a little distance, Beetie weeps quietly. "I brought him up," the old man says into the silence, "and he turned." His son is dead. The body has stopped twitching. His whole heart is in the sigh that fills the long minute before he says the last thing. "I kept him in this world, and I should have taken him out."

"Don't feel bad," Shar says, over Michael's head. "We do a lot of dumb things out of love."

Clary dips her head. "Or out of hate."

"He said you were dead," Michael says to Shar, to his mother, in the lull that follows the end. They have broken into the refreshment stand and eaten. Now they are lined up at the end of the dock, sitting with their feet hanging over while they wait for the first ferry of the day. Beetie and the broken old man have gotten back into their boat and gone; it seemed best to let them slip away before outsiders found them. By the time whoever gets here begins to ask questions, Shar and the Hales will have worked out the right things to tell them. "Dead!"

"Oh shit," Shar says, "he said a lot of things."

Clary says, "All lies."

"Born liar," Shar says. *Born.* Whatever drove him, he would have passed it on, she thinks, remembering that when the doctor told her there was never any baby, a part of her cried out at the loss. For the first time she is glad. Looking out over the water, she hugs her knees.

Michael is glad for the silence.

With no more emergency to give him momentum, no desperation to give him strength, he's gone digging into his storehouse of next steps and found he is completely out of next things. Now that the terror of pursuit and flight has ended, he is up against it. What to do. How to go on from here.

He turns to his mother with all this in his face. "Mom!"

Her own face is thin and bleached out from all those days locked in her sealed prison; it is stained with fatigue but it seems lighted from within. "Michael."

"So," Michael says to his mother. "What?"

Looking at him over Tommy's head, his mother shrugs. "It's OK. It is. It's over," she says, and with a look that they both understand she adds, "At least this part."

He has to make himself say the next thing. "And Dad isn't . . ."

This is the first time that they've let each other see into this hope and close the door for good. Clary says quietly, "No."

He lets his breath out carefully so she won't know how near he is to crying.

But she sees. She always does. And faces it head-on. "We're together," she says.

"What are we going to do?"

"We'll make it," she says.

He sees that slight and beautiful as she is and damaged as she is by losing Tom Hale, shaken as she is by everything that's happened to her, his mother is strong and fine. That she has always been stronger than he thought. And he understands as well that she's letting him know that for the first time since the officer came to the house to tell them the *Constellation* was missing, their lives are going to move forward. He is listening and he is aware that Teah is listening. Something inside him starts ticking, like the freshly repaired works in a stopped clock. "And we're OK?"

Because she needs to hear it as much as they do, Clary finishes. "We're going to be fine."